SHOWDOWN WITH A PSYCHO

In a crouch Cheney made his way across the room into a small foyer just off the dining room. It was darker than the other rooms, no windows, just the moonlight filtering in through the slightly open door.

Cheney picked up a broom, and used it to open the door a little wider.

Nothing but moonlight.

Cheney set the broom down and walked out into the backyard.

In the distance he saw a beautiful lake.

That was when something fell out of the sky, and wet grass jumped up and smacked him in the face like a giant frothing dog.

And then there was just darkness.

Books by Stephen Smoke

Pacific Blues
Tears of Angels
Pacific Coast Highway
Black Butterfly

Available from HarperPaperbacks

PACIFIC ◆ BLUES ◆

Stephen Smoke

HarperPaperbacks
A Division of HarperCollins*Publishers*

HarperPaperbacks   *A Division of* HarperCollins*Publishers*
10 East 53rd Street, New York, N.Y. 10022

Cover illustration by Danilo Ducak

First printing: April 1996

Printed in the United States of America

HarperPaperbacks and colophon are trademarks of HarperCollins*Publishers*

❖ 10 9 8 7 6 5 4 3 2 1

For my father

One

The Round Table was in session.

"What we do here is important," said Mark.

The others nodded. He did not look directly at them, but he could see their reflections in the mirror.

"What we do here, and out there, in the real world, is important. It's not enough that *we* know what we do is right. Others must know, and they will. They will talk about what we do here, and things will change."

The others nodded.

"Fear is what it's all about," said Mark. He looked at the others gathered at the table. At Carl. At Diana. At Malcolm. At Dennis.

"Fear brings a person out of his safety zone. The safety zone is the place where most people stay. It's a place they protect with money, power, sex, religion, whatever they hope will insulate them from their sins. But nothing can save a man from his sins."

Mark pulled on the Partagas Limited Reserve

Royale. It wasn't Cuban, but it was a lonsdale that compared very favorably with its famous counterparts. It was an exquisite creation. Packed with spice and pepper flavors, its filler grown in Mexico, the Dominican Republic, and Jamaica, its binder from Mexico and a wrapper from Cameroon, the cigar was six and three-quarter inches of decadent pleasure. At eight dollars a pop, Mark considered it underpriced. Some products really were better than others. Some Scotch really was better than other Scotch. Certain cabernets really were better than others. There were real reasons. Not snobbish, meaningless reasons. If you investigated, if you were interested, you could find quality.

Mark was the kind of person who liked fine things. He never bought off the rack. Not because he thought such extravagance would impress others. He did so because his standards were higher than theirs. Better than theirs. All of his suits were made by a tailor who knew Mark's build and how to accent his physical strengths and downplay his weaknesses. For nearly ten years he had gone to the same barber/stylist. Not because the stylist was the most expensive—though that was certainly true—but because the man understood the shape of Mark's head, the way his problem cowlick splayed this way and that.

Mahler's Ninth played in the background. As the fragrance of elegant smoke haunted the room. As Mark caught a glimpse of his suit in the mirror. As he touched the nape of his neck, sensing the perfect inch between the bottom of his hair and the beginning of his starched Armani collar. As he savored the bouquet of the Sterling cabernet.

There was a sense of perfection in the air. His senses were filled with it. The Round Table was filled with it.

"I'm a little sick a' that classical shit," said Carl. He was into country-and-western music.

"This is my night," said Mark firmly, without sounding adversarial. Mark respected Carl. He had earned his place at the table. And he was not to be trifled with. He was strong. Very strong. And unpredictable. Still, Mark could control him. Had to control him.

"Fine, but do we have to listen to that classical shit the whole fuckin' night?"

Mark picked up a remote control and turned down the London Symphony's version of Mahler's Ninth. Turned it down, didn't turn it off. Carl had to be handled. Giving in to him could have disastrous consequences. Carl was the kind of personality that could overwhelm. Dominate a group. Mark knew that and he resisted. In a sophisticated way. Looked him in the eye. Eye contact was important. Animals knew it, sensed it. So did humans. Don't look away, don't look down. Most of all, don't show fear. Because, like the animal he was, Carl would surely tear him to shreds. Mark knew that as surely as he knew his reflection in a mirror.

Still, Carl had his uses.

"We must remain focused," said Mark, not acknowledging Carl further.

"I'm next," said Diana.

"Yes. And yours will be a special mission."

Diana smiled. She knew. She had waited a long time.

Malcolm sat with his feet up on the table, looking out the window. Bobbing his head to some rock-and-roll song playing in his head. Mark let it go. Malcolm was important, too. But not tonight.

Dennis sat staring directly at Mark. Mark felt closest to Dennis. Yet that fact scared him. Carl was erratic. Diana had her . . . limitations. Malcolm was unfocused. Each had assets and flaws.

But Dennis was different. He stared straight ahead. Looked through Mark. He was there and he was not there. He seemed always to be in what could only be described as a calm rage.

Dennis was dangerous. More dangerous than the rest. Even more dangerous than Carl. He would have to be watched.

Mark raised his glass toward the others. He saw them in the mirror. Each drank. Even Dennis. Mahler played in the background. It was ritual.

When the Round Table had adjourned, Mark walked out upon the lawn. Toward the lake. Black Water Lake. The lake, the grounds, and the house had been left to him by his father.

Mark sat alone on the soft, smooth bank of the lake. Sipping his wine.

Ritual.

Looked out upon the lake. He had named it Black Water after his father died. The night of the funeral Mark had asked to be left alone. He had sat alone against the weeping willow between the house and the lake. Sat there sipping his father's best cabernet. Sterling. Like tonight.

That day had been frightening, yet exhilarating. He was finally free. Heir to a fortune. Heir to the pain and the legacy of pain and ghosts that came along with it. Still, he was free.

A root of the willow rose up out of the dew-drenched shadows like a boa constrictor frozen in time. Mark downed the rest of the cabernet and smashed the wine glass against the serpentine root. Burgundy drops splattered onto green leaves of grass. Pieces of glass took root in soil. Images flashed in his mind of ants crawling over a giant sugary piece of glass in the morning, like creatures finding an unexplained monolith in their world. The explanation was simple, but the ants would never know. Never figure it out.

Perhaps that's the way it was with people, Mark thought, the warmth of the cabernet washing over him now like a familiar and comforting blanket. People built religions, killed themselves, sold themselves because they could not answer life's important questions. But just because people couldn't come up with the answers, didn't mean there weren't answers. They were there. Out there somewhere.

Maybe the earth is just somebody's broken wine glass and we're the tiny ants incapable of explaining where life's sharp and shiny edges came from. Yet we throw ourselves against the edges daily, and, bleeding, unable to explain our existence, we eventually deify that which we cannot explain.

Mark felt good. Good company, Mahler, a Partagas Limited Reserve Royale, the Sterling. Bathe the senses in ecstasy. Sit by the lake and ponder the meaning of life.

It was ritual.

Mark stood and walked closer to the lake.

The half moon cast a reflection like a diamond necklace around the Black Water. It had always looked like black water to Mark. He had swum there. Fished there. Walked its banks. It was not polluted, but he had never seen its bottom. Secrets lived deep beneath the water's surface. *That's why they call them secrets,* his father had said.

And that's what Mark had always believed. Always wanted to believe.

He walked down to the dock, got into the small boat and adjusted the oars. Ritual.

Rowed out into the middle of the lake.

Looked back toward the shore. Sensed the others looking at him. Even though he didn't see them.

He knew what he had to do. Knew how to keep a secret.

As he sat there in the middle of the lake, oars idle, the moon skittering off the black water, he sensed the presence. It was the presence they all felt. It was the presence that had brought them together. Made them do what they did.

It was the presence.

It was justice.

It was . . .

Ritual.

Two

Frank Curtis always liked the Christmas season. He no longer believed in Santa Claus. No longer believed in peace on earth—at least not in his lifetime.

But he still cried every time he saw *It's a Wonderful Life*. Still believed that people were capable of being inspired by the spirit of the season, and that "miracles" could, and often did, come from such inspiration. Clearly, people genuinely felt more connected to their fellow man during the season when bells chimed, carolers sang in five-part harmony, and people gave gifts to people they wouldn't give the time of day to any other day of the year.

Frank tried his best not to be cynical. Not because he thought that a positive attitude would change his life for the better, but because he truly believed, wanted desperately to believe, there was a possibility that his daughter Molly's life might be changed for the better.

He viewed his own cynicism as merely the proper uniform of the day.

But, being an ex-cop, with alimony and a real life to slip
into every morning when he got out of bed, he still held
out hope that there was something better in the world for
people who believed that better things were possible.

The elevator door opened and Frank walked out of
the elevator, past the shopping mall guard. It was about
ten, and there weren't that many cars left in the subter-
ranean garage.

"Merry Christmas," said Frank to the young man. It
was going out on a limb, risking being politically incorrect. After all, Frank didn't know if the guy might be
Jewish, Buddhist, or Muslim. Last month he had read
an article in the *Trib* listing the newspaper's politically
incorrect taboos. Couldn't say "pow wow"—that
would offend Native Americans. Couldn't say that
"things are looking black" because that would offend
African Americans.

The security guard just smiled back and said, "Back
at you." The man was black, but Frank hadn't noticed.

Frank walked down the ramp out of the guard's
sight. The only sound was his shoe leather on cement
and his keys jingling in his hand as he pulled them from
his pocket.

Chilly, he thought. For Los Angeles. In the midfor-
ties. Rain, snow or temperatures under fifty degrees
always led the news in LA. Unless there was a riot, an
uprising, or a superstar charged with a sex crime. Or
even a minor celebrity charged with murder. He would
be glad to get back home, which these days was
Crestview, about ninety minutes north of LA. He'd be
home before midnight.

Frank walked to his Lexus ES300. Not the really
expensive one. Not the LS400. He had bought the car

used, for about twenty grand. Divorced, semi-retired, living on a cop's pension, a guy needed to know how to cut corners. Still, he liked the car. He hit the alarm button on his keychain as he approached, and it chirped once. He was looking forward to listening to the John Mayall CD on the way home. Blues, good blues, always relaxed him.

Frank walked to the driver's side door, reached for the door handle, and felt the sensation of cold steel pressed against the back of his head.

"Don't move, you fuck!"

Frank was electrocuted with fear. Paralyzed. Unable to speak or call out. His attention was riveted to one square inch of sensation at the back of his head.

"Please don't," were the only words that came. He had envisioned such situations a million times. Elbowing the fucking prick in the gut, ripping the gun away and saying something clever. Kicking the shit out of the guy, while waiting for the cops to show up. When it happened, for real, all he could say—plead—was, "Please don't."

"Fuck you, asshole!"

"Take the money. Hell, you can take my car, too."

"If all I wanted was your money or your car, I'd just take 'em. You got no power here, you stupid fuck!"

Frank swallowed hard, all the moisture in his mouth and throat had dried up.

"Please, for the love of God, don't kill me!"

"You love God? *Before* I put a fuckin' gun to your fat fuckin' head, did you love God?"

"Look, I got a wife and daughter—" Frank had an ex-wife, but under the circumstances, it didn't seem like a lie.

"Big fuckin' deal. I ain't got *nobody*. 'Cept now . . . I got you, muthufucka'."

Frank heard the sound of the gun hammer clicking.

"My God, no! Please!"

"Get down on your knees."

"What?"

"Don't fuck with me, asshole. You heard me."

Frank tried to swallow again, but the muscles worked without effect. He got down on his knees, his back still turned away from the assailant.

"Turn around."

Frank did as he was told.

"Lick my shoes."

Frank started to look up at the man . . .

And got a knee to the face.

"Don't look at my face!"

"Okay, okay," said Frank, the left side of his face on fire with the pain of bone on bone.

"Lick my fuckin' shoes, asshole!"

Frank slowly lowered his face toward the man's tennis shoes. *Is this it? Will my last act on earth be licking some psychopath's dirty running shoes? Running shoes? Is that important? Stop being a cop. Just live long enough to see Marge's face again. Molly's. And Lilly's.*

The granules of dirt and sand felt foreign to his tongue. There was a logo on the shoe, but Frank couldn't make it out.

"Lick the bottom." The man raised his shoe so that the bottom of the shoe was in Frank's face—ground-in dirt, remnants of gum and oil in the crevices of the contoured sole.

Frank realized he had no choice. He licked. And shook like a frightened child. He knew that death was six inches away down a slick steel chamber.

Suddenly the licking faded in Frank's consciousness as though he were drowning, and he was flooded with memories of his ex-wife, his daughter, his mother, his father, his ex-partner, Lilly.

Faces danced in front of him. Memories. People who loved him a long time ago. Perhaps the only people who ever really cared about him. In a blazing instant he realized how lucky he was. It happened so fast he didn't *intellectually* understand why he felt so fortunate, only that he felt immersed in his own gratitude.

Even if it had all turned to shit years ago when . . .

All sensation registered so rapidly now that Frank felt each mini-tremor as though it were a shock to the bone, but he still did not really understand what was happening to him. One thing he understood was that in spite of the fact that he was involved in a humiliating and life-threatening situation, his mind was deluged with a barrage of sensations the likes of which he had never known.

"Look at me, you pitiful fuck!"

The threatening and obscene words fell on Frank like emotional depth charges, slowly settling upon him through deep water, then exploding. Destroying the safe haven of memory.

Frank did not want to look at his tormentor. For many reasons.

"Look at me!"

"No."

"What?" said the man incredulously.

"No."

"Why not?"

"You know."

"Tell me."

Silence.

Frank felt the man's knee against his cheek again. "Tell me, you stupid fuck!"

"If I can identify you, you'll kill me."

The man laughed. "You've been watching too much TV."

"Just take what you want and go. I won't file a complaint."

"Really?"

"I swear."

Silence.

"I don't believe you."

Again the knee against the face.

Frank winced, recoiled, and still refused to look his assailant in the eye.

"I figure you're going to report this."

"Why?"

"You know why."

"I don't know what you're talking about."

Again the knee.

Again the pain, only this time worse.

"I mean, you're a cop, right?"

"What?"

"You heard me."

Frank instinctively pulled back. "Yeah, I heard you, but I don't know what you mean. I'm not a cop. You must've made a mistake."

"I haven't made a mistake, Frank."

"How do you know my name?" Suddenly Frank knew that he was going to die. "Oh, fuck! Don't, please, don't do this."

"You deserve to die, Frank."

"Why? What in the fuck are you talking about?"

"You know, Frank."

"I don't, I swear."

"Look at me."

In a moment of sadness, fear, and surrender, Frank realized that it wasn't going to make any difference one way or the other. He was a dead man.

He looked up.

At the gun.

Heard the explosion.
Felt a burning sensation on his forehead.
Felt his head jerk backward.
Felt his soul lift out. Into . . .
The Light.

Cheney sipped his Stag's Leap chardonnay as he lay by the fireplace, leaning against a white chair, his arm around his wife, Elizabeth. He had broken his self-imposed vow to drink only very good, under-fifteen-dollars-a-bottle chardonnay. Stag's Leap, the private reserve, was closer to thirty. What the hell, he was full of the holiday spirit. Besides, he and Elizabeth had their own version of the twelve days of Christmas. At breakfast he had given her a scarf he'd purchased at Bullock's. Tonight she had given him the chardonnay.

Stag's Leap by the fireplace, Cheney playing Christmas standards and romantic tunes on the baby grand, Elizabeth singing along, these things had replaced the old traditions. The kids--his and hers— were grown and had young families of their own. This Christmas, Cheney and Elizabeth would go over to his son's house and watch his granddaughter, Erin, rip apart a mountain of gifts and toss aside clothing in search of toys. Cheney remembered one Christmas when Erin was almost three, she sat for over an hour playing with discarded ribbons and wrapping paper, while the contents of the packages remained untouched. She got over that quickly enough. Paper was out. Anything that required a battery or a microchip was definitely in.

Cheney took in the smell of his wife's hair and the burning oak, the feel of her smooth, warm skin against his, the sound of embers crackling in the fireplace, the

taste of the oaky four-star wine in his mouth, the sight
of the shadows dancing to the tune played by the flickering fire. All these sensations washed over him, baptiz-
ing him in a kind of cocoon he realized, at fifty-five,
most people longed for but never knew. He had never
known it before Elizabeth. Before her, as an LAPD officer and detective for nearly thirty years, he had learned
how *not* to feel.

Cheney considered himself a very, very lucky man.

There was a knock at the door. Cheney and
Elizabeth exchanged looks. Who would be out at this
time of night? It was nearly eleven thirty. Petty, their
live-in housekeeper, was spending the night with her
sister.

"I'll get it," said Cheney.

He looked through the peephole first—Pacific
Palisades was a great neighborhood, but it was still on
planet Earth. Tony Boston, Cheney's protégé and current chief of detectives, stood on the front stoop.

A relieved Cheney opened the door. "Eh, Tony,
come in."

"We should talk out here."

Suddenly Cheney felt chilled.

"It's Frank."

Cheney didn't ask the question. Perhaps, he
thought, if he didn't ask it, Tony would never answer
it. But he knew that wouldn't happen. He would just
wait for Tony to speak.

"He's dead, Cheney."

Cheney's heart, which was beginning to beat rapidly,
skipped a beat. He gasped slightly. Started nodding,
teeth clenched, looking at Tony, or rather through him
like a dazed fighter who had no idea where he was. He
tried to speak, but he could not unclench his teeth. So
he just kept nodding slowly.

"How ah . . . how ah . . . what happened?"

"He was murdered in a shopping mall garage in Santa Monica."

"Robbery?"

Tony didn't answer immediately. "We're not sure yet."

Cheney nodded again. Took a deep breath.

"Cheney!" shouted Elizabeth from inside.

"I'll be right in," he yelled back. He looked at Tony. Suddenly he focused on how hard all this was for his friend. Cheney had been in Tony's position a hundred times. But the toughest times were the ones where you knew the family. Even though Cheney and his ex-partner, Frank Curtis, had drifted apart the past few years, Frank was still family. "Does Marge know?"

"Yes."

Cheney was thankful for that. "Is there anything I can . . ." The words didn't come.

"Nothing," said Tony. "I'll call you tomorrow, okay?"

"Yeah, sure," said Cheney. He shook Tony's hand, walked back inside and closed the door.

Tony walked down the driveway toward his Lincoln Town Car. Just as he put his hand on the door handle, he thought he heard a woman begin to cry inside Cheney's house. It was the sound of pain. Tony had heard it before. He got in his car and rolled up the windows.

Ray Malzone tossed back his bourbon, straight, and looked out at the Pacific lapping up on the shore like a sick dog. He wondered, not for the first time, if the water in the Santa Monica Bay had ever really been anything other than diseased. It had looked this way all the twenty-one years he'd been here.

The poker game had broken up at four, but Ray couldn't sleep. As a reporter—the *Trib*'s best reporter, or so the local awards had declared seven out of the past ten years—he was used to crazy hours. Used to poker games with other reporters and cops and any other refugees from the divorce courts looking for something to do that made them feel as though they still had a game to play and a stick to play it with. When you're ten years old, that stick's a baseball bat. When you're eighteen years old, it's something else.

When you're over fifty, which Ray was, it was a handful of cards and a glass full of something that stings when it goes down.

When Cary Ann had told him to move out of their Van Nuys home last summer, Ray was sure he knew the drill. Women, lots of women, had told him to hit the road. In fact, he'd left a few himself. But this time, the thing that made it so hard for him was that it was so easy for her.

He still held out hope he'd get back together with Cary Ann. They continued to see each other every week or so, and they talked every other day. If it were up to him, he'd move back with Cary Ann in a minute. But too many broken promises and morning-after excuses had taken the matter out of his hands.

This time it was taking him longer to snap back. Just like it was taking longer to reincarnate from the previous nights' hangovers. Ray had a solution to the latter problem—as long as he wasn't sober, he could never be hung over.

As the sun painted the day alive, slowly, in shadow, Ray sipped his Wild Turkey. So far, the morning was a still life, except for the joggers, whom Ray resented mightily. The joggers reminded him that he was not nearly as healthy as he used to be. He used to jog five miles a day, seven days a week, rain or shine. Went to the club and jogged indoors if the weather was bad.

Not anymore. Not for about four years now. Fifteen pounds heavier, he got out of breath playing tennis. With old men.

Nobody's life ever turned out to be what they thought it was going to. At least that's the way Ray figured it. And he had lots of evidence to back him up. No one in the weekly poker game had come close to their career targets. Even people Ray knew who were very successful had told him that they were successful at things they had not set out to do.

Ray wanted to write novels. The kind that professors at universities analyzed fifty years later for structure, allegory and character development. That was a dream worth having.

Ray would never drown in the sanctimonious pity of paradise lost. But there were times when he treaded a little bourbon and had trouble staying afloat.

His friends considered him cynical. He considered himself a realist. He had been at Kent State when four students were gunned down by the National Guard—he had been visiting from nearby Antioch when the shooting started. He had marched with Martin Luther King. Twice. Not arm-in-arm, but he had been there. Been counted. He had written his first published articles about the Vietnam War—how the government, and the people who "owned" that government were profiting from the war, from the deaths of America's children. He had written with glee about Watergate. It was, in fact, a series of articles on this subject for a Cleveland newspaper that got him his first job with the *Los Angeles Tribune*.

But Ray didn't write about corrupt Republicans anymore. All politicians were corrupt. This was not a cynical opinion, he had told his poker buddies on several occasions. He had enough dirt on virtually every politician in Los Angeles politics to run them all out of office. But then, every good reporter had the same information. He no longer used that information to "change the world," but merely as currency to endear himself to other politicians at the opportune moment.

Ray Malzone had changed. With his long hair and cocky attitude, he had been hassled by the cops more than once when he'd come to LA. Now a couple of his best friends were cops and he saw what it was like midnight to dawn on the streets, which were no longer mean. They were rabid. On those streets he saw the world from the bottom up. Real life. Not TV. Nobody called the cops if you were having a rational disagreement. They called the cops when somebody high on PCP was slicing off a piece of somebody's face. They called the cops when parts of someone's skull and brain were decorating the cigarette rack behind the convenience store cash register. They called the cops when some child lay dying in a pool of his own blood because his mother happened to be wearing red instead of blue.

Most of the time cops dealt with criminals. It wasn't like sixties TV when the cops always got the wrong guy. That made for interesting fiction, but in the overwhelming majority of cases, the cops usually got it right.

In twenty-two years, Ray had changed. The world had changed. Sometimes he wondered if he had just grown into it.

Ray Malzone had no clout in Moscow, London, or New York, but if the story was Los Angeles, and it was important, his byline always led the story.

The phone rang. It startled him. It was almost six in morning. Who in the hell? It better be World fucking War Three, thought Ray as he scraped himself out of the chair. Left the ocean behind.

"Malzone here." He listened. "Fuck me. Are you sure?" Listened some more. "Jesus, I'll be right there."

Three

Cheney was very familiar with the office he sat in this morning. It had been his for ten years before he had handed it over to Tony Boston, his handpicked successor. Like a quarterback, the job of chief of detectives was a skill position. A powerful position. A political position. It had meant little to Cheney, except that it had given him the power to tell people where to go and not have to draw them a map. Which, at the end of the day, left Cheney with more time to do what he really wanted to do, which was to be a cop.

At least that's the way it had been during the good times. The bad times, from which some type of political stench had always emanated, were what eventually drove Cheney from the job. That and a promise to Elizabeth to get out while they were still young enough to remember which parts fit into which holes. And why.

One of the reasons Cheney had been able to walk away was Tony Boston. Cheney had been his mentor.

Tony was a cop. An honest cop. That's all he ever wanted to be. Tony's father and his uncle had been cops. Cheney had known that Tony would use the power of the office as he himself had used it—wisely, for his people, for the city, and with the street smarts to know how to deal with the politicians who believed the LAPD was merely another lever of their own power.

"Coffee?" said Tony.

"No, thanks. I've been up all night. I'm running on caffeine and adrenaline."

Tony shook his head. There was so much to say and no words to adequately express it.

"I'm so sorry, Cheney. God*dammit*!"

Cheney thought about saying that Tony had nothing to be sorry for. That someone—one poor excuse for a human being—had a lot to be sorry for. To answer for. That one sorry son of a bitch was walking around unaware that he was really a dead man. You don't kill the ex-chief of detectives' partner and expect to walk away from it. You might expect to, but you'd be wrong.

One way or the other.

But all Cheney said was, "Thanks."

Silence.

After a while Cheney said, "So, what've you got?"

"Not much."

Cheney nodded. He hadn't expected the killer to drop his business card at the scene of the crime. It would take time. But that was okay with Cheney.

"Wrong place, wrong fucking time," said Cheney, shaking his head in disbelief. "How can a person protect himself from random violence? From every crazy fucking lunatic! Jesus, Tony, what's goin' on?" Cheney looked at his pupil, his friend. He didn't expect an answer, only understanding.

It wasn't easy for Tony to meet Cheney's eyes. Or hold them. He had never seen Cheney this emotionally wrung out—except when Elizabeth had lain in a coma two years ago, close to death. It was difficult to see your friend, especially someone as worldly and street-wise as Cheney, this way.

"It might not have been random."

Cheney blinked and focused on Tony. "You can't be serious. Frank didn't have an enemy in the world."

"We all have enemies, Cheney—real or perceived. We both know that. But that's not what I mean."

"Was he singled out because he was a cop? My God! Don't tell me—"

"I don't know. All I know is that the killer left a signature."

"A signature?"

"Yeah. We found a blue ribbon on Frank's body. It was folded kind of like those red AIDS awareness ribbons."

"Jesus," said Cheney, taking it all in, letting his head fall back against the high-back chair. He sucked some air and leaned forward. "What does it mean?"

"I don't know, I was hoping it might mean something to you."

"Why me?"

"We're looking for a motive. My first thought was that the killer might be someone Frank put away. Maybe when you two worked together."

Cheney shook his head.

"Think about the ribbon thing, okay? Let me know if anything clicks."

"Right." Cheney was still in kind of a daze.

"Cheney."

"Yeah?"

"There's something else." This was hard. "I wish I

didn't have to tell you, but you're going to find out anyhow when you look at the paperwork."

Cheney waited. For the fist to the face.

"We found material on Frank's tongue that was consistent with . . ." Tony paused and sighed, ". . . with the, uh, fact that the killer made Frank lick his shoes."

Cheney felt his teeth clench. He swallowed hard. He thought he nodded.

Tony looked at the man sitting on the other side of the desk. He owed Cheney a lot more than his job. Tony had known Frank, too, but they had never been close. In a strange way, Tony long ago had realized that he'd been, well, almost jealous of Frank. Tony's father had died when he was fifteen. Cheney had filled a lot of roles for Tony over the years: teacher, best friend, confessor, father.

"Look, Cheney, I know I can't keep you out of this, but we need to establish ground rules." Since his retirement, Cheney had been "unofficially" invited to handle certain cases the department deemed too delicate for the LAPD to become involved in. Cheney had been perfect for those jobs. He had retired prematurely. Everyone knew it. Just as everyone knew that he was desperate to keep his hand in.

"What kind of ground rules?"

"This is personal, very personal. A doctor doesn't operate on his own family, and a detective doesn't run the investigation into his ex-partner's murder. Still, you're the best detective I ever knew. I, that is we, the department, could use your help."

Cheney just listened.

"But you've got to remember, I'm in charge. Officially and unofficially. If I get the sense that you're out of control or jeopardizing the investigation, you're out of the loop. It's my call and my call alone. I don't want any procedural or prejudicial fuck-up that some lawyer's going to use to buy this guy a get-out-of-jail-free card. I want this bastard and I want him bad. Maybe not as bad as you, but I want him. And I'm not going to let anything, even our relationship, get in the way. You know that if the positions were reversed, you'd do exactly the same thing."

Cheney nodded.

"So, I'm going to need your word that you won't interfere."

"What does that mean, exactly? You want me to help, but . . . "

"I'll give you all the information I've got, when I get it. But the moment you start acting like Charles Bronson, you're out."

Cheney nodded again.

"I gotta hear you say it, Cheney. Promise me you're not going to do anything stupid if you get the chance."

"I promise." Cheney knew that was what Tony wanted to hear. He knew that that was the only way he was going to be dealt in.

And he also knew that he was lying.

Outside, as Cheney walked to his car, the strings of Christmas lights looked dead against the cobalt morning sky. Church bells chimed in the distance, an ancient alarm to a day of celebration and family. But to Cheney they sounded more like funeral bells.

Cheney and Elizabeth sat at their kitchen table nursing cups of coffee. Cheney stared out the window a lot and Elizabeth stayed close to him, holding his hand.

"You okay?"

"No, not really."

"What about Marge?"

"She's been told. I called her a little while ago. She sounds okay."

"How long have she and Frank been divorced?"

"About ten years, I think."

"Maybe it helps—having the distance, I mean."

"Maybe. I told her I'd come by, but she said to give her a couple of days."

"You know, you and Frank hadn't seen a whole lot of each other since he moved up to Crestview."

"I know, but whenever we got together it was like we were still as close as we'd always been."

Elizabeth just nodded. "This is going to be a tough one, Cheney." After a long pause, she said, "What are you going to do?"

Cheney dragged his left hand over his weary and drawn face. "What do you mean?"

"You know what I mean."

"Tony's dealing me in. But," added Cheney hastily, "with ground rules."

"You going to follow them?"

"You know me better than that," said Cheney, with as innocent a look as he could muster.

"That's the problem."

Cheney squeezed his wife's hand.

"So, what *are* you going to do?"

"I'm going to write Frank's eulogy." Cheney stood, went into his study and closed the door.

Four

s Cheney walked down the hallway, the smell of
marijuana hung heavy in the air. It was a familiar smell. Being a cop for nearly thirty years had
made him an expert on all kinds of illicit activity. On
the scale of one to ten, ten being the serial killing of
nuns with a Swiss Army knife, smoking pot was somewhere around *footnote* on the scale. Still, it was illegal
and a guy smoking pot was breaking the law.

Cheney continued down the hall that emptied into
the living room of the double trailer.

The man sat in a fully extended La-Z-Boy chair, ear-
phones on, eyes closed, his head swaying to the beat.
Cheney thought he detected the strains of Gershwin's
Rhapsody in Blue.

When the man opened his eyes, he looked startled.
"What the fuck!"

Cheney stopped in his tracks. He said nothing.

The man took off the earphones. "Derek. What in

the fuck do you think you're doing sneaking up on me like that? I could've had a heart attack, for crissake!"

"Sorry, Dad." Cheney felt a little foolish. The only person on earth who called Cheney by his first name was his father.

"Jesus, Derek, you almost scared the living shit outta me." He paused and smiled what, to Cheney, seemed a rather sheepish smile. "You want a brownie?" The old man tilted his head toward the plate on his lap.

Cheney took a moment to try to figure out exactly what was wrong with this picture, and sat down in the chair next to his father.

"You got somethin' on your mind?"

Cheney thought a moment before he spoke. "Are you smoking dope?"

"No, son, the Oldtimers Disease finally bent me so far I decided to smoke what's left of your mother's ashes."

"For crying out loud, Dad!" said Cheney, wincing.

"What the fuck do you think I'm smoking, for crissake." It was not a question.

Daren picked up a joint, lit it, inhaled, held it in, then slowly exhaled. "You want some brownies?" he repeated.

"Brownies?" said Cheney incredulously. "I didn't think you liked sweets."

"I've kind of developed a sweet tooth lately."

"I'll bet." Cheney shook his head. Maybe this was just a bad dream. "Correct me if I'm wrong, but didn't we have a conversation about thirty years ago during which you told me that smoking marijuana was bad for the chromosomes—I think you had it mixed up with LSD—and that it would ultimately lead to the decay of civilization as we know it?"

Daren gave his son a condescending look. "And I was right."

"Maybe I'm missing something here. If you were right then, you're wrong now."

"Why?"

"Why? Because you're sitting here smoking dope, your head swaying back and forth to Gershwin, and you're stuffing your face with brownies. That's why."

"So, what's the problem? You don't like Gershwin?"

"I love Gershwin—"

"So don't be such a schmuck. Look, Derek, I've listened to *Rhapsody in Blue* a thousand times, maybe more. I love the fuckin' thing. But I never heard it like this."

"Like what?"

"I hear all the instruments. Every note. It's very cool."

Cheney nodded. "That's just great. Maybe you could be a music critic for the AARP magazine. Perhaps you could do a retrospective on your favorite Grateful Dead albums."

"Don't be so sarcastic. I put up with a lot of your artsy fartsy music when you were a kid. Besides, this is art, Derek, real art."

"So, Dad, what's this all about, really?" said Cheney.

"What do you mean?"

"The last time I saw you wearing earphones you were at the Smithsonian listening to an account of the moon landing."

Daren Cheney set the earphones and the brownies on a side table, which was covered with recent copies of *Sports Illustrated*. After a moment he said, "Do you ever think of yourself as old?"

"I don't think about it much."

"You will. The first time I really thought about being old was when I had my sixtieth birthday. Sixty's old. I thought thirty was old when I was eighteen. But sixty's old by anyone's lights. But even then, I still didn't *feel* old." Daren paused and looked out the window toward the beach. His double trailer was just across the highway from the Pacific Ocean, between Santa Monica and Malibu. It was, in fact, larger than the house Cheney had grown up in. And it had a hell of a lot better view.

"The first time I actually felt old was when your mother died. It seemed like I didn't fit in this world anymore. You didn't need me, I wasn't working. I was just living off the pension and a couple investments. I had no place in this world, no purpose. And without your mother, the world became a very, very empty place. I had to figure out reasons to get out of bed in the morning. And when I looked in the mirror I didn't recognize the person looking back."

"What exactly are you trying to tell me here?"

"Yeah, well . . ." Daren shifted in his chair uncomfortably.

"I want an answer."

"Do you now? You sound like my father."

"I sound like you. So, tell me."

Daren lit the joint again, took a toke off it and said something that Cheney couldn't quite make out because he said it while not trying to exhale.

"What?"

After exhaling, Daren said, "I've got glaucoma."

The word slapped Cheney and stopped him cold. A few years ago, a friend of his had been diagnosed with glaucoma. He had money and access to the best medical care. His doctor had also prescribed, among other things, marijuana. But in the end, nothing had worked. And he had gone blind in three years.

"I didn't know," said Cheney.

"I didn't know myself until about a month ago. Hit me hard at first."

"At first?"

"It's scary, Derek, I won't lie to you. It's like one of those paint-by-number paintings in reverse. Instead of having a picture come to life, it's like the world's disappearing a little piece every day. It gets darker and darker and finally . . . well, I don't know about that part yet."

"How bad is it now?"

Daren smiled. It was a sad smile. "I got my legs, my arms, the pump still works. All in all, I guess it could be a helluva lot worse."

Cheney looked at his father and realized that he didn't care what it was as long as it made him feel like getting up another day. Cheney knew that he no longer needed his father, not in a way that he had as a child. But he needed him now in a different way. A selfish way. Cheney had never known a world in which at least one of his parents did not exist. It was an emotional, invisible marker in a world where the signposts and directions were forever changing. Cheney's last "permanent" orientation point would be gone when his father died. And he knew that the world would forever seem a more empty and foreign place.

"What do the doctors say?"

"One of 'em said he was sorry. That made me feel real good."

Cheney smiled. At least the sense of humor was not fading. As he grew older, Cheney realized just how underrated a sense of humor was in the scheme of things.

"They're doing what they can, Derek. I trust the kid."

"Kid?"

"Hell, he can't be a day over fifty."

"Any chance it can be reversed?"

"Reversed? No. They can slow it down some. But who knows, maybe they'll come up with a cure. The

kid gave me some brochures on an experimental procedure where they drill into the eyeball to relieve the
pressure—that's what it's all about. All that pressure
eventually destroys the retina."

Cheney was still stuck on the concept of drilling into
the eyeball.

"What's the doctor's name?"

"Why?"

"Maybe I could talk to him."

"What, you gonna go in there and tell him you used
to be chief of detectives, LAPD, and that if anything
happens to your father you're gonna bury him in some
Turkish prison? I don't think so."

"You know I wouldn't do that. I'm just concerned.
You're not exactly the perfect person to ask about your
illness. You could have a stake through your heart and
you'd be asking for some Tums."

"I appreciate your concern, Derek, I do. But no one
cares about this more than I do. I don't want to live in
a world where I can't see. I couldn't bear it. I'm too
old to adjust to it. So, just back off and let me handle
it. Like I said, I trust the kid. He comes well recommended, believe me."

Cheney nodded. He wasn't giving up finding out
who the doctor was, but he knew he was not going to
get the name today.

"So, I guess I'm being a rude host. What the fuck
brings you all the way out here?"

"Do I have to have a reason?"

"Usually."

"Nothing, really."

"C'mon, Derek. I'm in a good mood, let's talk,"
said Daren, lighting what remained of the joint.

"Frank's dead. He's been murdered." Cheney figured his father hadn't heard—for the past five years

Daren had refused to watch or listen to the news, except sports. And because he'd retired twenty years ago, his buddies on the force were almost all dead. Cheney hadn't asked him to go to the funeral because Daren had told him the day before Frank's murder that he wasn't feeling well.

"Good lord," said Daren, setting the joint down and expelling whatever smoke he had retained. "Why the fuck didn't you say so?"

"I got distracted."

"Jesus."

Cheney knew that his father, a lifetime cop, would understand what it was like to have your partner murdered, even if both partners were long retired.

"What happened?"

Cheney explained the details as they had been explained to him by Tony.

"Who did it?"

"I don't know."

"Somebody he put away?"

"It's possible, we're looking into it."

"We?"

"Tony's letting me in. For a couple of reasons. Not the least of which is he knows I'd get involved one way or the other anyhow. All I know is that I feel like shit and I didn't know where else to go."

"You came to the right place, son."

Cheney smiled at his father. "I know."

Two hours later, as Cheney pulled his car out of the short sandy driveway next to his father's trailer, he was still bothered by something that his father had said. *I don't want to live in a world where I can't see. I couldn't bear it.*

Cheney hit a button and the windows of his new champagne-colored J30 silently closed tight. Suddenly the wind off the Pacific had a distinct chill.

*   *   *

Cheney got back home about three thirty. Elizabeth was at work in her Westwood office. Petty was whipping up some low-fat sour cream in the food processor.

"How you doin'?" said Petty.

"Okay," said Cheney absently. He poured himself a cup of coffee from a pot he'd brewed that morning.

"I'm sorry about Frank."

"Thanks. What's for dinner?" Cheney didn't want to talk any more about it.

"Vegetable casserole, baked potato with low-fat sour cream and fat-free yogurt chocolate pie."

"Sounds great." He knew that Petty was trying her best to be nice to him. In a way he wished that she would treat him with the same disrespect she always did. He wanted things to be back to normal—Frank Curtis alive and his father healthy. "Any calls?"

"Ray Malzone called. Sounded like he really wanted to talk with you."

Cheney picked up his coffee and went into his study, which looked out over the large back yard. Even though there were houses in back of his and on each side, they were not visible from the back yard. Hedges of holly and ivy hugged a high wood-and-chain-link fence, providing the privacy that had originally attracted Cheney to the house. He picked up the portable phone, walked to the window, and dialed Ray's number.

"Ray?"

"Cheney?"

"Yeah."

"We need to talk."

"About Frank?"

"Yeah. You okay?"

"Yeah, I'm fine," said Cheney, but he wasn't.

"You don't sound fine. Look, when can we get together? Sooner the better."

"Tomorrow. Where would you like to meet?"

"Palms in Pasadena."

"I think I remember. If I forget, I'll just follow the smell of cheap Scotch."

Both men snickered halfheartedly. It was small talk. Banter. They each had a lot to say, were feeling a lot, but this was not the time to say it.

"One o'clock?"

"I'll be there."

Cheney heard the click on the other end of the line, pressed the End button on his portable phone, and stood silently looking out over his garden. He felt something brush up against his leg, and looked down.

Ace looked up at him through a pile of wrinkles. It never ceased to amaze Cheney that the dog could see at all, his eyes peering out from under about a dozen layers of black skin. Ace was a shar-pei, a Chinese fighting dog. Most of the breed's bad temper had been bred out over the years. At least that was so in Ace, whom Cheney referred to as a "lean, mean, sleeping machine." Ace could bark loudly and deeply when the need arose—when the mailman attacked the house with a handful of junk mail, or when an errant cat had the audacity to set paw on his turf. But he was more a lover than a fighter. In the year that Cheney had owned him, Ace had sired two litters and bitten no one. In fact, at the annual Cheney Fourth of July barbecue Ace had spent most of the time hiding under one of the picnic tables. He was a lovable dog. Loyal, affectionate, a good companion, which was Cheney's real checklist, not necessarily in that exact order.

With Elizabeth still keeping up a full roster of

patients, there were only so many hours Cheney could play golf at the club or search quaint wine shops for a decent bottle of chardonnay for under fifteen dollars. He always said that it was no great feat to find an excellent chardonnay for twenty-five dollars. Cheney enjoyed the quest. Maybe, his wife had suggested, that was one of the reasons he had been such a good detective.

Elizabeth was starting to cut her hours back. She no longer worked Saturday or Sunday. And she was usually home early Monday, Wednesday, and Friday. He knew that she was trying, but still it was an effort for him to find things to do to fill his day.

"You wanna go outside?"

Ace's tail, which was curled and to one side so that it could, as the breed books put it, "hold a quarter," began to wag madly. Cheney looked into the face that only a dog lover could love. And even some dog lovers thought the shar-pei looked a lot like an ugly pig.

Cheney smiled at Ace. He thought his dog looked quite elegant and handsome.

As was their habit after dinner, Cheney and Elizabeth adjourned to the living room while Petty cleaned up in the kitchen. After she finished her chores, Petty popped a bowl of low-fat popcorn and retired to her bedroom to watch TV.

Cheney had decided not to tell his wife about his father's glaucoma. He knew that sooner or later he would tell her, but tonight was not the night.

"I hate the idea of you going after Frank's killer," she said to him.

"You make it sound so dramatic. Tony's going to keep me up to speed and I'll have some input. That's all."

"Cheney, this is me, Elizabeth. You don't have to measure every word for the six o'clock news. Even if Tony hadn't given you his official blessing, there is no way you are going to stay out. You know it, I know it, and so does Tony."

"So what are you saying?"

"I think I already said it." Elizabeth sipped her cognac. "The job always has a way of sucking you back in."

"Is that bad or good?"

"Neither. It's just the truth."

"Ray wants to talk," said Cheney, changing the subject. Kind of.

"About Frank?"

"Yes."

"You, Frank, and Ray. The Three Musketeers."

"Yeah, we trusted each other, drank with each other, did all kinds of things together. Ray was the only newspaper man Frank and I gave information to. We knew that if we asked him to put something off the record we could count on it. We've been friends all these years, until Frank moved to Crestview . . . "

"And Ray married your ex-wife," said Elizabeth, putting her cognac back to work.

"He met her through me," said Cheney. He had said it before. This was always a difficult subject.

"Share and share alike. Isn't that the musketeer philosophy?"

"I doubt it. At least not in the context you're alluding to. Cary Ann and I were divorced for at least a year before she and Ray got married."

"So you say."

"Look, why are you busting my chops?"

"Sorry."

"You've always had a thing about Cary Ann."

"She hasn't treated you well over the years."

"You mean she hasn't treated *you* well. Look, she's all right. She never said anything bad about me to my son. I'm out of the marriage and happy with you, so what else matters, right?"

"I suppose."

Silence. Ace rubbed up against Elizabeth's leg. Cheney had already fed him, but he liked to spread himself around. There was always the chance Elizabeth might not know Cheney had fed him. It had happened before. Ace was a dog, but he knew how to work a room.

"Who do you think killed Frank?"

"I really don't know," said Cheney.

"You think it has something to do with an old case?"

"I don't know that either."

"If it goes back far enough, it could be a case you and he worked together."

"I never thought of that," said Cheney, although he had.

"You tell me how smart I am and sometimes you treat me like I'm an idiot. Why?"

"Because I love you," said Cheney, with a smile.

"That's bullshit, Cheney, and you know it. Just be careful. I'm too good-looking to be a grieving widow for long."

"Gee, now I feel a lot better."

"I'm just telling you to stay alive, that's all. Remember, you promised to love, honor, and obey."

"Obey? I thought that was your line."

"They ought to put you in a museum somewhere, Cheney." Elizabeth smiled, finished her cognac, and stood. "I'm going in. You about ready?"

"In a minute."

Ace got up also. He shot Cheney a squinting look through the folds of black skin, then padded off after Elizabeth.

Cheney walked to the window and looked out over the back yard, which was lit by floodlights. He thought about his ex-partner and how they had defied death together. Tonight Cheney stood there with a glass of cognac in his hand feeling very vulnerable, while Frank's body lay in a grave, after an autopsy that had cut his body up into measurable pieces. Each piece weighed and analyzed, all the numbers duly recorded on the autopsy box score. It all added up to the same thing. Frank lost.

Cheney thought about his father and what he must be going through. For as much as he cared for both men, Cheney could only understand these tragedies from a distance. Suddenly he wondered what it would be like to never see Elizabeth's face again. To never again be able to look into Erin's innocent eyes. To never again be able see Ace's sad and wrinkly face.

He tossed down the rest of his cognac and walked out of the living room toward the bedroom.

For some reason he left the light on in the back yard.

Five

M arge Curtis had married Frank two years after he'd joined the force. That was in 1965, when he was in his early twenties and she had just turned nineteen. The first year had been good, or so Frank had always told Cheney. But it had been rocky from the second year on, culminating in a divorce about ten years ago. Frank and Marge had been civilized enough to wait until their daughter, Molly, was off to college.

Cheney pulled up in front of Marge's one-story, two bedroom house in the bedroom community of Chatsworth. It wasn't fancy but it was sturdy enough to have survived the '94 quake, which had been centered less than ten miles away.

When she opened the door, Marge looked as though she had been crying. But then, Cheney thought that Marge often looked as though she'd been crying. "Come in," she said. She knew why he was there.

Marge fixed Cheney some coffee and they talked of more pleasant times.

"He was very proud of you, Cheney. Very proud. You two being such macho types, I don't know if he ever broke down and told you just how he felt. Chief of detectives . . . who would've figured. Kind of crazy the way things work out. You, Frank, and Ray, three young Turks. And now Frank's gone, Ray's married to Cary Ann, and you're off living like a fuckin' prince in the Palisades with some shrink." Living twenty years with a cop tended to spice up a person's vocabulary, especially when talking with others in the brotherhood.

"I'd hardly call it princely."

"Close as any of us are gonna get. All and all I didn't do too bad. I got Molly. She's a veterinarian, you know."

"I know," said Cheney, smiling respectfully. "Frank showed me a picture of her standing by a horse she'd patched up. Famous racehorse, if I remember correctly."

"A racehorse, anyhow. Yeah, I took that and sent it to Frank. Horses, dogs, cats, whatever. The kid loved animals since before she could talk. She's happy, Cheney, doin' somethin' she wants to do."

Cheney sipped his coffee.

"Ray was by yesterday. That was real nice of him."

"I've got an appointment to see him at one," said Cheney.

Except for the sound of birds chirping in the large oak outside the front window, and the permanent freeway hum that was the background music to the endless movie that was LA, there was silence. But it was a weeping silence. A silence so filled with sadness that Cheney felt like reaching over and wiping away the tears from Marge's frozen face. But he couldn't do that. She never revealed that much of herself anymore.

Marge took a deep breath and coughed a little. "So, who's Tony think did it?"

"He doesn't know."

"You gonna get involved?"

"I don't know," said Cheney.

"That was a stupid question," said Marge, smiling just a little. "I know you. How can I help?"

"I don't know. Is there anything that comes to mind?"

"Well, as you know, Frank and I haven't lived together for ten years. But he came to dinner every once in a while. And we talked on the phone."

"Did he ever mention any threats against his life?"

"No. And if there had been any, he'd probably have mentioned them to you first. You two stayed in touch."

Cheney nodded. He and Frank had stayed in touch, but it wasn't like before, when they were partners. After Cheney became chief of detectives it wasn't quite the same. Just as Frank and Marge had grown apart, Frank and Cheney had drifted apart as well. They had still talked, but it was mostly small talk. After Cheney retired, Frank had stayed on with the LAPD two years, then he'd moved about seventy miles north to Crestview, which was really just a suburb of Santa Barbara. They'd talked even less after that. In fact, Cheney hadn't seen Frank in almost six months.

Cheney sometimes wondered what had changed. Had he changed, or had Frank? Or was it just the natural order of things?

"Was Frank seeing someone?"

"You mean a woman?" asked Marge.

Cheney nodded.

"If he was, he didn't tell me about her. But then, I doubt if he would have."

"You doubt if he was seeing someone, or that he would have told you about it?"

"Both. You know, Cheney, people get older and their priorities change. Sex was never my big attraction to Frank. The older I got, I guess I forgot exactly what the original attraction was. It was mutual, though. Frank lived for the job and his booze. Long as he had a dose of each every day, he was a happy man."

"Was it the drinking that led to your divorce?"

"I dunno. It's hard to say it was one thing. He didn't beat me up, he brought home most of the paycheck, he didn't cheat so I'd notice it, and he always remembered anniversaries. In this day and age, twenty years of that kind of relationship qualifies as an outstanding marriage."

"So why did you get divorced?"

"I won't lie to you, I wanted more. Halfway around the track I could see that it wasn't going to happen. So I guess I just tried to find a place to stand where I wouldn't get buried under all the shit. I'm a survivor, Cheney. I got no big regrets."

The two sat swimming in the sad silence again, neither knowing exactly what to say next, or indeed, if there was anything left to say.

"Frank was a very troubled man, Cheney," she said finally.

"What do you mean?"

"He was not at peace with himself."

"Most people aren't. Especially after they retire. That plus the fact that he had no family anymore—none living with him anyway."

"It was more than that."

"What was it?"

Marge just shook her head and stared out the window past Cheney.

"Why did Frank move to Crestview? All his friends and family are here."

"Guess he wanted to get away."

"From what?" asked Cheney.

"I dunno."

"You ever visit him up there?"

"Nope. He never asked me up." Marge looked at Cheney again. "Maybe I shouldn't tell you this, but Frank was seeing some kind of therapist."

"What for?"

"He never said."

"Lots of people see therapists. I have. Lots of cops do. Hell, my wife would be out of business if people didn't need a little emotional support now and then."

"Yeah." She knew Cheney was trying to put a positive spin on it.

"You know the therapist's name?"

"No. All I know is that he said once that he wanted to stop by and say hello because he was going to be in town to see his therapist. That's as far as it went."

"Did Frank ever see a therapist while you were married? A marriage counselor or anyone like that?"

"No. The reason I mentioned that he was seeing a therapist lately is because I thought maybe he was seeing a department shrink, or someone the department referred him to."

"I'll look into it."

Cheney looked at his watch. "I better be getting along, Marge. I've got to meet Ray."

They both stood and started toward the door. "You tell him I said hello and that I appreciate him stoppin' by yesterday."

"Sure will."

Cheney kissed Marge on the cheek, opened the screen door and headed for his J30.

"Cheney?"

He turned back around. "Yes, Marge?"

"You get this son of a bitch," she said, uncharacteristically choking on raw emotion.

"I will."

"You promise?"

"I promise, Marge."

The Palms Bar and Grill was located in an old brick build-ing on Raymond, just north of Colorado in Pasadena's Old Town district. The building was seventy years old, which made it ancient by Los Angeles standards.

The Palms wasn't trendy. Its decor hadn't changed much since it opened in 1934, a year after Prohibition was repealed. Over the years the owners hadn't wasted much money on paint, or any other kind of embellish-ment, for that matter. But the long mahogany bar with brass fittings still worked fine. It kept most patrons upright and retained enough inherent dignity to serve as the working desk for some of the city's most notorious barflies. The place poured honest shots and there was no wine by the glass. Or by the bottle either. It was like an opium den for serious drinkers.

When he walked in and his eyes adjusted, Cheney saw Ray sitting in a corner booth.

"Thanks for coming all the way to Pasadena," said Ray as Cheney sat down and ordered a tap beer, which was delivered promptly by the bartender, who doubled as a waiter. It was easy duty, especially at one in the afternoon. Food was something of an obstacle to the commonly desired effect.

Ray Malzone was tall and slim, what baseball announcers called lanky. At fifty-four, he had all his hair, though three-quarters of it was now gray, and most of his teeth. Over the years he had spent a lot of time in the California sun, and it showed in a leathery complexion that wrinkled easily when he smiled or frowned, both of which he did often, almost compulsively. Cheney thought Ray was starting to look like Ace.

"Marge says hi, and thanks."

Ray nodded. "She doesn't look long for this world."

"Nobody is."

"Yeah, but she looks so sad. Like she's waiting for a bus to heaven." Ray sipped something from a half-glass. It smelled like whiskey to Cheney.

"How's Cary Ann?" said Cheney.

"Same as ever," said Ray, lifting his eyebrows in a gesture of helplessness. "You were married to her first, you should have warned me."

"I tried to, but you were too drunk to hear me."

"I think you just fixed me up with her so that you could stop paying alimony."

"For the record, I didn't fix you up. Seems to me you were sniffing around Cary Ann while we were still married."

"I never . . . well, you know, until you two separated."

Cheney didn't argue. Everyone's cover stories had been in place for a long time and Cheney considered it water under the bridge. He hadn't always been so non-chalant about the details. But after he met Elizabeth he found that he no longer needed answers to such questions. And there were reasons for letting bygones be bygones. First, there was Donald, his and Cary Ann's son. And then there was his friendship with Ray.

Finally Cheney brought up the subject he knew was on both their minds. "So, you did the obit on Frank?"

"Yeah. But I was thinking about doing more than that. You got anything on the guy who did this?"

"Not yet."

"You wouldn't be holding out on me, would you?"

"Me, hold out on the press?" said Cheney, trying to keep a straight face.

"It's not the press, it's me, buddy. You've told me a lot of things over the years that I would've given my left nut to print, but I didn't because I gave you my word that I wouldn't."

"You're a noble soul," said Cheney, sipping his beer. "So, Father Theresa, what's this all about?"

"Look, I know you're going to be right in the middle of this thing. I have two angles on Frank's murder. First and foremost, Frank was my friend and I want to see the bastard who killed him get nailed but good. Second, I think it's a good story."

"And you haven't had one of those in a while."

"Things've been a little slow. C'mon, Cheney, the cops could use some good ink for a change."

"Don't even *think* about bullshitting me, Ray. I know to the penny what you stand to get out of something like this. What I want to know is, what do *I* get out of it?"

Ray knew what Cheney meant. Cheney was not referring to money. He wanted to know how Ray could help him get the guy who murdered their friend.

"I have contacts, too. You know that. I've fed you a lot of good leads over the years. People clam up when the cops come around. They see me, it's different. I'm good with people."

"Especially when you can interview them in a bar. In that arena, I have to admit, you are without peer."

"C'mon, Cheney, cut me some slack. I'm serious."

"You're also a little drunk."

"I'm a functioning alcoholic." An indignant look flickered on Ray's face for an instant but it died quickly of embarrassment. "Look, Cheney, this could be my last chance. The *Trib's* cutting back and the bean counters are always looking for reasons to unload the upper-end salary guys. If this story goes anywhere, and if I've got an exclusive, I'm safe."

"For another year."

"A year can be a long time."

Cheney sipped his beer, not because he was thirsty, but because he just needed a moment to focus. "Look, Ray, Frank's got rights here, too. You turn this thing into a tabloid story . . ." Cheney didn't finish the thought. He just let it lie there, like a ticking bomb that would surely explode if Ray ignored it.

"C'mon, man, I'd never—"

"Maybe not intentionally. But these things have a way of getting out of control. We don't know where this story could lead. When you dig into a man's life, any man's life, there are always things that he kept private for a reason. Do we understand each other?"

"Of course."

"The bottom line is that I need you to feed me things I can't get from Tony," Cheney said.

"Like what?"

"You tell me, Ray. That's the deal."

"Fair enough." He smiled a whiskey smile that lit a small, dark corner of the bar in the middle of the afternoon. The smile was weaker than it used to be and it turned on much earlier than it used to. Maybe that was because it had a hell of a lot more darkness to fill.

Sierra Madre was a little town in the foothills just north and east of Pasadena. About the only time it ever got mentioned in the news was during the fire and mudslide seasons. It was a quaint town with a short main street, a hardware store, several curio shops, a bar, a nearly deserted theater, a couple of churches, a park, a market where clerks called customers by their first names, and a seafood restaurant touted by a well-known LA restaurant critic.

As Cheney drove down the sleepy main drag, a warm breeze caressed his cheek. Two mothers pushed children on swings in the park, a teenage couple, each with a backpack full of books, walked hand in hand across the street, and off to Cheney's right, a man in a green T-shirt and jeans walked uncertainly out of the bar, apparently having just sucked up a liquid lunch.

It was 1995, but it could have been 1965. For all its laid-back, folksy charm, Sierra Madre was home to an affluent and often creative populace. In LA, if you had more dreams than money and you wanted to be in the eye of the "Hollycane," you rented in Echo Park, Silverlake, or the Hollywood Hills. If you managed to turn some of those dreams into money, and you wanted to get out of the line of fire, Sierra Madre was as good a place as any. Better than most.

Cheney parked his J30 in front of a large old house. He thought it looked Victorian, but his take on architecture was not as good as it was on a lot of other things. A wooden sign hung between two black iron poles read: *MOLLY WALLACE, VETERINARIAN.*

Cheney hadn't seen Molly since she was a teenager, when he was married to someone else, and Frank was still married to Marge.

The waiting room was full of dogs. A guy with hair down the middle of his back had a black cocker spaniel on a leash. A black guy with his initials shaved in his head was petting a Great Dane while the dog dribbled water from its mouth like a leaky faucet. A gray-haired woman sat in the corner with a large English wolfhound that looked as though it needed a saddle more than a leash.

"Is Molly Wallace in?"

The woman behind the counter looked up over her horn-rimmed glasses at Cheney as though he were naked.

"I, uh, don't have a pet," said Cheney.

"Everyone should have a pet," the woman admonished.

"I have a shar-pei at home."

The woman smiled as though Cheney had just convinced her that he was not carrying the plague.

"I'm a friend of Molly's. I'd like to talk with her for a few minutes."

"Your name?"

"Cheney. Derek Cheney."

The woman disappeared through a door into a back area.

Cheney took a seat. The longhaired guy with the cocker spaniel was trading paper-training stories with the old woman with the wolfhound. Then they both started talking to the black guy about how cute the drooling Great Dane was. It was amazing to Cheney what a common denominator a pet was.

Molly opened the door to the reception room and smiled. "Cheney?"

"Hi, Molly."

"C'mon in."

Her office was decorated with diplomas and photographs. The photographs were mostly of men, including a couple of movie stars Cheney recognized. There were also a few of Molly and her mother, but there were no photographs of Frank. Molly sat behind her desk and Cheney sat opposite her. She had gained about forty pounds since he had last seen her. She wore little, if any, makeup, and she looked tired.

"Long time, no see," she said, leaning forward on her elbows.

Cheney thought she seemed genuinely happy to see him. And why not? Even though they hadn't seen each other for some time, there was about a fifteen-year stretch while she was growing up that they saw each other at least once a month. He'd always liked her and, he felt, she had liked him, too. Cheney remembered taking her to the movies once when Frank was in the hospital getting his appendix removed. Marge had wanted to stay with Frank and she had asked Cheney to take Molly to see some Disney movie. He had bought Molly popcorn and a Coke. And a box of Black Crows. Funny the things you remember, thought Cheney.

"I wish we were meeting under happier circumstances," he said.

Molly just pushed her lower lip into her upper lip a little and nodded slightly.

"I missed you at the funeral."

"I, uh, couldn't get away."

"Look, Molly, I know this is a tough time for you, and I realize you've got people in the waiting room, so I'll get right to it."

"You're looking into my father's murder?"

"Unofficially. Naturally, I'm giving everything I get to Tony."

"I don't know how I can help you."

"Well, I know your mother didn't see Frank very often anymore, and I'm trying to find out what was going on in his life just before his death. Anyone who might have had a grudge against him, somebody he put away who tracked him down, that kind of thing."

"You're really asking the wrong person. I haven't seen the man in more than seven years."

"That seems kind of strange."

"I have friends who haven't seen their parents since they moved out the house. It happens. There's nothing sinister about that. And I don't know anything about Frank's death."

"I was just hoping that you might know something about his life in Crestview."

"I don't. Whatever I know about it, which isn't much, I know from my mother."

Her mother was her "mother." Her father was "the man" and "Frank."

"What did your mother tell you?"

"I'm sure she's already told you."

"Never hurts to go over it again."

Molly took a deep breath and let it out. If it had been anyone but Cheney, she would have looked at her watch and declined to answer any more questions. "I know he was living in Crestview. Dingy-looking little burg. I remember passing through it a few years ago on my way up the coast."

"What was he doing up there?"

"What does anyone do when they retire?"

Cheney didn't answer. He scoured wine shops for good inexpensive chardonnays, made pasta by hand, and played golf at the Riviera Country Club. He didn't imagine that was what most retired people did. "Why did he move up there? Why not retire in the Valley, or somewhere closer to home?"

"Maybe there wasn't any 'home' for him here anymore."

Cheney nodded. Marge seemed to have lost her feeling for Frank and certainly Frank was not welcome in Molly's house. And, thought Cheney somewhat guiltily, he had not made any special efforts to maintain his connection with his ex-partner. But then, neither had Frank.

"Look, Cheney, it's good to see you, honestly. Why don't you and—you got married again, right?"

"Yes."

"Why don't you and your wife give me a call sometime and have dinner with me and my fiancé? But now I've got work to do and I really don't know anything about my father's murder."

"But—"

"You liked my father, didn't you?" she said, standing and looking Cheney in the eye.

"Yes, I did."

"What happened between my father and me is private. And it will remain private for several reasons, not the least of which is because I choose to keep it that way. Let this part of it go, Cheney. For you, my father died a few days ago. For me, he died a long time ago. You try to remember the good times, and I'll try to forget the bad. In the long run, the rest of it doesn't really matter much. Not anymore."

She looked at her watch and smiled, the way Cheney remembered her smile. "I've got a room full of sick puppies."

"That's funny. Your father and I used to say the same thing when we were working outta the Ramparts Division."

Cheney and Tony Boston walked along the Santa Monica Pier. A couple of surfers leaned against the railing, next to their boards and wet suits. A trio of old-timers, one of them a woman, walked toward the end of the pier, tackle box in one hand, rod and reel in the other. Tony was munching on a hot dog he'd bought from a vendor. He raved about the tiny stand having the best wieners in town, but Cheney preferred Pink's on La Brea. Cheney stuck his hands in his pockets. The wind off the Pacific in December could get mighty chilly at twilight.

"We found out what Frank was doing at the mall."

"Christmas shopping, I'd imagine."

"Probably. He bought a glass unicorn."

"It wasn't found with the body."

"I know. But a receipt from a store in the mall was found in his wallet. We checked with the store. He bought a twenty-five dollar unicorn about fifteen minutes before he was killed."

"So the murderer took the unicorn, left Frank's car, his wallet with a hundred bucks in it, and all his credit cards."

"Doesn't make sense," said Tony.

"Souvenir."

"What?"

"The killer took a souvenir." Cheney shook his head and looked out over the Pacific. "This guy's going to kill again, Tony."

"I was afraid you were going to say that." Because he had already arrived at the same conclusion.

"Was Frank seeing a shrink?"

"If he was, I didn't know about it."

"But if he was referred by the department, before or after he turned in his badge, you could find out."

"I could. Want me to?"

"Yes."

"What does it have to do with anything?"

"I don't know. Until we find the guy who killed Frank, I don't know what's important and what isn't. Also, I'm beginning to think I didn't know my own partner half as well as I thought I did."

"What do you mean?"

"Either I was oblivious to what made Frank tick, or he changed a lot in the past few years."

Tony stopped, wiped some mustard off his lips with a napkin, and tossed the napkin into a trash can. He turned his back to the wind and faced Cheney. "Be careful the questions you ask. You just might get answers."

"What's that supposed to mean?" said Cheney, though he was pretty sure he knew.

"I know you want to help find Frank's killer. All that's fine and good, but when you go digging up a man's past, there are always certain things that are better left buried."

"When you and I work murder investigations, are we that considerate of victims who aren't our friends?"

"This is different. Because Frank's your friend, the information isn't just something you write down in a report. It's something that can change the way you look at the man. Forever."

Cheney just faced into the wind, past Tony's fluttering hair, toward the Pacific that was churning on the axis of an ancient and timeless passion. Baby boomers despaired that teenagers had no sense of perspective or history and were doomed to repeat the mistakes they had made. Senior citizens felt the same way about baby boomers.

Cheney looked out at the ocean again as two teenagers strutted and swayed past him. They were talking about "gettin' a piece" of some guy, about "gettin' a piece of ass" later on. Seemed to Cheney everybody wanted a piece of somebody else these days, one way or the other.

He turned up his collar to the wind. Suddenly Cheney felt very tired. And very old.

The Round Table was in session.

"What we do here is important," said Diana.

The others nodded. She did not look directly at them, but she could see their reflections in the mirror.

"What we do here, and out there, in the real world, is very important. It's not enough that *we* know what we do is right. Other people must know. And they will. They will talk about what we do here and things will change."

The others nodded.

"Fear is what it's all about," said Diana. She looked at the others gathered at the table. At Mark. At Carl. At Malcolm. At Dennis.

"Fear brings a person out of his safety zone. The safety zone is the place where most people stay. It's a place they protect with money, power, sex, religion, whatever they hope will insulate them from their sins. But no one is ever safe from their own sin."

Diana caught a glimpse of herself in the mirror. She was not a babe. But then neither was she unattractive. She was a blonde with a solid, though not particularly round, figure. Angular, she would say. She was smart and her intellect had served her well over the years. She was the only female in the group. She liked that. Used it.

In the background the New Age sounds of pianist Margaret Lam Khai filled the room with soft tones. Diana smoked a filtered cigarette that she had read somewhere was nonaddictive. Besides, she rarely inhaled.

There was an aura of her femininity in the air and her senses were filled with it. The Round Table was filled with it.

"I'm a little sick a' that New Age shit," said Carl. He was into country-and-western music.

"This is my night," said Diana firmly, without sounding adversarial. Carl was unpredictable. Still, Diana could control him. Had to control him.

"Okay, but do we have to listen to that shit all fuckin' night?"

Diana picked up a remote control and turned down the piano music. Didn't turn it off. Carl had to be handled.

"Let's get down to business," said Diana, not acknowledging Carl further.

Malcolm sat with his feet up on the table, his head bobbing to some real or imagined rock-and-roll song playing in his head.

Dennis sat staring directly at Diana. He didn't need music. Diana felt closest to Dennis. Yet that fact scared her. Carl was erratic. Mark had his limitations. Malcolm was unfocused. Each had some personality problems. But Dennis was different. Dennis stared straight ahead. Looked through them all. He was there and he was not there. He seemed always to be a hair's breadth away from a homicidal rage.

Dennis was dangerous. More dangerous than the rest.

Diana raised her glass toward the others. She saw them in the mirror. Each drank. Even Dennis. The New Age music played in the background. It was ritual.

When it was over, Diana walked out upon the lawn, toward the lake. She sat alone on the smooth wet bank of the Black Water. Sipping her wine. Ritual.

Looked out over the lake. Sat there sipping a sweet wine.

Diana downed the rest of her wine and tossed the glass out into the lake. In the moonlight she could see the ripples undulating out in concentric circles from where her glass went down, died, in the water. Circles within circles. Life was like that. Her life was like that—endless waves emanating from a single event.

Eventually touching everything. Everyone.

Diana felt good. She stood and walked closer to the lake, down to the dock. She got into the small boat and adjusted the oars. Ritual.

Rowed out into the middle of the lake.

Looked back toward the shore. Sensed the others looking at her, even though she didn't see them.

She knew what she had to do. Knew how to keep a secret.

As she sat there in the middle of the lake, oars idle, in the middle of the Black Water, she sensed the presence. It was the presence they all felt. It was the presence that had brought them all together. Made them do what they did.

It was the presence.

It was justice.

It was . . . ritual.

Six

C restview was about ninety minutes from Pacific Palisades. Driving north up the Pacific Coast Highway, Cheney went against morning rush hour traffic. He loved his new J30. He had traded in the Mercedes 300E for a couple of reasons, not the least of which that he really liked the look, feel, and value of the Infiniti. The leather seats, the real wood, the CD, the Bose speakers. It didn't cost as much as the 300E, but he liked it as much, if not better. The ocean looked more peaceful today, especially with Pat Metheny playing guitar and Bruce Hornsby playing piano on the CD.

He pulled off PCH and onto Crestview's main drag a little before eleven. Christmas decorations, about a dozen strands of bells and candy canes, danced out of sync in the wind over the deserted streets. To Cheney the green-and-red decorations seemed like guests who had overstayed their welcome.

Cheney got directions to Frank's apartment from a teenager at a self-service gas station. In the old days, days Cheney could still remember, the kid would have been at the pump with a dirty rag in one hand and a squeegee in the other. The kid Cheney talked to sat behind a counter watching a portable TV and seemed irritated that the out-of-towner wanted something other than to put a ten or twenty in pump number one, two, or three.

Five minutes later Cheney pulled up in front of a duplex. He hit a button on the dashboard and the jazz simmered down inside the Bose speakers. He walked up three flights of steps to 3300 ½ Overlook Way. He knew Frank's apartment was empty so he knocked on the neighbor's door. No one answered.

He went downstairs and over to a blue house with a fence around it. The gate was open; actually it was broken in a way that made it difficult to close. The yard needed mowing—about a year ago. Cheney knocked on the door. He heard someone moving around inside and finally the door opened.

"Yeah?" A young man who looked to Cheney to be in his late teens stood in the doorway. His hair was black, long, and tied in a ponytail. He wore cutoff jeans, even though the temperature was near fifty, a T-shirt with a Chinese character on it, no shoes.

"I'm a friend of Frank Curtis. One of your neighbors," explained Cheney, pointing up the hill toward Frank's duplex.

"Right, the retired cop. I heard he was murdered in LA. Is that true?"

"I'm afraid so."

"You a cop?"

"I'm his ex-partner."

"C'mon in," said the man.

The decor was early orange crate, and there must

have been well over a thousand books lining every wall
and stacked on tables.

"You must like to read," said Cheney while he
moved a pile of books so that he could sit down.

"I like to write even more. That's why I'm here."

"Oh, you go to UC Santa Barbara?"

"No. I'm here because this is where Ross
MacDonald lived. And died."

Cheney nodded. He wasn't much of a reader, but he
had read MacDonald's Lew Archer books and liked
them. "He was quite a writer."

"The master. I worship him," said the young man,
using present tense. He extended his hand. "My name's
Douglas. Douglas Lee."

"Cheney," said the ex-cop, shaking hands. "Just the
one name."

"Like Dylan."

"In a way," said Cheney, not wanting to argue.

"Frank mentioned your name."

"Really? How well did you know Frank?"

"We'd buy each other beers and talk. Mainly he'd
talk and I'd listen. I'm writing my first private eye novel
and just being in Santa Barbara, where Ross
MacDonald walked and talked and wrote, shoots me up
with a shitload of inspiration. But I always need more.
I'm hungry for real life, you know what I mean?"

Cheney remembered. "Yes."

"And who knows more about real life than a cop,
right? Talking to Frank was like listening to a professor.
A professor of the street. Actually, I think he got something out of our relationship, too. It seemed like as
much as I needed to listen, he needed to talk."

"What did he need to talk about?"

"Like all of us, he was trying to rid himself of
demons."

"Anything more specific?"

Douglas laughed. "Don't worry, I'm not going to drown you in a sea of clichés. Frank talked about real specifics. Real cases, real stakeouts, real busts, real shoot-outs. Real life." Douglas shook his head as though in awe—not of Frank, but of the richness of real life. "The most amazing things I remember were the details, the little asides he'd make. Crazy things that if you put them in a book, people would think you're making them up. Real life is always more bizarre than fiction, don't you think?"

"I don't know. I don't read that much fiction. Did Frank make any enemies up here?"

"Frank?" Douglas made a face as though Cheney had asked him if he wanted to put money on the Cubs to win the World Series. "Are you serious? No way."

"Did he mention that maybe somebody he put away had contacted him?"

"Nah."

"Did he ever mention going to down LA regularly on business?"

"No. He'd go down to LA a lot, but he never told me why. I never asked. I mean, he used to live there, right? Worked there all his life. It's only ninety minutes away. He could've had a thousand good reasons. Why?"

"No reason."

Douglas smiled, didn't laugh. "So that's the way it is. I answer your questions, you don't answer mine."

"I don't know why he went down to LA," said Cheney. "Like you say, could be a lot of good reasons. Since he was killed in LA, I'm just asking, that's all."

Douglas looked at Cheney. Didn't nod, didn't say anything that would make him look or sound stupid.

"Frank have any other friends up here?"

"A few."

"Anyone special?"

"You mean like a girlfriend?"

"Whatever."

"There was Lilly. She's a waitress down at Jake's. That's a little bar down on Central. It's got sawdust on the floor, old songs on the jukebox, cheap beer, peanuts on the table, that whole nine yards."

"She working tonight?"

"Yeah. She works five nights a week. I'm pretty sure she's working tonight."

"Does she know that Frank's dead?"

"Yeah. We talked about it. Actually, we drank about it. She was pretty broke up when she heard."

"You know where she lives?"

"No, but she starts work around four. Want me to take you over there?"

"Sure."

"On one condition."

"Which is?"

"Tell me about a couple of your most interesting cases."

"You got it." Cheney stood and headed for the door.

"Four o'clock. I don't have a car. You mind picking me up?"

"No problem."

Cheney was halfway down the sidewalk toward his car when Douglas said, "Cheney?"

Cheney turned back around.

"I better warn you," said the young man with a smile. "Lilly might not be what you expect."

Jake's was a college bar. College-age crowd, alternative music, with a heavy mix of old and contemporary blues and a one-dollar cover. It was open-air, at least the wall to the left of the band, from waist-level up, was. The hole in the wall looked out over a parking lot that was a temporary berth for about a dozen decaled motorcycles and a variety of bumper-stickered entry-level-priced cars, most of which were banged up some.

The motif was Mexican, or maybe someone's cheap Tequila-dream idea of Santa Fe. The decor seemed to fit a budget more than the room that gave it sanctuary. The plaster walls were painted yellow with orange trim and they were covered with blanket/wall hangings and posters of what looked to be sepia-tint photos of Mexican bandits with big guns and mustaches. The occasional poster for the bands Nirvana, Soundgarden and Stone Temple Pilots gave Cheney cultural whiplash.

Douglas and Cheney took a booth near the kitchen. Lilly, who seemed pretty busy, waved at Douglas.

"So, what do you think?"

"Of the place or of Lilly?" asked Cheney, unable to take his eyes off the woman. She was young. Very young. Cheney pegged her at about twenty-two or -three. She was slim, wore her dirty-blonde hair so that it teased her shoulders without ever touching them. She had ferretlike features, and the easy smile that accompanied youth in which innocence had not yet been trampled by the crush of a daily grind. But Lilly didn't carry herself as an innocent. And, thought Cheney as he watched Lilly move, twenty-two was looking and sounding older every year.

"The place."

"It's cool."

Douglas smiled.

"What?" asked Cheney.

"I love it when old people use jargon from their

generation. It's like the language comes alive," said the young writer.

"That's groovy," said Cheney, bending his face into a half scowl.

Lilly walked over to their booth, tray in hand, and stuck out her hand. "You're Cheney." It was not a question.

"Nice to meet you."

"Same here. Frank used to talk a lot about you. Most of it good."

Cheney smiled and, despite himself, he wondered if she meant what she said or if she was just being glib. And if she wasn't, what did she mean by "most of it"?

"I gave you the booth next to the kitchen so I can stop and talk to you as much as I can."

"You get a break?"

"Actually, I've got one coming now. Let me just take this order in back, then I'm yours for ten minutes." With that, she dove between two battered swinging doors.

"Isn't she great?"

"Yeah," said Cheney, mainly because he didn't know what else to say.

"I brought you guys some Heinekens," said Lilly when she returned and sat down next to Douglas, opposite Cheney. "I was going to go to the funeral, but, well, I just didn't think that would've been the right thing to do."

"Why?" asked Cheney, even though he thought he knew. But a good cop let other people fill in the blanks.

"Well, you know. I imagine his ex-wife and daughter were there. I didn't want to make things any more difficult than they already were."

"What exactly was your relationship with Frank?"

Lilly laughed. It was an easy laugh that seemed

genuine. Cheney remembered such laughs, but it took
firing up a pretty good-sized cluster of remaining brain
cells to recall having heard one up close and personal.

"You mean was I fucking him?"

"Well, I wouldn't have put it as delicately as that."

"Irony. I love irony," said Douglas.

"But that's what you really meant, right?" said Lilly.

"I suppose." Cheney had to smile. At himself. He
was only out of harness a couple of years, and he felt
uneasy asking obvious questions, in the language people he asked would understand. Questions that needed
to be asked. And answered.

"Yeah. I was seeing Frank for about a year or so.
Exclusively."

"I see."

"I doubt it. You think Frank was playing hide the
sausage with some young, brainless bimbo. That ain't
the way it went. I liked Frank. I loved Frank, actually.
Least as close as I ever got to it—love, I mean. He
came in for about six months before we ever went out
on a real date. And even then, it was another six
months before we had sex. Frank and I had something.
Sex was part of it, but it wasn't the most important
part."

"What was the most important part?"

"He understood me."

When Lilly let it lay there, Cheney said, "I don't
mean to be rude, but isn't that a little vague?"

"Maybe to you. Men don't listen to women. Oh,
some of them put up enough of a show so they can
plant the old flag in pay dirt, but they hate to have to
sit there for very long not talking about themselves.
Frank and I talked and talked. About everything. Cop
stories, cars, beer, working for a living, dysfunctional
families, sex, the meaning of life, and where to get the

best waffles in town. Everything and nothing. Sometimes nothing's the best thing to talk about." Lilly leaned back in the booth, a light from the bar catching her and painting half her face yellow, the other in shadow. "By the time Frank and I went to bed, I knew more about the guy than most women know about their husbands after ten years of marriage."

"Which is why I want to talk with you. No one I know in LA seems to know much about his life after he moved up here."

"Maybe nobody wanted to know."

Cheney felt a twinge of guilt, but he shook it off. "Did he seem afraid or apprehensive lately?"

"No. In fact, he seemed in a pretty good mood. I mean, it was Christmas time and we . . ." The easy smile disappeared deep for the first time. "We were going to go skiing in Tahoe."

"Skiing?" asked Cheney incredulously.

The smile did an encore. "Yeah, I know. It's not a pretty picture imagining Frank on skis. But I wanted to go and that was going to be his Christmas present to me—that and a unicorn."

"What?" said Cheney, his hair standing on end. Tony had told him Frank had bought a glass unicorn the night he was murdered.

"Yeah, I have a collection. I told him I wanted a particular kind. It was kind of rare, but he told me he'd get it for me. And I believed him. Frank always followed through."

"I'm sure he would have."

Someone called Lilly's name loud and she yelled something back. "Look, I gotta go. Maybe we can get together after I get off."

"Sounds good," said Cheney. "Anyhow, thanks. I appreciate your candor."

"Why not? I got nothin' to hide." Then she disappeared into the kitchen.

"So whatdya think? Not what you expected, right?"

"I expected her to be a little older," said Cheney.

"Her body's young, but she's got 'years between the ears,'" said Douglas, pointing to his head with his beer mug. "Real street smart. She gets hit on four, five times a night, six nights a week. But she doesn't let it throw her off balance, you know what I mean?"

"I do. My wife's a little like that."

"She a waitress?"

"No, but she listens to people's problems all day and she still gets guys' attention when she wears a skirt."

"He liked you, a lot, Frank did. Sometimes it'd just be Frank, Lilly, and me, sitting around here at one o'clock. Nobody here but us and the bartender. He told us about the time he and you busted that transsexual stripper who had a derringer in the crotch of her pantyhose and she shot Frank in the arm."

Cheney smiled. "Neither of us wanted to search the guy. We were young. And pretty fuckin' stupid."

"He was proud of you."

"Oh?" Cheney wasn't sure he wanted to hear this.

"He was proud that you went on and became chief of detectives, and that he used to be your partner."

"He was a good man," said Cheney, sipping his beer and staring off into the past. Wondering why he hadn't said that he was proud of Frank, too.

"He was the kind of person I always wanted to meet," said Douglas, sucking down the rest of his imported, on-the-house beer. "The kind of person I needed to meet."

"What do you mean?"

"I'm a writer, right?"

Cheney didn't argue.

"I know grammar, I can string words together, but I lack experience. That's why I came to Santa Barbara—to walk the ground that Ross MacDonald walked."

"I don't mean to be a wet blanket, but coming to a shrine and paying homage isn't the same thing as experience."

"I know. But the funny thing is, when you pay your respects, like I have to my guru, things happen. What happened for me was that I met Frank. I have about ten hours of tapes of things Frank told me about his life, about his experiences as a cop. Things from the heart, you know?"

"But it isn't the same as *being* a cop."

"I understand that. But with a few exceptions, most writers, even the good ones, including MacDonald, weren't cops. After spending time in New York, LA, and now soaking up my experiences with Frank, I really think I've got something to say."

"Those tapes . . . you still have them?"

"Of course. They're my prize possessions."

"Could I listen to them?"

"Sure. And if there's anything you'd like to add to any of Frank's stories, I'll take notes, okay?"

"Okay."

The next couple of hours were buried under the sound of a band that played too loud and, for Cheney, far too often. Finally, he couldn't take it anymore. Lilly said she'd see them later at Douglas's place. Cheney told Douglas to stay, that he had some calls to make, and that he'd meet him at Douglas's apartment about one—Lilly said she'd be by after two.

When Cheney stepped outside the bar, the fresh air and the silence were welcome friends, warmly embraced. He had stepped into a strange world. His ex-partner's best friend and lover were in their twenties.

Early twenties. Some mystery writer wanna-be Frank felt comfortable enough with to pour out his life on tape, and some slim-hipped, flat-stomached waitress to share his bed.

Cheney needed some air. Two questions kept running through his head as he drove down the side streets back onto the Pacific Coast Highway. Lilly reminded Cheney more of Frank's daughter than of his ex-wife. He wondered if Frank saw it the same way.

But most of all, Cheney wondered what was on the tapes.

The woman looked into the mirror . . .

And a strange face stared back. She sat still for a moment. Took it all in. She was not beautiful. She was not ugly. She was middle-aged. Barely. She was not a drinker, never did drugs, and she watched what she ate. She had never married. She'd had two significant affairs in her life—both with married men who, she thought, for various and good reasons, would eventually leave their wives. For her. For the life the two of them had talked so long and so passionately about, usually between the sheets. But the men had not left their wives. Not fulfilled the fantasy. Not lived up to their promises.

Yet she never felt desperate. Or at least she never showed it. She was successful in other ways.

She looked into the mirror . . .

And applied the last touches of makeup. She had a date. A date with a man who loved her. Not like her father. Not like that son of a bitch. He had told her he loved her. Said all the right things. Done all the right things.

But he had done other things, too.

She remembered the first time.

She was twelve years old, a little gangly, a little unsure. The kids at school didn't know how to react to her. She was pretty, but she was tall, too tall. That was fine for basketball, at which she excelled. All the guys wanted to learn her moves on the court, but never asked her out on dates.

The woman remembered every real or imagined slight. And they all left scars as real as gunshot wounds.

But someone noticed. Finally. Gratefully.

Her father noticed that *such a pretty girl shouldn't be sitting home alone on a Saturday night*. Her mother had been gone that first time.

But even though she had felt a little uncomfortable, her father had made her feel good. Feel pretty. Grateful. And, just a little . . .

Afraid.

Andrew Mason looked in the mirror . . .

A strange face looked back at him. He sat still for a moment. Took it all in. He was not handsome. He was not ugly. He was middle-aged. He was a drinker, had done drugs off and on over the years, and tried, with varying degrees of success, to regulate his diet. He had failed at marriage. Failed at being a father.

But he had fulfilled the fantasy.

Andrew did not look at himself as a bad man, although he knew that others would. Others did.

For a while it would all calm down. The crazy pictures in his head would fade like dying embers from a firestorm. Even the most raging fire always burned down to embers. But unless the evil glow died, the flames would start again . . . if they landed on something flammable. And in Andrew's world, he was never far from images that could be inflamed. How he wished the embers would die forever.

But they never did. The crazy pictures always came back. He would get up in the morning and try to think positive thoughts, watch TV, listen to the news, and . . . and *goddammit* nothing would help. Eventually, he would get up one morning and there, in the background, a background no one else could see or hear, it would be there.

A darkness that shrouded his perception. Made the flowers look diseased. Made loving pets look like hounds from hell. Made minor events seem apocalyptic.

The darkness was not something he could ever explain to therapists. They listened, they nodded, they prescribed.

But they never understood. Not really.

The darkness was a black veil through which he saw the world. It removed color, texture and joy from a universe apparently replete in all those aspects. For him, the color, texture, and joy had never existed.

Because the madness always came back, no matter how he tried to push it away. Medication. Hypnosis. Group therapy.

Everything helped.

Nothing worked.

The crazy pictures always returned.

Was what he had done really so bad? Hadn't others done worse? Why was he so hard on himself? No one had died.

And that was how it always started.

The rationalizations.

And why not? Suicide was the only other answer. If not that, then he must learn to live with . . . it. What was it the guy on the radio said. *He is not a bad man. He is a man who has done a bad thing.* That made him feel better.

For a while.

Nothing made him feel good for very long.

The crazy pictures always returned. Always made him feel like a freak.

It was a bad feeling, being out of control. Andrew often thought that most people were out of control, if they really thought about it.

People fell in love with the wrong people. They were overwhelmed by the sight, the fantasy, the smell. . . . Out of control.

Andrew was always attracted to the wrong person. Overwhelmed by the fantasy. Out of control.

He took another shot of vodka and looked at himself in the mirror. *What a fuck-up!* And he raised his glass toward his image.

Suddenly he felt very afraid.

Fear was something she had learned to live with. She tasted it now as she walked along the beach, just the hint of ocean spray moistening her cheeks.

She felt her heart pumping, felt the dampness of wet sand seeping through her tennis shoes.

She heard the barefoot runner before she saw him. Heard his feet splashing and slapping against the wet sand. Getting closer. Very close now.

He saw the angular blonde in front of him. Walking. Slowly. He had never seen her before. Often he would come across the same people when he ran. Other people had routines, too.

He ran past her without looking back.

Which was why he never saw the knife.

Diana plunged the blade into the middle of Andrew Mason's back and he screamed and went down. She withdrew the knife and plunged it again. And again. And again.

After the third . . . incision, Andrew Mason stopped screaming. They were several hundred yards from the nearest house. Diana had planned it that way. Andrew Mason was the most meticulous man she had ever observed. But that was not why she had to kill him. He knew. And just in case he didn't, she turned the body over, plunged the knife once more into the dead man's heart, took something out of her pocket and dropped it on the open and bloody wound.

She put the knife in a plastic bag, stuck it inside her coat and walked back toward where she had parked her car. She felt good.

She knew the other members of the Round Table would be proud.

"Mind if I smoke some dope?"

Cheney smiled. "You mean, will I arrest you if you do?"

"Not exactly. It's just that Frank did a little smoke now and then—nothing more than that, I swear," said Douglas defensively. "He said lots of cops smoke weed."

Cheney shrugged. He didn't know if he would say "lots," but he knew a few cops who did. A little. Nobody tripped over themselves to make citizen's arrests. Most cops he knew drank. More than a little. Cheney was not his brother's, or even his partner's, keeper.

"It makes me feel good, you know?"

"No problem," said the ex-cop. He accepted a beer from Douglas, who had a joint in the other hand.

"I really loved Frank."

"Me too," said Cheney.

"He'd seen it all, you know." The young writer sucked the sweet smoke deeply into his lungs.

"Now you can never be president."

"Who'd want to be." Douglas exhaled. "Most people know what they know from other people. From TV. Frank knew what he knew from experience. Real experience. He *lived* the street. He didn't just read about it or see it on some cop show. I learned from him, I really did."

"Me too." Partners learned from each other. Cheney had learned from Frank, and Frank had learned a lot from Cheney. "About the tapes . . . "

"Right. I've got everything on my computer. All the topics on the tapes are indexed and cross-referenced. You looking for something special?"

"How about the most recent tapes? Say, the last month or so."

"No problem." Douglas punched up the list on his computer, found what he was looking for, walked over to his entertainment center, and ran his fingers along a row of neatly stacked cassettes, each with a number on its spine. He plucked out a clear box, opened it and put the tape into a dual cassette player. He walked back to the couch and sat down next to Cheney. He picked up a remote and aimed it at the cassette machine. The room was filled with a low hissing sound, then the unmistakable deep tones of Frank's voice. Cheney just had to smile.

Frank was laughing. He sounded as though he was half in the bag. But Frank could always hold his liquor. He could go through a fifth of whiskey in one day, not every day but now and then, and still fool most people—at least those outside of breathing range.

Frank was telling old war stories, all of which Cheney knew by heart, although he noticed some of the details were, well, somewhat more colorful than he remembered them. The tape was punctuated by occasional and appropriate laughter, and Douglas's "Wow" and "No shit!" every once in a while.

Cheney listened to ninety minutes of the tape that Douglas said was the last one he recorded with Frank. And there was nothing on it but Frank having fun mugging for the kid. He seemed to be having a great time. He didn't sound like a man who thought he was about to die.

There was a knock at the front door, and it opened almost immediately. Lilly walked in with a six-pack under her arm. It was about two thirty and Douglas was starting to sink under the weight of the marijuana and Frank's monotone voice.

Lilly went to the kitchen and returned with three beers. She handed one to Cheney, one to Douglas, twisted off the cap of the third, and sat down on the couch.

"You look a little tired, partner," said Cheney to Douglas.

"Man, I'm wasted. I got up at ten."

"You know what they say about the early bird," said Cheney, trying to keep a straight face.

"Feel free to use the place. I'm gonna turn in."

"Thanks. I'll talk to you tomorrow."

"Later." Douglas stood, beer in hand, and waved, not bothering to look back. The bedroom door shut and Cheney and Lilly were alone.

"Guess it's just you and me." Lilly took a swig of beer and set the bottle between her legs.

"I'm glad."

Lilly looked at him.

"I don't mean that the way it sounded."

"Look, Cheney—I can call you Cheney, can't I?"

"Of course."

"I don't need a map to find my way out of a phone

booth. I know you aren't trying to put the moves on me. I know you want to talk about Frank. Lighten up."

"Yeah, well . . ." Suddenly Cheney felt like a horse on skates. He usually did the pushing and shoving.

"To Frank." Lilly raised her bottle and Cheney tapped his beer against hers.

"To Frank."

They sat in silence for a moment, remembering the man as they each had known him. Cheney knew how he remembered Frank. He was wondering how much different Lilly's vision of the man was from his own.

"You said something tonight. You said you and Frank talked about everything. I think you mentioned dysfunctional families. Did Frank think his family was dysfunctional?"

"I don't know exactly what to say. Frank told me things in confidence, you know? I mean, I'm sure if you kicked off, you wouldn't want some guy coming around and making your wife tell him everything you told her in private."

"I'm not just some guy—I'm Frank's friend. And I'm not making you say anything. If there's something you think Frank would have wanted to remain private, it's your call. I'm just trying to get a firm fix on what Frank was all about in the last part of his life. When I knew him, he seemed . . . different."

"You tight with Marge?"

"He talked about his wife?"

"What's the deal—cops never answer questions?"

"Marge and I are friends," said Cheney lamely. But in his heart he knew it wasn't true. Frank had been their common bond and when he was no longer in the picture, Marge became just Cheney's partner's ex-wife.

"Maybe she was just a Christmas card friend,

somethin' like that," said Lilly, picking up on Cheney's equivocation.

"I don't send Christmas cards anymore."

"I've come to the conclusion that people don't have that many real friends in a lifetime." Lilly sipped some more brew.

"Did Frank actually use the term 'dysfunctional family'?" said Cheney, trying to steer things back on track.

Lilly thought a moment. Not about the question, but whether or not to answer it. "Yeah, he did."

"Do you know why he and Marge got divorced?"

"Do you?"

Cheney smiled. Lilly was wasting her time serving booze. She should have been a cop. "I think so. I don't think it was anything so horrible. Two people just grew in different directions."

Lilly smiled knowingly. "You been divorced?"

"Yeah."

"I thought so."

"Nothing disgraceful about it."

"Not anymore."

"Most adults have been married more than once."

"So I guess that makes it okay."

"It's not okay with you?" asked Cheney.

"I don't know. I never tried it."

As much as he admired the way she danced, Cheney knew the points were for style and not substance. "Look, I'm not trying to turn over every rock and shine a light on everything that moves. I'm trying to find the guy who killed my friend. I went to see his daughter the other day and she didn't seem too broken up about his death. That struck me as odd. Then I show up here and you look a lot like his daughter, only more so—"

"What do you mean by that?"

"Younger. The way I remember her before Marge

and Frank were divorced. Then you mention out of the blue something about a dysfunctional family and it gets me to thinking."

"About what?" said Lilly, looking the ex-cop straight in the eye.

She wasn't being defiant, she didn't look nervous. There was nothing on her face Cheney could read. It was like looking at a sheet of paper covered with foreign characters. He couldn't make it out. "I'm not sure."

"Let me tell you what you're thinking," she said confidently. "You're thinking you might not have known Frank as well as you thought you did. You're thinking maybe he likes young girls. Maybe young girls who look like his own daughter. Maybe he likes me 'cause I look a little like her. Am I getting warm?"

"I don't know, I—"

"Then maybe you're too close to the case, Cheney. After all, he was your partner. Because if I were you, that's what I'd be thinking. You want another beer?" she said as she set down her empty bottle and headed for the kitchen.

"Sure."

"I thought you might."

A moment later she returned with two beers, one of which she handed to Cheney. "So, where were we?"

"I think we were to the part where you were handing me my balls on a platter."

"Gee, I love that kind of talk. Reminds me of Frank."

"So, what do you think?"

"You mean do I think Frank was fucking his daughter?" asked Lilly.

Cheney just looked at her. He wasn't sure, but it felt like he was holding his breath.

"If he was, he didn't tell me," she said.

"What's your personal opinion?"

"I don't have one."

"You must."

"That's where you're wrong, cowboy. I don't have to have an opinion about that. I really—and I mean really—never thought about it. I know he had some problems with his daughter, and I know he was dating me. He always treated me like a woman, never like a child. He was a pretty straight guy—sexually, I mean. I'm not going to give you details, but he didn't make me dress up in cotton panties and pigtails, and lick a lollipop."

"I take it you wouldn't have gone for that."

She smiled. "I dunno, I never tried it."

This was a very interesting woman, thought Cheney. A blind man could see what Frank saw in her.

"He talked about you more than he talked about his family," said Lilly.

"Really?"

"Yeah. He said he admired you more than anyone he'd ever known."

Cheney nodded. He didn't know exactly what to say. After a while he asked, "Anything else?"

"Yeah. He said he missed you."

Seven

"Can I come in?"

"Hey, Cheney, what's up?" Douglas looked pretty chipper for eleven in the morning, thought Cheney. But then, Douglas'd had more sleep than the ex-cop.

Cheney walked into the young man's apartment, turned down offers of wine, beer, and the remnants of a joint. He settled for coffee, which the writer proudly brewed, describing the process and the machinery as he went. When they were seated on the couch in the living room, Cheney said, "You said you had an index about what Frank said on the tapes."

"Very complete. I cross-referenced every main topic he talked about. You looking for something special?"

"I'm looking for anything he said about his daughter."

"Okay." Douglas went to his computer and fired it up. He waited for a moment, sipped his coffee. Punched a few keys. "Daughter." Douglas shook his head. "What was her name?"

"Molly."

Douglas tapped a few more keys and smiled. "Got it. Tape five, number three-five-seven."

"Three-five-seven?"

"I put the tape in, at the beginning, and set the counter at zero. Then I fast-forward to three-five-seven and *voilà*—he'll start talking about Molly."

Douglas walked over to his entertainment center, found the tape, put it in, set the counter at zero, and fast-forwarded it to the right spot. "I don't think he said much about her. Otherwise I would've remembered. In fact, this is the only reference."

On the tape: "*My daughter used to think of me that way.*"

"*You have a daughter?*"

"*Yeah.*"

"*You never mentioned her.*"

"*I haven't told you* everything *about my life in two months, Doug.*"

"*Right. You say she* used to *think of you as a hero. Not anymore?*"

"*Things change. Not always in the ways you want them to.*"

"*Where is she?*"

"*She lives in Sierra Madre. She's a veterinarian.*"

"*No shit. An animal doctor. That's great.*"

"*Yeah.*"

"*She married?*"

"*Not anymore.*"

"*Where's Sierra Madre?*"

"*In the foothills above Pasadena.*"

"*You see her often?*"

"*I haven't seen her in about five years or so.*"

"*You're kidding! Hell, Pasadena's just a couple hours from here.*"

"Yeah, I know. Could we change the subject?"

"Sure, no sweat. But I'm trying to be a writer here, you know. I mean, this is an interesting topic."

"Not to me."

"What I mean is, you love your daughter, right?"

"Yes."

"You're within easy driving distance and you don't see each other. So, if you love her, that means she's got a problem with you."

"Let's just drop it, okay?"

"C'mon, Frank. This is conflict. This is drama. This is real life. Nothin' like real life—isn't that what you always say?"

"It's something private that I want to stay private. If that's all you want to talk about, fine, I'm outta here."

"Okay, okay. Sorry, Frank. I'm just trying to be professional."

"Yeah, sure."

"So, what do you want to talk about?"

Silence.

"I'm really not in the mood anymore, Doug. Let's call it a night."

Douglas hit the remote and the tape clicked to a stop.

"What do you make of that?" asked Cheney.

"I don't know. Obviously he didn't want to talk about his daughter. Other than that, I don't know. Quite frankly, I was less interested in Frank's personal life than I was in his professional life. Hell, I've got a personal life to draw upon. What I was collecting was war stories, you know?"

"Yeah, I know."

"What do you make of it?"

"Nothing really," said Cheney.

Douglas smiled. "I wonder. It seems strange that

you specifically ask me for anything Frank said about his daughter. And Frank refuses to talk about her on tape. It gets me to thinking."

"About what?"

"I'm not sure, but I'd like to know what you're thinking right now."

"Can't always get what you want, Douglas."

"The Rolling Stones."

"Pardon?"

"Famous Stones song. 'Can't always get what you want.' Goes on to say, 'But if you try sometime, you just might find . . . you get what you need.'"

"Think that's true?"

"I know I can't always get what I want. Learned that a long time ago. Far as getting what I need, I don't know. Depends on what that really means. Sometimes I think I need an extra ounce of smoke. Sometimes I think I need to get off the stuff. Sometimes I think I need to get laid. Sometimes I think I need to stop thinking about fucking and get down to work. I guess you could make a case for the fact that everybody gets what they *need*—to survive, at least—until they die. I mean, if you're alive, you're obviously getting what you *need*. Thing is, some people need more."

"I know they expect more."

Cheney decided it was time to go. He thanked Douglas for the coffee and the information, and said he'd try to arrange a ride-along with some LAPD detectives the next time Douglas was in LA. The young writer seemed pleased. Cheney advised him to leave his dope in Crestview. He gave him a card and left.

Cheney got in his car and pointed the Infiniti south toward the Pacific Coast Highway and home. He hit a button and the driver's side window slid down silently. The sea breeze filled his senses like the perfume of a well-remembered lover. He put in a Keith Jarrett CD, *The Köln Concert*. And started thinking about Frank.

Had Frank always gotten what he wanted? Of course not. No one did. Had he gotten what he needed? Debatable. Had he gotten what he expected from life? After listening to the tapes and talking to Lilly, especially about the Tahoe skiing trip, Cheney doubted that Frank expected that he was going to die. Not now anyhow.

Cheney's ex-partner had carved out a life in Crestview that was very different from the one he had had when he and Cheney were close. And as different as it was, it appeared to have been a happy one. Someone admired him, talked with him, was interested in everything he had to say.

And someone loved him. Someone young, pretty, sexy, and sassy. Someone who could tell the real thing from the crap—regardless of the label. She saw the real thing in Frank, and Cheney figured that Frank was grateful for that.

He had figured that Frank had run away from LA because of the divorce and the . . . unpleasantness, the as yet unnamed unpleasantness, with his daughter. Maybe that was true, maybe it wasn't. Cheney had expected to find some old broken-down alkie cop, living on TV dinners, ready to order booze and bullets for his last meal.

But it hadn't been that way at all. Cheney was happy that Frank had found some peace and happiness. That was the good part. But things still didn't add up when it came to Molly. Cheney tried to focus on the portrait of a happy Frank skiing down the slopes with Lilly and drinking into the night with Douglas, his own personal Boswell.

But something was wrong with that picture.

* * *

"I appreciate your meeting with me, Mr. Wallace," said Ray Malzone.

"That's okay. I've read some of the articles you wrote for the *Trib*. Good stuff. Honest."

"Thanks."

"I heard about Molly's dad. That's tough."

Harry Wallace used to be married to Frank's daughter, Molly. He was not at all what Ray had expected.

Wallace ran a gym in Rosemead. Lots of mirrors, Stairmasters, treadmills, leotards, muscle shirts, and sweat. Ray had figured the veterinarian's ex-husband would be a bookworm with glasses and a pristine white collar. But Wallace had no collar and he wore baby blue contact lenses.

"Nice place."

"Thanks. I built it from scratch. We've had some of the chains sniffing around, seeing if I was interested in selling, but I'm in no hurry to sell. I like calling the shots."

Ray sat in Wallace's office, which was large and glassed-in on three walls, all of which had a view onto various parts of the gym. The door was closed.

"I remember Frank mentioning your name," Wallace said. "Weren't you at Molly's graduation?"

"Yeah. Frank, Cheney, and I go way back."

"Yeah, Cheney. Frank's ex-partner. He was chief of detectives for a while, right?"

"Right. He's retired now."

"I liked the guy. He was all right."

"Yeah, me too. Look, Harry—may I call you Harry?"

"Sure."

"I don't mean this in any way to sound, well, offensive, but how did someone like you wind up married to someone like Molly?"

Wallace coughed a laugh out his nose. He had heard that before. "You gotta remember, this was ten years ago. Molly was in grad school and I was a senior majoring in business, minoring in physical therapy. We met through a mutual friend and we liked each other. In the beginning, it was a very physical relationship. On both sides. Molly was quite a number before she started to let herself go. No offense, I know you're a friend of the family. It's just that she had some decent twenty-three-old, uncorrupted genes and with a little help from me, she got into the best shape in her life."

"So, you two got married."

"Just after she got her B.S. By then, I had this place, but it was a shell of what it is now. I only had a few machines, a bunch of free weights, space for aerobics classes, and that was about it. I made my money selling diet programs and food supplements." Wallace smiled. "I was pretty broke then, but all the dreams were intact. It wasn't so bad. You know what I mean?"

It had been a long time since Ray's dreams were intact, but he nodded anyway. "So, what happened between you two?"

"Things happen."

"Yeah, well, my experience is that they usually happen in someone else's bed."

"We grew apart. 'Nuff said."

"Gotcha. I'm actually here about Frank."

"I didn't kill him," said Wallace with a smile.

Ray laughed. "Yeah, I know. I'm just doing some background. I plan to talk with Molly and I just thought you might be able to clue me in a little."

"About what?"

"Oh, I don't know. Maybe her relationship with Frank. I remember she used to idolize him."

"What?" said Wallace incredulously.

"She used to idolize her old man."

"You really *are* missing a few pages. She hated Frank. Least for the last few years."

"Why?"

"Who the fuck knows. Shortly after things went south for us, she developed a real attitude about Frank, too."

"Did he have anything to do with you two splitting up?"

"Absolutely nothing. He was still friends with me, but he made it clear his loyalty was with Molly. Who the hell knows why. But she despised the fuckin' guy."

"That wasn't always so. I remember all kinds of Norman Rockwell scenes with Molly and Frank. Something must have triggered the change."

"Molly changed when we split up. Her attitude, her politics, the way she dressed, everything. Suddenly she was a fuckin' victim."

"Victim? How so?"

"All of a sudden I'm like Frankenstein's evil twin. I'm supposed to have beaten her, verbally abused her, basically held her back in every way a 'man' could. The word *man* became like a profane term to her. She didn't say the word, she spat it out."

"You say she changed when you two split up. You mean like one day you moved out—"

"She threw me out, actually."

"So one day she throws you out, then the next day she hates men?"

"Not exactly. Like I said, we had our problems. I moved out, got my own place. Molly, with my insurance, started seeing a shrink."

"Why?"

"We both thought it would do her good. For my part, I thought it might help get us back together. This went on for a couple of years. One therapist, then another. Finally, she ends up with this one nut, and suddenly there's not only no chance for reconciliation, but I'm the cause of all her problems."

"And Frank?"

"Yeah, well, whatever I wasn't responsible for, he was."

"How was Frank responsible?"

Wallace scratched his nose absently and looked out at an aerobics class in progress a few yards beyond his office window. "I'd rather not say."

"We can do that part off the record."

"How do I know?"

"You say you've read my work. I'm not a tabloid hustler. You can trust me."

Wallace considered the matter for a moment, then shook his head. "I don't know what possible good it can do now."

"Who knows. Give it a try. We're off the record."

Wallace sighed deeply and leaned forward a little. "She said that Frank had, you know . . . "

"What?"

"You know, molested her."

"You're kidding."

"No."

"Did you believe her?"

"No. But, hell, I don't know what the fuck to believe anymore about anybody. You know what I mean?"

"Yes, but that's very hard to believe. I remember Molly and Frank getting along so well."

"Yeah, I know. Frank and Marge, sometimes just

Frank, used to come over for dinner almost every week when Molly and I were first married. Molly couldn't cater enough to Frank. It just doesn't make any sense."

"You say things changed when you two split up. Could you be more specific?"

"You mean dates and time? No. But I can tell you that everything changed when she started seeing that last therapist. That's when I pulled back my insurance. Hell, if she was gonna crucify me, I wasn't gonna pay for the fuckin' nails."

"You happen to know the name of that therapist?"

"No."

"Maybe some insurance receipts?"

"I throw that shit away as soon as the IRS statute of limitations runs out."

"Could you check?"

"Sure, but don't get your hopes up. Besides, this part of our conversation is off the record, remember?"

"Right."

Ray Malzone had gone in not knowing exactly what he was looking for, except maybe a miracle. As he got into his car and punched Cheney's number into the cell-phone, he was starting to believe he'd gotten one.

"I'm telling you the woman hasn't had a decent night's sleep in nearly a year because the bird starts making the sound of a smoke alarm every morning at five A.M."

"You've really got to stop listening to so much talk radio."

Petty waved her hand at Cheney, dismissing his non-responsive reply. "No, seriously, what would you do?"

"I'd put a sprinkler system in the birdcage that would be triggered by the sound of a smoke alarm."

Petty turned back toward a bowl full of dough she

had working, nodded and mumbled to herself, "Good answer." She also spent too much time watching *Family Feud*.

The phone rang and Cheney said, "I'll get it."

"Like I'm gonna race you for it," said Petty over her shoulder.

Cheney pretended not to hear. There was no point.

"Cheney here."

"You just get back?" said Tony Boston.

"Little while ago."

"I left a message."

"I haven't played the machine."

"You busy?"

"You mean now? I could spare an hour or so. Why?"

"We need to talk."

"About Frank?"

"Meet me at Marty's in an hour."

"See you there." Cheney hung up and wondered why Tony hadn't answered his question.

The bartender got the bottle of chardonnay they kept for Cheney just below the bar, poured him a big-tipper's dose and slid the wine and Tony's tap Miller Genuine across the bar. Tony picked up the drinks and took them to a corner booth where Cheney waited.

"So, what's up?" said Cheney.

"Last night a guy named Andrew Mason was murdered on a Malibu beach. Stabbed. In the back and through the heart. Whoever did it whistled while they worked. And a woman was seen running from the scene."

"Frank was shot . . . by a man. What's the connection?"

"The blue ribbon. We found one on Mason's body just like the one we found on Frank's body."

"What?" It wasn't that Cheney hadn't heard Tony, it was that he couldn't believe it. "That's crazy," was all he could say while he tried to sort it all out.

The two men sat in silence for a moment. "You say the killer was a woman. That means someone saw her."

"A jogger saw her from a distance. He was about fifty yards away. Said the murderer had blonde hair and that he was sure it was a woman. Last he saw of her the woman was running up some wooden stairs to the Pacific Coast Highway."

"What've you got besides that?"

"Not a whole helluva lot. The killer wore tennis shoes. Reeboks. But there weren't many good tracks and it doesn't help a lot unless we get a suspect who was stupid enough to keep the shoes for us to find."

"What about the knife?"

"Took it with her."

Her. The word fell like a wrench into the gears of knowledge Cheney had gained as a career cop. Women killed. With passion, sometimes even with relish. But they rarely were serial killers. Yet that was not the mind-jarring thing. "Maybe the 'woman' was a man wearing a wig," he said.

"Maybe. But it's more than that. If the killer had used the same MO and just tossed on a wig, then I'd say, sure, no problem. With most serial killers, the whole process is a kind of ritual. I don't have to tell you that, you taught me that. Killer gets up at the same time of day, eats the same thing, dresses the same way, and he sure as hell uses the same method of killing."

"This link, the blue ribbon. You got anything?" asked Cheney.

"Nothing. Generic kind of thing that could be bought at any fabric store, gift shop, drugstore, or supermarket."

"But the way it's shaped and the fact that it's left on the victims' bodies, it must mean something."

"It means something, but I don't know what the fuck it means." Tony toyed with his drink and looked up at Cheney. "I need your help, Cheney. The department is on me about this one, because of Frank. It's not the mayor screaming to the papers that he wants my head on a platter, like in the movies. It's personal, you know. The chief takes Frank's death personally and it's my shoulder he's looking over."

"I understand."

"I got nothin'. Whoever this person is, or these two people are, they're beatin' the shit outta me. So, I'm thinking out loud here. Let's say there are two killers. Man and a woman."

"Okay."

"All right, so, what's their relationship? Are they boyfriend and girlfriend? Husband and wife? Ex-husband and ex-wife? Brother and sister? Whatever that relationship is, it would tell us a lot."

"You don't have a good enough description of either murderer to make any assumptions. The only thing you know for sure is that the man had dark hair and the woman was blonde. And lots of blondes aren't natural blondes." Cheney shook his head. "What do you know about Andrew Mason?"

"He was forty-seven. Divorced. Worked as a graphic artist for some ad agency up in Topanga Canyon. Lower-level type."

"At forty-seven?"

"At this point, I'm just reading from the sheet. I'm interviewing his boss tomorrow."

"Want some company?"

"I thought you'd never ask. Want me to send a car?"

said Tony only half-kiddingly. The closer he got Cheney to this case, the better he felt.

"What else do you know about the guy?"

"Not a lot. He rented an apartment in Malibu. Neighbors said he was quiet."

"Which means they never talked to him and didn't know jack shit about him."

"Basically, yes."

"We've got to find out."

"I know."

"You know why?"

"Because if the murderers aren't the same, the victims probably are. And if there is more than one killer and they're killing people at random, then it doesn't make any difference what you and I do. We'll never catch them until they make a mistake. If we can find a common thread between Frank and Andrew Mason, then maybe we've got something we can work with."

"Right."

Cheney checked his watch. Elizabeth would be getting home about now.

Tony tossed down a ten and the two men stood. "About tomorrow. Around ten I'm stopping by the place the guy worked, then I'm going to the apartment where he lived. Here's the address of the ad agency." He handed the card to Cheney, who pocketed it.

Outside in the parking lot Cheney had another thought. "You said Mason was married."

"Right."

"Any children?"

"One."

"A daughter?"

"Yeah. How'd you know?"

"Just a guess. Where does she live?"

"I don't know."

"Find out."

"You've got to think this through," said Elizabeth. They had a corner booth at Vito's in West Los Angeles, a few blocks east of incorporated Santa Monica. It was their favorite Italian restaurant. Cheney and Elizabeth were not snobs, but they were sticklers for pasta. Not the sauce, but rather the noodles themselves. This was especially true of Cheney, the self-proclaimed, make-it-from-scratch-with-a-hand-crank-machine "master" pasta maker. Usually, restaurants boiled pots of pasta and merely reheated the noodles when they were ordered. Vito's fresh pasta was boiled *after* the order was placed. So, when Cheney ordered pasta al dente, it arrived al dente. He had gone into several Italian restaurants with good reputations and spoken with waiters who either didn't know what al dente meant, or simply said that they could not control how the pasta was cooked—presumably because it had already *been* cooked.

Cheney set his fork down, picked up his napkin, wiped a pine nut sliver from the pesto sauce off his upper lip. "What do I need to think through?"

Elizabeth took a deep breath and leaned back in the red leather booth. Picked up her Stag's Leap cabernet sauvignon, sipped, and replaced the glass on the white tablecloth. "Exactly how deeply do you want to dig into Frank's life?"

"I want to find out who killed him."

"Tony will do that. Eventually."

"Maybe," said Cheney, realizing that he was being evasive.

"What I mean, Cheney, is exactly how much do you really want to know about Frank?"

The remark just lay there like a hissing snake. He didn't answer.

After a moment, Elizabeth said, "You can't change the past, Cheney. But you can irreversibly alter the future."

"What do you mean by that?"

"I mean, you can't bring Frank back. But you can learn things about him that will change the way you think about him for the rest of your life."

"What exactly are you talking about? Just because Frank had a daughter—"

"Who wouldn't talk to him."

"And this victim has a daughter—"

"Which seems to be about the only thing the victims had in common."

"So far," said Cheney defensively.

Elizabeth said nothing. She didn't have to.

"Just think about it," said Elizabeth. She wrapped her long, slender fingers around her husband's hand. "It's okay not to be perfect. You know that, don't you?"

"I know."

Elizabeth smiled. "We all get blind spots when it comes to the people we love."

Blind spots, thought Cheney. In the land of the blind, the one-eyed man was king. Cheney had two eyes, but he didn't feel like a king.

He felt like a voyeur.

Eight

When Cheney pulled up at the Topanga Canyon address Tony had given him the night before, Tony's car was already in the parking lot, along with a Jeep Cherokee, a Range Rover, and a couple of less expensive Japanese cars. Much of Topanga Canyon, physically and spiritually, had been carved out by the hand of the sixties. In 1995 they still had health food stores and restaurants, a nudist colony, lots of people with long hair, and probably more Volkswagens per capita than any city on earth. Not that that was bad, thought Cheney as he got out of his car and ducked under a wind chime. That was just the way it was.

Donald Beekman, Andrew Mason's boss and owner of the small Beekman Advertising Agency, was a slight man with a receding hairline. Beekman looked rather dashing with a dark, bushy mustache that curled up slightly at both ends. Every once in a while he would touch his upper lip with his right thumb. Cheney knew that was a common habit for a man who has recently trimmed his mustache. A framed photograph on Beekman's desk had the date July 4, 1994 engraved on a small plate beneath it.

The second-story office had windows on three sides, all of which looked out upon rustic scenery—untrimmed trees and bushes, birds, squirrels, butterflies. Not a telephone pole, billboard, or golden arch in sight.

Cheney had counted five people sitting at computers in a large bullpen area just outside Beekman's office. The receptionist made six.

"Andrew was the most meticulous person I'd ever met," said Beekman, after introductions had been made all around.

"I thought artists were, well, not known for being particularly *regimented*," said Tony.

"I never really looked at Andrew as an artist." Beekman raised his eyebrows and cocked his head in a condescending gesture. "I know that's not a politically correct thing to say. These days if a person shits on a piece of paper you can get ten percent of the population to agree that it's art. I've got creative people and I've got the nuts-and-bolts types. Don't get me wrong, you need both."

"Give me an example."

"My creative person will come up with a concept, based on what we believe the client's looking for. Once the idea is set, the creative person will turn it over with a couple of preliminary sketches and detailed instructions to a nuts-and-bolts person. He or she executes the creative person's vision, in great detail, while the creative person comes up with another concept for another client. Most nuts-and-bolts types want to be creative types. It's a constant struggle keeping egos intact. But Andrew was different."

"In what way?" asked Tony.

"Andrew was comfortable being a nuts-and-bolts guy. Never expressed any desire to do anything else. And he was very, *very* dependable and good at what he did."

"How long was he employed here?"

"Four-and-a-half, five years."

"Ever have any problems?"

Beekman smiled. "Just getting Andrew to take his vacations every year. I explained to him it's only two weeks per year and that's it. If you don't take the two weeks during the calendar year, you can't roll them over into the next year."

"Most employers should have such problems," said Tony.

"Why do you think he didn't want to take vacations?" asked Cheney.

"Off the record?"

"Sure," said Tony. Mainly because he knew it would keep the man talking.

"He had no life outside the office. At least none that I ever heard about. He was divorced—I know that from his application. He didn't date anyone."

"How do you know?"

"About six months ago I had a little barbecue out at my house here in the canyon. I have the cookout every year, and every year since Andrew's been here, he always had some lame excuse why he couldn't make it. This year I twisted his arm and told him that he *had* to come. Anyhow, I got a couple glasses of spiked punch into him and we had our only 'real' conversation. Ever see that Steve Martin movie, *The Lonely Guy*?"

Cheney and Tony nodded. Cheney had seen it. Tony had not.

"Andrew would've made The Lonely Guy look like Don Juan in Rio during Carnival. I almost felt like crying when I was done talking with him."

"Why?" asked Tony.

"The guy had no life. None. Zip, zilch, zero."

"What about his ex-wife?"

"Hasn't spoken to her in years."

"Does she lives in the LA area?"

"I don't know."

"I understand he had a daughter."

"That's right. Again, I don't know anything about her. And he didn't keep a picture of her on his desk."

"Did he socialize with anyone in the office?"

"No."

"Was he close to *anyone*?"

"I wouldn't say close. Bob, Bob Keltner, he's our newest artist. He doesn't own a car, so he'd get Andrew to give him a ride every now and then if it was on Andrew's way home. I imagine Bob spoke with Andrew more than anyone else."

"Mind if we take a look at Andrew's desk?" asked Tony.

"Be my guest."

The three men stood and walked into the outer office.

Andrew Mason's desk was in a corner, behind a six-foot-high Chinese screen. The surface of the desk was neat—an Apple Quadra 840AV, keyboard, monitor, and mouse. An in-basket with marked-up printouts of a sneaker ad set off to the left of the monitor. An empty, and recently washed, coffee cup with a color painting of a fox staring at tracks in the snow sat just to the right of the monitor, on a coaster depicting a lush English countryside. Besides that, the desk was clean. The oak surface looked dusted. The wastebasket was empty.

Cheney opened the only drawer. Inside was a manual entitled *Company Book of Style and Layout*, a copy of *International Ads in Print '94*, and a calendar. Cheney leafed through the books, mainly to see if anything fell out. Nothing did. He looked at the calendar, which included an occasional doctor's appointment, dentist's appointment, several car maintenance checkup appointments—with the appropriate mileage next to each entry— and, on every Wednesday night, the abbreviation "mtg."

"Meeting," said Tony. "Maybe he was in a twelve-step program."

"Most twelve-step programs meet more than once a week."

"Some, but not all. Maybe he only needed it once a week."

"Hi," said a young man approaching Mason's desk. He had brown hair down to his shoulders, which were wide and square. Cheney pegged him for twenty-two or -three.

"You Bob?" asked Tony.

"Yeah. Don said you'd like to talk to me about Andrew."

"That's right."

"I don't know much about the guy. I mean, like, who did, right? Real loner. Not a bad guy. I don't mean he was a bad guy. Just kept to himself. Nothing wrong with that. Whatever works for you, you know?"

"I understand that Mr. Mason often gave you rides."

"Yeah. My girlfriend's a waitress at Henri's down on Pacific Coast Highway, it's on the ocean. You know it?"

Tony nodded.

"Anyhow, it was on his way home, so he didn't mind."

"What did you two talk about when he gave you a ride?"

"Nothing. Actually, I guess I did most of the talking. Andrew wasn't much for conversation. Nice man, though, never made any waves."

"We understand you don't want to speak ill of the dead," said Cheney, trying to get the young man to level with them. "What we want from you is a realistic portrait of Andrew, through your eyes. Okay?"

"Sure."

"Did he ever talk about his family?"

"No."

"Did he seem troubled about anything?"

Bob shrugged. "Andrew always seemed a little troubled to me. But not by anything in particular. Just by life in general, if you know what I mean."

Cheney didn't know exactly, but he nodded as though he did. "Did he ever talk about a meeting he had on Wednesday nights?"

Bob arched his eyebrows, flipping through the mental files, searching for the right answer. "Yeah," he said, with the smile of an eager pupil who had just remembered the right answer. "Some nights, if we left at exactly the time Andrew had to leave, he would drop me by Henri's. But never on Wednesdays. He said that was because he had something to do."

"Something?"

"That's what he said at first. Then, after a few times, I pressed him on it. It was a card meeting."

"Andrew played cards?"

"He didn't play cards, he traded them. Baseball cards."

"You've really changed since the last time I saw you."

"The last time you saw me I'd just graduated from college. That was about ten years ago," said Molly.

"You look great," said Ray Malzone. He really didn't think she looked great, but it seemed like the right thing to say.

"I really don't have much time," said Molly, looking

at her watch. She had agreed to meet Ray at a tiny out-door cafe a couple of blocks from her Sierra Madre office.

"I know you're busy and I appreciate you taking the time."

A waitress brought Molly a cup of Red Zinger tea and Ray a Heineken.

"Look, Ray, I know you were a friend of my father's." Ray nodded while Molly poured hot water over the tea bag in her cup. "Why do you want to talk to me?"

"I'm just filling in some background about Frank."

"What kind of background?"

"Oh, just the usual."

"Don't treat me like a child, Ray. Because I'm not a child anymore. I'm a woman."

"Okay. I'll cut to the chase. I talked with your ex-husband and he said you and Frank were estranged."

"I can't imagine that muscle-bound lummox using the word 'estranged.'"

"Maybe he didn't. What I'm asking is, did you and Frank have some kind of falling out?"

"It was much more than that."

"What do you mean?"

"It's none of your business."

"Did Frank molest you?"

Molly just stared back at Frank as though he'd just made a rude noise.

Finally Ray said, "Is it true?"

"If it is, will you put it in the article?"

"I don't know."

"Damned right you won't. You're his friend. You're a man and you're not going to write about it. Fact is, you probably don't even believe me, anyhow."

"Why would you say that?"

"People stick together. Men stick together. It's a

conspiracy of silence, Ray. There's not any more child molestation going on today than yesterday, it's just that people, *some* people, are less afraid to talk about it, that's all. But still, things haven't changed that much. Most people would rather just sweep it under the rug."

"You're right. But I've written a number of articles over the past few years on this very subject. I think you'll find me a sympathetic listener."

Molly toyed with her tea bag and assessed Ray. "Why would you be willing to hurt your old friend?"

"That's not my intention. I don't want to make him look bad. On the other hand, if he's done something awful, it's not my job to shield him either."

"He molested me, Ray."

Ray shook his head and looked as sad as he could for Molly. He knew that he could have done a better job if he had a buzz on, but he didn't, so he did the best he could. "I'm really sorry to hear that, Molly. Really. I remember the two of you together. He was so proud of you and, at least you *seemed* to be proud of him, too."

Molly sighed, picked up her cup of tea and drank, then set her cup down. "That was before."

"Before what?"

"Before I knew that he molested me."

"What do you mean before you knew?"

"Children block out things that are too painful to remember."

"You mean you forgot that your father molested you until you were an adult?"

"It's very common, Ray. And if you've written at all on child molestation, as you say you have, I'm sure you're familiar with the phenomenon. Sometimes a person is just unable to process the emotional content of a traumatic event and, therefore, she blocks it out."

"What made you remember?"

"I recalled the molestation during therapy."

"Therapy?"

"I was seeing a therapist to help me deal with my divorce. During our sessions, with considerable effort and pain, we were able to recover those lost memories."

"We?"

"My therapist and me."

"What was the therapist's name?"

"Why?"

"Just curious. Don't worry, he, or she, wouldn't tell me anything even if I got a court order. Like I said, I've done a few articles on this subject. Maybe I know this therapist."

After a moment, Molly said, "Stanley Craig."

"In the Valley?" Ray was fishing.

"No. He's got an office in the Marina."

Ray pretended to search his memory. "No, never heard of the guy. Do you still see him?"

"Sometimes. Not regularly like before. I'm a lot better now that I know what the source of my pain has been. Besides, the goal of therapy is to be able to eventually leave it. At least that's what Dr. Craig says."

"About the memories . . . There's no doubt in your mind that they're real."

"Absolutely none," said Molly, suddenly rigid in posture and attitude.

"Some people don't believe in repressed memory."

"Some people used to believe the world was flat. The memories I have are vivid, they're not made up. And, more importantly, when I recovered that part of my life, my whole life changed. I became a whole person again. In short, the proof is that it worked."

Molly checked her watch. "I've got to go." She stood.

"Thanks for seeing me, Molly." Ray stuck out his hand and Molly shook it perfunctorily. Then she turned and walked away.

Ray sat there for a moment, watching her walk away. *The proof is that it worked.* He wondered what constituted "working." She was divorced and unmarried. She despised her father with a haunting hate that carried beyond the grave. Ray thought he was a pretty decent judge of character, particularly because he saw so many flaws in his own. Although he had not spent much time with Molly, he could tell that she was not a happy person.

Of course, there was much more to life than being happy. Ray was happy, or what passed for happy, whenever his blood alcohol level hit point-one-zero.

Out of the corner of his eye Ray spotted a small bar across the street. He tossed a five-dollar bill on the table and hurried over. The place was nearly empty.

"What'll it be, pal?" said the heavyset man behind the bar.

"Best single malt you got. A double."

The bartender poured a Glenlivet, neat, set it in front of Ray, and slid a cocktail napkin underneath it. "Five bucks."

Ray put a ten on the bar. While the bartender took the bill back to the cash register, Ray tossed back the booze.

Happiness was just a shot away.

Cheney followed Tony west through Topanga Canyon over to Pacific Coast Highway and north to Andrew Mason's Malibu apartment. The building looked like a shoe box on stilts. A two-door garage fronted PCH. A wooden walkway along the right side of the shoe box led to a short enclosed hallway off to the left, and two doors. The first door was Andrew Mason's. Or at least it used to be.

Cheney and Tony walked past the uniform at the door and stepped inside. The living room and kitchen, separated by a counter bar, took up most of the apartment. A small bedroom and bath just to the left of the front door completed the floor plan. The bed was made, the cap was on the toothpaste, the dishes were put away. It looked to Cheney like a model home. A place where someone was *supposed* to live, but didn't. Not really.

"Find anything interesting?" asked Cheney, taking in the view.

"We found a family album—pictures of Mason's daughter and wife in happier times. Couple of original paintings, signed by Mason himself. No guns, no drugs."

"What about baseball cards?"

"No."

Cheney nodded and continued to look out over the Pacific. He knew there wouldn't be any. "An address book?"

"A metal flip-open job by the phone."

Cheney noticed two paintings resting against the wall of windows that looked out over the Pacific. He squatted down and looked at them. He felt like a mortician peering into the eyes of a dead man. The hardened oil paint was all swirls of red and yellow. Lots of confusion and passion for a man who lived in an orderly box. The painting style reminded Cheney of Van Gogh's swirls of yellow and blue in *Starry Night*. But whereas Cheney felt peaceful when he viewed *Starry Night*, he felt a sense of unresolved chaos in Andrew Mason's work. He could make out no clearly defined images. There was an occasional eye peering through the hellish maelstrom, but even those were not distinct. Cheney wasn't sure whether or not he was seeing eyes or if, like when looking at cloud formations, he was merely perceiving a shape subjectively. After a moment, he started feeling uneasy. He stood and turned away.

"Where's the family album?"

Tony picked up the book from the kitchen counter and handed it to him. Cheney sat down in a dark green leather chair, just under a hanging plant that needed some serious talking to or at least some water, and started leafing through the photographs. There were lots of smiles, hugs, rabbit-ears-behind-unsuspecting-subjects, even a dog. Three good-looking people—mother, father, and daughter—hamming it up in scenes that would've made Ozzie and Harriet look mean-spirited. But people never recorded the incidents that blew a family apart. Yet those, more than the magic moments, were the indelible images that lasted a lifetime. That eventually obscured the hundreds of pieces of nicely colored Kodak paper.

Cheney removed a photograph of Andrew kneeling down with his arm around his daughter, while she had her arms around an Irish setter. On the back it read: *Carla, Andrew, and Red Rover, May 6, 1975.* Cheney recognized Andrew's handwriting from the calendar at his office. He was meticulous even back then, thought Cheney.

"Daughter's name is Carla," said Cheney.

Tony picked up the address caddy, punched the letter C and the lid flipped open. There were two listings. One for "Catering," which was followed by the name, address, and phone number of a local caterer. The other was a listing for "Camera," which was followed by the name, address, and phone number of a local camera shop.

"Let's try Mason," said Tony. "Even though she might be married, maybe he filed her under the family name." There was only one listing under M— "Market," which was followed by the name, address, and number of a local market, with the words home delivery under the entry.

"Look under daughter," said Cheney, turning and facing the ocean again.

"What?"

"D for daughter."

Tony punched the letter D. There were three listings. "Dishwasher," which was followed by the name, address, and number of a repair service. "Dentist," which was followed by the name, address, and number of a local dentist.

And "Daughter," which was followed by the name Carla, an address, and a phone number. "Bingo, 818," said Tony, referring to the phone number's area code. "She's local."

Tony walked to the counter, picked up the phone, which had already been dusted, and push-buttoned Carla's number. After two rings a woman's voice said, "Yes?"

"Carla?"

Silence. Then, "Who is this?"

"My name's Tony Boston. I'm the chief of detectives, LAPD." Silence. Tony put a hand over the receiver and whispered to Cheney, "I don't think she knows."

"I think she'll be able to handle it," said Cheney, not bothering to look at Tony, still staring out at the ocean.

"Is your father Andrew Mason?"

Silence. Then, "Why?"

"I take it that's a yes?"

"I haven't seen my father in nearly five years."

"I'm afraid I have some bad news, Mrs. . . ?"

"Carter. It's Ms. And I'm divorced."

"Ms. Carter, your father was murdered last night."

Silence. Then nothing.

"Are you all right, Ms. Carter?"

"I'm fine," she said evenly.

"I wonder if you're planning to be home for the next couple of hours?"

"Why?"

"I'd like to ask you a few questions about your father."

"As I've already told you, I haven't seen my father in a very long time."

"It would just take a few minutes and it might help us catch the man who killed your father."

"I doubt it."

"Please."

Silence. Then, "I'm going out now. Come by around seven-thirty. But I'm going out again at eight, so I'll only be able to spare you a few minutes. That's the best I can do."

"Do you know how we can reach your mother?"

"She died seven years ago."

"I'm sorry." Tony looked down at the address in the book, read it off, confirmed that hers was the same as the one in the book, and hung up.

Cheney walked over to Tony. "Pretty broken up, eh?" he said sarcastically.

"She can see us at seven-thirty. Wanna come?"

"Definitely. Why don't you swing by and pick me up. I'll buy drinks on the way back."

"I'll be there at six forty-five."

"Mind if I take the address book?"

Tony handed Cheney the address caddy. "It's been dusted, but it's still evidence."

"I'll give it back to you tonight. What about the neighbor?" said Cheney, tilting his head toward the apartment's shared wall.

"Candace McCoy. She hasn't been in since last night."

"I thought I heard something next door a few minutes ago."

Cheney and Tony walked out of Andrew Mason's apartment, into the short hallway. "Did someone just go into the apartment next door?" Tony asked the uniformed officer.

"Yes, sir. Ms. McCoy."

Tony nodded and he and Cheney walked the few steps to the woman's door. It was open, but the screen door was closed. Inside they could see a blonde taking groceries out of a double-bagged paper sack.

"Ms. McCoy?"

The woman turned around. She didn't look startled. Cheney's instant take was that she looked like a woman who didn't startle easily. She walked to the door, didn't bother to open the screen. "You cops?"

"Yes, ma'am. We'd like to ask you a few questions," said Tony.

"About Mr. Mason?"

Tony nodded. Candace showed the officers in, offered them drinks, hard and soft. Cheney declined everything, Tony settled on a Diet Pepsi.

"Nice place," said Tony, taking a sip of his soft drink. He and Cheney sat on a white leather couch, while Candace took the matching chair opposite them, her long tanned legs curled up beneath her. She wore white shorts and a yellow midriff, which served as a frame for the work of art that was her brown, washboard-flat stomach.

"It's great. And I drive a new black Porsche Carrera. It's great, too."

"You must have a great job," said Cheney, playing along while trying to keep a straight face.

Candace made it easy. She almost started laughing. "A job? I don't think so. Not that I have to tell you this, but I'm what the older generation calls a 'kept woman.' You know what I'm saying?"

Cheney nodded. He was part of that older generation, and he didn't need a translation.

"Look, it's not as though I'm selling drugs or something. It's like being married except I'm the one in control. You know what I'm saying?"

Cheney nodded again. "About Andrew Mason . . . "

"Incredible. I mean, murdered? You see it on TV, but, shit, not this close. One wall away." She shook her head and shivered a little. To Cheney, it seemed like a practiced move.

"How well did you know Mr. Mason?" asked Tony.

"Not well. We said hello when we passed each other, that's about it."

"How would you characterize him, generally?"

She lifted her eyebrows, inhaled deeply and exhaled slowly through pursed, pouty, pretty lips. Again, a practiced pose, thought Cheney. "Kind of weird, I guess."

"How so?"

"He was quiet. I mean, I know that's not weird. Fact is, that's cool—a neighbor being quiet. But he was like weird quiet, you know what I'm saying?"

This time neither man nodded. "I'm not sure I do," said Tony.

"Well, sometimes I wouldn't hear any noise coming from his place for days at a time, even though I knew he was home."

"How did you know?"

"I could see him. Sometimes I'd get home late at night and walk in without the lights on. Being right on the ocean, I don't like to advertise that I'm not home. And when I'm home, I like to get comfortable, you know. And with two windows facing the ocean . . . "

"You could close the drapes."

"I'm not a drapes person, you know what I'm saying?"

Neither Cheney nor Tony knew for sure, but they thought they got the picture.

"Anyhow, I'd come home and look out at the

ocean. Sometimes I'd see the lights of a ship in the distance. Sometimes I'd see the moon glistening off the water, right up to the shore. And sometimes I'd see Mr. Mason sitting on his balcony, just staring out at the water. For hours. All night sometimes. He'd sit there alone, hardly moving. It was spooky."

"Did he ever—"

"Spy on me?" Candace laughed. "I don't think I was his type, you know what I'm saying?"

"No."

"I never saw him with a woman. He lived alone. He was real quiet, like I said, and he never came on to me. Men always come on to me, you know what I'm saying?"

That, both men understood completely.

Cheney said, "Did you ever see him with any men?"

"Come to think of it, no. But I've got a pretty good instinct for that kind of thing."

Cheney was going to ask what kind of thing she meant, but he thought he knew what she was saying.

Outside, Cheney sat in his Infiniti, talking with Tony through the open window. "See you tonight," said Cheney.

"Right. You know, the witness said he saw a blonde running from the scene. Candace *is* a blonde."

"She is today," said Cheney as he pulled away.

"What's for dinner?" said Cheney as he passed through the kitchen on his way to his den.

"Oh, I'm fine. And you?" said Petty sarcastically.

"Sorry. How was your day?"

"You really want to know?"

Cheney stopped and willed himself to turn around. "Yes."

Petty smiled. "You wouldn't believe what they had on *The Tony Bishop Show* today."

"That's a pretty safe bet."

"This guy"—she paused for emphasis—"left his wife . . . you ready?"

"Petty, please just shoot me, okay?"

"C'mon, guess."

Cheney started to argue, but experience had taught him the foolishness of such a strategy. "He left his wife for her brother?"

Petty shook her head. "Nah, that was a year ago. You ready?"

"As ready as I'll ever be."

"He left his wife for the neighbor's dog."

For a moment Cheney just stood there and looked at his housekeeper, trying to figure out which one of them was crazier. Petty for watching such programs, or he for listening to her talk about them. "That can't be," he said simply.

"It was on TV."

"Superman's on TV. The Easter Bunny's on TV. Even the Menendez brothers are on TV. But that doesn't mean you're supposed to believe they're real."

"Ha, ha, Mr. Cynical. They actually had the dog on the show, too."

"Oh, well, then I stand corrected. Did Bishop interview the dog?"

"Dogs can't talk."

"I'll bet Bishop didn't say that."

"But this dog understands sign language."

"That's it," said Cheney. He turned and walked out of the kitchen. He knew she was not stupid. And Elizabeth had assured him just a few months ago that Petty wasn't getting senile—he had asked. It must be the TV, thought Cheney. Her addiction to the tube was turning her brain to Swiss cheese.

Cheney closed the door to his den, happy to have something to do at that moment. He checked the digital clock on the desk. It was one o'clock. He had almost six hours to kill before Tony picked him up.

Cheney set Andrew Mason's address caddy in the middle of his desk, punched A, took out a paper and a pen, and started copying the names, addresses, and phone numbers. There were seventy listings in all. And all but ten had been listed categorically first. Ten listings had names and phone numbers only, no category designation. Cheney picked up the phone and called the first number on the list.

"Hello," said a man on the other end.

"Is this Chip?" asked Cheney, reading the man's first name from Mason's phone book.

"Yes. Who's this—?"

"I just wanted to make sure the Wednesday meeting is still on."

"What meeting?"

"Sorry, I must have the wrong number." Then Cheney hung up quickly.

He tried the other nine names. Three gave essentially the same puzzled reply that Chip had given. Cheney got no answer or answering machines when he called the other six numbers. He decided to take a nap and try again later. But before he did, he knew he had one call to make first.

"Hello," said a sleepy female voice.

"Lilly?"

"Yeah, who's this?"

"Cheney."

"Oh, hi. You know what time it is?"

"About two."

"Yeah. I don't get up till four. I'm a night person, remember?"

"Sorry."

"No sweat." Cheney heard her yawn. "What can I do for you?"

"I wanted to ask you something about Frank."

"Sure."

"You two got together almost every night, right?"

"Just about. Sometimes he'd tell me he had things to do."

"What about Wednesday nights?"

"Yeah, Frank had a thing about Wednesdays."

Cheney felt his heart skip a beat. "What do you mean?"

"He'd never miss Wednesday nights. It's blues night at the club where I work. I don't know if you knew this about Frank, but he knows his blues. Some nights he'd flake out on me, but never Wednesdays. Why do you ask?"

"Nothing. Thanks."

"Sure. And Cheney."

"Yes?"

"Next time, remember—two in the morning is okay, but not two in the fuckin' afternoon."

"I'll remember."

Cheney hung up and went into his bedroom to take a nap. Happy to leave at least one nightmare behind.

At five thirty Cheney started in on the list again. Three more "What meeting?" answers, three more names crossed off.

"Hello," said the next man on the list.

Before the man could ask who was on the other line, Cheney said, "Hi, Hal. I just wanted to make sure the Wednesday meeting is still on."

"I guess. You mean because of what happened to . . ." Silence. Then, "Who is this?"

"I'm a friend of Andrew's. I'd like to talk with you."

"Who *is* this?" said Hal. He tried to make his

voice sound demanding, but Cheney could feel the fear in it.

"Look, Hal, we can do this the easy way or—"

"How do you know my name?"

"My name's Cheney. I'm with the LAPD," said Cheney, fudging the truth just a little.

"My God!" The man hung up.

Cheney tried the number again, but the line was busy. Cheney tried for the next ten minutes, with the same result.

Cheney push-buttoned another number. "Tony?"

"Yeah, I'm just leaving."

"I need an address for a phone number."

"Shoot."

Cheney read him the man's number.

"Anything important?" Tony asked him.

"Could be."

Carla Carter lived in an apartment complex in Encino, just off the Ventura Freeway. The place was all plants and earth tones—a beige couch, two brown leather-and-chrome chairs, a solid oak coffee table, on top of which were recent issues of *Time* magazine, *New Woman, Western Hiker,* and a copy of *The Guerrilla Handbook For Female Survival in the '90s.*

Carla Carter was not a solicitous host. She had offered no drinks or snacks, only a seat and a glassy stare. She sat with both feet on the floor in one of the chairs, wearing a pair of jeans and a sweatshirt bearing the Pepperdine University logo. She had medium-length blonde hair pulled back and tied with a rubber band. She wore little makeup.

"I've got to leave in twenty-five minutes."

"If you'll excuse my saying so," said Tony, "you don't seem very upset by your father's murder."

"I'm not," she said flatly.

"A lot of daughters would be."

"My father and I had a rather unique relationship," she said with a sneer so explicit in her voice that none was necessary on her face.

"How's that?"

"I don't have to tell you. You're not my therapist."

"That's true. But I am a police officer. And I am investigating a homicide. I can do a lot more than you might think. Legally."

"Is that supposed to be some kind of threat?"

"No. I'm just letting you know where I stand. I've got a job to do and the taxpayers expect me to do it. One way or another, I get it done."

"That's really admirable. Very macho," she said, the sneer coating her words with so much bitterness that they appeared to drip from her mouth as much as emanate from it.

"Are you a molestation victim?" asked Cheney. But he already knew the answer.

"I am an incest survivor. Not a victim."

There it was, out on the table, thought Cheney. With Carla checking her watch every minute, there was no time to do the dance. "Your father molested you," said Cheney. It was not a question.

"Yes." She volunteered no more. Clearly, Carla wasn't going to make it easy.

"And you hated him."

"Wouldn't you?"

"You hated him very much?" said Tony, ignoring the woman's question.

"Yes. More than I've hated anyone in my life."

"Enough to kill him?"

"Definitely. But I didn't."

No one spoke for a moment. Then Tony said, "You mentioned on the phone that you hadn't seen your father for five years."

"That's right," said Carla, holding her chin up.

"You're what, about thirty-five?"

"Thirty-one."

"Sorry."

"Not every woman relies on a man lying to her in order to develop a positive self-image." The sneer was back in her words, and in the room, like some kind of invisible bitter poison.

"So, you stopped seeing your father when you were twenty-six."

"So?"

"How was your relationship with your father until then?"

"It was a joke. An illusion. I deluded myself into believing what I had to believe in order to survive."

"What do you mean?"

"That's none of your business."

"You said your mother died seven years ago."

"That has nothing to do with anything."

"That must have been very tough," said Cheney. "My mother dying was one of the most difficult experiences of my life. And I was a good deal older when it happened than you were."

Carla nodded and the sneer disappeared. For a moment, Cheney thought, she appeared almost vulnerable. Even soft. There was a flash of the girl he had seen in the family album with her father and her dog.

"A lot of people need help getting through that kind of grief. I know I did. My wife's a psychiatrist. It helped a lot to have someone to talk to."

"Yeah," said Carla, nodding again.

"A good therapist is hard to find. But when you find the right one"—Cheney paused—"it can be a lifesaver."

"That's true. And getting the wrong therapist can be devastating. Especially when they don't recognize the signs."

"What signs?"

"The signs of sexual abuse are obvious to the trained professional. Ask your wife. The other therapists I went to, mostly men," she said bringing back the sneer, "said my problems stemmed from all kinds of things. Some of them even said I didn't have a problem at all. My life's been one problem after another and some idiot listens to me for a hundred dollars an hour and all he can tell me is that I don't have a problem."

"But you found someone who recognized the signs," said Cheney.

"Yes. It was clear to him that I was a victim of molestation. And with his help, I've become a survivor, *not* a victim."

"That's good," said Cheney. "Then, did you confront your father?"

"Finally, yes."

"And what did he say?"

"Of course, he denied it. At first."

"At first?"

"Obviously, he was in denial."

"You say 'at first.' Did he finally admit it?"

"Yes. One night he just broke down crying, begging for my forgiveness. But how can you forgive someone for ruining your entire life?"

"When did you confront your father?"

"About six months after I started therapy, I decided that in order to start healing, I had to confront him with what he'd done to me. And it was a couple of months after that that he confessed."

"What do you do, Ms. Carter?" asked Tony.

"My degree is in mathematics."

"Is that what you do—you're a mathematician?"

"As I'm sure you know, there is a tremendous gender bias against women in the mathematics field. Little boys are supposed to be good with math and little girls are supposed to be good in home economics."

"So you're unemployed?"

"I'm on disability. I take it one day at a time, but I'm surviving better and better every day."

"Your rent, your therapist . . . these things all cost money."

"I get alimony from my ex-husband, and my father kept up insurance payments for my therapy. I know what you're thinking," she said with a sneer. "That I'm living off men. Nothing could be further from the truth. If it weren't for those men, I'd be leading a full and productive life on my own right now. If they gave me every penny they made for the rest of their lives, they could never make up for the damage they did to me."

"You said that your father admitted that he'd molested you . . . "

"I know what you're going to ask—do I have any proof?"

"Yes."

"He didn't put his confession into any legally incriminating form, if that's what you mean. But he admitted it to me, face to face. Like I said, he broke down crying. That was enough for me."

"Enough for what?"

"So I could begin my healing. So I could verify that my memories were real. So that I could get on with my life."

"How long ago did the molestation take place?"

"That's none of your business."

"Could you tell us how we can contact your husband?"

"Why? You think I'm nuts?"

"No. It's just routine. Was he in contact with your father?"

"I don't know. I haven't communicated with my husband for the last three years, ever since the divorce was final."

"You must know how to reach him. You said he sends alimony checks."

Carla looked at the two men for a moment, trying to figure out whether it was worth resisting. She stood, walked over to a desk, wrote something on a piece of paper, and handed it to Tony. "That's his number," she said. "Now, I've gotta go."

"One last thing, Ms. Carter."

"Yes?"

"Where were you last night between eight and eleven?"

"I was teaching a women's study workshop at the Women's Center."

"For three hours?"

"Two and a half. Class was over at ten thirty, but I stuck around and talked to some people afterward. I locked up a little after eleven."

Thirty minutes later, Tony and Cheney pulled up in Tony's car to the curb outside an old Craftsman-style house on Kensington Drive in the Hollywood foothills. The house belonged to Hal Carlisle, the man who had been scared shitless a few hours earlier when Cheney had spoken with him about the Wednesday night meeting.

"You believe Carter's alibi?" asked Tony.

"We should call to check it out, but yes, I believe her. If she's actually teaching the class, we can verify all the information she gave us with one phone call. If she didn't show last night, or the class ended at nine, she just hanged herself."

"Yeah, I believe her, too," said Tony. "But I'll—" He stopped in midsentence.

Tony and Cheney were just about to get out of the car when a man with short dark hair, wearing tan slacks and a light black jacket hurried out of the house, locking the front door, and almost running to his late model, powder blue Toyota Corolla.

"Wanna go for a ride?" asked Tony as he pulled away from the curb without his headlights on.

Tony tailed the Corolla down Franklin, where it turned left on Argyle, going past Hollywood Boulevard, Sunset, and Santa Monica Boulevard. The car turned right on Willow and slowed down like the driver was looking for a parking place. Tony just drove on by and turned right at the next corner; he could see Carlisle easing his Corolla into a parking spot.

Tony and Cheney got out of the car. They were just turning the corner on foot when a porch light went on and Carlisle disappeared inside a two-story house. Then the porch light went off again.

"We don't have a warrant," said Tony.

"I'm not a cop."

"We might be tipping our hand."

"Let's keep it unofficial. I'll go in alone. LAPD was never here."

"What if you need backup?"

"Carlisle doesn't strike me as the rough type."

"You don't know who's inside. Or how many. Take my gun, just in case."

"Tony, I don't—"

"It'd make me feel better."

Cheney took Tony's gun and stuck it down his pants in back, under his jacket.

"Feel better now?"

"As soon as you're in, I'm going to the side window just to make sure."

Cheney nodded. He knew that Tony had another gun in an ankle holster.

Cheney climbed the three stairs up to the porch, and knocked on the door. No one answered, but Cheney heard voices inside. Finally, the porch light went on again and a man, not Carlisle, opened the door. He looked to Cheney to be in his late thirties. He was lean, a little over six feet, with short black hair, and a salt-and-pepper mustache. He was dressed in an inexpensive pink short-sleeved shirt, khaki slacks, and sandals, no socks. There were pockmarks on his face, unhealed scars of adolescence.

"Yes?"

"I'd like to speak with Hal Carlisle."

"There's no one by that name—"

"Don't even bother. I just saw him walk inside."

The man swallowed hard. "Who are you?"

"I want to ask Hal some questions about Andrew Mason."

The man swallowed hard again. "You a cop?"

"No, but I can get a couple carloads of 'em here in ten minutes. Sirens, flashing lights. Kind of thing that gives the neighborhood a festive feel. Everybody standing around pointing, asking questions. It's a real party. I'm not much for parties, though. I'm better one-on-one. But it's up to you."

The man quickly sorted through his options. He obviously wasn't used to making these kinds of decisions, especially this quickly. "How do I know you're not the person who murdered Andrew?"

"I guess you don't. But I'm not. If I wanted to kill Hal, I wouldn't have followed him, let him walk inside a house, then knocked on the fuckin' door."

"We have nothing to hide," said a voice inside. "Let's get this over with."

The man opened the door, turned off the porch light and showed Cheney into the living room. There were three others, including Carlisle. They all stood there and just looked at Cheney. One older man, with a shaved head, stepped forward. He didn't offer his hand.

"I take it this is an emergency meeting of the Wednesday night club," said Cheney.

"What exactly do you want?" said the bald man.

"Is this where Andrew Mason used to spend his Wednesday nights?"

"Yes."

"Mason was pretty secretive about the meetings."

"Not everyone would understand."

"Understand what? That he gets together with a bunch of child molesters every week?"

The bald man inhaled deeply, shook his head slowly, and sat down. The others slowly took their seats, including Cheney.

"How did you know?"

"Educated guess. You know, I could get a warrant for this place—"

"You can huff and puff all you want, Mr. . . ?"

"Cheney."

"Mr. Cheney. You won't find any child pornography here. You won't find any children here. This is a support group. For some of us, it's all we've got to hold onto. We no longer give in to . . . to that part of ourselves. We must be vigilant, and we must be available for each other at any time, day or night. But we do *not abuse children any longer!* Period!"

"So why do you have to be so vigilant?"

"I didn't say we were never tempted. But we do *not* act out anymore."

"There would be a lot of psychiatrists who'd say that isn't possible. That people like you should be behind bars forever."

"This is not a normal twelve-step group. We're kind of a splinter group. We take what works from other groups and put it together with what works for us. If anyone acts out, he's out of the group. Forever. In fact, we vow to turn in any member to authorities if we have knowledge that he's acting out. This is not just a self-help group, it's the only thing standing between us and hell."

The man sounded sincere. Cheney didn't know if he agreed with him or not, but that really wasn't why he was there. "Do any of you have any idea who might have killed Andrew Mason?"

"No," said the bald man.

"What about someone he molested, or maybe some victim's parent?"

"We don't name names and places here."

"I thought you said you vowed to turn each other in if a member . . . had a slip."

"Each member can talk freely about his or her past. And that's what it is and where it'll stay—in the past. Even so, we find it's an intelligent safeguard not to name names. If a member got in trouble, he might use . . . certain facts as leverage against another member. This way we can speak openly about what we did without feeling that we're putting ourselves in a compromising position."

"I see." Cheney paused for a moment and looked at the men, each of whom looked back at him anxiously. All except for the bald man. Whatever demons were chasing him, he seemed to have outrun them, at least for the moment. "You do want to help find Andrew's killer, don't you?"

Finally the bald man spoke. "Honestly?"

"That's always my first choice."

"Yes and no. Of course, we want the murderer found. Andrew was our friend. Part of our family. But our family, in order to remain together, requires privacy. If the investigation, or a subsequent trial, shines a light on us, well, it doesn't take a genius to figure out that the press might be, well, shall we say less than kind in portraying us."

Cheney thought about arguing, but it was just reflex. He knew the man was right.

"Besides, I really don't think Andrew's problem had anything to do with his murder."

"Does a blue ribbon, worn like the red AIDS awareness ribbon, hold any special significance for you?"

Cheney scanned the faces for any hint of reaction, and found none.

"No," said the bald man. "I'm sure it means something these days, but it doesn't mean anything special to us."

"I never met Andrew, and I'm trying to get a handle on who he was. Tell me a little about him."

After an initial and strained silence, the bald man nodded toward Hal Carlisle. A little self-consciously and with a dry mouth, Hal said, "Andrew was a nice guy. Never made trouble. Always very punctual. Sometimes I'd catch a ride with him over here and he'd always arrive at exactly the minute he said he would. It was as though he'd been sitting outside in his car timing himself so that he'd walk up to my door when the second hand swept twelve."

"Yeah, he was very punctual," said the man with the mustache. "We could always tell when it was eight o'clock—that's when we start our Wednesday meetings. Andrew would knock on the door and we'd know it was exactly eight."

"Besides punctuality . . ." said Cheney.

"Andrew was a profoundly disturbed man," said the bald man without passion. A simple statement of a simple fact.

"Could you be more specific?"

"Andrew didn't have his demons in a box yet. What I mean by that is, each of us knows that we have demons that can rip our world wide open at any moment. People like us know that because it's happened to us many times. Gradually, with the help of our group, we put the demons in a box and lock them in. We own the box. We have the key to the lock. But sometimes the demons can be very seductive. They can lure us into errant thinking and we forget the excruciating pain that ultimately accompanies the pleasure.

"Andrew had never completely contained his demons. They haunted him in a form that was just as real as you are to me, and I am to you. In time, I believe he would have been able to lock his demons away. But he had no peace. He wrestled with his madness night after night. Wednesday night was the only night he could sleep well. He told us what he could tell no one else. He told us that he had committed unspeakable acts, contemplated unspeakable acts, illegal acts. We let him know that we understood, and that we would not turn away as long as contemplation or temptation never turned into reality. For him it was like six days of pumping air into a tire until it was ready to burst, then coming here on Wednesday and letting most of the air out."

"How long had he been a member?"

"I'm not sure."

"Four years," said the man with the mustache. "He joined about a month or so after I did, and I joined a little over four years ago."

"If you have any idea who could have killed Andrew, it would be in your best interest to tell me."

"You mean because maybe the murderer might start killing us?" said the bald man with a raised eyebrow. "I think not. But if another of us is killed, then I'll be wrong and you'll have a wonderful clue."

"In other words, you're not going to volunteer any personal information."

"Would you?"

Cheney thought about it. Of course the man was right. Cheney could be some small-time blackmailer. They had never seen him before. He knew, as any cop knew, trust was always earned. He withdrew a card that had his business phone number on it—he had three lines at home: his and Elizabeth's unlisted number, Cheney's business number, and Elizabeth's private line that she gave to her patients to use in case of an emergency. Each had a distinct ring. Cheney had insisted on it after being awakened two nights in a row at three in the morning by one of his wife's more colorful patients.

At the door, Cheney spoke privately with the bald man. The others seemed content to stay in the living room.

"Look, I have a lot more clout than you might think—"

"You're Derek Cheney," said the man with a smile. "I saw you on TV when you were the chief of detectives. And I remember the Yamaguchi case and that serial killer case two years ago with that film director."

"Okay, so then you know I'll give you a fair shake."

"What exactly does that mean?"

"It means that if you try to cover something up or lie to me, I'll find out, and I'll hang you out to dry. But if you play it straight with me, I'll keep you out of it."

"I believe you," said the man. Then he shut the door.

As Cheney walked down the steps, he wondered if he felt the same.

It was later than Cheney had anticipated they were going to finish up, so he gave Tony a rain check on the drinks. It was raining when they pulled onto the Santa Monica Freeway and headed west toward Pacific Palisades.

"What do you think?" asked Tony.

"I don't know. This is the strangest case I've ever worked."

"Maybe it's just because it's Frank."

"Maybe. But Frank wasn't a part of this group. Frank was shot in a parking lot by a man. Mason was killed on the beach with a knife by a blonde woman. Sounds like two entirely separate homicides."

"Except for the blue ribbons."

"That plus the fact that both men's daughters hated their fathers. Mason's daughter said he molested her, and his being in that group more or less confirms that."

"You think Frank molested Molly?"

Cheney didn't answer. Not because he didn't have an answer. It was just that the only one he had, he didn't want to give.

"What do you know about child molestation?"

"I beg your pardon?"

Cheney fastened a button on his yellow pajama top, shut off the bathroom light, padded across the thick blue carpet and got into bed. He loved their bed. It had cost as much as his first car. King-sized, down mattress, down pillows, down comforter. When he got into bed it took about thirty seconds before he sank completely, elegantly to the bottom of the mattress.

"From your professional experience," he said, feeling

himself sandwiched in between down comforter and mattress. He propped two large pillows up behind his back and pulled the comforter over his chest. It was a warm and predictable slice of heaven.

"I know a great deal about child molestation. After all, I'm a psychiatrist. You'll have to be more specific."

"Do you think it's the psychiatric flavor of the month?"

Elizabeth put down her book and turned toward her husband. "By that I assume you mean, is it overly diagnosed."

"I guess that's a polite way to put it."

"Apparently this isn't a matter of idle curiosity. What exactly is your question?"

"I'm not sure." He thought a moment. "Do you think a child molester can be rehabilitated?"

"I used to think so. I'm not so sure anymore."

"What about a twelve-step type of program for molesters?"

"I imagine it could help. But all it takes is to fall off the wagon once every ten years to destroy a lot of people's lives."

"Have you ever treated a child molester?"

"I've treated many people who have been molested, but I've only treated a couple of perpetrators."

"How did their treatment work out?"

"They're no longer patients."

"That's really not an answer."

"One was a father who had molested his daughter. In fact, I first met him in a session with his daughter and his wife. The daughter was my patient. She described the abuse and I initiated the joint session. At first, the father refused to come, but eventually he came in."

"Did he admit that he'd abused his daughter?"

"Kind of."

"Isn't that a little like being kind of pregnant?"

"I wish it were that simple. All the man would admit to was being very affectionate. He said he would often pat his daughter on the bottom—even when she was a teenager. The daughter said that she remembered him kissing her goodnight on the lips when she was about ten years old. The father admitted that he kissed his daughter when he tucked her in. Sometimes on the forehead, sometimes on the cheek, sometimes on the lips, but never—he said—in an inappropriate manner. The daughter said that he used to spy on her when she was a teenager and she would be taking a shower. He admitted that a couple of times he'd gone into the bathroom unannounced—he said it was to brush his teeth when he was late for work, or to retrieve something out of the bathroom. He said there was only one bathroom in the house and that sometimes 'harmless invasions of privacy' couldn't be helped."

"What did you make of it?"

"I was leery of his initial resistance to coming into the office."

"Maybe he was afraid of being misunderstood."

"Maybe he was afraid of being discovered."

"I suppose they're both legitimate fears."

"It's not my job to pass judgment or to put people behind bars—that's your job, darling," said Elizabeth.

"And don't you forget it," he said with a smile.

"I must admit that I believe some therapists *project* a diagnosis."

"Like when *all* a particular therapist's patients wind up having been molested?"

"Yes."

"This happens sometimes, particularly with the crowd. A person will go to a number of therapists and eventually wind up going to one who will diagnose him or her as having been molested as a child."

"Isn't that just a crock of shit? I mean, most therapists I've heard interviewed on the subject say that their patients have trouble *forgetting* their molestations, not remembering them."

"It's not that simple. The conference I attended last summer in Denver had a special panel on this subject. One doctor recounted an experience he had had as a three-year-old child. He remembered being kidnapped and then rescued by his nanny. He recalled the event vividly, down to the the kidnapper's mustache and the color of his hair.

"It turned out that on her deathbed the nanny told the family that she had made up the entire story."

"You mean she staged it?"

"No. She didn't even stage it. She merely told the parents that she had foiled a kidnapping attempt because she was afraid of losing her job."

"But the details the doctor remembered . . . "

"That's the interesting part. He had been told the story so often, and had told it himself so many times, that he actually had a 'memory' of the event."

"An event that never happened?"

"Exactly. Today, when a therapist puts a subject under hypnosis and gets her to recall certain events in her life, an imaginary event can become a real memory."

"What do you mean exactly, a 'real memory'?"

"Let's say I tell you to close your eyes and recall our first meeting."

Cheney closed his eyes and, after a moment, said, "All right."

"Where are we?"

"In the hallway of the courthouse downtown."

"What am I wearing?"

"I'm not sure."

"Concentrate."

"Okay, you're wearing a suit, a white jacket and skirt."

"My hair?"

"It's uh . . . about shoulder length and tied back. Kind of that schoolmarm look for the jury."

"Am I carrying anything?"

"Ummm . . . a briefcase."

"What color?"

"Brown, kind of beige."

"Okay, open your eyes."

Cheney did so.

"You feel comfortable with that recall?"

"Yes."

"You're sure?"

"Pretty much so, yes. I mean, after all, it was the first time I saw you. You know what they say about love at first sight."

"Okay. I wore a pantsuit, and my hair was cut short that summer. I had no briefcase, although I had a number of visual aids already set up in the courtroom."

"How can you be so sure?"

"There was a photograph in the *LA Tribune* of me walking in the courtroom that day. I was the main witness that convicted the guy you arrested."

"I remember that," said Cheney a little defensively.

"I'm sure you do, darling."

"Let me see that picture."

"Okay." Elizabeth went to the closet and returned with a scrapbook. She handed her husband the book, open to the appropriate page. "See, that's you in the background."

"Yeah, yeah," said Cheney as he closed the book and handed it back to Elizabeth, who had resumed her place in bed.

"The point is, if I had taken what you just said as gospel, then whatever scenario we would build on top of that foundation would be groundless, even though we might both agree to it.

"One of the interesting things that came out during the conference is that most therapists do absolutely nothing to verify the accuracy of these repressed memories."

"Wouldn't that be impossible?"

"I don't mean verifying the accuracy of an intimate encounter between two people in a bedroom, where it's one person's word against another. What I mean is, let's say one of the memories had to do with a child being kidnapped by satanists and flying over a large body of water on a weekly basis. That's unlikely if, say, the child grew up in the desert. And it's even more unlikely if a number of the therapist's patients had similar memories, but grew up in different parts of the country, particularly if they've never been aware of those memories before."

"So you're saying that repressed memories are bogus," said Cheney, even though he suspected Carla Carter's repressed memories were, in fact, genuine.

"I'm not saying they're *always* bogus. I'm saying that they *can* be. I've had patients who'd blotted out things that were simply too painful to process emotionally. It's a black spot in their memory and sometimes it will come out during therapy."

"Then what exactly is your professional opinion?"

"My opinion is that memory is a tricky thing. It's not as absolute as we used to believe it was. Ask either spouse in a messy divorce to give you an objective description of why the marriage broke up. Many times they will describe the same rooms, but recall entirely different versions of what was said and done in those rooms. And they'll both be convinced they're telling the truth.

"And the other thing, of course," said Elizabeth, sighing and setting the scrapbook on the side table next to the bed, "is that child molestation does happen. I think that we missed a lot of it in the past, and maybe we're seeing it now even in places it doesn't exist. It's part of my challenge as a therapist to be diligent enough to discern reality from imagination."

"You said you treated two molesters. What about the second one?"

"The other guy was much different from the father I'd seen with his daughter. This man sought me out. A friend of his had recommended me. In the first session he told me that he had molested several young boys, and that he had never been caught. This was before I met you," she said, giving her husband a sideways glance. "If I'd known you then, I'd have given you his address and you and your cop thugs could've gone over to his place and hung him by his balls."

"I think that'd be fair." Cheney paused. "But not legal."

"But it's moral."

"A lot of women think it's moral to cut off their husbands' penises if they fool around with other women."

"So, what's your point?"

Cheney smiled and hit the light. "I'm sleeping on my stomach tonight."

The Round Table was in session.

"What we're doin' here is important," said Carl.

The others nodded. He did not look directly at them, but he could see their reflections in the mirror.

Duane Eddy's guitar wept mournfully in the background. Carl tapped his fingers to the beat on his beer can. The others—Mark, Diana, Malcolm, and Dennis—sat quietly.

"People're gonna talk about what we do here . . . and out there."

"Fear is what it's all about," said Carl. "Fear brings people outta their shells, where they feel safe. They try to protect themselves with money, power, sex, religion, whatever they think will save them from their sins. But nothing and no*body* can do that forever. The past eventually catches up with 'em. *We* catch up with 'em," said Carl with a crooked and malevolent smile.

Carl caught a glimpse of himself in the mirror. He was a good-looking man. Not boyishly handsome, but strong. He wore jeans, a black cowboy shirt with white piping on the front and back. His belt buckle was brass, worked into the image of a bucking horse. He wore new leather boots. He'd hardly ever worn this pair. But then, this was a very special occasion.

Carl shook a Marlboro cigarette out of a hardpack and lit it. The smell of burning tobacco, the sound of Duane Eddy's guitar, the solid feel of leather boots as he shifted his weight from one foot to the other and stood at the head of the table . . . there was a sense of his machismo in the air.

"I hate this shit-kicking music," said Mark, preferring the complexity of Mahler to what he considered inferior ear pollution.

"This is my night and we're gonna do it my way," said Carl firmly. He wasn't going to be pushed around by some fucking pretentious asshole.

No one said anything.

"All right, let's get to it," said Carl finally.

"I'm next, after you," said Malcolm.

"That's right."

Malcolm sat with his feet up on the table, his head bobbing to some real or imagined rock-and-roll song playing in his head.

"I'd like to propose a toast," said Carl. "To Diana. Congratulations on a mission accomplished."

The others raised their glasses in Diana's direction, then drank.

"Two down and three to go," said Carl.

"At least three," said Dennis.

"At least."

Dennis sat staring directly at Carl, as though looking through him. Through them all. He was there and he was not there. He was a ticking bomb.

When the meeting adjourned, Carl walked out upon the lawn. Toward the lake. He sat alone on the smooth, moist bank of the Black Water. Sipping his beer.

Carl downed the rest of his beer and tossed the can out into the lake. In the moonlight he could see the ripples undulating out in concentric circles from where the can died in the water. Circles within circles. Life was like that. His life was like that—endless waves emanating out from a single event.

Eventually touching everything. Everyone.

Carl felt good. He stood and walked closer to the lake, down to the dock. He got into the small boat and adjusted the oars. Ritual.

Rowed out into the middle of the lake.

Looked back toward the shore. Sensed the others looking at him. Even though he couldn't see them.

He knew what he had to do. Knew how to keep a secret.

As he sat there in the middle of the lake, oars idle, in the middle of Black Water, he sensed the presence. It was the presence they all felt. It was the presence that had brought them all together. Made them do what they did.

It was the presence.

It was justice.

It was . . . ritual.

Nine

The next morning Cheney got up with his wife. In the kitchen he sparred a little with Petty, who told him she wanted the following Wednesday off because she and her sister had gotten tickets for *The Tony Bishop Show*, which was going to be taping in Hollywood all next week. Then he put a healthy dose of coffee in his LAPD commuter mug and was out the door before nine. He was in Chatsworth by nine thirty.

If Marge was surprised to see Cheney, she didn't show it. She seemed happy to see him. She poured them both some juice and they sat down. The TV was on, but the sound was muted.

Marge was dressed in white slacks, which showed her figure to be a lot fuller than when she was married to Frank. She had on a light green short-sleeved blouse and white tennis shoes. There were no photographs in the room, just paintings; prints, actually. Most were cheaply framed and all were of famous biblical figures performing some recognizable event from the holy story.

Cheney remembered Marge as a reticent person, more content than happy. Frank told the stories, she listened, laughed in the right places, and served drinks and sandwiches. Cheney had never seen Frank abuse Marge physically, or even verbally. He knew men who spoke of their wives sarcastically or disparagingly while both were in the presence of others. Cheney always recognized it and never liked it. It made him feel uneasy, like he was being made to witness a public flogging.

But Cheney also had never seen Frank show any outward displays of affection toward Marge. At the time, he had just figured Frank was one of those men who was uncomfortable with that kind of thing. Cheney had lots of friends like that. He used to be like that, but Elizabeth had changed him.

A Siamese cat leaped up on Marge's lap. In the background Cheney noticed a game show contestant jumping up and down, becoming so excited that he threw himself on a car, which he had apparently just won.

"Is the juice okay?"

"Yeah, it's fine," said Cheney. "Marge . . ." This wasn't going to be easy.

"I squeezed it myself. Molly bought me one of those juicers for Christmas last year."

"It's good."

"You can really tell the difference. Least I can."

"Marge, I spoke with Molly."

"Really? That's nice. Doesn't she look great?"

"Yes, she does."

"I'm so proud of that child."

"Marge . . ."

"Yes?"

"What happened between Frank and Molly?"

"What do you mean?" said Marge with the innocence of a nun being asked about the intricacies of S
and M sex in the boudoirs of the rich and famous.

"Something happened. They're not . . . they *weren't*
close for a long time."

"I'm sure I don't know what you're talking about."

After a moment Cheney looked Marge in the eye
and said, "I'm sure you do."

Silence. It was a painful silence for them both.

Finally, "Would you like some more juice?" It was not
a serious question. She knew Cheney didn't want any
more juice. Just as certainly as she knew that she
would, ultimately, have to answer his question. But the
more time she put between the question and the answer,
the longer she could live in her dream world.

"Why does Molly hate Frank?"

"She doesn't hate Frank."

"Something happened, Marge, and the sooner you
admit it, the faster you can get on with it."

"With what?"

"The truth."

Her mood suddenly changed. The naive smile disappeared. "What do I need with the truth, Cheney? My
husband is dead. My daughter is alive. Some things are
better . . . "

"Yes?"

"I don't want to talk about it."

"About what?"

"Nothing." Marge started to stand, but Cheney
caught her by the wrist. Not threateningly, but firmly.

"You've got to talk about it, Marge."

"Why?" she said angrily. "What good will it do?"

"It might have something to do with Frank's murder."

"No," she said, as if saying it made it so. "Molly
didn't kill Frank. She was here with me that night. So

what difference does it make to me? None. It won't bring Frank back, and there's no reason to—"

"To what?"

"Every family has private things."

"You call Frank molesting Molly a private thing?"

"How *dare* you!" said Marge with more venom than Cheney had ever thought her capable of.

"I dare because I know," said Cheney, gambling.

Silence.

"Every family has its misunderstandings," said Marge, trying it again from a different angle.

"What do you mean by a misunderstanding?"

"A misunderstanding is something that's misunderstood."

"This misunderstanding . . . it had something to do with Frank . . . abusing Molly."

"Frank never molested our daughter!"

Cheney took a shot. "Molly said he did."

"Molly doesn't know what she's talking about."

"She told you that's what happened."

"She misunderstood."

"What exactly did she misunderstand, Marge?"

Cheney could see that her eyes were starting to water up. Tears weren't flowing, but there was a watery glaze. Apparently this was a familiar pain.

"Frank was always very affectionate toward Molly, you know that, Cheney."

"Being affectionate and molesting a child are not the same thing."

Suddenly Marge started shaking her head. The tears came. She buried her head in her hands and started to sob. Cheney moved to her side and held her, patting her back comfortingly for a few minutes, until she grabbed a Kleenex from the side table next to her chair and tried to pull herself together. Cheney resumed his seat.

"This is very difficult," she said through her sniffles.

"But it's necessary."

"Why? I really don't think so. There's nothing to be gained by trying to answer unanswerable questions."

"What do you mean 'unanswerable questions'?"

"It's one person's word against another's." She looked Cheney hard in the eye, with as much strength and defiance as he had ever seen in her. "When the two people are your husband and your daughter, there's no right answer."

"Maybe you just don't want to know the answer."

"Life isn't that simple, Cheney. Maybe it is for you, but it's never been for me."

"What did Molly tell you Frank did?"

Marge fixed Cheney with a look. In that instant he felt something he had never experienced from her. Hate. She hated him. For his question. For not backing down. For not letting it go, the way a *real* friend would.

"She said that Frank touched her."

"Where and—"

Suddenly Marge exploded. She stood and screamed, "Where did he touch you! Was he drunk at the time! Did he threaten you in any way! Did your mother know! Did she believe you when you told her!" Marge was hysterical.

Cheney stood and embraced his old friend, trying to soothe her as best he could. She broke down in his arms. Cheney recognized what was happening. He was confronting her with her denial and he was not letting her walk out the same way she had walked in. She had heard the questions before, given acceptable answers, and been able to maintain a distance between herself and the truth.

Cheney refused her that luxury now. Not because he didn't want to. Because he couldn't.

"He didn't do it, Cheney. You knew him," said Marge. But it was more a plea than a credible defense.

"I knew part of him," said Cheney. He guided Marge to the couch, where he sat her down as though he were a dancer gracefully leading his partner into position. He continued to hold her hand. He was not trying to manipulate her. He was trying to comfort his friend.

After a moment, Marge looked up at Cheney. "Do you believe we all have a dark side?"

Cheney thought about the question for a moment. "I believe we're all tempted. I believe we all have given in to temptation at one time or another."

"That's not what I mean. Having sex before marriage, or outside of a marriage is giving in to temptation. Having sex with your own child, your own blood . . . that's something else. Don't you think?"

"Yes." Cheney thought it was something else. And at the same time he was reminded of the gradation of sin philosophy. Sin was sin, some would say. Evangelists would preach that fantasizing about having sex with your best friend's wife was the same as having sex with her. Cheney no longer believed that was true. He believed that finding your best friend's wife sexually attractive, acknowledging that in the privacy of your own thoughts, then making a conscious choice, for whatever reason, not to have sex with the woman, deserved more praise than damnation. If free will was the grease that put humanity on the highway to hell, then exercising that free will in the pursuit of a higher good—even if it was merely an act of loyalty to your best friend—must be acknowledged as good.

"I don't believe Frank ever had sex with our daughter."

Cheney spoke as gently as he could. "You don't believe it, or you don't want to believe it?"

"I don't believe it."

"What exactly did Molly say?"

Marge inhaled deeply, then blew the air out as though trying to purge the blackness from the room. "She said that Frank had touched her inappropriately when she was a child."

"Why don't you believe her?"

"She never said it when she lived under my roof."

"When did she make these accusations?"

"A few years ago, when she was going through her divorce."

"She'd never mentioned it before then?"

"No. And when she brought it up, she blamed me."

"Why?"

"Because she said I should have known."

"If it was going on, maybe you should have," said Cheney.

"I didn't. I swear. I think the pressure of the divorce broke an emotional dam and all kinds things just came flooding out."

"What kinds of things?"

"She believed she was sexually abused by Frank. She believed she was emotionally abused and betrayed by me. She believed she was physically and verbally abused by her husband."

"And you don't think any of that was true?"

Marge blew her nose, sat upright and blinked her eyes as dry as she could. "Do you know what it's like to be sexually abused?"

"No, I don't."

"I do. I was fondled by my uncle nearly every Sunday for a couple of years when I was ten and eleven years old. That was long before there were a hundred times more lawyers than gas stations. Long before tabloid TV, feminism, Anita Hill, and Paula Jones. This happened during a time when you just didn't talk about such things. First, no one would've believed you. Second, your accusations would've only hurt yourself. Third, the climate was such that society in general believed that, unless you had a deranged psychotic living under your roof, these things just didn't happen. But it happened to me."

"And you told no one?" asked Cheney. This was by far the most intimate he had ever been with Marge. He wondered if she had ever told Frank.

"I told my mother eventually."

"And?"

"And she patted me on the head and said that it must've been my imagination. But I know she really believed me. Back then, there was nothing she could do except take me away somewhere. Farthest she'd ever been from home was fifty miles."

"How did you feel about that—her not backing you up?"

"At first, I hated her for it. But then I understood. I didn't understand my uncle. I just understood that there wasn't anything my mother could do about it."

"So, what's your point?"

"My point is, I got on with my life. I tried to forget and get on with it. And, quite frankly, I think I did all right."

"You tried to forget. Isn't that odd?"

"You think trying to forget something painful is strange?"

"No. It's strange that you spent a lifetime trying to forget, but it took Molly almost twenty years to remember."

"I know. That's what I can't understand. I know how I felt when my uncle put his hands on me. It was a horrible feeling. I felt so helpless, so dirty. And he reinforced those feelings until I was more frightened than he was that someone would find out. But I also feel guilty now."

"About what?"

"That I can't help take away some of Molly's pain. She has vivid memories of what Frank did to her. I wasn't in the room when she says he molested her. I honestly don't believe it happened. But then, when my mother said she didn't believe me, I felt betrayed. It was almost worse than the molestation itself."

"You say all this came out during Molly's divorce."

"Yes. It was the most traumatic, well, maybe the second most traumatic time of her life."

"How does her ex-husband feel about all this?"

"I'm not sure. We haven't been that close since he and Molly split up."

"Maybe I should talk with him. Do you have his address?"

"Yeah." Marge stood and walked out of the living room into an adjoining bedroom.

Everything Cheney had heard were things he didn't want to hear. His ex-partner had, in fact, been accused by his own daughter of molestation. And the second victim's daughter had made the same accusation, which had, essentially, been confirmed by the fact that her father was in a twelve-step program for child molestation.

"Here you go," said Marge as she walked back into the room and handed Cheney a piece of paper with Molly's ex-husband's name and phone number on it.

"Thanks. You okay?"

"No," she said with a whimsical smile.

"You know our number, Marge. You can always call."

"I know, and thanks. And Cheney?"

"Yes?"

"Don't hurt her."

"What?"

"Don't hurt Molly. No matter what. Frank's already gone. She's still alive. Promise me."

"I promise." He kissed his old friend on the cheek. "Call me, okay?"

"Yeah."

Cheney walked out, got into his car . . .

And didn't have the heart to look back.

"I saw a weepy card in the store the other day for Birth Mother's Day. Just what we need: another official group of victims with tearstained faces. Their own fucking card," said Daren Cheney, shaking his head in disbelief.

"Lighten up, Dad," said Cheney. They sat in the waiting room of Dr. Nathan Pollard, ophthalmologist. Although he had protested, Daren had allowed his son to accompany him—drive him, actually—to his appointment.

"And there were more people out protesting the execution of a serial killer yesterday than showed up at Frank's funeral."

"C'mon, Dad."

"Mr. Cheney?" A woman in a white nurse's uniform appeared at the door. Her smile looked sincere to Cheney.

Daren stood up. "Stay," he said, as though speaking to a dog. Cheney knew the remark was meant for him.

Cheney's father and the nurse disappeared into the bowels of the office and Cheney sat thinking about how things had changed without his really noticing. Somewhere along the line the father had become the son. Not that the shift was acknowledged. Not that it ever would be.

Cheney had always looked up to his father. The cop.

For many years Cheney had been referred to as "the cop's son," or "Daren's son." Gradually, he had developed his own identity, but he had still followed in his father's footsteps. In the beginning, some skids had been greased by the old man, but Cheney had earned his success. In fact, he had worked twice as hard just so there would be no doubt about it.

But now, especially with his mother gone, Cheney was more parent than child. His father was getting older, less strong physically, and to a degree, mentally. Daren put up a strong front, but Cheney knew that his mother's death had pulled the pins out of a reality his parents had created and shared for fifty years. At seventy-eight years old, his father played tennis several times a week, and took a two-mile walk on the beach every night after dinner. He was in great shape for a seventy-eight-year-old man. But still, he was a seventy-eight-year-old man.

Cheney looked up, and through the open reception window saw Dr. Pollard walk over to a file cabinet and withdraw a folder. Cheney stood and walked to the reception desk. "Doctor?"

"Yes?"

"I'm Daren Cheney's son. May I have a quick word with you?"

"Certainly."

Dr. Pollard opened the door and led Cheney into his office. When the doctor closed the door and waved Cheney to a seat, the ex-cop knew the news was not going to be good.

"We have just a couple of minutes while Daren lets his eyes adjust to the drops I just gave him," said the doctor as he sat down in a black leather chair behind his desk.

"How is my father?"

"What has he told you?" asked the doctor, ignoring Cheney's question.

"I know he has glaucoma. I've done some reading on the subject and I know there's no cure."

"That's correct."

"But I've also read that there are several promising new treatments."

"That's also correct. And I'm sure that, in the future, glaucoma will be another one of those once-feared, easily treatable diseases."

"In the future . . . "

"The treatments you're referring to are experimental. They're promising, but they're not ready."

"But if there's no hope anyhow, why not give them a try?"

"For one thing, if the treatments don't work they can cheat the patient of the few remaining days of sight he or she has left."

Both men were silent for a moment. The doctor was not going to volunteer information, yet he was not entirely unsympathetic to Cheney's concerns.

"How bad is it?"

"How bad would you say it is if you knew you were going blind?"

Cheney didn't answer immediately. Finally he said, "How long?"

"Till he can't see anymore? That depends. My guess is that he might have another year or so until . . ." The doctor sighed. "Look, I know this is tough. My own grandfather had glaucoma. I would have given anything to save his sight. Quite frankly, seeing him go through what he went through was the main reason I decided to specialize in ophthalmology. He's dead now, but if he were alive, I still couldn't save his sight."

"He didn't die of glaucoma, did he?"

"Not directly."

"What do you mean?"

"Glaucoma is not a fatal disease. But sometimes . . ."

"Yes?"

"Sometimes the idea of not being able to see . . . well, it just changes things. Changes them so much that some people just can't take it."

All the way back to his father's trailer park, Cheney made sure they didn't talk about his father's appointment. There was the perfunctory, how'd it go?, how you feeling?, but no details. Cheney knew that his father knew the same facts Pollard had told him, and they weren't going to change no matter who said them.

Cheney pulled into a parking spot next to his father's trailer, got out, and coaxed the old man into going for a walk on the beach across PCH. The sun was hot for this time of year. The wind was strong, the surf up. For nearly a half hour the two men walked along the beach, hair and collars blowing, the sound of the ocean constant, grinding and, in its way, comforting. They stopped beneath a pier that jutted out under a restaurant. Daren sat down. Cheney sat down next to him.

"So, how're ya comin' on Frank's murder?"

Cheney brought his father up to date. As it had in the past, talking it out, just running down the details to his father, helped Cheney organize the facts better in his head. Daren nodded, took in all in, much the same as he had when he'd been briefed on hundreds of other murders. This time he wasn't sitting behind a desk; he was sitting with his son, staring out at an angry ocean that seemed, to him, to be getting farther and farther away.

"You really think Frank molested Molly?" asked Daren, not bothering to look at his son.

"I don't know what to think."

"You don't want to think so. This other guy . . . ."

"Andrew Mason."

"Did you have a hard time believing he molested his daughter?"

After a slight hesitation, Cheney said, "No."

"If you want to find Frank's killer, don't get soft about Frank. You're a good cop, Derek. Can't believe you quit so young. Pussy-whipped."

"C'mon, Dad."

"Okay, okay. Anyhow, you gotta be a cop now. If you wanna be Frank's friend and make sure nothin' happens to his memory, then back the fuck off. Now. If you really want to nail the son of a bitch who killed him, save your sentimentality for after you fry this bastard's ass. You gotta look at it cold and hard and not be afraid of what's lookin' back. You know what I mean?"

Cheney nodded, and continued to stare out at the ocean. "Yeah," he said. "It's just that . . . "

"What?"

"This suppressed-memory thing. According to Marge, Molly didn't even remember that Frank had molested her till she was in her mid-twenties."

"Memory's a hard thing to get hold of, Derek."

"For some therapists it's big business. How do you feel about it?"

Daren Cheney didn't answer immediately. He just sat and stared out at a fading world. "You're asking the wrong person, son. I put a lot of stock in memories. These days, that's about all I've got left."

* * *

"You know how I feel about you, Ray," said the man. He was clearly uncomfortable.

"Like a brother. I know that, Bob. So why the clandestine meeting?" Ray Malzone sat in a red vinyl booth at the Midtown Steak and Ale in downtown Los Angeles, which was within walking distance of the *Los Angeles Tribune*'s main offices. It was a living, breathing canvas of suits and ties, and skirts of a politically correct length. The waiters wore red vests and black bow ties that matched their pants, belts, and shoes. Their hair was trimmed and there wasn't an actor in the bunch. Ray nursed an Absolut martini while Bob Stuart drank a Classic Coke with lemon.

Stuart cleared his throat. "This isn't easy, Ray, I hope you know that."

"What isn't easy? You can tell me anything, Bob."

"We've got a problem."

"We?"

"The *Trib*. You've been a great reporter—more than a reporter, really. And I'm sure you'll be great again, but it's just that . . . "

"What? I know things've been a little slow lately. I'm just going through one of those dry spells."

"You haven't gone through a dry spell since before Woodstock." Ray knew the situation must be grave; Stuart didn't even crack a smile.

Both men were silent for a moment, then Stuart took a deep breath, looked Ray in the eye, and said, "You're a drunk, Ray."

"What?" said Ray, doing his best to look surprised. "You mean because of this?" he said, tilting an open palm toward his martini. "This is my first drink of the—"

"It isn't your first drink of the day. I smelled alcohol on your breath when you sat down. And it isn't just today. Frankly, if the work was, well, if it was up to your usual standard, I might have been willing to look the other way. Again."

"I've just got a little writer's block, that's all. Sometimes the alcohol helps."

"Obviously, it isn't helping anymore. You've been drinking hard for the past ten years, probably longer than that. You say it helps you write, but even though you come into work smelling like you've slept in a vat of Scotch, you haven't written anything worth a shit in almost a year and a half."

"I won a Pulitzer," said Ray defensively.

"And you earned it. But that was a long time ago. You haven't earned your salary in nearly two years and we—that is, the *Trib* is tired of subsidizing your bar tabs."

"So what exactly are you saying here, Bob?"

Stuart sighed again. "I'm saying you're fired, Ray."

Ray's heart skipped a beat. "You can't be serious."

"I couldn't say it to your face unless I was more than serious, Ray. I'm one of the last friends you've got left. I'm telling it like it is."

"Oh really? I'm supposed to thank you for ripping the rug out from under me? Fuck you!" said Ray. He picked up his drink and tossed down what was left in the glass.

"I hate this, Ray, I really do."

"Yeah, well, I'd rather be on your side of the table than mine."

Neither man said anything for a moment. The sound of lunchtime chatter, plates being piled, silverware stacked, orders shouted, all blended together to fill the silence. Finally Ray spoke. "I'm working on something very big, Bob."

Stuart just looked at Ray.

"It's about that cop who got killed."

"Your friend?"

"Yes. He and Cheney and I go way back. Cheney's giving me the inside track."

"Last time I checked, Cheney was no longer employed by the LAPD."

"No, but Tony Boston is. Tony is Cheney's protégé. Cheney wants the guy who killed Frank, wants him bad, and Cheney's feeding me the inside story. For old time's sake."

Stuart ran his hand over his face as he considered what Ray had just told him. "Is it a random killing?"

"Doesn't look like it." Ray suddenly felt like a used-car salesman. Buying time, saying what the buyer wanted to hear. Anything to make the sale. Work out the fucking details later.

"Because if it's a random killing, well, of course that's very unfortunate, but not much of a story."

"But if it's not . . ." Ray tossed out the bait again.

"Then that's something else entirely."

"I'm hearing it might be a serial killer." He hadn't heard that, but he needed to close the deal.

"Are you serious?" said Stuart, suddenly very interested.

"Nobody knows. Not yet. But with Cheney as the point man, I'm first across the finish line."

"A serial killer who killed a cop. Hmmm. Of course you know that the *Trib*'s book division has first right of refusal on all book proposals that come from an employee covering a story for the paper."

And that was when Ray knew the deal was done. "I know, Bob. So, what do you say?"

"You could be lying to me."

"I'll eventually have to put up or shut up."

"If you don't put up, then you're still fired."

"Still? If I'm fired now, then I'm officially a free agent."

"How long till you know something solid?"

"Couple weeks, tops."

"Give me something in a couple of weeks and we'll talk. In the meantime . . ."

"In the meantime, I'm still working."

Stuart sifted through his options.

"C'mon, Bob. I've worked for the *Trib* for over twenty years. What the fuck is two weeks? If I'm wrong, you're only out small change. If I'm right, the company's got big numbers for a couple of weeks and a bestseller for six months. Whatdya say?"

"Two weeks. After that, you're out. And don't think about taking the story somewhere else. You started the story with us, if it pans out two months down the line, you owe us. That's the deal, take it or leave it."

Mainly because he had no choice, Ray reached across the table, shook Stuart's hand, and said, "Thanks, Bob. You won't be sorry."

Stuart looked at his watch. "I gotta get back. See you later, Ray."

"Right."

When Ray was sure that Stuart was gone, he waved the waiter over and ordered another Absolut martini. A double.

Calypso McGuire was easy to talk to. Whenever she introduced herself people always asked her about her name. She told them that her mother had been a dancer and that Calypso had been the first word that popped out of the new mother's mouth when her baby was born. It was a good story and it explained Calypso's unique name as well as anything could. Of course, Calypso had no idea if the story was true or not. She'd never met her mother and had no clue who her father was.

The sound of scrambled bowling pins echoed off the cavernous walls of the twenty-lane bowling alley. Calypso sat at a booth in the bar, shoes off, feet up on the seat opposite her, drinking well Scotch and smoking a Salem menthol. She was celebrating her fortieth birthday, but she looked fifty-five. The remnants of four cupcakes sat on the table in front of her. Her three girlfriends were bowling in a lane about fifty feet from the bar. They looked like they were having a good time. They were laughing and mugging for the guy she brought. Munro Gates. Munro was thirty, looked about forty, but he was a lot of laughs. He was a salesman at the shipping company where Calypso worked. Always quick with a joke, a wink, a pinch. He had told her on a number of occasions that she was the only one he could pinch on the ass anymore and not get fired. She guessed he meant it as a compliment.

Forty years old. Calypso drained her Scotch and held her glass in the air until the waitress saw it. She wondered what her kids were doing tonight. Her kids . . . those memories were of a long time ago. A world away. As though it were someone else's life.

But it was not someone else's, it was hers. She'd been wrong. She'd been sorry. Usually she'd just been drunk.

But that was before people started introducing themselves with a handshake and their particular brand of survivorhood. Back then, she wasn't "Calypso and I'm an alcoholic." She was just a drunk who occasionally left the trailer park with one of any number of lowlife dogs for an hour of cheap booze and bargain-basement sex. Left her kids in the trailer park. Left her husband a few times before he finally left her.

She remembered sitting alone in the trailer, drinking the last of a bottle of Scotch, looking around at four walls that threatened to eat her raw, and realizing there was nothing left to leave.

That had been how she rang in her thirty-third birthday. Tonight Munro was here telling jokes. Three girls, her closest friends, her only friends, had sprung for cupcakes, bowling and a bar tab. But, if anything, Calypso felt even more alone than she had felt that night seven years ago in the trailer. At least then, she figured it couldn't get any worse.

"Eh, Caly," said Munro, who had finished bowling and led the three women back over to the table. "Happy birthday, kiddo." He leaned down, kissed her drunkenly on the mouth, sat down in the booth beside her, pinching her subtly as he did.

"Thanks."

The three women sat down with their beers.

"So, the big four-oh. How does it feel?" asked Munro.

"Pretty shitty, Munro. Pretty fuckin' shitty."

There was gallows laughter all around.

"C'mon, Caly. Forty's nothin'. You got half your life still ahead of you."

"That's a pretty depressing thought. I mean, where's fuckin' Kevorkian when you need him."

"Boy you *are* glum, honey," said Alice, one the three women, each of whom was roughly Calypso's age.

"I passed glum twenty years ago."

"Hell, she's so fuckin' down, she takes speed so she can get depressed," said Munro, laughing out loud at his own joke.

The waitress delivered another well Scotch and set it in front of Calypso.

"I'll take that," said Munro, grabbing the tab off the waitress's tray and tossing a ten-dollar bill in its place. "Thanks, honey. See ya later."

The waitress, who seemed to be familiar with Munro, walked away but could just barely be overheard to say, "In your dreams."

"Umbrella," said Munro. He was past the point of no return. His blood alcohol level was so high the cops would need oxygen just to be able to read it. But he'd been there before. Most every night of the week, in fact. He was flying on automatic pilot.

"Umbrella?" said Alice. "C'mon, Munro, I gotta drive."

"Don't worry, I'll drive you home. But don't forget I'm gonna want a tip."

Alice blushed and Munro laughed even though nothing humorous had been said. "Umbrella," he said again and, holding his cocktail glass to his lips, he turned it upside down, making it look like an umbrella, while he gulped down the contents.

After only a little more coaxing, the three women did the same.

Calypso sat looking at her full glass. Umbrella. That's exactly what I need, she thought. Because when it came down this hard, you needed something to keep the shit out of your eyes.

Carl sat in his car listening to Alabama singing about the advantages of living in a small town. Carl knew that a town was made up of people and it was people that made the difference. He had grown up in a small town. Lots of good folks.

But devils lived there, too.

His car was parked under a tree with lush white flowers in bloom. He thought that was odd—a tree with flowers in bloom this time of year. But California was different. No seasons. Not really. Some flowers bloomed in winter here when snow smothered Mother Nature almost everywhere else.

They smelled good, the white flowers did. He couldn't place the fragrance exactly. A little like lilacs, but then he wasn't sure.

He checked his watch. She was late. Which was good, really. Carl wasn't sure why it was good, but he tried to put a positive spin on it. Which wasn't hard, really. He reached in his pocket and withdrew the vial. Popped the plastic lid and shook a blue capsule into the center of his palm. He snapped the lid back on the vial and put the vial back in his pocket. He tossed the Pacific Blue into his mouth, worked up some saliva, and swallowed the tiny pill. He'd already had two.

It wouldn't be long now. She would come home. He would be flying.

And another devil would be slain.

Power to the fuckin' people . . .

"I made the pasta myself," said Cheney.

"I bought the sauce myself," said Petty. "And let me tell you, I spent more time standing in line at that fancy-schmantzy store you sent me to than you did making this pasta—" Petty paused as though she were about to reveal a dark secret—"with a machine."

"I thought you said you made pasta with that hand crank machine," said Tony.

Elizabeth just smiled and twirled a small bite of pasta on her fork.

"The crank broke," said Cheney, shooting Petty a look out of the corner of his eye.

"It's good anyhow," said Tony.

"Anyhow?"

Petty just smiled contentedly. "Anyone for coffee?"

Later, while Petty cleaned up the dishes and Elizabeth went into the study to catch up on some paperwork, Cheney and Tony walked around the perimeter of Cheney's back yard. The back yard, which by itself measured five thousand square feet, was surrounded on all three sides by holly that hugged a wood-and-chain-link fence as though it were fluffy hair on a dog. It was neatly trimmed each week by a Japanese gardener whose services Cheney had inherited, and continued to pay well for, when he and Elizabeth had bought the house. The color in the back yard came from the many rose bushes; there were always some in bloom. The yard was ringed by nearly sixty Malibu lights. During the day Cheney could see the Santa Monica Mountains over the back of the fence facing north. Tonight all he saw was a spotlight in his neighbor's back yard.

Tony took a deep breath of fresh air. His condo looked out on another condo. The closest he came to breathing air like this was an evergreen air freshener put in his car each week by the guys at the car wash.

"So, how's your dad?"

"He's hanging in there," said Cheney, which was what people said when there was nothing much else to say.

"He's somethin', man. I mean two hours of tennis five days a week. Shit, that's fucking unbelievable. That guy's going to outlive the two of us."

"Yeah. So, this shrink treating Frank," said Cheney, changing the subject.

"Dr. Alan Spellman. I told him about you, that you used to be Frank's partner. For what it's worth, the doctor seemed to know who you are, either from reputation, or from Frank. Anyhow, I told him that you'd like to talk to him about something. Very discreetly."

"He went for it, just like that?"

"He's not going to spill his guts to you about Frank. He said he's willing to meet with you and answer some questions, if he can. I take that to mean that he's going to be giving you mainly answers of the yes or no variety."

"Meaning that he won't sit still for a fishing expedition into his patient's life."

"Actually, I admire the guy for that. I wouldn't want someone I told my innermost thoughts to telling everybody after I croaked what kind of a pervert I was."

"So, essentially, he may be willing to verify what I already know, but unwilling to give me anything I don't already know."

"That's my take."

"So, when am I seeing him?"

"Tomorrow morning, nine A.M., before his first patient. I've got the address right here." Tony reached in his jacket pocket, pulled out a piece of paper, and handed it to Cheney, who looked at it and stuffed it in his pants pocket.

"Anyone want more coffee? I made it myself from *scratch*," said Petty, a black figure framed in the light from the living room.

"Sure, I'd like another cup," said Tony.

Petty walked back into the kitchen without waiting for Cheney's reply.

"You mind?"

"Hell no," said Cheney. "You're welcome to stay all night as far as I'm concerned."

"Yeah, well, I've got nothing else to do."

Calypso McGuire closed the door, locked it and leaned against it. She stayed there until she heard Munro's car pull away. He had dropped her off last. She knew why, but she would have none of it. Not tonight. Maybe never again. Rolling around for two minutes in the sack with Munro was preferable to few activities short of opening your veins with a chain saw.

Calypso set her purse down on the table by the door, flipped on the light switch, and collapsed onto the couch. She picked up the remote control, aimed it at the TV, and a black-and-white movie appeared. A woman—Calypso thought it might be Lana Turner— was holding a small blonde girl in her arms. The girl was crying and it was raining. "I love you, Mommy," said the little girl through her tears. "I love you, too, honey. More than you'll ever know," the mother answered. The music came up.

Calypso hit the Off button on the remote control and the screen went dark. She went to the entertainment center that housed her TV, a cheap stereo, and her booze. She opened the cabinet doors, took out an unopened bottle of Glenlivet. Her boss had been given the bottle last Christmas, shortly after he had driven home drunk one night too many and knocked down half of his two-car garage. In order to get his wife off his back, he became a regular at a convenient AA meeting and Calypso had inherited the Scotch. She had been saving it for a special occasion. For better or for worse, she thought, this was about as special as it got.

She took the bottle out of the box, then out of its waxed paper container, and opened it. She poured a three-shot dose into a clean wine glass that was sitting on a silver tray next to where the Glenlivet lived.

Calypso walked back to the couch, reaching up and shutting off the light from the wall switch as she did so. She sat in the darkness and drank. Alone. The darkness and the silence were her best friends. Not because they helped her, but because they were familiar and they didn't hurt her.

She picked up the remote control and felt for the CD button. Suddenly the room was filled with the country sounds of Vince Gill. He was singing about losing a love and that the only way he could get over it was to die.

As he moved into the room, Carl thought it was bizarre how sometimes life danced on the head of a pin, in perfect balance. Suddenly it was as though he was in the middle of a country-and-western music video. He saw Calypso before she saw him.

Calypso polished off the last of the premium Scotch and tossed her head back. The quality liquor was working its spell. Finally, everything was starting to feel all right. Or numb. Whatever. Everything was starting to make that kind of perfect sense that it always made when enough alcohol was applied to the problem. She heard Vince Gill's voice. She heard herself breathing heavily.

And then she heard something else.

Carl moved closer to the woman on the couch. He was directly in front of her by the time she opened her eyes. She looked shocked, he thought, as he leaned down toward her. As though she didn't know him.

But he knew her.

He had seen her face in a million nightmares.

•   •   •

Oh my God! This can't be happening! That was Calypso's first thought. Her last was . . .

God, forgive me.

"Kind of a unique name," said Tony as he stood in the middle of the tiny living room.

"Never knew anyone named Calypso," said Cheney. "Never heard the word except in a song."

"Wasn't Cousteau's boat named *Calypso*?"

"Good to see you again, Cheney," said Detective Paul Knight. Knight was a good-looking guy, little over six feet tall, blond, strong. Cheney thought the man had put on a little weight since he'd seen him last. Knight had always looked younger than his age, and now, at forty-five, he looked to be in his mid- to late thirties.

Cheney nodded and shook the man's hand.

"Sorry about Frank."

"Yeah. So, you were the first one on the scene here?"

"Right. We got a call from a guy named—" Knight looked down at the notepad in his hand— "Munro Gates. From what I gather talking to him, he was tryin' to tomcat his way into Ms. McGuire's bed. Gates couldn't pass a sobriety test if you took off two points for good behavior."

"He still around?"

"Yeah, he's holding up a tree over there," said Knight pointing through the window to a tree in the front yard. "I'm letting him slide on the DUI."

"Why?"

"He's been very helpful, and he's sober as a judge now. Apparently he can nail the time of the murder within thirty minutes."

"If he's telling the truth," said Tony.

"Easy enough to corroborate. The ME's inside right now. Stupid thing to lie about."

"Thanks," said Tony in a tone that let Knight know that he was being dismissed. Knight flipped his pad closed, and moved into the bedroom.

Cheney and Tony walked outside. The one-story house was more a bungalow than a house, but it probably still sold for six figures in Glendale. Cheney wondered if the woman had owned or rented. The grass, what little there was of it, looked as though it hadn't been mowed in several weeks. The yard was not cluttered with garbage or abandoned cars or machinery, but it didn't look kept up.

It was eleven thirty-five, time for Letterman or Leno or Koppel, but for this sleepy residential block the entertainment of a lifetime was taking place outside their bedrooms. Lots of people in tennis shoes and robes stood around sharing theories of who, what, why, and how. Three news helicopter flew overhead. *Man, this was just like the fuckin' movies.*

"I don't like this," said Cheney, making sure no one could overhear him.

"I know. It doesn't make any fucking sense," said Tony, shaking his head in disbelief.

"Frank is shot by some guy in a parking lot downtown. Then some guy gets stabbed by a woman on the beach. Now a woman—a *woman*—is murdered. All completely different MO's, but that fucking blue ribbon ties them all together."

"Yeah, that's why Knight called me."

"If it wasn't for the blue ribbon, there's no way I'd believe the three murders were related."

"Maybe there really are three different perps."

"A serial killer group?" said Cheney incredulously.

"I don't know, Cheney. Right now, I'm willing to consider anything."

The two detectives walked over to the man leaning against the tree, who had been watching them nervously.

"You Munro Gates?" asked Cheney.

"Yes." Gates looked pretty sober to Tony. Fear and the adrenaline that rode it home did a lot more to sober a person up than a pot of coffee.

Tony introduced himself and Cheney. Munro had the attitude, familiar to both of them, of an innocent eager to prove himself so. Cheney used to think it strange that innocent people always seemed to be the most frightened, while criminals and psychopaths were content, happy to leave the lying to hired guns. Innocent people were smart enough to know that everyone had something to hide. Guilty people knew that someone had to prove their guilt, and that wasn't nearly as easy as it used to be.

"I dropped her off around ten."

"You'd been out together?" asked Tony.

"With three other people."

"Did you give those names and addresses to Detective Knight?"

"Yes. We all went bowling. It was Caly's birthday. I think she would've been forty."

"Would've been?"

"She told me she was actually born at eleven fifty-seven P.M." Munro looked down at his watch. "Just about now," he said with a weak smile that was more sad than anything else.

"Did you know Ms. McGuire well?"

"Well, you know, not real well. We worked together. All the girls and me, we work together at Nowell's Shipping, here in Glendale. I'm a salesman there. Been there nearly twenty years."

"How long have you known Ms. McGuire?"

"I met her a few years ago. She worked up front and I always schmoozed her when I was in the office. She is . . . well, she *was*, great. A real broad, you know what I mean?"

"No."

"Well, I mean, she was a woman who didn't mind being called a broad. Hell, I think she took it as a compliment."

"Did you mean it that way?" asked Cheney.

"I sure as hell did," said Munro, as though defending a chivalrous act.

"Detective Knight said you dropped Ms. McGuire off at approximately nine forty-five."

"That's right."

"But that you came back a half hour later."

"Yeah," said Munro, the chivalrous tone gone from his voice.

"You forgot something?"

"Not exactly."

"Then why did you come back?"

"I was drunk, okay?"

"What does that mean exactly?"

"It means I was drunk. I knew Caly lived alone. I mean, it wasn't like we hadn't done it before."

"You'd had sex with Ms. McGuire before?"

"Yes. So, anyhow, I just figured that it being her birthday and all, well . . . "

"You'd give her another gift to unwrap."

"Something like that."

"Neither one of you is married?"

"No. I've been divorced for about ten years. Kids're grown and my wife lives in Seattle with my ex-best friend. Caly's been divorced ever since I've known her."

"Any boyfriends?"

"I imagine you mean Caly. She meets people, but there hasn't been anyone steady as long as I've known her."

"What about you? You her steady?"

"I guess that depends on what you mean by steady. We've been having sex a few times a month for a year, year and half, something like that. But we never talked about getting serious. I guess we looked at each other as kind of a safe harbor until the real thing came along."

"You both felt the same way about it?"

Munro sighed a little. "I guess the older you get the more you figure the real thing either ain't comin' or else it passed you by when you weren't looking."

Cheney knew there was another possibility—the real thing passed you by when you *were* looking. Perhaps that was the most bitter pill of the three to swallow.

"So, you came back around what time?"

"Ten fifteen, something like that. I walked up the sidewalk and knocked on the door. When I didn't get an answer, I went to the front window."

"You peered in Ms. McGuire's window?"

"Don't make it sound like that, okay? She and I were very tight, intimate. I'd spent the night here dozens of times and I knew she was home. I didn't want her to be alone on her birthday."

"And, of course, you didn't want yourself to be alone on her birthday," said Tony.

"Okay, so I'm a fuckin' asshole 'cause I was drunk and wanted to get laid. I never raped nobody. I never forced myself on Caly. I just didn't want to go to sleep alone, and I thought, it being Caly's birthday and all, she'd feel the same way. That's the fuckin' truth, okay?"

"So you looked through her front window."

"That's when I saw . . . well, you know. I went directly to my car phone and called 911."

Tony looked at Cheney out of the corner of his eye. He was handing the man off to his mentor. Cheney caught the look.

"Did Ms. McGuire ever talk about her ex-husband?" he asked Gates.

"Not really. That was a long time ago."

"What about kids?"

"She had two boys. They lived with her husband."

"And you say that she was forty years old. How old were her kids?"

"I'm not really sure. Couldn't be more than early twenties at the most. Probably late teens."

"Would you say that she was close to her kids?"

"Not hardly."

"Why would you say that?"

"Well, for one thing, her ex-old man and the boys live somewhere in the LA area. I mean, if they live that close and they don't get together for Mother's Day, no card, don't call on her birthday, no Christmas presents—what would you think?"

Cheney knew what he thought, but he said, "What did *you* think?"

"I figured probably her ex poisoned the kids against her. That's what my ex did."

"Didn't you think that was odd, the father ending up with custody instead of the mother?"

"Not really. Nothing surprises me much anymore. He probably just had a better lawyer. That's the way it works, right? I mean, you guys know that better than most people."

"Did she ever talk about her kids?"

"Some. Not a lot."

"When she did, would you characterize her remarks as motherly, affectionate, hostile?"

"Definitely motherly, affectionate. Never hostile. I

can tell you that for sure. I mean, I remember last Mother's Day, I was riding her a little about why her kids hadn't called or even sent a card—we spent the afternoon at her place, just in case one of the little assholes decided to call. Anyhow, I challenged her and she made up all kinds of crazy excuses why they hadn't called. No, never hostile, that's for sure."

"You say her kids and husband live in the LA area?"

"I think her husband lives in Santa Monica. He owns a record distribution business. Nothing big-time. One of those New Age kind of businesses. Synthesizer music and pyramids. I met him once. Quite coincidentally— me and Caly happened to be at the same restaurant at the same time. He seemed like a nice enough guy."

"Were the boys with him?"

"One of 'em was. He stayed in the booth, though. Ignored Caly. I felt like walkin' over there and giving him a slap upside the head, you know? Caly felt horrible about the whole thing. That was the last time we went over to the Westside for dinner, just so we wouldn't run into her ex and her kids. Bullshit. You know what I mean? Real bullshit."

Later, when Cheney and Tony stood in the shadows of the homicide circus, Cheney said, "Deal me in tomorrow. And see about getting a line on her ex-husband."

"It's already in the works. Call me when you're done with Frank's shrink. I should have something by then."

Some people knew a city by street names and landmarks. Ray Malzone knew LA by its bars. He knew the places with the best happy hours and the most generous drinks. He memorized bartenders' names like kids memorized batting averages of their favorite players.

Over the years, knowing bartenders on a first-name basis had come in handy when he wanted to gather information on a story. These days, it came in handy when he needed to convince someone to cut him some slack on his tab.

Lee's was one of a couple of well-known cop bars in Chinatown. Ambrose Lee, the founder's grandson, ran the place and did most of the bartending during the week. He liked having cops in the bar. His cousin was a cop, so was an uncle in Hong Kong. Having cops around was good for business for at least two reasons. First, even though it was Chinatown, people felt safe coming in and having a drink. Second, cops drank a lot. In fact, Lee knew of only three people who could drink more than Ray Malzone and not die of alcohol poisoning. All three were cops. One was a woman.

Someone said, "Eh, Ray."

"Eh, Mike, sit down."

Mike Brown sat down in the booth opposite Ray, who waved Ambrose over, ordered another Scotch for himself and a Johnny Walker for Brown. The two men made small talk for a while, asking about family, work and health. Brown knew why he was there. Ray needed something. But that was okay. It worked both ways. Ten years ago when Brown's son needed a summer job to earn some extra money for college, Ray got him a job driving a delivery truck for the *Trib*. The kid didn't like the hours as much as he liked the pay, but the old man was happy. Five years ago Ray had given Mike some information on a TV commentator who was doing a hatchet job on the cops five nights a week. The information found its way to the TV guy and suddenly the attacks stopped. He even did a puff piece the following week about what a fine job the boys in blue were doing. During the commentary he had tried to smile. Not so that he could come across better, but mainly to try and cover the fact that he was scared shitless.

"So, Ray, you're tellin' me straight that you got this deal with Cheney?"

"Swear to God, Mike. It's just that Cheney expects me to pull my weight. Our deal's worth shit if he just feeds me information. I've got to give him something he doesn't already have."

Brown nodded. He believed Ray. Sure, he knew Ray was a drunk. Hell, everyone did. But the only person anyone ever caught him lying to was himself. "This is very sensitive, Ray. If the tabloids get wind of what I'm going to tell you, it could burn up all the leads we've got."

"I understand."

"Okay, here it is. Frank was murdered by a serial killer."

"What?" Ray was stunned. He had told Bob Stuart that there could be a serial killer involved, but he hadn't believed it for a minute. "You can't be serious."

"I'm not only serious, there's absolutely no doubt."

"But how—"

"A blue ribbon's been found on each of the three victims' bodies."

"Three?"

"That's not all. The craziest part of it all is that the third victim is a woman."

"Good lord! What kind of a serial killer would kill men *and* women?"

"It gets even weirder." Brown told Ray all he knew about the case.

A couple of whiskies later, Ray said, "I don't suppose you have the names of the last two victims."

Brown smiled. "I thought you'd never ask."

Ten

"I trust Detective Boston explained the ground rules," said Alan Spellman as he shook hands with Cheney. "Yes. Thanks for seeing me."

Alan Spellman stood just under six feet tall, was bald on top of his head and had bushy black hair on either side. He wasn't muscular, but he was very thin, and Cheney noticed the square shoulders that came with regular exercise, particularly exercise that took place during the formative teenage years. The psychiatrist's hair was tied in a short ponytail that barely touched his starched collar. He wore Armani—shirt, belt, shoes, slacks—like some people wore sweats, thought Cheney. The man looked very comfortable in the clothes and, on him, they looked casual, as though he probably had a tux in the back room for work.

Cheney didn't know Spellman, but through the department he knew of him. He was a straight shooter, not some quack who coddled every asshole who wanted a disability check. The word was, if you didn't want to get better, you went elsewhere. Spellman made you work. At least that was what Cheney had heard.

The office was deserted, not even a receptionist was present. Spellman had told Cheney that she would be in at nine forty-five. Sharp. Which Cheney took to mean that he should be gone before then.

"You have a good reputation," said Spellman. He sat behind his large mahogany desk in a high-backed leather chair. The view through the window behind him was of the ocean, which was about five miles away. "And Frank spoke very highly of you. He cherished his friendship with you."

Cheney sat in a matching leather, regular-back chair opposite Spellman. "Thanks. He was a good man. A very good man."

"You two didn't see much of each other after you got promoted."

"That wasn't a conscious decision," said Cheney, a little defensively.

"I didn't say it was." Spellman was a man as comfortable with being in control with patients as Cheney was with suspects.

"I need to find out something about Frank."

"I'll tell you what I can, ethically."

Cheney nodded. There was no sense beating around the bush. The clock was ticking. "Was Frank molesting his daughter? I'm sorry, that's not an easy question to ask."

"It's not an easy question to answer." Spellman didn't look shocked. He laced his fingers together and put them behind his head. He coughed and said, "Perhaps I could best answer such a question in, shall we say, a hypothetical manner."

"All right," said Cheney. He had no choice.

"I once had a patient—not Frank, I want that made perfectly clear."

"Okay."

"This patient came to me and he was very distraught. Seems he had been accused by his daughter of molesting her. She had been away at college, and during the course of therapy she was receiving for something else, she had had certain 'memories' that her therapist said were indisputable.

"My patient loved his daughter. That Christmas there was an 'intervention' by the mother and the children—the daughter had secretly spoken with her brother and another sister. After several hours, the man finally broke down and confessed."

"So he actually *had* molested his daughter?"

"That's the interesting part," said Spellman. "You have to understand that this man loved his daughter very, very much. And after hours of being accused of denying his 'crime,' he became convinced that he had, in fact, done certain things that his daughter had interpreted as inappropriate behavior. And he felt very guilty about having caused his daughter any distress.

"Well, he immediately went into therapy—with me, in fact. It turns out that the facts of the case weren't as simple as his daughter's therapist wanted them to appear. In fact, while my patient did remember certain acts that could have been misinterpreted—a kiss on the cheek, a look while the daughter was getting out of the family's swimming pool—he could not recall the major transgressions his daughter accused him of committing—actual sexual intercourse, oral sex, et cetera."

"Maybe he didn't want to."

"Perhaps. That's what the daughter's therapist said. In fact, the therapist said that the father would never recall those incidents because if he admitted to them he would go to jail."

"That's possible."

"Very possible. However, I'm not a spectator in this field. I'm a player, and a very good one. This patient wanted to get it all out, let the chips fall where they may. Whereas he admitted to what I already mentioned, I am convinced that the charges made by his daughter were not true."

"Why would she lie?"

"She wasn't lying."

"But—"

Spellman held up a hand. "Under hypnosis, or any number of other techniques, I could get you to see very vivid mental pictures that mixed certain things about your past that were real and certain aspects that were, well, not real. When the real and unreal aspects of your memory get mixed together, it becomes difficult to distinguish what is real and what is imagination. And if you have an authority figure tell you that your imagination does not lie and that the mental pictures explain your symptomology perfectly, and I put you into a support group with people who share a similar therapeutic experience, you could eventually become convinced, utterly one-hundred-percent certain, that all your memories are absolutely real."

"Is that what happened to Molly and Frank?"

"I don't know. Like I told you, this is the experience of another one of my patients. His experience may, or may not, give you some insight into Frank's situation."

"So, your opinion is that this person did not molest his child."

"My opinion is that he did not. But let me tell you something, Cheney. I really don't have a problem with what other therapists do, if it does some good. But when unscrupulous, or merely unprofessional therapists make unfounded charges, it trivializes a serious problem. It's like crying wolf too many times, when people like myself see that we're really surrounded by wolves.

"A few years ago, some brilliant media person put the phrase 'children never lie' into the contemporary vernacular. Everyone is capable of lying. You, me, our children, our parents. A few years ago I did a paper on that very subject. You ask a child the same question seven days in a row and you might get the same answer six days in a row. Then on the seventh day the answer is different and he can go into great detail on the new answer. Children have a very vivid imagination."

Spellman allowed himself a smile. "It was quite shocking, really. The kids I wrote about were mine—we have two, boy and a girl. I them asked if there were monsters in the back yard. After telling me no for six days in a row, on the seventh day my son said, 'Sure.' Then he proceeded to tell me about the horns on the monster's head and about the giant claws on its feet. Then he told my daughter and, for the first time, she told me she'd seen the monster, too.

"There are monsters out there, Cheney. But the children aren't going to slay them. It's up to people like you and me. And if we're going to be effective, we can't waste our time chasing ghosts."

Spellman looked at his watch and Cheney knew that was his cue.

At the door, he stopped and turned to the doctor. "One last thing, just out of curiosity."

"If I can."

"When you get a patient you're sure is, in fact, a molester, what do you do?"

"I encourage him to turn himself in and to go through the process, no matter how painful that might be, then to make amends to those he's hurt. Basically, to take his medicine."

"And if he doesn't want to?"

"I tell him to get the fuck out of my office."

Cheney nodded and walked to the elevator. As he rode down, he thought about the fact that Spellman had never thrown Frank out. Maybe that was something.

Maybe he was just grasping at straws.

Cheney called Tony from the car phone. They had a noon lunch meeting scheduled with Calypso McGuire's ex-husband, Trey. Cheney wrote down the address and found it in the Thomas Guide. That left him with nearly two hours to kill, so Cheney decided to take a walk on the beach.

Fifteen minutes later, he knocked on his father's aluminum trailer door. "Dad, it's me."

Daren Cheney opened the door wearing nothing but a towel wrapped around his waist. "What are you doing here?"

"Glad to see you, too."

"I'm glad to see you, I just wondered why you didn't call ahead."

"I was just a few minutes away, so I decided to take a chance. Besides, if you weren't here, I was going to take a walk on the beach anyhow."

"Daren? Who is it?" said a woman's voice.

Cheney and his father looked at each other as though they had just uncovered a ticking bomb, but neither wanted to be the first to dive for cover.

"It's acupressure."

"What?"

"For my health. It's a health thing. Like acupuncture except without the needles."

"What are you talking about?"

"Ah, hell, c'mon in."

Cheney followed his father into the trailer. Sitting on his father's bed, wearing shorts and a halter top, was a woman Cheney figured to be in her mid-fifties. But it was hard to tell. She looked pretty fit. Legs with not only tone, but muscle. Her eyes looked a little Chinese, like she'd had a face lift, or two, because she was definitely not Asian.

"Lanie, this is my son, Derek. Derek, Lanie."

The woman stood and shook Cheney's hand.

"Lanie's into the healing arts."

"Pleased to meet you."

"She knows about my, uh, problem and she was trying to help."

"What problem is that, Dad?" said Cheney wryly.

"My glaucoma, what do you think?"

"I don't know, maybe you've got other problems I don't know about."

"Very funny. I hope you're not trying to embarrass my friend." To Lanie, Daren said, "Derek's always been a little bit of a prude."

"I'm sorry if I offended you," said Cheney to the woman. "I really should have called ahead." He turned to go.

"I gotta go, anyhow." Lanie stood and kissed Daren on the cheek. "See you later?"

"Yeah."

And with that she was gone.

"Later?" Cheney asked his father.

"They got the Seniors' Twilight Special over at Tiny's On the Beach. All the shrimp and oysters you can eat for seven bucks. Guy my age needs his oysters."

"I'll bet. She a senior, too?"

"How old do you think she is?"

"Fifty-five, or thereabouts. Which would make her twenty-three years younger than you."

"Which means?"

"Which means that when you were forty, she would've been seventeen."

"Age differences don't mean anything after both parties are adults, in case someone forgot to tell you. And when both parties get past fifty, there're no more cradles to rob."

"Still . . ."

"Still what? Lanie's sixty-five. She was a Rockette for three years. She teaches the aerobics class in the trailer park. I'm proud that she wants to hang out with me. And I'm sure it'll come as a shock to you that she fancies me, too."

"Fancies?"

"Grow up, Derek. I have sex. You weren't delivered by storks."

"I know, but—"

"But it seems odd to you because I'm not having sex with your mom. I understand, but give me a break, son. When your mother died, all I wanted to do was crawl into that grave after her. Any way you slice it, my time's just about up. And now with the glaucoma, I'm not sure how much longer I wanna keep goin' through the motions anyhow.

"So sure, it's great having some babe thirteen years younger than me thinkin' I'm something special. She sits around listening to my war stories thinkin' I'm a cross between Rockford and Sam Spade. I'm not, but it's fun havin' someone think so. You know what I mean?"

The last was not a rhetorical question. Cheney knew that his father was really asking if Cheney knew what he meant. In a way Cheney did, in a way he did not.

Cheney had never been that lonely. Not yet. For a moment he tried to put himself in his father's position. He pictured himself nearly twenty-five years into the future, without Elizabeth, eyesight irreversibly failing. The sands of time were not running out, they were sprinting.

"I think I know what you mean."

"Hopefully, you never will." Daren Cheney nodded and started to put on a pair of shorts. "Still feel like that walk?"

"Yeah."

In less than five minutes they were strolling beside the Pacific Ocean. Neither had said anything since they left the trailer. Both were embarrassed by the intimate nature of their conversation. They should not have been, and that, in a way, was part of their discomfort.

As they walked, Cheney watched his father. Watched him walking, talking, noticed the way his hands moved while he explained this point or that. Noticed the way his salt-and-pepper hair blew in the ocean wind. Just as his father was carefully noting the subtleties of a world disappearing before his eyes, Cheney was watching the man who had most influenced his life, going through the last motions of his own life. In a year, two years, or three, Cheney knew that his father may no longer be there. No longer be there if he had two hours to kill and wanted to take a walk on the beach. They walked, talked, laughed a little, reminisced about Cheney's mother, and skimmed a few flat stones off the ocean.

"You set for Erin's birthday party tomorrow?"

"Actually, I wanted to ask you about that," said Daren a little sheepishly.

"What?"

"Do you think anyone would mind if I brought Lanie?"

Cheney's first reaction was to respond as though his father had asked if he could bring Hitler to a Jewish Defense League meeting. But he stifled himself. "Why?"

"Why? Because she's my friend and I'd like to bring her to the party."

"You're not going to make some crazy announcement like you're going to marry her or anything like that, are you?"

"Are you on medication, Derek?"

"No, dammit, it's just not that easy to take."

"It?"

"Lanie."

No one said anything for a moment. Then Cheney said, "Sure. No problem."

"Thanks." Daren stopped on the beach and faced his son. "Look, Derek, she's not your mom. She's my friend. I'm not asking you to treat her like your mom, but I don't want you to treat her with any less respect than you would give any of my friends. Do you understand?"

Cheney nodded. "It just takes some getting used to."

"Then get used to it. Fast. Do you realize how your mother and I had to adjust to every one of your girlfriends? Frankly, we never liked your first wife. But we bit our tongues. It was your life. It was a mistake, but—"

"Okay, okay. I get the point. See you tomorrow."

Cheney helped his father walk across the Pacific Coast Highway back to the trailer park. Daren had trouble seeing the *WALK/DON'T WALK* sign. Cheney wondered how he crossed the road, on which some cars traveled at speeds of up to eighty miles an hour, without help. Without Lanie. Without anyone else around to give a fuck.

Suddenly the woman's presence in his father's life seemed considerably less threatening.

. . .

Trey McGuire was tall, about six three, wore jeans, tennis shoes, and a plaid shirt. His store consisted of five rooms. Three were filled, floor to ceiling, with tapes and CD's of New Age music. Another room was partially filled with merchandise, but it was primarily a shipping room. The fifth room was McGuire's office, which had a couch, a desk, a coffee table, a computer, and a couple of unmatching chairs. The one window looked out over a supermarket.

McGuire had already ordered lunch. Three different kinds of soup—lentil, vegetable and vegetarian chili—and three different kinds of salad—Caesar, chef and Chinese chicken. The three men divided the soups and salads according to their taste, and made small talk while they ate.

When they were done, McGuire talked about his ex-wife. "I'm not really sure what I can tell you about Calypso, at least about her life lately. The kids and I are her past. We've been divorced for about ten years."

"When was the last time you saw her?" asked Tony.

"I ran into her by accident at a restaurant not too long ago, but the last time we got together on purpose face-to-face was about a week before the divorce was final."

"What about the kids? When was the last time they saw their mother?"

"It's been several years."

"You got custody," said Cheney.

"That's right."

"Isn't that kind of unusual?"

"Not really. Not anymore."

"When the father gets custody, particularly sole custody, with the mother living thirty miles away, and she hasn't seen her kids for years . . . yeah, that's still unusual."

"Calypso was a very, how shall I say this, a very unique individual."

"What do you mean?"

"I mean, it isn't polite to speak ill of the dead."

"Sometimes dead people were real shits. Sometimes that's why they ended up dead. Our job is to find the person responsible for her death, and now isn't the time to hold back."

"Maybe you're right."

"There's no maybe about it, Mr. McGuire," said Tony. "We're not here to slander your ex-wife. We don't write for the newspapers. We just want the truth as you know it."

"'The truth, like beauty, is in the eye of the beholder.' Guru Santayanda," said Trey, tilting his head toward the photograph of a man who looked, to Cheney, like a blond-haired, blue-eyed surfer he'd once arrested for selling dime bags in Venice. It wasn't the same guy, this Guru Santayanda in the photograph, but the resemblance was striking.

"Yeah, well, I know what you're saying. All we want to know is the truth from your point of view, Mr. McGuire."

"All right. Our marriage was a mistake. From the beginning. I didn't know what I was getting into. Neither of us did, really. We were young, and Calypso was pregnant."

Cheney noted that McGuire used his ex-wife's full name, while her new friend Munro Gates called her Caly. Perhaps Munro had been on a more familiar basis with the woman than had her ex-husband.

"I was twenty-one and she was nineteen."

"So you have a twenty-one-year-old son."

"Almost twenty-one. But how did you know that?"

"I just did a little quick math," said Cheney. "Last night was your ex-wife's birthday. She was forty."

For an instant, the distance narrowed in McGuire's eye. The distance between now and then. Between order and chaos. Cool control and hot passion. He recalled her first birthday they shared together. They had been too poor to afford presents. He had written his pregnant wife a song. He'd baked her a cake and played her the song that night. They had made love and talked about the future. About how it would be when his songs were being played on the radio. Talked about their son—they were both sure the baby would be a boy—and what he would grow up to be.

The songs never got played on the radio. The son grew up, but he never spoke to his mother anymore.

And Calypso McGuire was dead long before her time.

"You have another son," said Tony.

"Yes. He's eighteen. Both boys still live with me."

"In Santa Monica."

"That's right. I've got a rent-controlled apartment there. Lived there for almost fifteen years."

"You say you haven't seen your ex-wife for some time. How often did you talk on the phone?"

"Not often. Few times a year."

"What did you talk about?"

"I didn't really talk about anything. It was usually Calypso. She'd be on one of her drinking binges and she'd call in the middle of the night. Every time the phone'd ring after midnight, I'd know who it was. Lots of times, I just let the machine pick up, then I'd unplug the phone."

"But not always."

After a moment, McGuire said, "No, not always."

"When you didn't hang up, what did you talk about?"

"Like I said, Calypso did most of the talking. She'd say how she screwed up her life, our kids' life, our life. She'd say she was sorry and how she'd changed. But it was just the booze talking. All the time she was talking about how she was going to turn over a new leaf, she was so drunk she was slurring her words."

"But you listened."

"Yeah, I listened. I used to love the woman. I never remarried, except to my work. Between work and raising two kids I never got serious about anyone else. And Calypso was my first love. You know, sometimes when she'd call at two in the morning and she'd be crying and talking about how she was going to change, for a moment—and *just* for a moment—I'd want like hell to believe her."

"Why did you two split up?"

"I don't see how this has anything to do with her murder."

"Maybe we will," said Cheney.

He breathed deeply and exhaled. "Calypso was a slut."

"She had sex with someone else?"

"No. She had sex with *everyone* else. I know you think I'm exaggerating, and obviously I am. But not by much. It would not be stretching the truth to say that Calypso'd had sex with more than twenty different guys by the time we called it quits. I think she was a nymphomaniac. She was also a drunk. I'm not sure which came first."

"You had proof of this, then."

"Enough to get a judge to give me sole custody of the boys. I refused to expose these kids to that kind of out-of-control lifestyle. I don't know if either of you have ever lived with an alcoholic, but if it isn't the worst experience in this life, I don't want to know what's worse. Sometimes I'd come home and Calypso would meet me at the door, give me a kiss, have dinner on the stove. The kids would be doing their homework or watching TV, everything would be right. The way it's supposed to be.

"Then some nights—and the frightening part was that I'd never know when—I'd come home and the kids would be hiding in their room, the dishes would be unwashed and stacked in the sink, she'd have a Jack Daniels bottle in her hand and she'd stink of some cheap men's cologne. She'd give me a big sloppy kiss and fall back on the sofa—if she was lucky—and lay there, spreading her legs like some kind of animal. If it would've just been me, maybe I could've dealt with it better. I'd still have gotten out, but it wouldn't have hurt so much. But it was the kids. They saw it all. When she'd start drinking, it was like she didn't care anymore. The only thing that mattered was throwing some raw meat to the beast between her legs. I'm sorry," said McGuire, shaking his head, trying to free himself from the grasp of old memories that slept but never died.

"Those nights, when she'd call you and you'd listen . . . Did she ever mention anyone she might've been afraid of?"

"No, not that I recall."

"Maybe some jilted lover, someone at work, whatever."

"No. Calypso never seemed afraid of anything except growing old by herself."

"You say that one of your sons is almost twenty-one?" said Tony.

"That's right. Brad. He's graduating from USC next fall. He's got a three-point-six grade average."

"Smart kid."

"I'm very proud of him."

"I wonder if we could talk to him."

"About what?"

"Nothing in particular. It's standard procedure to interview the victim's family."

"Brad, Zack, and I are family. That's it. Calypso wasn't family anymore."

"Nevertheless, she was his mother and I'd like to ask him some questions."

"What if I refuse to allow it?"

"You can feel free to sit in, Mr. McGuire. Neither you nor any member of your family is a suspect in your ex-wife's murder. I assure you we're not trying to open old wounds. Like I said, this is just standard procedure."

"I'll ask him."

"How can we reach him?"

"He works here part-time. He'll be here in a couple of hours."

"Thanks. We'll stop by a little later."

"I'm doing a piece on your father's murder. I got your name from the police," said Ray Malzone. He walked briskly, trying to keep up with Carla Carter as she walked across the campus of Pepperdine University, books clutched to her chest.

"I don't have to talk with you."

"I know, but I would really appreciate it if you did. How about helping out a fellow alumnus," said Ray pleadingly.

Carla stopped. "You graduated from Pepperdine?"

"Yep, class of '67." Ray had been in the class of '67, but it was Ohio State.

Carla wondered if the university had been around

then. It seemed so long ago. And this guy looked so old.

"What paper are you with?"

"The *Trib*. In fact, I won a Pulitzer a few years back."

Carla looked impressed. "Really? What did you write about?"

"It was an article on the plight of California farm workers."

"No kidding?"

"No kidding," said Ray with a straight face. Instantly he knew he had struck gold. Actually, the article that had won him the Pulitzer had been about the life, and murder, of a black cop who had dedicated his life to fighting gangs in South Central. But Ray knew that wouldn't have played as well as the farm worker story. He'd written that one, too, but he hadn't gotten anything special for that besides his paycheck.

"So, you're writing an article on my father's death."

"Right."

"What's so special about him? I mean, why is some Pulitzer Prize-winning journalist interested in my father?"

"You make him sound so insignificant," said Ray, trying to deflect the question while he thought of an answer that would sound logical.

"He was to me."

"Why?"

"Because he was a user. And you didn't answer my question. Why is someone like you interested in my father's death?"

"He was murdered. People are always interested in murder."

"You say the cops gave you my name. Then they must have also told you that I have no idea who killed my father."

"Yeah, I know. It's just that I'm putting together a little background on Andrew Mason, the man, the father."

"Good luck. He was a terrible father and he wasn't much of a man either."

"Ouch. You sound very bitter."

"What do you want me to say?"

"The truth. Sometimes the truth hurts." Ray's conversation with Molly had given him a scent. He couldn't tell Carla what he was thinking. Couldn't tell her that her father was killed by a serial killer. But he could use what he had learned from Molly to work on Carla. Discreetly.

"Kind of odd, your father being murdered and you feeling all this hostility."

Carla was silent. They stood on a sidewalk in the middle of an open campus. A man tossed a Frisbee, and a German shepherd ran it down. A young couple sat on a blanket, talking animatedly.

"Did something happen between you and your father?"

Still Carla was silent. Finally, she looked at Ray and sneered, "*Everything* happened between me and my father."

"Everything? What do you mean?"

"My father was a sick man."

"He molested you? Sexually?"

After a moment, she said, "Yes."

This was what Ray was hoping for—a confirmation of his hunch. Cheney wasn't going to give him everything. He was still trying to earn his way back into Cheney's graces. Trying to prove that the bottle hadn't killed all the instincts.

Ray did not wish Carla any harm, but then, whatever harm was done had been done a long time ago and there was no taking it back. He was an investigative reporter, one of the best—at least he had been once. He felt this one in his gut.

"I don't know you well, but you seem to be an attractive, well-adjusted young woman." Instantly Ray regretted the "attractive" reference. But the word, by itself, had not been enough to kill the deal.

"I'm a survivor," she said defiantly.

"Yes, I can see that." Ray's heart was beating fast. Bottom of the ninth, two out, bases loaded, down three runs. He was going for the grand slam. "You must've had some help."

"I beg your pardon?"

"Therapy. You must've had a good therapist."

"As a matter of fact I did."

Brad McGuire was a good-looking kid. He had blond hair, square shoulders, a bronze tan, and white teeth. In his shorts and sleeveless T-shirt he looked like a model for California sportswear. But he wasn't. He was just some kid earning money as a part-time shipping clerk in his dad's business. A kid about to graduate from college. A kid whose mother had been murdered.

The young man suggested that the three of them, Cheney, Tony, and himself, go downstairs to the coffee shop. More privacy, he said. And some "killer coffee."

The coffee had a nutmeg aftertaste and the crowd was eclectic. Guys with suits, women in tennis shoes and T-shirts, panhandlers who looked as though they'd just stumbled in after having begged enough change for a cup of java.

"Sorry about your mother," said Cheney.

"Yeah," said Brad, looking away, out into the Santa Monica street where a big blue bus was momentarily blocking the view. In a moment it chugged away and Brad looked back at the two men.

"How do you feel about your mother's murder?" Cheney would never have asked such a question under normal circumstances, when the answer would be obvious.

"How do you think I feel?" said the young man defensively.

"I really don't know, Brad. I was told that you haven't seen your mother for a long time, that you didn't call her on holidays. That's, well, kind of peculiar when your mother lived only about thirty minutes away."

"Yeah, well, my mother is—was—a peculiar person."

"In what way?"

"Look, my father told me he's already talked to you. I agreed to talk to you just because . . . "

"Because why?"

"I don't know, really. Maybe it wasn't such a good idea."

"You wanted to help," said Cheney, guiding the young man.

"Yeah, I guess."

"And that's good." Cheney was the point man on this interview. He could see that Brad immediately deferred to him, perhaps because he was older. Tony didn't mind.

"Your father told us a little about why he divorced your mother. You were about what—nine, ten?"

"I was ten when we moved out. Eleven when they actually got divorced."

"How did you feel about the divorce?"

"I dunno," said Brad shrugging his shoulders absently.

"You must have felt something."

"It was inevitable. My folks didn't get along

anymore and, well, my mother wasn't much of a mother, there toward the end."

"In what way?"

"She wasn't acting like a mother, you know."

"What do you mean?"

"Nothing." Brad drank some of his coffee and stared out at the street again. Clouds were painting a bright afternoon into something gray.

Cheney kicked Tony under the table and made a subtle movement with his eyes.

Tony stood. "I gotta hit the head."

Cheney leaned across the table, closer to Brad. "Look, I want to ask you a couple of personal questions. I think maybe you'd want it off the record, so maybe I should ask you when Tony's in the john."

"So what? You'll just tell him anything I tell you."

"But it's off the record—he's official LAPD, I'm not. You could always deny anything you tell me because it's just you and me and I'm not wired. That's the way the system works."

"Look, I don't know what the fuck I'm doing here in the first place," said Brad nervously. "You think I had something to do with killing my mother, you gotta be outta your fuckin' mind."

"You didn't want to kill her? Sometimes?"

"No."

"Never?"

"Maybe a long time ago, when I was a kid, but I didn't do it, okay?"

"Why did you want to kill your mother, Brad?"

"None of your business. Look, I gotta get outta here." Brad made a movement as if he was going to stand.

"I know why you wanted to kill your mother, Brad." That stopped him cold.

"You don't know *nothin'*, man!" Suddenly hatred

burned in the young man's eyes, like a toxic acid, melting his attractive features into something distorted and ugly.

"Did your mother molest you?"

"What?"

"You heard me. Did she?"

"No way, man."

"What about your younger brother? Did she ever molest him?"

Cheney braced himself. He knew the look. For an instant, it looked as though Brad was going to come across the table at him. "That has nothing to do with anything, man! You understand?" It was not a question. It was a threat. The young man looked Cheney hard in the eye. "It's your party, you pick up the fuckin' tab." And with that, he got up and walked out.

"I would've bet against it," said Tony as he and Cheney walked back to the parking garage.

"So far child molestation's the only common thread."

"But a woman molesting her own sons? It's a little off the beaten track, even for me."

"I had to take a shot," said Cheney.

"So what does it mean? Molly, Carla, and apparently Brad say that their parents, all murder victims, molested their children. I still don't buy Frank molesting Molly, but I think we can assume that Andrew Mason molested Carla. Now Calypso looks dirty. Even so, I still don't understand how it all ties together."

"I don't either," said Cheney. And he wasn't sure he wanted to know. Not that he didn't want to find Frank's killer. It's just that if finding the killer meant finding out for sure that his ex-partner was a child molester . . . Sometimes it was just better to let the dead rest in peace.

Cheney was thinking about that as he got into his J30 and it started to rain. It never rained in California, or so the saying went. As he drove home through the sudden downpour, the sun peeked through the clouds.

Cheney looked around for a rainbow, but he couldn't find one.

The Cheney home was the site of Erin's tenth birthday party. Petty had baked a chocolate cake with white icing. On the top was a figure of a palomino. Erin had a collection of horses, many of which Cheney and Elizabeth had given her.

Erin was the daughter of Cheney's son, Donald, and his wife, Samantha. The guest list included Cheney's ex-wife, Cary Ann, Erin's favorite grandmother. Cary Ann was currently, though not happily, married to Ray Malzone, whom Cheney had known longer, and liked much better.

Over the years the divided family had learned to coexist in a civil manner while managing not to damage furniture or egos too badly in the process. Donald was a feature writer for the *Trib*. By pulling a few strings, Ray had managed to get Donald a job there. Donald had kept the job, and been promoted several times, based solely on the high quality of his work. In fact, he was generally regarded as equal to, if not better than, his counterpart at the *LA Times*. Samantha was a stay-at-home mom who volunteered for everything from selling snacks at the concession stand during T-Ball games, in which Erin played, to teaching remedial reading classes to seniors twice a week—she had been a teacher before marrying Donald.

Donald and Samantha had an agreement that when Erin went away to college, Samantha would start a business and Donald would support her in that effort. Erin's college fund had been started by Cheney when Erin was born. "The greatest law of the universe is that of compound interest," Cheney had said at the time. Not an original line, but appropriate. The money had never been touched, and because it had been placed in a highly profitable mutual fund during the mid-eighties, college would not be a problem when Erin was ready to go.

So that meant that most of Donald and Samantha's savings could go into her business when the time came. When Erin was ready for college, Samantha would only be forty-one. Time enough for another lifetime, she figured.

"What did you get me, Grandpa?" said Erin.

"What do you mean?" said Cheney innocently.

"My present?"

"Present? Why?"

"It's my birthday, silly."

"You're kidding. I guess I forgot."

"You didn't forget." Erin laughed that cute little laugh that always stole everyone's heart. If you wanted to meet anyone, Cheney always said, take Erin someplace. Strangers would come up to him and comment on what a cute little child this was. She was beautiful, warm, and trusting. Cheney knew, more than most people, that that would all change. When he looked into his granddaughter's eyes, he always cherished the look he saw, felt, coming back. Nothing lasted forever. And innocence was usually the first thing to go.

"Maybe I can find something," he said with a smile.

"If you can't, it's okay, Grandpa." It was comments like that, that so endeared this child to Cheney.

"Eh, Cheney," said Ray Malzone as he and Cary Ann were ushered in by Elizabeth.

"Cheney," said Cary Ann, politely.

"Hi, you two."

"Erin, come here, honey," said Cheney's ex-wife, kneeling down.

Ray leaning close to Cheney in a conspiratorial manner. "Can we talk?"

"Sure."

"I mean alone."

"What about?"

"I might have something interesting for you about Frank's murder. Tony here?"

"He's working."

"We need to talk."

"Okay."

"You still have any of that Hennessy XO around?"

"For special occasions."

"Hey, it's Erin's birthday. What's more special than that?"

Though Erin had taken to Elizabeth as warmly as she had to Cary Ann, she had never seemed to open up the same way to Ray as she had with Cheney. That was okay with Cheney. For lots of reasons.

"Meet me in the study in a half hour," said Cheney.

"You got it."

The doorbell rang, and for some reason that Cheney could not completely explain, his heart skipped a beat and he got a funny feeling in the pit of his stomach.

Elizabeth opened the door and guided Daren Cheney and his *date*, Lanie, into the living room and began introducing her around. Daren was dressed in a Guess sweatshirt Cheney had bought him last Christmas, a pair of jeans, and a good-looking pair of Western boots. Lanie wore high-heeled shoes, black pantyhose, a flower-print skirt that stopped a couple of inches above her knee, a white blouse, and a shawl, the colors of which matched her skirt. Her red hair was teased, but not so much that it qualified as "big hair."

Cheney was simply relieved that she had not shown up wearing a leotard.

"Hi, Dad," said Cheney. He had made himself scarce while his wife performed her hostess duties. He tried to convince himself that he wasn't hiding. And when that failed he tried to figure out exactly who and what he was hiding from.

"Hi, Derek. You remember Lanie."

"I don't think we were officially introduced the other day," said the woman, holding out her hand.

"Pleased to meet you," said Cheney, shaking Lanie's hand.

"So where is the birthday girl?" she asked.

"She's around."

"I've got a little something for her."

"You shouldn't have, really."

"She insisted," said Daren. "She's got five great-granddaughters of her own."

"Plus three great-grandsons. You know, Daren, I'm a little hot from the drive over. You think you could get me a drink?"

"Sure. What'll you have?"

Lanie looked at Cheney. "You have margaritas?"

"Comin' up."

"Actually, I'd prefer if Daren got it for me." She added quickly, "He knows exactly how I like them."

"Back in a minute."

As Daren departed it was clear to Cheney that Lanie wanted to speak privately.

"You feel uncomfortable about me being here with your father, don't you."

"Of course not. He's a . . . well, yeah, actually, I do."

"I understand. I felt the same way the first time my father brought his female friend home for Thanksgiving dinner. He was sixty-seven, divorced for eight years, and the 'home wrecker' was sixty. I was still married at the time and even though I intellectually understood that there was nothing illicit about my father bringing this woman home, I had a gut reaction to it. Plain and simple. No sense pretending you don't feel something when you do, right?"

"Right."

"Anyhow, I just want you to know that I know how you feel—as much as anyone can know how another person really feels. And I'm aware that I'm not your mother. I'm Daren's friend."

"What exactly does that mean—friend?"

"I'm a different kind of friend than the guys he plays cards with. Least I hope so—these days a person can't be too careful about her sexual partners."

"Oh, jeez."

"I'm kidding, okay? You gotta lighten up a little, kid. You know, Daren warned me about you."

"What do you mean?"

"He said you're a little on the conservative side."

"He didn't," said Cheney, a little defensively.

"Actually, he said you're a bit of a tight-ass."

"Oh, that's nice. So, what does that make him, a loose—"

"Here you go, Lanie," said Daren, handing her a margarita.

"Thanks, baby. Is that Erin?" she said, pointing through a patio window.

"Yes."

"Hold this." Lanie gave her drink to Daren and walked outside.

"She's really something, isn't she?"

"She's something, all right."

"I want to thank you for inviting us."

"You're always welcome in my home, Dad. You know that."

"Yeah, I know that, but I'm just glad you didn't make a big deal out of me bringing Lanie."

"Yeah, well . . ."

"Because coming here and seeing Erin . . ." Daren didn't have to finish the thought. "She's so beautiful," said Daren finally.

Cheney wasn't certain which female his father was talking about. It didn't matter. In a way, in a way Cheney completely understood at that precise moment, it was equally true of both.

"This is smooth shit," said Ray Malzone, referring to the Hennessy XO.

"Enjoy."

Cheney noted that it obviously was not Ray's first drink of the evening and was certainly not going to be his last. "Nice to see you and Cary Ann together."

"Yeah, well, we still don't live together, but we still see each other."

"I hope it works out."

"Yeah, me too," said Ray with a sigh. "To Erin," he said, changing the subject and raising his snifter toward Cheney.

Cheney felt strange toasting his granddaughter's birthday with cognac, but arguing the matter didn't make much sense. He pointed his glass in Ray's direction and both men drank.

Cheney sat in a high-back red leather chair and Ray sat in a matching chair just off to Cheney's left, a mahogany side table between them.

"I think I might have something for you," said Ray. He planned to milk this for all it was worth. He needed this. Needed it bad. He had to prove he still had it. Prove it to the *Trib*. Prove it to Cheney.

Prove it to himself. They said the road to hell was paved with good intentions. The road back wasn't paved at all, or at least that's the way Ray saw it. It was a dirt road without signs. That's why most people never found their way back. Ray had neither good intentions nor a map. What he had was gut instinct, a sense of direction, and a nose for a good story.

"I'm all ears," said Cheney, the sound of the birthday party serving as background to this closed-door conversation.

"What's the common thread between Frank's murder and Mason's murder?"

"How do you know about Mason?"

"You're not my only source, Cheney. This is my job, remember? And, in case you forgot, I'm still pretty good at it. So, what's the common denominator between the two murders, besides the blue ribbon?" Ray tried not to gloat.

And Cheney tried not to show it, but he was impressed with what Ray had been able to come up with, and keep quiet about, on his own. "You tell me."

"Child molestation."

"Molestation is *alleged* in each instance," said Cheney. He would forever reserve judgment on Frank. Despite the evidence.

"Right. And this third murder . . ." Ray paused for effect. "I haven't spoken to anyone involved with that one yet—Calypso McGuire was the victim's name, right?"

Cheney nodded, refusing to give him the satisfaction of an audible answer.

"After talking with the daughters of the first two victims—"

"You spoke with Molly?" said Cheney. It was as much an accusation as a question.

"Well—"

"You had no right."

"Relax, Cheney."

"She probably agreed to see you because you and Frank and I used to be friends."

"So?"

"You didn't go see Molly as her father's friend. You were there as a reporter. You used her."

"I didn't use her, Cheney. I'm like you—I'm trying to find out who killed Frank."

It was true that they were both trying to find Frank's killer, but Cheney didn't think it was for the same reason. "You're just trying to save your ass. You're trying to climb back into the big time on the bones of our old friend."

"Bullshit. I admit I need to make something happen, professionally, but I wouldn't use Frank's murder like that. I really think this is an important story, especially now that we're dealing with a serial killer."

Cheney was getting irritated. After a moment he said, "You said you had something for me?"

"You talk to Calypso McGuire's kids yet?"

"One of them."

"Was that child molested?"

Cheney hesitated slightly. "I'm not sure."

"Was the child seeing a therapist?"

"I don't know. Why?"

"I think it's important."

"Why?" repeated Cheney.

Ray Malzone smiled like a man holding four aces and a trump card. "You got the husband's home phone number?"

"Yes."

"Call him."

"Look, Ray—"

"Call him and ask him if his kids are seeing a therapist."

"I've got to know where you're going with this."

"You got a pen?"

Cheney picked up a pen from the side table and handed it to Ray.

"I'm going to write down a name. If the husband says this name to you, I'm still the slam-fucking-dunk son of a bitch I was when you used to respect me. If he doesn't say that name, I'm some fucking rummy loser who doesn't deserve to be sitting here drinking your hundred-dollar-a-bottle cognac."

Cheney watched as Ray wrote a name on the label of the cognac bottle, then turned the label away from Cheney. "Make the call."

Cheney walked to his desk, looked through some scraps of paper, and found Trey McGuire's home phone number. He picked up the portable phone and push-buttoned the number.

"Hello."

"Mr. McGuire?"

"Yes."

"This is Derek Cheney. We met yesterday."

"Yes."

"I'm sorry to bother you at home."

"My son was very upset after talking with you."

"I'm sorry."

McGuire did not respond. He did not accept Cheney's apology.

"Mr. McGuire, I need to know something."

"What?"

"Your sons . . . is either one of them seeing a therapist?"

"I don't know that that's any business of yours. Our

family's problems are private, and they certainly have nothing to do with Calypso's murder."

"I understand."

"I wonder," said McGuire bitterly. "Do you have children, Mr. Cheney?"

"Yes, I do."

"How would you feel if I, a complete stranger, came into your home and asked your child intimate questions that even you, as his father, found difficult to ask?"

"I'm sure I wouldn't feel comfortable with that."

"You sure as hell wouldn't. Tonight Brad and I got into a shouting match. He ended up slamming doors and stomping out of here. That's never happened before between us. You said something to my boy today that hurt him. Hurt him bad. Now you want something else. And next week when you're off on some other case, my sons and I will be left wallowing in the shit you left in our house."

Cheney didn't feel like arguing. He could defend himself, but the man was not wrong.

"I'm very sorry, Mr. McGuire. You have a right to be upset."

"I don't need your permission to feel upset."

"That's true. Look, I just need you to answer one question, then I'll leave you alone, I promise," said Cheney, hoping that, in the long run, he could back it up.

After a long silence, McGuire finally said, "What's the question?"

"Like I said, I'd like to know if either of your boys is seeing a therapist. And if so, I'd like to know the therapist's name."

"What if I tell you the person's name?"

"What do you mean?"

"I mean, I know that there's a legal confidentiality

between therapist and patient. Does it work both ways? What I really mean is, I don't want this to come back legally on me, or in any way on my sons."

"So there is a therapist," said Cheney, not answering McGuire's question.

"The man has helped heal our family. Do you understand what I'm saying?"

"I understand that you feel a loyalty to him."

"I do. I don't want him to get hurt. I wouldn't want him to think he's getting harassed by the police because I gave you his name."

"We're not going to harass anyone."

Silence. Finally Cheney said, "Can you please give me his name?"

In Cheney's study, Ray listened to Cheney ask the question, nod, say thank you, press the Off button on the portable phone, then set it down on the side table between them.

"Well, did he give you a name?" asked Ray, as Cheney returned to his leather chair.

"He did."

Ray picked up the Hennessy XO bottle, poured himself another shot, and handed the bottle to Cheney.

Cheney looked at the label. "I'll be damned."

Ray Malzone just smiled and sipped his cognac.

Eleven

Dr. Stanley Craig's office was in Venice, a couple of blocks from the ocean. It was on the second floor of a building that looked as if it had probably been a warehouse a long time ago. The entire first floor was taken up by a New Age bookstore. Business was brisk even though it was only ten in the morning.

Tony and Cheney decided to go in unannounced. In the doctor's reception area, Tony handed his card to a middle-aged woman in a nurse's uniform. She looked impressed. Tony wasn't sure by what—him or the card and what it meant.

"I'll tell the doctor you're here," she said, and scurried off down a hallway.

The waiting room was decorated with cheaply framed crayon drawings, a stack of *People* magazines, and a couple of women's magazines.

The door opened. "If you'll come this way," said the nurse.

She led Cheney and Tony down a short, carpeted hallway that opened into a large room. "Doctor will be with you in a minute." She left immediately, closing the door behind her.

The room was like no other doctor's office Cheney had ever been in. There was no desk. The ceiling was probably thirty feet high. One wall was all windows, which looked out onto a parking lot. What seemed to be a real tree loomed over half the office, which must have been close to three thousand square feet. A dozen colorfully painted barrels were strung together to form a tunnel. There was a jungle gym and a sandbox, in which were buckets and shovels. Soccer balls, footballs, and basketballs lay strewn about. There was a lowered basket and backboard off to the right of the sandbox. Posters of famous sports figures lined the walls.

The door opened and Dr. Stanley Craig walked in. He stood about five-ten, Cheney estimated. Hundred sixty pounds, slender, still had most of his curly brown hair. He wore a Hawaiian shirt, beige slacks, and high-top athletic shoes. He shook the detectives' hands.

"Please, sit down."

Cheney found a beanbag chair shaped like a baseball glove, Tony situated himself on a barrel with a padded seat, while Dr. Craig leaned up against the trunk of the tree.

"So, what can I do for you?"

Tony took the lead. This was official, on the record. "We'd like to ask you a few questions about some of your patients."

Craig smiled and cocked his head. "Yes, well, as I'm sure you know, I'm not obligated to answer such questions."

"In fact, you *are* obligated to answer certain questions, while other questions may be covered by doctor/patient privilege."

"Well, let's see what we can do without getting the lawyers involved," said Craig, transforming his condescending smile into a good-natured one.

"Is Molly Wallace a patient of yours?" asked Tony.

"Yes."

"What about Carla Carter?"

"Yes."

"And Zack McGuire?"

"Yes, but what's this all about?" The smile was gone.

"It's about murder, doctor."

"My God! Murder? What are you talking about?"

"Molly, Carla, and Zack each accused one of their parents of sexual abuse. All of those accused parents have been murdered recently."

"Good lord!" Craig took a deep breath, shook his head in disbelief, pushed off the tree trunk and walked to the wall of windows. He looked out the window for a moment, then turned back around to face the detectives. "What does it mean?"

"We were hoping you could tell us."

"I assure you, I'm as shocked as you are."

"You gotta admit, it's quite a coincidence that all three victims had a connection to you."

"The connection is that all three murder victims allegedly abused their children."

"Actually, we're not sure about that," said Cheney. "Right now, the charges of molestation are just allegations. It's not our job to prove or disprove those allegations. We just want to find out who killed these people."

"This is incredible," said Craig, shaking his head in bewilderment.

"Are Molly, Carla, and Zack in some kind of group therapy?"

"No. At least not through this practice."

"Would they have any way of knowing each other?"

"They might have met in the waiting room, but that's not likely. Hold on." Craig left the room and returned in less than a minute holding a large book.

"Let's see," he said, turning pages and sliding his finger down the entries. "No, not likely at all. Molly, Carla, and Zack have regular weekly appointments, but not on the same day of the week."

"Do you know if they've attended any other therapy groups?"

"Like survivor support groups?"

"I suppose, yes."

"If they have, I am not aware of it. You'd have to ask them."

"You see the position we're in here, doctor," said Cheney. "I mean, it's quite a coincidence that the only common factor in all three deaths is you."

"You keep saying that and it's not true. I'm a therapist. I treat people here. The common denominator is child molestation, not me."

"I hear you, but it isn't that simple. If each of the victims had simply been abused, then, yes, you're right. But all the alleged victims said they were abused and all were your patients. That's very strange. No, you're the common denominator."

"This is outrageous. You can't be seriously considering me as a suspect."

Neither Cheney nor Tony responded.

"Maybe I should call my lawyer."

"If you feel that you have something to hide, maybe you should."

"Child abuse is a very sensitive charge. A person in my position, with the knowledge I have, must be very careful about what he says."

"Is there anyone else who could have had access to your records?"

"None. Confidentiality is crucial in order to gain the patient's trust."

"Then we're right back where we started."

"Wait," said Craig, as though he had just remembered something important. "There might be another explanation."

"Yes, doctor?" said Tony.

"Six weeks ago someone broke into this office."

"Was anything taken?"

"No, but the file drawers were unlocked and the copy machine had been used extensively."

"How could you tell the copy machine had been used?"

"We keep track of the number of copies we make in order to comply with our service contract. Nearly five hundred copies were made the night of the break-in."

"I don't suppose you reported the break-in to the police," said Cheney skeptically.

"As a matter of fact, I did. I called the police as soon as I discovered it. Two officers came out. There must be a report somewhere."

"What day was this?"

"Like I said, about six weeks ago. Just before Thanksgiving."

"We'll check on it," said Tony. He stood, and Cheney did the same.

"You have a home phone?" asked Cheney.

The doctor gave them his home number, and the detectives made a note of it.

"I guess that'll be all for now," Tony said. "We appreciate your cooperation."

"Of course. For a moment there, you really had me going," said Craig, obviously still shaken by the thought of being accused of murder.

The two detectives headed for the parking lot. "What do you think?" Tony asked Cheney as they reached the car.

"I don't know. The guy seems squirrelly to me."

"Maybe you get a little strange talking to people about child molestation all day long."

"Maybe. You notice all the kids' toys upstairs?"

"Hard to miss. Why?"

"Just wondering."

"What?"

"I don't know, but I can't picture people Molly's age climbing around on a jungle gym."

"Well, did I earn my XO?" asked Ray Malzone. He sat in Blackie's, a Wilshire Boulevard bar a block and a half off Main in Santa Monica. It was dark. Ray was working on his second Scotch—he told Cheney it was his first. Cheney didn't believe him, but then Ray didn't expect him to.

"You mean did Dr. Craig collapse into a pool of Jell-O without his lawyer present and confess to being a serial killer?"

"Hey, I still believe in Santa Claus."

"You believe in the power of the next drink." Cheney looked at his watch. "Even at eleven in the morning."

"Look, Cheney, I know you're my-friend, I know you're just trying to do the right thing, but, you know, some people just perform better when they're running on high-octane fuel. I'm working and I'm giving you good information, right?"

"Right."

"I'm not saying you wouldn't have figured it out, but I worked my ass off figuring it out first. *Before* you did. That's what I do, Cheney. That's why we're still friends."

"That's not why we're still friends, Ray."

"Bullshit. If I was some rummy-ass who couldn't pay the fucking mortgage, couldn't pay his car payment, couldn't fucking produce, and I still lived off Vitamin A—"

"Vitamin A?"

"Alcohol. Get with it. Anyhow, if I still couldn't get it up anymore, you'd write me off. Am I right?"

"You're wrong."

"Bullshit, I'm wrong."

"I'd write you off as someone I could depend on, but I wouldn't write you off as a friend."

"Gee, Cheney, I'm touched."

"You're not touched, you're drunk."

"But I was right, wasn't I?"

"You gave us a good lead. I'm grateful."

"How grateful?"

"Deal's the same. The story's yours when we bring the guy down."

"Even if it's not this guy."

"Deal's a deal."

"You working on an expense account?"

Cheney knew where this was going. He motioned toward the bartender and pointed at Ray's nearly empty glass. There wasn't any point in arguing anymore. Ray would have eventually bought the drink himself. Besides, Cheney was impressed by what his friend had done. Cheney's primary motivation was to find Frank's killer. Regardless of all the things Ray was not, he was a good reporter. A digger. He wasn't afraid to go places, ask questions that other reporters were, for various, and sometimes good, reasons afraid to ask.

"So, what do you want me to do now?"

"I'm not sure. What's your gut with this guy, Craig?"

"Never met him," said Ray, initiating the Glenlivet. He had instructed the bartender to upgrade his drink to Glenlivet if the other guy was buying. "Sorry, this is still a work in progress."

"Okay, look into this Craig's past. Get me the kind of thing that won't come up on a computer printout. Find out what kind of doctor he is. Check with the AMA. See how his colleagues feel about him. His office was burglarized six weeks ago, see if there's anything more to it. Find out what he did before he came to LA. Who're his parents? Does he have brothers and sisters? Talk to people who knew him in high school, that kind of thing."

"Gotcha. In fact, I'm following up a hunch tonight that could answer a few of those questions, or at least point me in the right direction," said Ray. He was feeling good. He had been right, or at least he had given Cheney good information, about Craig. He would have a long lunch with his editor about how fantastically the story was shaping up. How the cops were fawning all over him. How this story was going to set this fucking town, this whole fucking country, on its ass.

It was going to be good for a few days, a couple of dozen drinks. Ray Malzone wasn't used to planning much beyond that. A couple of bottles of good Scotch was about as far into the future as he could see anymore.

"The guy's clean," said Tony Boston. He sat at his desk, feet up, fingers laced behind his head.

"What were you expecting, he had warrants out for being a serial murderer in ten states?"

"No. But I was hoping for at least a parking ticket. And that break-in he told us about? It happened. November twenty-second. He told the Venice PD basically what he told us."

"So?"

"So maybe someone really broke into the doctor's office, rifled through the files, copied some of them, and decided to become the masked avenger."

"Possible."

"Makes sense. Fact is, it makes more sense than a pillar of the community, after having never done so much as jaywalk, suddenly getting the urge to go out and kill people."

"Any other burglaries in that area in a five-week window either way?"

"Are you serious? This is Venice we're talkin' about here."

"Check it out, okay?"

"Okay. I should have a full report later this afternoon."

"Good, and let's find out how Craig advertises."

"Reason?"

"If he was burglarized, I'd like to know how someone knew there was something there to find."

"Maybe it was a patient. A patient would know best. He'd know what Craig's specialty was, know where the files were."

"So would anyone who worked for Craig."

"Right. My guess is that it's a patient," said Tony.

"Why?"

"Motivation. Opportunity. The guy, and/or the woman, is going to Craig because he believes his life has been destroyed by a child molester. This person knows that Craig's files are full of such cases, complete with the names—the only place these names appear—of the perpetrators. So, one night this person either stays after an appointment, or figures out a way to get in, copies the files, and suddenly becomes Charles Bronson."

"So why leave the file drawers unlocked for Craig to see in the morning?"

"Maybe he didn't have a key."

"If you know enough to pick the lock in the first place, and you go to the trouble of copying that many files and putting them back so you won't be discovered, you should know enough to lock the drawers again. And why not bring your own copier, camera, even a small video camera, or simply take notes about the perpetrators?"

"I'm not following," said Tony.

"Okay. The burglar breaks in. It's midnight, he's alone. He doesn't need five hundred pages of information."

"That's how many pages Craig said was copied."

"I remember. But why so many pages?"

"Maybe the killer needs to know everything. Maybe he wants to be sure. Maybe he wants every piece of information he can get about the people he intends to kill. Makes sense to me. I mean, you don't want to make a mistake."

"But he made a mistake. A big one."

"Which was?"

"Why let anyone know you were there? Get in, make the copies, take notes, whatever the fuck you need to do, but why in the hell would you leave a file cabinet unlocked and run up five hundred copies on the office copier counter?"

"I don't know."

"I don't know either. Because the person or persons we're dealing with who committed the first three murders is many things, but he sure as hell isn't stupid."

"You think Craig's dirty?"

"I didn't say that. I just think we can't cross him off the list."

"Okay. Is Ray checking him out?"

"Yes."

"Good."

"So what else do you recommend, short of a rubber hose?"

"This is your investigation, Tony, I'm just along for the ride."

Tony smiled. It was not the truth, Cheney was testing him. Truth was, Cheney was going to get Frank's killer, with Tony's help or without it. Both men knew that. Tony's preference was to bring the guy in officially. But it was only a preference.

"So we talk to his colleagues. People in the building where he works, where he lives."

"I'd do that," said Cheney.

"Find out about current girlfriends."

"Or boyfriends."

"Okay. I'll call you when I've got something."

"How exactly does Dr. Craig get his patients?" asked Tony.

Craig's secretary looked up at the detective as though he were asking her to work overtime and she was already late for a hot date. "You know, you really ought to talk to Dr. Craig."

"Apparently I just missed him and I need this information," said Tony. In fact, he had waited in his car outside the office until he saw Craig leave.

"Well, there's word of mouth—patients telling other patients. But mainly it's phone book advertising."

"You advertise in the Yellow Pages?"

"Everybody's Yellow Pages. When I was a kid there was only one."

"Yeah, well . . ." said Tony nodding his head as though he agreed with something the woman had meant, but had not really articulated.

"People call in and I ask them what page they're calling from."

"What page?"

"Since we advertise in four or five phone books and the ads are pretty much the same, I need to keep track of how many people call from each ad. The page is different for each phone book. That way, at the end of the year we figure out how much money each ad brought in and how much each ad cost. We're very high-tech around here."

"Sounds like it. I don't suppose you have a copy of the ad somewhere?"

"Sure." The woman picked up a phone book from under her desk, opened it to the Yellow Pages section and flopped the open book on top of the counter. "My cousin did the drawing. He wants to be an artist."

"Looks great. Why is that kid holding a sheep?"

The secretary arched an eyebrow disapprovingly. "It's a dog," she said.

"What's that?"

"Craig's ad in the Santa Monica phone book," said Cheney. "Tony just faxed it to me."

Elizabeth picked up the piece of paper and perused the advertisement.

"More coffee?" Cheney was already on his feet.

Elizabeth handed him her cup and he poured them both some fresh-brewed Colombian Vanilla Supreme he'd picked up from Starbucks on the way home. He added about an ounce of nonfat milk to each cup and returned to the table.

"Thanks," said Elizabeth as she took her coffee without looking up at Cheney.

"So, what do you think?"

"It says he specializes in treating 'the chronic effects of childhood trauma,' which is just a euphemism, really."

"For?"

"For saying he treats child molestation victims."

"Is it that clear?"

"Like a neon sign. Which, I suppose, is good because it is, after all, an advertisement."

"That means that anyone with a Santa Monica phone book had access to Craig's address and phone number, and knew that he specialized in treating molestation victims."

"There aren't any initials after Craig's name."

"What?"

"Usually therapists taking the time and money to advertise themselves, put as many initials after their names as they can in order to impress potential patients."

"Maybe he's bashful."

"Bashful therapists don't advertise in the Yellow Pages."

The phone rang and Cheney picked up the cordless phone lying on the table. "Hello." Pause. "I can be there in thirty minutes."

The Ginseng-Sing was a natural-elixir bar in Venice, owned by an ex-cop who married a yoga instructor half his age. They met at an AA meeting. For the price of a call drink at the bar next door you could get an herbal concoction that would increase your libido, simulate an alcohol high, or simply mellow you out. All legally, at least for the time being. The drinks that increased the libido were far and away the most popular.

Jessie, the owner, greeted Cheney at the door and ushered him to a corner booth where Tony and another man waited.

"Whatcha' drinkin'?" said Jessie.

"I don't know. What would you recommend?"

"Try the stuff that'll give you the four-hour hard-on," said the man sitting opposite Tony.

"Sounds good to me." Cheney sat down next to Tony.

Introductions were made all around. The man was Ivan Mason, a Venice detective who worked Breaking and Entering. After Cheney's drink was delivered in an aperitif glass—the liquid was dark brown—Tony started the ball rolling.

"So, you investigated the break-in at Craig's office."

"Not much of an investigation. Or much of a break-in, for that matter."

"What do you mean?"

"The burglary took place in the early morning of November twenty-second. About nine o'clock we got the call from Craig's office."

"Who called?" asked Cheney.

"The secretary. So anyhow, we go out there and talk to Craig. He's very indignant that someone would have the nerve to break into his office."

"Not unusual," said Cheney. "Lots of people feel that way when their homes are burglarized. The question is why would someone break into Craig's office, specifically, and copy his files?"

"Obviously, the burglar had something specific in mind. I mean, he didn't break into the office to steal money. Craig specializes in treating patients who were sexually abused. If the perpetrator knew what he was looking for, then he obviously knew Craig's specialty. So, the burglar walks in, copies the files—files he's got some use for—then he's outta there."

"Any similar burglaries in the area around that time?"

"None. There were no other doctors' offices broken into two months before November twenty-second or since." Ivan smiled uncomfortably.

"Something wrong?" asked Cheney.

"I gotta piss bad. Sometimes this herbal shit does that to you."

"We'll save your place," said Tony.

The big guy got up and hurried toward the restroom.

"So, whoever broke into Craig's office has a list of what he considers to be the scum of the earth," said Tony.

"Maybe. If that's true, then anyone who has ever been accused of sexual abuse by one of Craig's patients is now on some kind of source hit list, regardless of the credibility of the accusation."

Tony nodded. He knew that Cheney had tossed in the last qualifier, still holding out hope that Frank was innocent.

"Which means we're totally fucked," continued Cheney, "because that list is legally and ethically off limits to us. Forever. All we'll be able to do is confirm their names with Craig after we pick up the bodies."

"You think Craig's a healer by day, killer by night?"

"Well, it's either him or the burglar," said Cheney.

"I'm sure there are a couple of other possibilities."

"Those are the only ones I see. Unless you think his office manager is in on it."

"I don't. So, where do we go from here?" said Tony. It was something he used to say to Cheney, his mentor, all the time. The detectives who worked under Tony now would be surprised, perhaps disappointed, even disillusioned, if they heard him say these words.

But this was a private conversation.

"Continue running Craig through every computer-sieve you can. And set up another meeting with him."

"Why?"

"I want to find out what alibis he has for the nights of the murders."

The Round Table was in session.

"What we're doin' here, it's fuckin' important," said Malcolm.

The others nodded. He did not look directly at them, but he could see their reflections in the mirror.

In the background the sound of Jimi Hendrix's stretched, light-gauge guitar strings moaned a plaintive rock-and-roll melody. Malcolm tapped his fingers to the beat. The drugs were in place. They directed the visions. This was *fuckin' incredible, man*. He ruled. For a fuckin' change.

"What we're doin' here, people are gonna talk about it. Fuckin' TV movie, man. Sky's the limit."

"Fear is what it's all about," said Malcolm. He looked at the others gathered around the table. At Mark. At Carl. At Dennis. At Diana.

"Fear brings people out of their shells. They feel safe in there. They protect themselves with money, power, sex, religion, whatever they think'll separate them from their sins. But nothing and no one can do that forever. The past always catches up with everyone. *We* catch up with them," said Malcolm with a crooked and malevolent smile.

Malcolm caught a glimpse of himself in the mirror.

He was a good-looking man, handsome and strong. He wore jeans, a T-shirt with a Rolling Stones Voodoo Lounge Tour logo on the front. Tennis shoes. The shirt was a souvenir. He made sure he washed and dried it "logo in." He had thought that maybe he'd like to be buried in it—under a black sport coat, of course.

This was a very special occasion.

Malcolm took a drag off the marijuana cigarette, held the smoke in his lungs, then, reluctantly, greedily, exhaled. The smell of burning marijuana, the sound of Jimi Hendrix, the euphoria of the real and imagined pictures flashing through Malcolm's brain. There was a sense of his *power* in the air.

"I hate this rock-and-roll shit," said Carl, preferring the gentle twang of Duane Eddy's guitar.

"This is my night and we're gonna do it my fuckin' way," said Malcolm firmly. He wasn't going to be pushed around by some shit-kicking asshole.

No one said anything.

"All right, let's get down to it," said Malcolm finally.

"I'm next," said Dennis.

"That's right. Which means right now, tonight, it's your turn to shut the fuck up and help me."

"I'd like to propose a toast," said Diana. "To Carl. Congratulations on a mission accomplished."

The others raised their glasses in Carl's direction, then drank.

"Three down and two to go," said Malcolm.

"At *least* two," said Dennis.

"At least."

Dennis sat staring directly at Malcolm, as though looking through him. Through them all. He was there, and he was *not* there.

Dennis was dangerous. More dangerous than the rest.

When the meeting adjourned, Malcolm walked out on the lawn. Toward the lake. Black Water Lake.

He sat alone on the smooth, wet lake bank.

He picked up a stone and skipped it across the water. In the moonlight he could see the ripples undulating out in concentric circles from where the stone had died. Circles within circles. Life was like that. His life was like that. Waves of life emanating out from a single event.

Eventually touching everything. Everyone.

Malcolm felt good. He walked closer to the lake, down to the dock. He got into the small boat and adjusted the oars. Ritual.

Rowed out into the middle of the lake.

Looked back toward the shore. Sensed the others looking at him. Even though he couldn't see them.

He knew what he had to do. Knew how to keep a secret.

As he sat there in the middle of the lake, oars idle, in the middle of the Black Water, he sensed the presence. It was the presence they all felt. It was the presence that had brought them all together. Made them do what they did.

It was the presence.

It was justice.

It was . . . ritual.

Aubrey Mitchell was a broken man. He lived in an apartment complex in Glendale, by himself. One of his three children stopped by every month or so. The place was furnished, which was just as well because he owned no furniture and no longer had a job. He was living on his savings, which would run out by the summer.

His life hadn't always been like this. Three years ago

he had been the CEO of a Southern California software firm, with a house in the Encino Hills. Life had been good for Aubrey and his wife of nearly forty years. Sure, the house was a little big for the two of them, a little empty because the three children were grown and on their own. But he and his wife Karen had gradually redone the house with the children's departure in mind. They had turned one of the kids' rooms into a study for Karen so that she had an *official* space in which to pursue her poetry and article writing. Another room had been turned into a home gym, complete with floor-to-ceiling mirrors on two walls.

These were supposed to be the golden years, the best years of his life. Aubrey and Karen had scrimped and saved, given their children every advantage they could, and sent them off into an uncertain world armed with education, principles, and what they truly believed was a sense of self and empowerment.

Aubrey thought he had planned for everything. He hadn't planned for this.

Eighteen months ago his world exploded. He remembered the night, the phone call, just as some people remembered every detail about where they were when John Kennedy was assassinated. Aubrey had been sitting in his living room with Karen. They were watching *LA Law* when the phone rang.

Aubrey answered it. It was Cathy, his eldest daughter. She seemed cold and businesslike and had told him that she wished to speak to her mother. Aubrey didn't think much of it at that moment. Over the years, when Cathy was going through various crises, she had felt more comfortable confiding in her mother. Aubrey understood and respected that.

Of the three children, Cathy had always seemed the most vulnerable, the most troubled.

After speaking with her daughter for a moment, Karen had handed Aubrey the phone and told him she would take the call in the bedroom. He recalled the look on his wife's face. It was a strange look. You live with someone for forty years, you get to know and read every look that person has.

He had never seen that look before.

When *LA Law* ended and his wife had not returned, Aubrey began to feel uncomfortable. His first thought was that something terrible had happened to Cathy. But he couldn't shake the look his wife had given him before she'd left the room.

Finally, an hour later, Karen came back into the living room. Aubrey could tell that she had been crying. He remembered getting to his feet and moving apprehensively toward his wife. He'd felt a sick feeling in his stomach. "My God, Karen, what is it?"

"Stop!" she had said, holding up her hand.

"What?"

"Don't touch me."

"What are you talking about?" Again Aubrey made a move toward his wife.

"Stop!" screamed Karen. "How could you have *done* such a thing! You bastard!" Then she began to weep.

Although his wife did not calm down, Aubrey was able, after some time, to find out what his daughter had said. Cathy had informed her mother, with the help of her therapist, who had been on an extension phone in order to give support and corroboration to Cathy's account, that Aubrey had sexually molested Cathy on a number of occasions. The mother's initial skepticism was overcome by the therapist's assurances that this was unquestionably true. The therapist further implied that Karen, as the mother, should have known what was going on under her own roof, and that for her to "continue not to believe your daughter raises the question of collusion with your husband and ethical, perhaps even legal, culpability."

That night as he stared into the eyes of a woman who had been his lover, his soulmate, his shelter from all of life's physical, emotional, and spiritual storms, he saw something he had never dreamed he would see there.

Disgust.

Aubrey had pleaded his case, both he and his wife in tears, but in the end Karen had told him that the evidence was irrefutable and that she felt a great sense of guilt and blame for not having protected her daughter.

That same night Aubrey had packed a bag and checked into a motel, for what he prayed would be a one-night stay.

He had never gone back home, had never been allowed to return. His wife and her attorney were adamant about that.

When word of the charges against him had spread, all but one of his friends deserted him, and he was fired from his job. His bank accounts were frozen by his wife—on her lawyer's advice, lest he take the money and leave the country.

A lifetime of trying to do the right thing, of sacrifice for his family, of remaining faithful to one wife, were completely obliterated in the blink of an eye. And regardless of whether he won his own pending suit against the therapist, his reputation would never be restored. His wife had already informed him that even if a court found him innocent, she was thoroughly convinced, as was one of his other children, that Aubrey would forever be guilty in the eyes of God.

It was not God that he was afraid of, it was the legal juggernaut that was steamrolling him. He firmly believed that that system could never prove him guilty.

But all the king's horses and all the king's men could never prove Aubrey Mitchell innocent again.

Sal's on Santa Monica Boulevard in West Los Angeles was not the kind of place people went to pick up some-one. It was the kind of place people went to drink in the company of like-minded souls. That didn't mean that occasionally two people didn't wind up going home together, but that was rarely the intended goal. The goal was walking into some dark hole-in-the-wall while the sun was still on fire, and walking out when it was gone and you were tired enough to go home and straight to sleep without thinking too much about the day you had just flushed down the toilet.

Ray Malzone was working on his second plate of happy hour appetizers, which consisted of French bread, Vienna sausage, Swedish meatballs, and Swiss cheese. He wiped his face with a napkin upon which was printed ten sports trivia questions, most of which Ray knew the answers to. He grabbed hold of his cocktail glass like a cripple grabbing hold of a cane, and made his move.

"Mind if I sit down?"

The woman looked up from her well Scotch. She did not answer immediately. "I guess it's okay."

Ray sat down. "My name's Ray," he said, extending his hand.

"Charlotte," said the woman, shaking Ray's hand weakly. Charlotte was forty-seven, divorced for ten years. Her brown hair was cut short because it was easier to take care of that way. And because she had been taught that middle-aged women don't wear their hair long. She wore a brown sweater and a black skirt. A few men in this bar had commented that she had nice legs. Not great legs, but nice. Not because they were muscled or well-shaped. Nice because they were slim, while most women her age were overweight and hid their legs under slacks. Nice because the men who told her this were always drunk and the youngest woman in the bar on any given night was in her early forties.

But Charlotte soaked up the compliments like a bone-dry sponge sucking up rain in a desert. Besides, she liked the men—some of them, anyhow.

Charlotte was working on her third drink—Ray knew because he was counting. He could tell by the way she handled herself that it would take two drinks for the alcohol to kick in, and three before she started to feel good. Ray knew the feeling—he'd just shot up his third Wild Turkey.

"I've never seen you in here before," she said.

"First time."

"Well, this is a nice place. Good people."

"To good people," said Ray and the two toasted. It didn't take much. They both would have toasted the sound of two glasses clinking together.

"So, what do you do, Ray?"

"Little of this, little of that," he said with a disarming smile.

Charlotte had heard that answer before. The spirits who haunted places like this weren't setting the world on fire. They got by, they weren't homeless, but they didn't run companies. At least not anymore.

"What do *you* do?"

"I run a doctor's office."

"Run? Are you a doctor?" asked Ray.

She laughed at the suggestion. "Hardly. I answer phones, make appointments, fill out insurance forms, help patients fill out medical histories. Makes watching paint dry look exciting."

"C'mon, now. You're being modest. I'll bet you wanted to be a doctor yourself."

Charlotte looked up in amazement at Ray. "How did you know that?"

"Lucky guess." Which was exactly what it was.

"I met my husband when we were both in college—UCLA. He went on and became a lawyer, while I raised the kids. When we got divorced I toyed around with the idea of going back to school and trying to get a medical degree. But it just didn't work out."

"Your kids . . . "

"They're grown. Jennifer's a lawyer in New York and Paul owns a bookstore in Chicago."

"You must be very proud."

"Yeah, I guess. We kind of grew apart during the past few years. Nothing serious, just life and distance."

Such answers, Ray knew, betrayed the fact that it was more life than distance that caused the separation. "So, what kind of a practice do you manage?"

"Doctor's a therapist."

"psychologist or psychiatrist?"

"Your guess is as good as mine," she said with a cynical sneer.

"What do you mean?"

"I mean you don't ask the people who're hiring you for *their* résumé."

"You're kidding, you mean the guy—"

"Who said the doctor's a man?"

"I just assumed—"

"Yeah, well, there are some great women doctors," said Charlotte indignantly. "I would've made a helluva doctor."

"Sorry," said Ray. Charlotte had the makings of a belligerent drunk. Which was okay with Ray. He just wanted to keep her talking. "So, are you saying the doctor's a quack?"

"Not necessarily. Who knows? I mean, you don't have to be a psychologist or a psychiatrist to treat kids for molestation."

"He treats people who've been molested as children?"

"That's his specialty. Seems to be pretty good at it, if the monthly balance sheet's any indication."

"He does pretty good, eh."

"Oh yeah. Hell, if P.T. Barnum was alive today, he'd be president. Everybody's a fucking victim."

"What do you mean?"

"You know what I mean," said Charlotte, looking Ray straight in the eye. There was a meanness in the look that he recognized. He'd seen it before in other drunks' eyes. Sometimes in a mirror.

"You think he's conning his patients?"

"Some of them, yes. You get these losers coming in, they're in their thirties and the handwriting's already on the wall—f-a-i-l-u-r-e. Well, nobody's supposed to fail or think badly about themselves these days. So in order to restore your self-esteem, it becomes necessary to find someone to blame. And who better to blame than your parents? We've all got 'em. And if you're thirty years old and you're all screwed up because your father touched your privates changing your diaper when you were six months old, who's going to argue?"

"A lot of people, I'd think."

"Well, sure, the parents would. But you've got people out there who are convinced that Elvis is still alive and that space aliens killed JFK. When it's your word against someone else's, most people usually come down on the side that's determined not by facts, but by their own beliefs. You know what I'm saying?"

"Yes, I do." To Ray, the woman seemed like a person whose life had run out of possibilities and justifications. Someone smart enough to know that she was really responsible, and too weak to do anything about it.

"What the fuck do I care, though, right? I make good money, end of story."

Ray signaled the bartender for another round. Charlotte didn't argue.

"So, where does this doctor practice?"

"Venice."

"Tough area. Friend of mine has an office down there," said Ray, recalling what Cheney had told him. "Guy's been burglarized twice in the past six months."

"Tell me about it. We got burglarized about six weeks ago. Probably, anyhow," said Charlotte as she downed the rest of her Scotch and accepted a replacement from the bartender, who slid another Wild Turkey in front of Ray.

"What do you mean probably?"

"I mean nothing was taken."

"Then how could it be a burglary?"

"Someone broke in and photocopied files."

"Why would someone do that?"

"Who knows."

"You got a theory?"

"I'd rather not say."

"Why not?"

"Because."

"Because why?"

"Because the guy who writes my checks is a wacko, that's why." Charlotte was feeling good. The social filters were evaporating. She could say and do things that she was unable to do without the booze. She could be gregarious, outgoing, rude, and vicious.

"You think he burglarized his own office?"

"Maybe."

"Why?"

"Like I said, he's a nut."

"You have any proof?"

"That he's a nut, yes. That he burglarized his own office, no. Just a feeling."

"Why would someone burglarize his own office?"

"I don't know. It doesn't make any sense to me either."

"So where's this guy from? Bet he's from the East Coast," said Ray.

"Pacific Point."

"Isn't that about an hour north of here?"

"Yeah, he goes up there sometimes on the weekend. Hey," said Charlotte a little tipsily, "what's all this interest in Dr. Craig?"

"Nothing. Let's talk about you."

"No, let's talk about *you*," said the woman drunkenly, looking at Ray as though he was a piece of meat and she was a vegetarian just about to fall hard off the wagon. It had been a long time since anyone had looked at Ray that way, but then, he thought, it had been a long time since he had been in the company of a woman this drunk.

"What are you thinking?" she mumbled thickly. But that was okay, Ray understood drunk-speak.

"I was thinking about what a looker you are," he said. But he was lying. He was really thinking about slipping out of the bar when Charlotte went to the ladies' room, going home and immediately to bed.

So he could get an early start for Pacific Point in the morning.

Twelve

"I don't know why we need to go over this again," said Dr. Stanley Craig. He relaxed against the live tree trunk in his office. Cheney and Tony remained standing.

"We won't go over anything we already covered. I don't want to waste your time," said Tony, who then proceeded to run down a list of dates and times during which the murders were committed.

Craig consulted his desk calendar and his private appointment book. After a few minutes he said, "I was at home each one of those nights."

"Which is where?"

"At my condo in the Marina."

"And I suppose you were alone."

"As a matter of fact, I was not alone."

"Then someone can corroborate your story?"

"It isn't a story," said Craig indignantly. "It's the truth."

"Does this person have a name?"

"Of course, this 'person' has a name. But I'd prefer to keep her out of this."

"I'm afraid that's not possible at this point."

"What are you talking about!" said the doctor angrily. "You come in here and I answer all your questions, make myself and my records available. And now you try to intimidate me by saying that it's not possible to keep my private life out of some lurid murder investigation that has absolutely nothing to do with me. That's ridiculous and it's insulting. Certainly I'm not a suspect here."

"Everyone's a suspect until we find out who murdered these people."

Craig tried to stare the two men down, but without success. Finally he sighed resignedly. "What do you want, exactly?"

"Corroboration."

"I feel so violated." Craig pushed himself away from the tree trunk as though suddenly he was touching something poisonous, and began pacing. "This is absurd."

"We need a name."

After a moment, Craig said, "Bridget. Bridget Colfax."

"She was with you each one of those nights?"

"I'm not positive about all of the nights you're talking about." Craig turned toward the two men. "But I'm sure we were together the night of the last murder."

"How did you meet Bridget?"

"We met a few months ago, I'm not sure of the exact circumstances."

"Think back," said Tony gently. "It might be important." That was exactly what Cheney would have said and how he would have said it. Not too strong, but keep things moving in the direction *you* want them to go.

Craig turned and looked out the window onto the parking lot, and beyond that, to the ocean through a lifting fog. "At a bar. I met her at a bar."

"Which bar?"

Craig turned around. "Is that important?"

Because the doctor had raised the question, Tony knew that it might be important. "Could be."

"I don't know how—"

"I want you to understand the process, Mr. Craig," said Tony, purposely not calling him doctor. "I ask the questions, you answer them, and then I evaluate the answers. It's kind of like in your business. Your patients come to you with their problems. You ask questions, they answer them, and you guide them into a personal realization."

The three men were silent for a moment. Finally, "I think it was, uh, Barry's. It's a place in West Hollywood."

Cheney nodded, along with Tony. They both knew the place.

"So, you say she can vouch for the fact that you were with her on the night of the last murder."

"Yes, definitely."

"Do you know how we can reach the lady?"

Craig coughed a little, sniffled. He didn't have a cold, didn't feel allergic, except maybe to answering Tony's questions. "She lives with me."

"Pardon?" said Tony.

"She lives with me. Bridget's lived with me for a while."

"How long?"

"Is it important?"

Tony smiled. He had already answered that question. He was in control and he was not going to answer the same question twice.

"A couple of months, I guess."

"You guess."

"Six weeks, eight weeks, something like that. What's the difference?"

"So, if we want to talk to Bridget, we can reach her at your home address and phone number?"

"Yes."

Tony nodded. "So, what can you tell us about Bridget?"

"She's my girlfriend, what else is there to know?"

Tony wasn't sure whether the man was being evasive or condescending. "What does she do?"

"She's between jobs."

"Okay," said Tony. Lots of women who lived with doctors were between jobs. Not a crime. "What kind of job is she between?"

"I'm not sure I know what you mean."

"I mean, is she a hockey player waiting to be called up by the Kings?"

"No need to be facetious."

"Sorry. I'm just trying to get a handle on who Bridget is and what she does."

"I don't know that much about her."

"She's lived with you for about two months, and you don't know that much about her?"

"All I know is that we hit it off, we dated for a short while, and I asked her to move in. Nothing illegal about that, is there?"

"No. Strange, maybe."

"Strange?" said Craig, looking Tony straight in the eye. "I don't think so. I have patients who've married after two weeks."

"Maybe that's why they're patients."

"My point is, many people are impulsive. In fact, most of us act impulsively about certain things, particularly when it comes to sex. And, just for the record, I haven't married Bridget, I merely asked her to move in with me."

"Okay. So, do you know how Bridget made a living before she met you?"

"I believe she was a hostess or a dancer, something to do with the club scene."

"Club scene?"

"I think that's self-explanatory."

"Which club scene are we talking about?"

"She worked in the Hollywood area. There are a lot of clubs in Hollywood."

"That's why I asked you a question that might help us narrow it down."

"I'm not sure."

"Then I guess the only way we can do that is to talk with Bridget."

"I guess so."

"You think she's home now?"

"I don't know. She's out a lot."

"Yeah, well, we're in the area. It'd be great to be able to kill two birds with one stone—I mean, us already being here in Venice, so close to the Marina. We're what . . . five minutes from your place?"

"Feel free to use the phone in the outer office. If she's home, I'm sure she'll see you. Tell her I said it's all right."

"Thanks."

Craig moved toward the door, indicating that the interview was over.

Cheney noted, as he stood, that Craig was obviously a man used to being in control. In this kind of a situation, it was usually the cop who ended the interview.

Neither Cheney nor Tony was surprised when they dialed Craig's home number and no one answered.

Pacific Point was a sleepy little town about an hour north of Santa Monica. The census set the official population at forty-seven hundred, give or take a few people. It was a town, not a city, where rich people felt comfortable sipping seven-dollar-a-glass chardonnays al fresco and poor people smiled politely while serving them, all the time dreaming that some day either hard work or a personal injury claim would gain them entrance into the platinum-card inner sanctum.

The *Pacific Point Lighthouse* was the only local newspaper. It was a weekly and it contained mainly society news, and a sports page that chatted up the exploits of the residents' sons and daughters in the local leagues. Most people who lived in Pacific Point got a number of daily newspapers—the *LA Times, Wall Street Journal*, and the daily *Santa Barbara Breeze*.

The *Lighthouse* office was located between a dry cleaners and a one-hour photo place. As Ray Malzone parked his car, diagonally, not parallel, in front of a digital read-out parking meter, he noted that Pacific Point must have more art galleries and French restaurants per capita than any place he'd ever seen.

A bell rang when Ray opened the front door of the *Lighthouse* office.

A man looked up from a computer workstation. He appeared to Ray to be in his mid-thirties. He was smiling. "Yes?"

"I'd like to speak to the editor-in-chief."

"I guess I'm he," said the young man.

Ray smiled and offered his hand. "Ray Malzone."

"Stephen Sample."

The two shook hands. Ray was surprised, unpleasantly, that the man had not recognized his name immediately. Lots of newspaper people, especially in California, recognized the name of a Pulitzer Prize-winning colleague, even if it had been almost ten years ago.

"What can I do for you?"

"I'm with the *Trib*, in LA."

"I know the *Trib*," said the man.

Who didn't, thought Ray, but he kept the thought to himself.

"I'm doing a story on someone who used to live here."

"Oh yeah, who?"

"Guy named Craig, Stanley Craig."

The name did nothing for Sample.

"So, you never heard of the guy."

"Must've been before my time. Truth is, I kind of inherited the *Lighthouse* from my uncle. He started the paper in '49—*nineteen* forty-nine," added the young man.

"Oh," said Ray. *Like I thought* your *uncle started the paper in* eighteen *forty-nine*. "He still live around here?"

"Sure. He owns a bar just around the corner."

"A newspaperman and booze, what'll they think of next."

"Pardon?"

"Nothing. You think he might be there now?"

"He's always there. You know, I'll bet you're about the same age as my uncle. Maybe you two can swap old war stories."

Ray resisted the impulse to reach over and slap Sample upside the head. Instead he just smiled and got directions.

∎ ▪ ▪ ▪

"Ray-fucking-Malzone. In my fucking bar," said Bobby Sample, shaking his head in genuine awe. He shook Ray's hand as though it were a cross between the Holy Grail and an old-fashioned water pump.

Ray had heard his name hyphenated that way before, but never by someone whom he respected more—a writer who actually owned his own bar. And there were those who did not believe in some grand design. Ray shook his head, dismissing such heresy.

At this time of day—morning, actually—the place was deserted, but Ray didn't mind.

"Whatcha drinkin'? On the fuckin' house, of course."

"Wild Turkey."

"Man's drink," said Sample as he poured. "Sometimes some prissy asshole gets lost and wanders in here off Main Street and orders some fucking tits-on-a-bull's-orgasm-fucking thing. Jesus, I hate that shit," said the man as he slid Ray's drink onto the pockmarked bar in front of him.

"Thanks. To your health," said Ray, raising his drink.

"Wait a minute." Sample poured himself a healthy dose of the same elixir. "Ray-fucking-Malzone," he said again as he set his glass down.

"What's a nice bar like this doing in a place like Pacific Point?"

"Yeah, well, you're not the first to ask. You notice I'm off the main *drag*. I was here before all this fancy-schmantzy shit. Before you could shoot up a canvas with a squirt gun full of pastel oil paints and sell it for the price of a decent house. Before rosé became blush wine or white zinfandel. But hell, you know what I'm talking about. You're Ray Malzone."

That required another toast.

As Ray got a refill on his Wild Turkey at ten in the morning, without so much as a minor judgmental out-of-the-corner-of-the-eye look, he was thinking that he might never leave.

"So, Bobby, I'm trying to find out something about a guy named Stanley Craig."

"Junior or Senior?"

In an instant Ray knew that he had come to the right man. "The guy I'm talking about is, I dunno, maybe middle forties."

"That'd be Junior. Senior's dead, anyhow."

"So, what do you know about Junior?"

"What are you looking for?"

"I don't know, really. Just start talking."

"Okay. The Craig family used to own this town. Big-time players. Junior's grandfather, Oliver Craig, was in oil. Lots of offshore drilling in the old days. Anyhow, Oliver purchased the best real estate in the county for his family, and he kind of ran Pacific Point like his own little kingdom right on up through the mid-sixties.

"His son, Stanley Senior, was cut from a different bolt of cloth. You see it all the time. One generation beats the odds, makes the money. The next generation inherits the money and privilege and they don't know their ass from a fuckin' hole in the ground. Senior was that way. He married the prettiest girl in town and built a mansion on his daddy's property and then . . ."

"Then?"

"The walls came tumblin' down."

"What do you mean?"

"Let me tell you." Sample freshened both men's glasses with the nectar of the devils and resumed his tale. "These days you ask about the Craigs in this town, nobody knows from nothin', unless you wander off Main Street and ask one of the locals about ancient history. Guy built this fuckin' town and nobody knows who the fuck he is anymore. These days it's TV and radio. Real time. By the time the news is in print, the only thing the paper's good for is lining a birdcage."

The man's attention was starting to wander, Ray thought. "So what happened to the Craig family?"

"Everything happened to the Craig family. First, there was the murder."

"Murder?" said Ray incredulously.

"Oh, yeah. Senior was murdered by an itinerant farm worker. The family had lots of strawberry fields to work and they employed hundreds of workers over a period of a year. Did well by most of them, from what I heard.

"Anyhow, Senior winds up dead one night after a fight over money with one the hired hands."

"Good lord. How old was Junior when this happened?"

"Let's see, that was probably about '65, he must've been a teenager at the time. I dunno, maybe fifteen, something like that."

"That must've been tough."

"Yeah, he took it hard. But that was just the beginning. About six months later, after giving birth to Senior's only other child, Senior's wife dies in a boating accident."

"My God!"

"It gets worse. About a year later, Oliver and his wife, Clara, die in an automobile accident while vacationing in France."

"So Junior's the only one left."

"And his younger sister, Clara."

"Where is she?"

"I don't know. Far as I know, she still lives out at the family house."

"How old would she be now?"

"Let's see, she was born around '65, that'd make her about thirty. Why?"

"Just curious. You say you haven't seen her recently."

"Nah. Haven't seen her in years. Frankly, Clara isn't quite right, if you know what I mean."

"I don't know what you mean."

"She's a little . . ." Sample raised his glass toward his head.

"Crazy?"

"Not like rubber-room crazy. She's just not real social. Very intense. Kind of stares at you when you're talking to her. Know what I mean?"

"Yeah."

"Strange family. Kind of like the Kennedys, but West Coast, if you know what I mean."

"I'm not sure."

"Cursed. More money than God, but who would want to go through all that shit."

"You ever meet Stanley Junior?"

"Meet him? Are you kidding? I knew Stan from way back. He was a precocious little son of a bitch. Real smart. Not much in the way of an athlete, which bothered the shit out of Senior, but, hey, what're you gonna do, right?"

"Right."

"I'd see Stan around town at least once a week. His father'd bring him by the restaurant—I used to own the best restaurant in town, before the foreigners came. Before they made the Point something it wasn't—like putting a skirt on a dog. I grew up here and I can't stand what they've done to the place."

"About the Craigs . . ."

"Senior was okay, least he was to me. But he was a wimp. His dad, Oliver, and I used to drink all night together and wake up on the fuckin' beach. He was a real man's man—you know what I'm sayin'. But Senior," said Sample, shaking his head and puckering up his face, effectively doubling his already abundant wrinkles, "when the guy walked, there was nothing rattling down there in the old shorts, if you know what I mean.

"And Junior . . . there was a *real* lost soul. I never actually got close to the kid. And by the time he was ready to graduate from high school—top of his class, I might add—he was essentially a rich orphan. Eighteen years old, no parents, no grandparents, and his sister was about three years old.

"But he got the fuckin' money. Can't feel too sorry for him."

"You keep track of what Stan Junior did?"

"Not really. I know he moved down to LA. That's about it."

"And you say his sister . . . "

"Clara."

"She lives out at the family estate alone?"

"Last time I heard. Like I said, I haven't seen her for years. Frankly, I haven't even thought about Clara in a long time. She's away a lot. When she's gone, I guess the place sits empty."

"Is it empty now?"

"I don't know."

"Is there anyone who might be up to speed with the Craig family these days?"

"The sheriff. Nate Oldfield. He's been sheriff since the mid-sixties. Good man. You'd like him. I think his first year on the job was when Senior was murdered. You know, he'll be in here later. Maybe we can all sit down and toss a few back."

"Maybe. You think he might be in his office now?"

"Probably. Tell him I gave you my stamp of approval."

"I'll do that."

Ray took his wallet out of his jacket pocket.

"Put that away," said Sample. "You're a fuckin' celebrity. Tell you what." The man took a small knife out of his pants pocket and handed it to Ray. "Carve your name in the bar and we'll call it even."

"You sure?" said Ray.

"Yeah. Just make sure you put the date under your name. Hell, I haven't had a Pulitzer Prize winner in here for a while."

"Oh yeah? Who was the last one?" asked Ray as he set about his task.

"Me. Most newspaper people, especially California newspaper people, know that," said Sample with a wry smile.

Sheriff Nate Oldfield looked to Ray to be in his late fifties, but he was carrying some extra weight and his face looked puffy, so it was hard to pinpoint his age. He was at least a couple of inches taller than six feet and he still had the squared shoulders that were usually the result of having been an athlete in his youth. After forty, a person could lose weight, he could pump up a little more muscle tone. But squaring the shoulders was not the same as strengthening the muscles on those shoulders.

Oldfield was reading the *LA Times* sports section when Ray walked in and introduced himself. The sheriff didn't appear surprised to see him, and Ray had the distinct impression that Sample had called Oldfield and told him to expect company.

After the introductions, Oldfield said, "You like tennis?"

"To be honest, I don't follow it."

"Me neither. Till a few years ago. That's when I realized that the only sport I could still participate in, besides golf, which I love, is tennis. That Sampras, he's somethin', isn't he?"

"Yeah," said Ray. He knew that much. Just as he knew that it was his line. Oldfield wasn't Ray's genial old grandfather, although he might have been to some kid. Oldfield was a cop who knew how to retain his job in a rich man's town and still get free drinks over at Bobby Sample's bar.

"So, the Craigs . . . pretty high-profile family," said Ray, dropping the conversation in a groove and letting it roll.

"Right."

Ray went over the ground he had covered with Bobby Sample.

"Stan Senior's murder . . . that must have been tough," said Ray.

"What do you mean tough?"

"Politically."

"What do you mean?" said Oldfield defensively. Like he knew exactly what Ray was talking about.

"I mean you must have been under a lot of pressure. Guy who owns the town—"

"Stan Senior didn't run this town, least he didn't run me. Maybe he owned the mayor."

"Who was mayor when Stan Senior was murdered?"

"I don't see how that's important—"

"I'm just trying to do my job. Trust me, that job does not include putting innocent people behind bars, or even embarrassing them. I'm just asking questions, okay?"

"Terrence McBain was mayor. He was a weak little weasel. He and his wife live in Florida now. He didn't have anything to do with it anyway."

"With what?"

Oldfield toyed with a pencil on his desk. After a

while he looked up. "This is a big can of worms, and it don't lead nowhere, anyhow."

"Let me be the judge of that."

"Why?" said the cop sincerely. "'Cause you got my best interest at heart?"

Ray looked the sheriff in the eye for a moment. Oldfield would not allow himself to play the fool, and Ray knew it.

"If I had a story that would burn your ass and make me a million bucks, they couldn't put a pen in my hand fast enough," said Ray. "I'm a whore, I admit it. But we're not on opposite sides here."

"This isn't easy, you know. I mean, no matter what I tell you, you go home to your family and you still got a job."

"So what is it you can't tell me that puts your life in jeopardy?"

Oldfield gave him a relaxed smile. "Maybe I'm exaggerating a little. It's not a matter of life and death, least not to me. It's just that this is a quiet town and the people who live here don't like any bad publicity. Except for the Bouillabaisse Festival and the Strawberry Festival, we really don't much care if anybody knows we even exist. A thing like this . . ." Oldfield's voice trailed off.

"Like what?"

"You put the words *rich* and *murder* together and you've got a tabloid headline. Facts and people's feelings don't make any difference. We just don't want *Hard Copy* coming in here with their cameras, dredging up ancient history . . . history this town would just as soon forget."

"Stanley Senior's murder."

"Right."

"Bobby Sample said it happened during your first year on the job."

"Yeah, I was twenty-one. Like everyone else, I knew the Craig family. Knew them enough to recognize them on the street or nod when they nodded at you first. Junior and I went to the same high school, but I was about six years ahead of him.

"Anyhow, Charley—the sheriff at the time—and I got called out to the Craig place about ten o'clock one night. Mrs. Craig, Senior's wife, sounded frantic over the phone. When we got there, Senior was lying there in his study, strangled."

"By one of the farm workers," said Ray.

"Yeah. And it was a real weird scene. On the one hand, Mrs. Craig was kind of bouncing off the walls, while the son was down by the boathouse working on his boat."

"Even after he knew what happened?"

"He knew. That's what made it so strange. There were sirens blasting, his mother was coming apart at the seams . . . "

"What did he say to you?"

"He asked me what I wanted him to do?"

"What do you mean?"

"I mean, he said something like, 'Okay, my father's dead, I wish he wasn't, but I've got to work on my boat. Do you need my help?'"

"Didn't you think that was odd?"

"I'm sure you don't mean to be insulting," said Oldfield, looking Ray in the eye with a laser-like gaze.

"Sorry. So, how did you and the sheriff determine the identity of the murderer?"

"The sheriff did most of the work—like you said, it was my first year on the force."

The force, thought Ray. In this two-bit town, you got one or two guys wearing badges. Hardly constitutes a fucking *force*. But what he said was, "Sample said you arrested a guy who worked for Craig."

"Guy named Fernando Rodriguez. He'd worked at the farm a couple of seasons. Worked his way up to foreman, actually. Craig liked the guy, and according to the people we talked to, Rodriguez liked Craig."

"So why did he kill him?"

"Money."

"Lack of, I imagine," said Ray.

"Yeah, most people don't kill you because you give them too much."

Given certain cases tried in LA courts recently, Ray knew that was a debatable point, but one that had no relevance here. In the real world, the sheriff was right.

"So, how did you wind up arresting Rodriguez?"

"Mrs. Craig said that Rodriguez had been in the house the night of the murder. As foreman, he was the spokesman who had come to Craig to air the workers' grievances. The two men were locked in Craig's study at about eight o'clock. Mrs. Craig had heard shouting, but after a while she went to bed. Forty-five minutes later she came downstairs and discovered her husband's body."

"Sounds pretty circumstantial."

"Except for the fact that we found fifty-five hundred dollars cash in Rodriguez's quarters."

Ray shook his head. "Let me get this straight. Rodriguez is a labor leader, at least among the immediate workers. He goes to the boss's house to plead their case. Then he murders the boss and robs him of five thousand dollars. Was he in his quarters when he was arrested?"

"He was on the grounds."

"So, if he did this, why didn't he run away?"

"I don't know."

"What did Rodriguez say about the fifty-five hundred dollars?"

"He said that he had had about five hundred under his bed. He said he had no idea about the other five thousand."

"What else did you have to tie him to the crime?"

"Fingerprints."

"In the study?"

"Yes."

"He didn't deny being in the study, did he?"

"No."

"What was his side of the story?"

"He said he had a screaming match with Senior, left about eight thirty, then went for a long walk, alone, on the property."

"Could've happened that way."

"Maybe. The theory that made much more sense was that Mrs. Craig was telling the truth when she heard Rodriguez and her husband arguing—"

"How did Rodriguez characterize his meeting with Senior?"

"He said they'd argued and wound up yelling at each other."

Ray nodded, and made a mental note.

"Continuing with the theory," said Oldfield, "the two men have a fight, Rodriguez strangles Craig in a fit of rage, grabs whatever cash is in the room, and runs away."

"And goes back to his quarters, stashes the money, then goes for a moonlight stroll?"

"The amount of missing cash matched the difference between what Rodriguez said he had and the total found in his room."

"Someone could have put it there."

"Who? I mean, what are the odds of someone killing Stanley Craig Senior, when he had never taken the opportunity to do so before, and this plan just happening at the exact moment that Craig was having a knock-down-drag-out fight with Rodriguez?"

"They were yelling. Lots of people could have heard the fight. Besides, no one said they were physically fighting."

"Still, the odds are against that kind of coincidence."

"They were against Rodriguez, because Craig was rich and Rodriguez was Mexican and poor?"

Oldfield did not answer immediately. The overhead fan in his office showered some of the cool sea breeze coming in off the Pacific over him like holy water. "That was part of it."

"Shouldn't have been."

"Nobody should be unhappy or homeless, but it happens."

"So, you arrested a patsy."

"We arrested a man a jury of his peers found guilty in a fair trial."

"Let me picture this. By a jury of his peers, you mean a jury of twelve itinerant workers."

"Get the fuck down off your high horse. You don't look that fuckin' naive. If you gave every defendant a jury of his peers, most of the time you'd have to go to the penitentiary and let out twelve criminals every time a case came to trial. The man got a fair trial, I was there."

"So, you believe he killed Craig?"

· "I believe it's the most logical explanation."

"That's not the same thing."

"Justice is not an exact science."

"Maybe it doesn't work."

"It works better in Pacific Point than it does in LA," said Oldfield with a confident smile.

Ray had no good answer to that. "Again, do you believe the man in prison for Craig's murder is the guy who did it? Your own gut feeling?"

"Rodriguez isn't in prison anymore."

"He got out?"

"He was murdered in prison."

"You're kidding," said Ray incredulously.

"I'm not a comic, I'm a sheriff."

After a moment, Ray collected himself. "That still doesn't answer my question. Do you think Rodriguez did it?"

"I honestly believe that it's the best explanation for what happened. I have my doubts, but then I have a certain amount of doubt about every case where the suspect denies the allegations. I wasn't there to know one way or the other. Let me put it to you this way— you ever interview a guy in prison who said he was innocent?"

"Yes."

"How many times?"

"Over the years, maybe six times."

"They made a good case the first time you talked to them, got their side of it, right?"

"Yes."

"Now, with some real time, and some real facts in between, how many of those people do you think were innocent?"

Ray knew that at least three of the people he interviewed under those circumstances were guilty—they later admitted their guilt. After getting the prosecution's side of things in two other cases, he was pretty sure those two prisoners were guilty. He remained convinced that the sixth man was innocent. Still, he took the point.

"Who was Rodriguez's lawyer?"

"Guy named Jacob Starn."

"Is he available?"

"Should be. He's the judge here."

■   ■   ■

"People generally see what they want to see," said Jacob Starn. "We're creatures blind to anything but self-interest. And that self-interest can be sexual, familial, financial, whatever."

"That must have been quite a trial," said Ray Malzone.

"Biggest trial Pacific Point ever saw. It was certainly my biggest up to that time. If the truth be known, I relished it. I was fresh from USC law school, second in my class, and here I was representing some itinerant farm worker against the charge of murdering the town's richest citizen—the victim's daddy excluded, of course. It was the trial of the century, least around here," said Starn. The lawyer, now a judge, looked to be in his mid-to-late fifties. He was slim, bordering on skinny. His face was dark and leathery from living most of his life in the beach community. Starn wore an Armani shirt, rolled up a couple of times above his Rolex. He wasn't wearing a tie, but, to Ray, he didn't look like a man who would be uncomfortable wearing one.

"Open-and-shut case?"

"Not really. Why would you say that?"

"The sheriff made it seem like all the evidence was stacked against Rodriguez."

"Oh, it was. But it was all circumstantial. Rodriguez denied having killed Stanley Senior. In fact, denied is a rather weak term to describe his innocent plea. Cold-blooded murderers deny charges against them. This guy got down on his knees, pleaded with me to believe him. Swore on his wife's Bible in front of me. Offered to do it in court."

"You believed him?"

"I was his lawyer."

"That's not an answer."

"In some circles it passes for one."

"In the circles I run in, it's the same as saying you don't believe him."

"Then you must get out more, Mr. Malzone. I believed Mr. Rodriguez was innocent, even though I knew he was going to be convicted here in Pacific Point. I was counting on the case being overturned on appeal."

"Why wasn't it?"

"Because Rodriguez died in prison. He was killed in his cell by another inmate."

"Strange."

"Strange, yes. Something I can use to convict the real murderer, no."

"The real murderer?"

"I have no proof."

"But you have a theory."

"I also have two legs, doesn't mean they'll carry me to victory in the Boston Marathon. And that's what it would have been—a marathon. Nobody cared about Rodriguez. And the witnesses against him were high-profile rich people with money, power and influence."

"Which means?"

"Doesn't take a calculator to figure it out. Rodriguez was going down."

"If you believe Rodriguez was innocent, then someone must have been lying."

"Or maybe skewing the facts in their favor."

"The rich witnesses?"

"Malzone, you ever hear the phrase 'let sleeping dogs lie'?"

"Yes, but in the newspaper business we don't take it too seriously."

"Maybe you should."

"An innocent man's reputation will be restored."

"Give me a fucking break, Malzone. You're not here to restore the reputation of a migrant farm worker who died thirty years ago. You're here for yourself."

After a moment, Ray said, "So, let's say I am."

"You are."

"Okay, now we've established I'm a son of a bitch. That still leaves us with the fact that you don't think your client murdered Stanley Craig Senior. And more than most people, you're in a position to know who did."

"I don't know, otherwise I would have gone back to court."

"Would you?"

"Maybe."

"Who do you think did it?"

"I really don't know. But I'll tell you something you don't know. A year later Oliver and Esther Craig, Senior's parents, died in an automobile accident in Europe."

"I heard that."

"Did you also hear that it probably wasn't an accident?"

"You mean they were murdered, too?"

"Not so you could prove it."

"So no one tried."

Suddenly the social veneer was gone. Starn leaned forward and looked Malzone in the eye. "You're getting in deep, Malzone. Too deep for your own good."

"Does that mean you think the murderer is still alive?"

"All I'm saying is that my advice to you is to back off."

"Then you know who this person is?"

"Why are you here, Malzone?"

"I wanted to talk to you about Rodriguez."

"I mean, why are you here in Pacific Point?"

"I don't have to tell you that," said Ray.

Starn looked at Ray with a knowing smile and leaned back in his chair. "That's true. That's very true."

Aubrey Mitchell tossed down the last of his cappuccino at the Rainbow Club on Brand in Glendale. He used to be able to pick up the tab for dinner and drinks at places much more expensive than this, but tonight he had eaten before he came. He was careful to apportion out his finite bank account in amounts that would stretch it out for as long as possible. Eat at home, have an after-dinner coffee, maybe a beer at the bar. This way, without spending more than ten dollars, he could sit for a couple of hours nursing a cheap drink in the company of strangers. People who did not know him. Did not know his daughter, or his troubles. Just other travelers who would be happy to exchange comments on how the world would end, and which bar had the best big-screen TV to watch it on.

After a few minutes a man sat down next to Aubrey as the Stones' "Midnight Rambler" came on the jukebox. Aubrey and the man talked amicably for nearly two hours.

Midnight came quickly and Aubrey felt good for the first time in a long time. He knew it had something to do with the drinks he'd had, but it also had something to do with talking to someone about nothing—sports, the commercialization of Christmas.

When there was no one else at the bar and the bartender started closing out the register, Aubrey didn't feel like calling it a night. Neither did the other man.

"Want me to show you something special?"

"Sure," said the man.

"It's about fifteen minutes from here, but it's really impressive."

"Okay, let's take my car," said the man.

About twenty minutes later, the two of them stood in front of Christ-on-the-cross spotlighted by twenty flood-lights. "Isn't this incredible?" said Aubrey. It was a religious display in the foothills above Pasadena, sponsored by a local church. At this time of night the place was deserted. The display was on a timer system that turned on about six o'clock and went off about three in the morning.

Aubrey knew this because he had been responsible for the display for six years, before he had been "politely excused" from his duties.

"You don't seem impressed," said Aubrey, noting his companion's lack of enthusiasm.

"It's okay, I guess."

"You don't believe?"

"In what?"

"Life everlasting, the resurrection."

"Maybe one life is enough," said the man.

"So, you believe that this is all there is."

"I hope so."

"But if this is all there is, then there's no ultimate justice, no redemption."

"So, you a sinner?"

"We're all sinners."

"Yeah, well, you some kind of big-time sinner?"

Aubrey looked at the man for a moment before he spoke. "That's an odd thing to say."

"Well, are you?"

"No, of course not."

"You know, lying's a sin, too. C'mon, Aubrey, tell me what you did."

"Nothing," said Aubrey. He walked onto the hill and sat down next to the electro-haloed Jesus

"Nothing?"

"Nothing."

The man walked over and sat down next to Aubrey. "The Bible says God is the father . . . "

Aubrey looked at the man strangely. "Yes."

"A father is important, don't you think?"

"Of course."

"A father sets the standards for his children. Shows them what's right and what's wrong."

"Yes."

"So, what's the problem?"

"Problem?" asked Aubrey, not knowing where the man was going with this.

"If you're the father, and you're the one who says what's right and wrong, then why are you such a fucking asshole." It was not a question.

"What?" said Aubrey, taken aback.

"You heard me."

"I heard the words—"

"You're a monster, Aubrey," said the man.

"What in the hell are you talking about?" Aubrey was beginning to get scared.

"You abused your daughter, didn't you?"

"Who are you?"

"Cathy. You destroyed her."

"How do you know my daughter's name?"

"Is that important?"

"Yes," said Aubrey firmly. He stood, his heart beating fast. Who was this man?

"Is it as important as you putting your penis into your little girl's mouth?"

"I never—I *never*—did such a thing." Aubrey turned like a mad dog on the man. Suddenly, he was more angry than frightened. "Who told you this garbage?"

The man just glared back.

"It's all lies!"

"I think you're lying now," said the man.

Aubrey lost track of time, of himself, and of all the rules he had lived by his whole life. He lunged at the younger man and grabbed him by the throat.

The man sensed what was coming, and used Aubrey's weight and movement to his own advantage. The two wrestled for a moment, only a moment, and suddenly Malcolm was straddling Aubrey's chest.

"All right, all right!" said Aubrey. "Get off me!"

"Fuck you!" said Malcolm with a rage in his eyes that sent a chill through Aubrey.

To the right of Malcolm's shoulder Aubrey could see the comforting face of the Electric Jesus.

And in that instant he knew he was going to die.

Cheney looked at the body as it lay sprawled lifelessly over the cross, prominently displayed by the spotlights shining on it. A wooden figure of Jesus lay on the ground nearby. Even though it was nearly three in the morning, a crowd of about twenty people stood staring at the bizarre tableau. Their attention was focused on Aubrey Mitchell, who gazed with dead eyes into the starless sky.

Cheney and Tony Boston were looking up at the blue ribbon pinned to the dead man's shirt.

"I called 911 about one o'clock," Charles Waits told the detectives a few minutes later. "I was out walking my dog, Bear, when I saw . . ." he said, pointing to the corpse on the cross.

"You usually walk your dog at one o'clock in the morning?" asked Cheney.

"My wife and I'd just gotten back from a party down

in Long Beach. I always take Bear for a walk before we turn in."

"Did you see anyone else?"

"Like I told the other officer, I saw a man kind of jogging down the road."

"Jogging?"

"Well, I mean he wasn't running full-out, or anything like that. But I did notice that, just before he saw me, he was walking."

"You say he was jogging. How was he dressed?"

"Street clothes. That's what made it seem odd, you know. I mean, jogging at one in the morning is strange enough. Though I know a guy who runs in the middle of the night. He used to be a drinker, so when he gets the urge to drink, he runs."

"But this man you saw tonight, he wasn't your friend."

"No."

"Is there anything else you noticed about him? Was he white, black, Hispanic?"

"I think he was a white guy. He was about fifty yards from me when I turned the corner, but I'm pretty sure he was a white guy."

"Any other features you can remember? Like, was he bald? Did he have any facial hair? Did he run with a limp?"

"He had hair. Not real long, but moderately long."

"Average length hair," said Cheney sarcastically. The remark went over Waits's head. The cop knew that this was yet another crime committed by a man of average height, weight, facial structure, hair length. The average man.

"He didn't seem to run with a limp, but then, I didn't really look for it. I don't think he had a beard, but I really wasn't close enough to tell if he had a mustache."

"Did he just disappear into the night, or did he get into a car?"

"He got into a car about a block on, up around Cedar Street," said Waits.

"Passenger side or driver's side?" Cheney wanted to know if there might have been someone else in the car who was driving.

Waits thought about that for a second. "Driver's side."

"Okay. You gave your number to the officer you spoke with first?"

"Yes."

"Thanks for your help." The two detectives turned and walked away. "Any other cars parked up here within a block or two?" Cheney asked Tony.

"I've already checked. Three cars were parked on the street within two blocks of here. As you can see, most of the people who live up here have driveways and garages. Two of the cars are registered to people who live at the addresses where the cars are parked. The third car is registered to a woman who lives in San Francisco, but has the same last name as the name on the mailbox. I figure she's down here visiting relatives."

"So, probably the victim came up here in the other guy's car."

"Or maybe his own and the killer drove it away. The victim still had his wallet, with twenty bucks and all his credit cards in it. Address on the driver's license says he lives at 117 N. Vista Lane, Encino."

"You dust the wallet yet?"

"Yeah, let me get it."

Tony returned with the wallet and handed it to Cheney, who snapped open the photo section of the billfold. There were seven plastic sheaths for photographs. Six were filled, one was empty. Cheney thought that was odd, but he knew there could be a lot of reasons for that. Apparently Aubrey Mitchell had three children, two girls and a boy, and a wife. They were pretty photographs, perfect. The kind that came with wallets. Cheney knew a man who kept the photos that came with his wallet and showed them to people as though the people in the pictures were members of his own family. The guy wasn't happy. He was a cop. Used to be, anyhow. He ate his gun a few years ago. For an instant, a vision of his father flashed in Cheney's mind. Then it was gone.

Cheney shook his head, snapped the wallet closed and handed it back to Tony. "Has the wife been told?"

"No. I figured you might want to go with me."

Cheney didn't *want* to go, but he knew that he should.

Malcolm rowed out into the middle of Black Water. The water licked the boat like a giant and friendly dog. The darkness enveloped him in its warm embrace even though the moon and stars were obscured.

Malcolm smiled as he recalled the image of Aubrey Mitchell on the cross. He sat back in the boat, let it drift, and breathed deeply the cool night air. In this darkness, he felt light. In this lake, as he drifted about tossed by tiny waves, he felt oriented and filled with purpose and direction.

After a few moments, he reached over the side of the small boat and pulled up a line attached to a white buoy. At the end of it was a small plastic bag. He brought it on board, untied the wire that clamped it shut and made it watertight. He removed the photograph from his pocket, put it in the bag, sealed the bag, and dropped it back into the lake.

Then he hoisted the stone he used as the boat's anchor back into the boat and began rowing toward the shore. Even in the darkness he could feel the eyes of the others upon him. He had done well. He was proud of himself.

He knew the Round Table was proud of him, too.

Thirteen

The porch light came on. "Yes?" The voice came from behind a closed door.

"Police," said Tony, holding his badge up to the peephole in the door.

"Just a minute."

Two minutes later a woman wearing slippers and a pink robe over a long flannel gown opened the door slightly, keeping it chained. "Could I see your identification again?"

Tony flashed his badge again. The woman took it. "I'm going to call to make sure," she said, not waiting for Tony's permission. She shut and relocked the door.

Cheney recognized her from a photograph in Mitchell's wallet.

A few minutes later the woman opened the door, handed Tony his ID, and showed Cheney and Tony into her living room. "You can't be too careful these days," she said.

"Of course," said Tony.

Karen Mitchell sat on a white corduroy love seat while Cheney and Tony sat on a matching couch. Her caution was now replaced by fear. Something had happened. Police didn't knock on your door at five A.M. unless something couldn't wait.

"Is your husband's name Aubrey Mitchell?" asked Tony.

"Yes."

"He's been murdered."

Karen sat there, looking at the two officers as though they had just said that the sun would come up in the morning. Tony's words had not registered. Neither cop was surprised. Shock played itself out in lots of ways, depending on the special way it ripped your heart out.

"How, uh . . . "

"He was strangled. In the foothills above Pasadena."

The woman nodded and her eyes glazed over. She bit her lower lip.

"Mrs. Mitchell," said Tony.

"Yes?" said the woman, coughing, inhaling deeply.

"Do you know where your husband went this evening?"

"Of course not."

"Pardon, ma'am?"

"Aubrey doesn't live here . . . oh, did you think he still lived here?"

"This was the address on his driver's license."

"He should have changed that," she said, as though admonishing a child.

"Where did he live?"

"I believe he had an apartment in Glendale."

"You never went there?"

"Why would I? I mean, why would I?" she said, her voice trailing off as if words and their meaning had become something unfamiliar to her.

"So, you were divorced?"

"Yes. No, that is, not yet. But it was just a formality."

"I see. You and your husband were getting divorced."

"That's correct."

"I wonder if I might ask why?"

"I don't think that's any of your business."

"Who initiated the divorce?" asked Cheney, pressing on.

"I did, but—"

"And the grounds for that divorce?"

"Irreconcilable differences."

"What differences?"

"Like I said, it's personal."

"Tell them, mother," said another voice.

Cheney, Tony, and Mrs. Mitchell turned their heads at the sound. Cathy Mitchell, also dressed in a robe and a flannel nightgown, walked into the living room.

Cheney and Tony stood. Tony said, "I'm Detective—"

"I know who you are. I've been listening to the entire conversation."

Cheney recognized the young woman from the photographs in the dead man's wallet.

"Then you know about—"

"My father? Yes."

There was no shock present in Cathy's eyes, only contempt. The kind of chronic, aching contempt that eventually made the person look bitter and ugly.

"Maybe you should go back to sleep, Cathy," said Karen.

"I don't think so," she said, and sat down next to her mother on the love seat. The two men resumed their seats.

"I'm sorry about your father," said Cheney.

"You may be the only one," said Cathy, looking Cheney hard in the eye.

"Are you all right?" asked Tony.

"You mean am I okay because I'm not bawling my eyes out? Yeah, I'm fine."

"I take it you and your father were estranged," said Tony. It was not a huge leap in logic.

"My father ruined my life, okay?" said Cathy.

"It's not right to speak that way about your father. He's dead," said Karen.

"Why not? He destroyed our family."

"You had a problem with your father," said Cheney, priming the pump. In fact, it was more like pouring gasoline on a fire.

"Problem?" said the young woman incredulously. "The only person with a problem was my father."

Cheney took a chance. "Did he molest you?"

The question hung in the air like a grenade with its pin pulled. Cathy and her mother exchanged looks. It was hard to tell what was passing between them. Whatever it was, it was evil and malignant.

"You bet your fucking ass, he did," said Cathy with an expression that dripped with a kind of venom Cheney, in thirty years of police work, had rarely seen.

Cheney nodded. "And the divorce was about this," he said to the mother. It was not a question.

Karen nodded, tears starting to fill her eyes. The anger that had sustained her all these months was beginning to give way to the reality that the man she had spent most of her life with was gone, the victim of a vicious assault. There was no taking anything back. Not anymore. Some questions would forever go unanswered. Important questions. Questions that poisoned the waters that had nurtured her most of her life. It was over. The finality of it was startling and just now beginning to set in. The lonely world she had inherited in the past few months was now, suddenly, even more lonely. The object of her anger was gone. It was as though a sun had burned out prematurely and she, as a planet around that sun, was now cold and dark, utterly without direction.

And, somewhere in all the insanity, that object of her hate was also the object of her love. The paradox left her reeling, as genuine shock began to take a stranglehold on her. The only thing that kept her from losing it was her duty to be there for Cathy. And that was as much from guilt as from obligation.

"What did your husband say about the charges?"

"Pardon?" said Karen Mitchell. It was as though she either had not heard the question or considered it so ludicrous that she wasn't sure she'd heard it correctly.

"Did your husband admit that he molested your daughter?"

"What in the hell did you expect him to say?" said Cathy. "You're a cop. The scum of the earth you bring in every night, I'll bet none of them ever say they're innocent."

"So he denied the charges," said Cheney, calmly.

"Of course," spat Cathy.

"Actually, he filed a lawsuit of his own," said Karen, softly, almost apologetically.

"Mother!" said Cathy.

"It's true," said the woman. Cheney was not sure what she was referring to, but it sounded as much like a tiny prayer as it did a statement.

"What's true is that he just wanted to molest me all over again, but this time in a courtroom. He was an *animal*!"

"You have other children?" asked Cheney.

"A son, Ralph, and a daughter, Melissa."

"And they back the molestation allegations?"

"To the letter," said Cathy, with fire in her eyes.

"Actually, Ralph—"

"Mother, please! You know that Ralph's in denial about all this. What more proof do you need?"

"What proof do you have?" asked Cheney in the calmest voice he could muster.

"What?" said Cathy, as though he had just slapped her in the face. "Men don't want to believe these things happen. And you know why?"

"Why?"

"You know why," said Cathy with a sneer. "Because men do these things. They've been getting away with molesting their babies forever. It's just in the past few years that we've blown the whistle on your depravity."

"I did not molest my child," said Cheney.

"Oh yeah?" she said accusingly.

"I did not," said Cheney firmly, feeling his face flush.

"You seem very defensive. I believe thou doth protest too much," said Cathy with a smug smile.

"Cathy, please," said her mother.

While Cheney tried to focus himself, Tony took over. "You mentioned your son, Ralph—is that his name?"

"Yes."

"How does he feel about all this?"

"He stands by his father."

"What do you expect?" said Cathy, shaking her head. "I'll tell you the truth, I'm very concerned about Sandra."

"Sandra?" asked Tony.

"Sandra is Ralph's six-year-old daughter." Karen turned to her daughter. "Maybe you should just go in and get some sleep. I'll be in shortly."

"When did you discover that your father molested you?" asked Cheney. He didn't want Cathy getting away without at least answering a couple more questions.

"When?"

"The address on your father's driver's license, which was issued two years ago, is this address. How long ago did your father molest you?"

"I'm not sure that's any of your business."

"Not in the last two years?" Cheney asked.

"No."

"Your mother said that the divorce had to do with the molestation. Either you knew about the molestation and never told your mother until lately, or you just found out recently that you were molested."

The two women exchanged looks again. "I found out recently," said Cathy finally.

"So, you're in therapy."

"That's correct."

"And the name of your therapist?" asked Cheney.

"That's confidential."

"Are you seeing Dr. Stanley Craig?"

The look in both women's eyes was all Cheney needed to see.

It was about six thirty when Cheney and Tony drove down out of the hills. The sun was up, dew glistened like zircons on the *Home Shopping Club*, and another day in Encino Hills was about to unfold like a crisp hundred-dollar bill.

They had managed to pry some basic information from Aubrey Mitchell's widow: his current address, the fact that he had been fired from a very good job when his "crime" was "revealed," that he had no current job. He had no friends. It had been difficult, but Tony and Cheney managed to get Ralph Mitchell's address; and after Cathy had gone back to bed, they had convinced Karen to give them the address of the lawyer who had filed her husband's suit.

"How do you feel about stopping by Craig's place to talk with his girlfriend?"

"It's six thirty in the fucking morning," said Tony.

"That's the point. I have a feeling that Dr. Craig is going to tell Bridget to make herself scarce for a while."

"So maybe he's already sent her out of town."

"If he did, we'll find out in twenty minutes."

"You da boss," said Tony, pointing the car toward the Marina Freeway.

The doorman at the Marina Blue Towers didn't argue much after Tony stuck a badge in his face. He called upstairs, and after several rings, told whoever answered that the police would be right up.

A woman opened the door. She wore a kimono, much shorter and thinner than the robes worn by Cathy and Karen Mitchell. She told the detectives that her full name was Bridget Colfax, and that she had met Stanley Craig a couple of months ago at a night-club. She had dark hair, a plain face, stood about five-feet-ten, and looked to be maybe ten pounds overweight.

Cheney wondered where Craig was. The police show up at your door, especially this early in the morning, most people are curious enough to put on a robe and join in.

"Where is Dr. Craig?"

"He's asleep. Do you want me to wake him?"

"No," said Cheney.

"So, you and Dr. Craig are . . . together," said Tony.

"You mean is he my boyfriend? Yes, I guess you could say that. Is there anything in particular I can help you with?" said Bridget sleepily.

"Last Friday . . . "

"Yes?"

"Where were you between the hours of nine and

eleven?" asked Cheney. Calypso McGuire had been killed last Friday around ten o'clock.

"Am I a suspect in some crime?"

"Just answer the question, please."

"What time again?"

"Nine till eleven."

"I was here. With Stan."

"What were you doing?"

"We watched some TV, fucked, and went to sleep."

"I see," said Cheney, doing his best to conceal a smile.

"What about last night?" asked Tony.

"Same thing, except we didn't watch TV."

"So, if Dr. Craig was here all night, and if you . . . well, then he's probably still here."

"He told me he doesn't want to talk to you."

"Why?"

"He said you've been giving him a hard time. And quite frankly, if what he's been telling me is true, I think he's got a case."

"A case?"

"Harassment."

"I doubt it."

"Yeah, well, I know a lawyer . . . "

"Don't we all," said Cheney. "But the bottom line is, Dr. Craig is not here."

"I'm here," said Craig, walking out of the bedroom and into the living room. His robe was YSL, dark blue. He also had on a pair of black Pierre Cardin slippers. He poured himself into an oversized black leather chair next to Bridget.

"Good morning," said Cheney.

"Is this really necessary?" said Craig. He looked very tired.

"It's routine."

"Getting law-abiding citizens out of bed at this hour is routine?"

"I hate to be the one to break the news, but another one of your patients' 'perpetrators' has been murdered."

Craig and Bridget looked blankly at Cheney.

"Guy named Aubrey Mitchell."

"Cathy Mitchell's father?" said Craig. "Good lord."

No one said anything for a moment.

"I'm sorry to hear it," said Craig, exhaling deeply. "I'll have to call Cathy later this morning."

"You don't look too shook up."

"Should I be?"

"You mean you believe that Aubrey Mitchell deserved to die?"

"No. First, I've never met Aubrey Mitchell, therefore I cannot pretend to be 'shook up' by news of his death. Second, my loyalty lies with my patient."

"Cathy seems to have hated her father," said Cheney.

"I imagine you might have hated your father if he did unspeakable things to you, or your sister."

"According to his wife, Aubrey Mitchell never acknowledged molesting Cathy."

"Denial is part of the perpetrator's pathology. Besides, in the litigious society in which we live, there are many very practical reasons people don't acknowledge even obvious culpability."

"You mention a litigious society. I understand that Aubrey Mitchell had filed a lawsuit. Were you one of the defendants named?"

After a moment, Craig said, "You ever been sued?"

Cheney nodded.

"Even the good guys get sued from time to time. People who've got the balls to put themselves on the line inevitably wind up being targets. Yes, that slimeball was suing me. So what?"

"What were you doing last night between the hours of ten and two?" asked Cheney, changing the subject.

"Whatever she says," said Craig, tilting his head toward Bridget.

"In your own words."

"We watched a little TV, then we went to bed."

"What time did you go to sleep?"

"After Letterman's monologue."

"Tell me one joke from the monologue."

"I don't know, I don't remember jokes."

"Think about it."

After a moment, Craig said, "Something about 'Gentlemen, start your injuns.' It had something to do with Indians. Not particularly politically correct." Craig looked at his watch. "Look, I have a patient at ten, and I'd like to get another hour's sleep. Unless, of course, you think I'm some kind of crazed killer and you want to arrest me."

Cheney bit his tongue. He stood, and Tony followed suit. "Thanks for your time." No one shook hands.

As they rode down in the elevator, Tony said, "What do you think?"

"I think I need some sleep."

"Yeah, me too. But what do you think about Craig and his girlfriend?"

"I remember the joke."

"The joke?"

"On *Letterman*. The joke about 'Gentlemen, start your injuns.' Elizabeth and I watched Letterman till about twelve-fifteen. I remember the joke."

"So, you believe him."

"I don't know what to believe right now. I'm out

seven hours of sleep. I know he's got the right answers. And as much as I think the guy's bent, I'm not sure he's a murderer. I mean, we camp around this guy's tent long enough, we could probably find out all kinds of things about Craig. But I don't know if he killed Frank."

"Yeah, I know what you mean. Why don't you get some sleep and call me about one. I'll get the address of Aubrey Mitchell's lawyer, then I'll see if we can set up a meeting with his son—apparently the last person on earth who believes Mitchell might not have molested his daughter."

"What about the lawyer?"

"The guy represents him. Doesn't mean he believes him."

Ralph Mitchell was an unassuming man, living in a modest two-bedroom house in Glendale. His wife and daughter were not home when Cheney and Tony stopped by. Because the detectives had called ahead to set up an appointment, they figured the absence of the wife and daughter was probably intentional.

"I'm sorry about your father," said Cheney.

Mitchell nodded. Over the course of the next ten minutes, the detectives covered with Ralph, gingerly, the same emotional killing ground they had gone over with Karen and Cathy Mitchell.

"My father did not molest my sister," Ralph insisted.

"How do you know?"

"Because I was there." Ralph Mitchell drank coffee from a cup that had a red heart on the side, just below the word *I* and above the words *San Francisco*.

"Sometimes we see what we want to see, or remember what we want to remember."

"My memory is clear."

"Maybe he did it when you weren't around."

"Why are you doing this?" said Mitchell, his face a punched-in mix of grief, anger, and confusion.

"I'm sorry."

"You're not sorry."

"We're trying to find out who killed your father."

"Really?"

"Really."

"My sister killed my father."

"Come again?"

"My father died of a broken heart."

That would make murderers of us all at one time or another, thought Cheney, but he kept it to himself.

"This whole thing with my sister has been a nightmare. You can't imagine what it's like unless you've been through it. I loved my father and I always will. My God." The man seemed overwhelmed. After a moment, he looked up at Cheney. "How do you explain to your six-year-old daughter why Grandma made Grandpa move out of their house, and why Aunt Cathy is saying all those awful things about Grandpa? I mean, this kind of thing wasn't covered in the basic parenting course."

"That's tough," said Tony.

"It's a helluva lot more than that. See the thing is, I love my sister, I love my mother, and I love my father. A thing like this doesn't allow you to be neutral. People and circumstances demand that you come down on one side or the other. And when you do, the other person, who you love with all your heart, attacks you. *Attacks you!*" he repeated, his eyes betraying the hard fact that he still did not fully understand the politics of the war he was living through. "Cathy as much as said that the only reason I didn't publicly denounce my father was because I was molesting my own daughter. 'Like father, like son,' she said. I can't begin to tell you how that made me feel."

"So, you blame your sister."

Ralph Mitchell looked up at Cheney, recognizing that the cop was trying to evoke a visceral response. "Blame? Yes, I blame my sister. Cathy is a troubled person. She's been through two marriages, failed stints as a songwriter, a poet, a children's book editor, and—using the last few dollars from her last divorce settlement—editor and publisher of a 'new woman's' publishing company. She managed to publish one book, *The Successful '90s Woman.*

"Her entire life, whenever things get uncomfortable either she leaves or joins some group intent upon legislating against that particular discomfort. Real life isn't always comfortable," said Mitchell passionately. "Sometimes it actually hurts, sometimes you don't get everything you want when you want it, sometimes it's just downright unfair. But that's the way life is. But guys like Craig—"

"Stanley Craig?" said Tony.

"Yeah, Cathy's therapist. Guys like Craig, they live off people like my sister. First he convinces them that they're victims. Then he tells them that somebody ought to pay for that victimization."

"He thought your father should pay for victimizing your sister," said Cheney.

"My sister was a victim of herself and her own soft-headed belief that she was *entitled* to go through life without experiencing discomfort. And when she felt uncomfortable, when things didn't work out the way she planned, then someone else always got the blame. My sister failed at everything she ever tried in her life. Some people are like that—if their short-attention-span ambition doesn't get results in ten minutes, they're off to the next thing. Success is not hopes and dreams. It's that plus a helluva lot of hard work. You don't *wish* your dreams into reality. Cathy thought she could. And when true love and personal achievement eluded her, and she hit the big three-O, something had to give. Either she had to grow up and take responsibility for not following through with her ideas or her marriages, or she had to blame someone."

"And she blamed your father."

"Perfect target, if you think about it. He was destroyed, and my sister was provided with excuses for the rest of her life."

"Had your sister seen any therapists before Craig?"

"Hell, yes. Both of her divorce settlements came with special open-ended 'therapy expenses'—for the 'hell' she'd been put through. My sister never wanted to grow up, simple as that. And this latest episode with my father accomplished two things. First, it guaranteed that she never has to grow up."

After a moment, Cheney said. "And?"

"And it killed my father."

"We were gonna nail that bastard but good," said Danny Clay, Aubrey Mitchell's attorney. He looked to Cheney to be in his late forties, early fifties. Clay was what Cheney called "hapless"—the lawyer was losing his gray hair, and the plugs in his scalp were arranged so randomly that they looked like a dozen dust bunnies that had blown onto his head and become stuck there.

Danny Clay's law practice was located in an old four-story office building in Santa Monica. On the West Coast, "old" could apply to anything that happened since a *Headline News* update. But this building could pass for old in most towns. Built in 1925, it had no central air conditioning, no valet parking, no floor-to-ceiling glass. This could have been a building straight out of a Raymond Chandler novel.

"Which bastard is that?" asked Tony.

"Stanley Craig, that son of a bitch."

Aubrey Mitchell had been cleaned out financially. Whether it was a result of his own sense of guilt or his wife's lawyer's keen grasp of the law and how it could be used to rob and steal, really didn't matter. What did matter was that poverty had led Aubrey to Clay. Clay saw the potential. If he could fend off the "ludicrous assault on this good man's character," the settlement with Craig's insurance company, plus the possible ancillary rights arising from a successful verdict more than made up for the risk. In fact, the only thing he could lose was his time. Nothing out-of-pocket. And for an attorney who wasn't working in one of the Century City towers, wasn't on retainer with a major corporation, such risks were worth taking.

"So, what happens now?"

"What do you mean?" said Clay. He swiveled his chair around toward the window and turned on the window air conditioner. Red-and-blue plastic streamers started waving in the fan's breeze.

"I mean, now that your client's dead, what happens to the lawsuit against Craig?"

"Let me put it this way—my client was my main witness. Now he's dead. It's not like I'm going down to my local Benz dealer to place an order for the new SL, if you get my drift."

"So this is a serious setback."

"You might say that."

"What kind of a case did you have before your client was murdered?"

"Fantastic."

"Look, Clay, we're not reporters," said Cheney. "Don't put a spin on it. Just tell it like it is."

Clay coughed a little, then righted himself. "It wasn't a slam dunk, okay?"

"Why? If your client's innocent . . . "

It was Clay's turn to get hard-nosed. "You're cops, you know the way the game's played. These days, the victim is king, an allegation's almost the same thing as a conviction. Even if you win, the client's still perceived merely as someone who beat the system. If you make a charge of child molestation against anyone, and I really mean anyone, no matter what happens in the courtroom, a certain percentage of your family and friends, and society in general, will always believe that you're guilty. That's the way it works, and that's the weapon attorneys hold over people's heads. With guys like Mitchell, it's not so much what people think, it's about principle, it's about truth. I felt sorry for the guy. He just didn't know how dirty it was going to get."

Cheney nodded. Tony just stared back.

"Aubrey Mitchell was a decent man. For the record, I believed the guy. But he just never got it."

"Got what?" asked Cheney.

"He wanted vindication. He wanted to prove his innocence."

"What's wrong with that?"

"I tried to tell him. I might have been able to get him off, but I could never prove he was innocent."

"What do you know about Craig? You must have researched the guy," said Tony.

"He's a minor guru to the repressed-memory crowd. Every loser in the world comes to him eventually, and *voilà!* they have not only a solution to their problems, but a villain who is responsible for every failure they'd ever experienced."

"Dear old dad."

"Sometimes dear old mom. Craig's an equal-opportunity assassin."

"So you think every parent that Craig's patients have accused is innocent?"

"Absolutely."

"I see." Cheney didn't see. Not really. Because he knew that in at least two instances—Andrew Mason and Calypso McGuire—there was a very good chance that the accused parents had, in fact, molested their children. "So, what if I told you that I could prove beyond a shadow of a doubt that some of Craig's patients' accusations were correct?"

"Then I'd say you're lying."

Cheney nodded. It was interesting to him that both sides in the child molestation question were equally inflexible. Aubrey Mitchell's daughter would settle for nothing less than her father's complete destruction, despite no physical proof, no corroborating evidence, and his tearful and poignant denials. And Mitchell's lawyer was unwilling to believe that *any* of Craig's patients were molested by their parents.

"What are you going to do now?" asked Cheney.

"About the case? I'm not sure. I have to be realistic."

"Of course."

Cheney and Tony stood, Clay did the same.

"One thing," said Cheney.

"Yes?"

"Were you the first lawyer to sue Craig?"

"Yes, as far as I could determine. And I looked into that."

"I'm sure you did," said Cheney. He knew the man had done so, if for no other reason than to see if he was going to have to stand in line if he won a judgment. "When did you file suit?"

"I'm not sure of the exact date."

"Approximately."

"First part of November."

Cheney didn't say anything. But he was thinking that that was just four weeks before Frank was murdered.

Daren Cheney answered the door and let his son in. Cheney had called ahead this time.

Several photo albums were stacked on the coffee table. The one on top was open.

"What's all this?" said Cheney as he sat down.

"I like to look at old photos while I can still see 'em. Sometimes I look at the albums twice a day. Sometimes three. Remember this?" said Daren. He pointed to a photograph of Cheney and his father standing in front of an apartment building on Gardner in Hollywood.

"Yeah, I remember," said Cheney. "Those were some great times."

"For who?"

"What do you mean?"

"I mean, what made you think times were so good back then?"

"I don't know exactly. Just a feeling. I was about ten, right?"

"Yeah."

"So, I was playing Little League ball, trading baseball cards with Paul. And there was you and Mom."

"Yes?"

"It was a family," said Cheney. "Not like today."

"What the fuck do you know," said Daren.

Cheney was taken aback by the strength in his father's remark. "What are you talking about?"

"You think that just because your mom and I stayed

together we didn't have the same kind of pressures people have today?"

"No, I didn't mean it that way."

"You didn't mean it that way, or you never really thought about it that way?"

"I don't know, maybe a little of both."

"When that picture was taken, I had just moved into a little studio apartment over on Sycamore Avenue."

"You left Mom?" said Cheney, startled at the revelation.

"She threw me out."

"But you were around."

"I was around when I needed to be. Being a cop, my schedule allowed for me to be gone nights, sometimes for a couple days at a time. You were used to that. I'd make sure I was there for your ball games, then I'd tuck you in and go back to my own place. You always thought I was working the night shift and that I got home after you went to school. I made sure I made enough appearances so you wouldn't catch on, while your mom and me figured out what we were going to do."

"I never knew," said Cheney.

"You weren't supposed to know." Daren looked at the photograph closely. "Your mother was a beautiful woman."

Cheney nodded.

"Memory's a funny thing," said Daren. "*You* look at this picture and you get filled with good feelings, *I* look at it and all I feel is pain. I almost lost your mother then and there. For a while, I thought I'd lose you both."

"But you didn't."

"I didn't know that then. And when I look at these snapshots I remember what I felt then. I guess I was just about as scared as I've ever been in my life."

"Why? I mean, what was it all about?"

"You really wanna know?"

"Why?"

"I'll tell you if you want to know."

Cheney knew what his father was saying. Daren was about to give him a glimpse behind the scenes. Children rarely knew, and for many good reasons, what their parents' lives were really like.

"Yes, I want to know."

"Being married to a cop ain't easy, but you already know that. Your mom knew what she was getting into—her father was a cop. But she was his daughter, not his wife. There's a big difference.

"Anyhow, we'd been married about twelve years and I was going through a tough period at work. I was—well, that part's not important. It was a bitch at work. I was doing a lot of stakeouts, so lots of nights I wasn't home. Your mom with her work schedule and me with my crazy, all-hours-of-the-day-and-night schedule, we just kept missing each other. It got so we became like strangers.

"Anyhow, I started to develop a friendship with a woman who was working Ramparts as a dispatcher. She wasn't Marilyn Monroe, but then, who is? We started going out for coffee. I'm sure I don't have to draw you a picture."

"And Mom found out?"

"Your mother was many things, but never dumb. She put it together and told me to move out until I made a decision. She wouldn't put up with me having an affair."

"She gave you time to decide?"

"It wasn't open-ended. After all, there was you— that was a major consideration with her. She gave me six months to make up my mind. If I didn't come back to her and promise her that it was over and that I would never, under any circumstances, do it again, she

would file for divorce. And, in those days, it was a fore-
gone conclusion that I would lose custody of you."

"What happened?"

"I moved out—not *in* with the lady in question. To
be honest, I was tempted. Your mother and I had been
together for almost fifteen years, married or dating. I
was very frustrated with certain areas of my life and,
well, frankly, the attention and company of an attractive
woman who thought I was the best thing since sliced
bread . . . hell, it wasn't as unrealistic an option then as
it sounds now."

"But you came back."

"You bet your ass I did."

"Why?"

"Why?" said Daren, smiling a little for the first time.
"Because I may be ignorant, but I'm not stupid. I honestly don't think I've ever met anyone quite like your
mother in my life. She was attractive, yes, but she had a
way about her. She had a sense of integrity, a great
heart and . . . she was the only woman in the world
who could lie to me."

"What?"

Daren coughed a laugh out his nose. "I'm a cop,
right? I can sniff out a liar at a hundred paces with a
clothespin on my nose. Your mother was even more
street-smart than I was. And she knew me. I guess she
trusted me not to pass up the best thing that would
ever come my way in this life."

Neither man said anything for a while.

"I miss her. God, I miss her," said Daren. The smile
was gone.

"Me too, Dad. But life goes on."

"For who? For you. You've got Elizabeth, Donny,
Samantha, and Erin."

"You have them, too."

"Children are wonderful, grandchildren are a great blessing. But how would your life change without Elizabeth?"

Cheney did not respond immediately. He needed Elizabeth as much as he needed air to breathe. Without her, he would have to create a new purpose for getting up every morning and going through the motions. And he could not imagine what that purpose would be.

"My life would change terribly," said Cheney finally.

"I miss your mother very much," said Daren, looking away from the albums out the window of his trailer toward the ocean.

"What about your new lady friend?"

"Lanie's very nice," said Daren, turning his attention back toward his son. "But you don't start things when you're seventy-eight years old, you end them."

"That's sounds very ominous."

"I'm just speaking from my heart, son. I'm so lonely without your mother that sometimes I just sit here and ache, it hurts so much."

"You know that I'm here for you, Dad. We get together regularly and we talk three, four times a week."

"Would that be enough for you?"

"To do what?"

"Never mind. Hey, feel like a walk on the beach?"

"Sure."

Daren Cheney locked up his trailer and he and his son crossed the Pacific Coast Highway at the light. It was a beautiful day. The low clouds had burned off and there was nothing but ocean, sand, and sky.

Daren wondered if he had done the right thing in telling his son about his affair. Had he in some way betrayed a trust, in some way made his wife look bad in her son's eyes? He didn't think so.

Cheney wondered if he had done the right thing in

asking his father to tell him about the affair. Had he in some way shared a secret that his mother would have preferred to have remained private? He wasn't sure.

Daren wondered if his son understood what today, this talk, this walk was all about.

Cheney wondered if maybe he shouldn't ask his father if he wanted to go on the cruise he and Elizabeth were taking this spring. Hell, he could even invite Lanie.

After not speaking for nearly thirty minutes, Daren stopped just under a pier—it was his two-mile marker. Two miles from the trailer. He'd worked it out with one of those hand-held distance counters Cheney had bought him a couple of years ago.

"You know that I love you, don't you?"

"Of course," said Cheney. "I've never doubted it."

"It's important. You know, even though I almost left your mom, I would never have left you. I swear to God, I wouldn't have."

"I know, Dad. I know." Cheney reached out and put his arms around his father. For a change, Daren hugged him back. Both men were uncomfortable with touchy-feely emotions, and after a moment, they resumed their walk down the beach.

"You know, Dad, Elizabeth and I are planning a cruise this spring. Why don't you and Lanie come along."

Daren Cheney stopped and looked at his son. He smiled a melancholy smile. It was odd, he thought, how two bright people could live through the same moment and see it all so differently.

"Dad seemed pretty depressed this afternoon."

"He's not working anymore, his wife is dead, and he's losing his sight. He's going to get depressed now and then."

"I suppose you're right."

Cheney sat with Elizabeth on the couch in their living room. He had played a couple of Eagles tunes, along with some country-and-western songs he'd recently picked up the sheet music to at a quaint music store in Brentwood. The fireplace crackled with a fire made of real, unprocessed logs Cheney had purchased from his neighbor's son. The young man had a cabin in Arrowhead, which he had offered to let Cheney use if he ever wanted to. Cops—especially high-ranking, high-profile cops—got offered all kinds of things. But not the rank-and-file cops. They retired and told war stories to people with nothing better to do than listen to some cynic who knew the world from its rotting core out.

Cheney realized that, in some ways, that described Frank. They had been partners for many years. They knew things about each other that their wives and children would never know, perhaps never understand.

Yet there was something else. Frank *might* have been killed because he *might* have molested his daughter. That possibility became more overwhelming every day.

If Frank had actually molested Molly, then Cheney felt that Frank had betrayed him. Had lied to him. But the worst part of it, at least for Cheney, was that if Frank had really been that troubled, that insane, why hadn't he felt safe enough to confide in Cheney. If he had . . .

"You okay?" said Elizabeth.

Cheney smiled weakly and told her what he was thinking.

"You can't blame yourself."

"But what would have happened if he'd told me?"

"You tell me."

Cheney looked into the fire. There were no safe answers, no comforting thoughts flickering there.

"I know you loved Frank—"

"I still do."

"Of course. And if you love someone, you've got to be able to overlook a lot."

"You mean, I should be able to get past the idea that he was a child molester?"

"I mean, that you don't have to dig into the intimate side of your friend's life."

"You mean his dark side?"

"I mean, you don't treat your friends as though you're working for *A Current Affair*. You allow them some privacy. That's why they call it privacy."

The phone rang. Petty answered it and yelled that it was for Cheney.

"Cheney," he said when he picked up the phone.

"It's me."

"Yeah, Tony, what's up?"

"Bridget Colfax, Craig's live-in girlfriend?"

"Yeah?"

"She committed suicide in her own apartment in Santa Monica about two hours ago."

Bridget Colfax's apartment was on Fourth Street in Santa Monica, about five blocks from the Pacific Ocean. When Cheney pulled up it was almost midnight. There were four black-and-whites and a couple of unmarked cars, one he recognized as Tony's.

The first thing Cheney noticed when he walked into the apartment was that it did not look lived in. It was organized, but not kept up. The dust on the furniture was so thick he could have written his name in it. The walls were bare. No plants. Cheney checked the date of a *People* magazine on the coffee table. November first. Two months ago. Everything seemed to be in its place, except for Bridget Colfax's body, which lay in the middle of the floor.

"You call Craig?"

"I left a message with his service."

"Machine or live?"

"Live. Don't forget, Cheney, the man's a doctor," said Tony sarcastically. "Well, kind of."

"What do you mean?"

"I ran down Craig's credentials. He majored in psychology and attended college at UC Berkeley."

"Can't put a guy in jail for that—not that you shouldn't be able to."

"Back off. My brother went to Berkeley and he's a card-carrying Republican."

"Okay, okay. So, where's the red flag?"

"Craig dropped out of school after two years."

"He never graduated from college?" said Cheney incredulously.

"Right. Now he's out in the real world with a big-time practice in Venice, healing people who could not be helped by other credentialed therapists."

"And tearing families apart in the process."

"At least that."

"So, what did you find here?"

"A lot. Maybe too much."

"What do you mean?"

"Let me show you."

Tony led Cheney upstairs to Bridget Colfax's bedroom. Again, Cheney was struck by the stark decor. A nondescript bed, a chest of drawers, two side tables. It was like walking through a furniture showroom.

Tony went to the closet and opened the door. Cheney stopped in his tracks.

"My God!" It was more an awed whisper than a shout.

There in front of him was a sort of shrine. The back wall of the closet was covered with photographs of the murder victims, thumbtacked or glued along with newspaper stories about their murders, plus photographs of people neither Cheney nor Tony recognized.

"So, Bridget Colfax killed . . ." Cheney could not bring himself to say it.

"Frank?" said Tony gently.

Cheney nodded. He was looking at a photograph of Frank. He recognized the background and the person Frank was with—he was coming out of the blues club in Crestview with Lilly Henley, the waitress he had been seeing just before his death.

"But the witness in Frank's murder saw a man running away," he said to Tony.

"It's easy for a woman to disguise herself as a man, in this context, at least. If Bridget dressed in pants and a shirt and a short-haired wig, the witness would have seen a man. People always assume that a killer is a man. Would it have occurred to you that a woman killed Frank? In one other case, witnesses saw a woman. As a woman, Bridget had the weapon of surprise. Her victim was older and probably not in the best shape."

Suddenly they heard a scream from the living room. Cheney and Tony ran downstairs, where they found Stanley Craig by the body of Bridget Colfax, weeping.

Thirty minutes later, Cheney, Tony, and Craig were sitting in Colfax's upstairs bedroom. Craig still looked a little pale.

"You all right?" asked Tony.

"No, I'm not. My God, what happened here?"

"Looks like your girlfriend got a fatal case of conscience."

"What are you talking about?"

"Mr. Craig," said Tony, refusing to use the term

"doctor," "what do you make of this?" He led Craig to the closet and opened the door.

The sight hit Craig like a heart attack. "Oh, no! No!" He backed away from the unholy shrine as though he were being chased by a band of lepers.

"She . . . she's the one?"

"What do you mean?" said Tony.

"Bridget stole my files? She was the one who broke into my office?"

"Why would you say that?"

"She had access. She could have taken my office keys, or had duplicates made, who knows," said Craig, shaking his head in disbelief.

"Why would she want to kill these people?"

Craig didn't answer immediately. He sighed and took a deep breath. "I was not completely honest with you regarding my relationship with Bridget. Before she was my, well, girlfriend, she was my patient."

"Is that so?"

"You can imagine why I wouldn't want to reveal that fact."

"Yeah, I guess you didn't want to tell us you were sleeping with one of your patients," said Tony. "Bridget came to you because she'd been molested?"

"Yes. She was a very troubled person."

"And you helped unburden her soul."

"There's no need to be sarcastic."

Tony didn't apologize. He and Cheney sat looking at Craig, who appeared to be visibly shaken. He was not going to—was not in a position to—demand an apology.

"We got very close, very fast. After all, I'm not a married man and, well, Bridget is . . . well, I found her attractive."

"She was nearly fifteen years younger than you."

"I'm forty-five and she was thirty-one. Is that scandalous? I don't think so."

"Tell us about Ms. Colfax."

"I'm her doctor and I—"

"Fuck you," said Tony, getting in Craig's face. "You're not a fucking doctor. You never graduated college and your therapy comes out of some fucking book anybody can pick up at the local bookstore. You're a fuckin' fake and I—"

"I am *not* a fake!"

"You're just a quack."

"I am *not*!" Craig stood.

Cheney got in between the two men. "This is bullshit!" he shouted.

Craig sat down first. Then Tony. Cheney sat down on the bed, in between the two men, and turned to Craig. "So, what can you tell us about Ms. Colfax that might help us here?"

After just the exact amount of silent bravado he figured he could milk from the confrontation, Craig said, "Bridget was a very unique case. She had been molested not only by her father, but by her mother as well."

"You say that's unique?"

"Not unheard of, but very, very rare. Usually, it's one parent. The other parent's complicity is that he or she remains silent."

"But Bridget's case was different."

"Yes, very. She was an only child, and being molested by both parents, you can imagine how helpless she must have felt. Who could she turn to? There was no one. She felt isolated. She submitted out of fear that her parents' threats would come true. They told her they would kill her dog. They told her they would lock her in the cellar. They told her they would cut off her allowance."

"Cut off her allowance?" said Cheney.

"Yes."

"That's not part of any satanic ritual, is it?"

"A parent knows how to manipulate his or her own child better than an outsider," said Craig condescendingly.

"I suppose. And you believed her?"

"Children don't lie about being molested."

"Is that so?"

"Anyone familiar with the field will tell you that. What possible motivation would a child have to lie about such a thing? And besides, you're missing the point here. Bridget was not ten years old, she was thirty-one. She *knew* what had happened to her."

"When did she know it?"

"Pardon?"

"When did she know she had been molested?" asked Cheney again.

"I'm not sure I understand your question."

"Was she aware of the molestation before she came to see you?"

"She knew about it, of course."

"Had she seen other therapists?"

"Yes."

"Then she must have confided in them about her molestation."

"I suppose."

"You're not sure?"

"The symptoms of Bridget's molestation were manifested in virtually every area of her life. Chronic illnesses—"

"Like?"

"Asthma. That's a frequent sign. You see the strangling effect of—"

"How else was it manifested in her life?" asked Cheney again, not loudly, just firmly enough to keep Craig from getting off track and giving a speech.

"As I said, in virtually every other area. She had

never been able to hold a job. She never realized her inner potential. And her relationships with both men and women had the fingerprints of a molestation victim all over them."

"I see."

"You have to understand that Bridget was always aware, subconsciously, of what had happened to her, even if she wasn't aware of it consciously. The mind protects us from traumatic events, the sensations of which our minds are not ready to process. A survival mechanism in the brain allows us to shut sensations off when they hit overload. Otherwise, we'd all go crazy."

"So, she didn't remember being molested until she came to see you," said Cheney. It was not a question.

"I think you're missing the point. You can't blame the doctor for finding the malignancy."

"And you help these people."

"I do, yes."

"Did you help Bridget?"

Craig looked Cheney hard in the eye. "Obviously not as much as I had hoped."

"So, she broke into your office and stole your files. Knowing what you know about her, as her therapist and her lover, what would you say her motivation was, *doctor*," said Tony.

Craig drew his hand down his face. After a moment, he looked up at the two cops. "Apparently she wanted to make them pay."

"Them?"

"Parents who molest their children. She got my files and went after perpetrators mentioned in those files."

"And you had no indication that this could be happening?"

"How could I?"

"Maybe because you were not only her doctor, you were also sleeping with her. That could have given you a greater insight."

Craig looked at Tony. "Can I go now?"

"Why?"

"Because I'm tired, I'm in shock. If you want me to answer any more questions, I'm going to have to call my lawyer."

"You can go, but we'll be in touch. Stay available."

Craig didn't bother to say thanks. He walked out of the room.

"What do you think?" asked Tony.

"I think he's an asshole."

"Yeah, but if every asshole was a murderer, you'd need a computer to keep track of the body count in this town. The question is, is he a murderer?"

"I don't know. You think Bridget's a murderer?" asked Cheney.

"Personally, I still think the multiple killer scenario, as untypical as it is, makes the most sense. I mean, how do we know that there aren't five people out there with closets full of the same pictures? Maybe Bridget got so she couldn't look herself in the mirror anymore."

"Maybe someone else in the group killed her and made it look like a suicide," said Cheney. "And if it is a group, then Bridget was probably the one who supplied them with information on their targets."

"If it is a group, then that means the group, minus one, still exists. Which means that those photographs in the closet, the ones we don't recognize, are the next targets."

"Maybe we should get Craig to compile a complete victim list based on any files Bridget could have copied."

"He's not likely to comply."

"Then we'll threaten him."

"With what?"

"Who the fuck knows," said Cheney. "We'll figure out the right buttons to push. Get everything you can on Craig."

"We need as much information as we can get. How's Ray doing?"

"I haven't heard from him lately. In any case, we've got to move fast. I don't want this group of self-appointed avengers killing somebody else just because we're waiting on a call back from Ray."

"Gotcha. So, if this is a group, how did it get together?"

"Actually, if this really is a group," said Cheney, coming down strong on the *if*, "then tonight it's a little more clear how they found each other. After Bridget took the files, not only did she cull them for targets, she probably also contacted the molestation victims."

"I don't know," said Tony. "If that's true, then you're saying that Molly—Frank's daughter and your goddaughter—is part of an inner circle of killers."

"Okay, okay," said Cheney, not wanting to believe it himself. "Try this on for size. Bridget copies, what, a hundred files?"

"Potentially."

"So she contacts a hundred molestation victims. She goes and talks to these people as a victim herself, so she's a sympathetic character."

"Sympathetic or not, are you going to agree to committing murder?"

"I don't know. According to Craig, his patients' lives are already devastated by the molestation. Most people don't know what they're capable of until it happens to them."

After a moment, Cheney walked to the window and

looked out. A chilly breeze blew in off the Pacific. "You ever see the movie *Strangers on a Train*?"

"No."

"Ah, you young people," he said, turning to face Tony. "It's a Hitchcock film in which two strangers meet on a train. They talk about how horrible their lives are and how much better they would be if one person, in each man's life, was dead. So they agree to kill the other person's nemesis and never see each other again. The idea being that the police would never be able to trace the actual killer because there was no motive attached to him."

"What are you saying?"

"What if Bridget copied the files, contacted a few victims, and they decided to get revenge—not for themselves, but for each other?"

"So, you've got a group of people filled with such hate for their own parents that they agree to serve as each other's executioner?"

"Another person who you know feels your pain."

"That premise still implicates Molly."

"Maybe, maybe not. Just because Bridget contacted her, that doesn't mean she went along."

"Then why would someone else agree to kill Frank? Why not target the molester of a victim who goes along?"

"I don't know. There could be lots of reasons."

"Like what?"

"Lots of reasons," said Cheney. He shook his head wearily. "It's been a long day. I'm going home."

"By the way, I forgot to show you something." Tony took a sealed plastic bag out of his jacket pocket and handed it to Cheney.

Inside the sealed bag was a note, its message spelled out in letters made of blue ribbons: *Children never lie.* He handed it back to Tony.

"Suicide note?" asked Cheney.

"Could be. It ties it all together."

The Round Table was in session.

"What we're doin' here is important," said Dennis. "No more fuckin' around. This is it."

The others nodded. He did not look directly at them, but he could see their reflections in the mirror.

In the background there was no sound. Except for the wind outside. Dennis stared into the future, into the dream. He felt the adrenaline exhilaration that dreamers feel when they are about to cross the threshold of their dreams.

Dennis felt in control. Not only was it his turn, but he knew, and he sensed that the others knew, he had always been in control. If someone had taken things in a direction he figured wouldn't work, he would have stepped in. Made that person alter the course.

"What we do here will be reported on television and radio, and in the movies. We're the real thing."

Everyone nodded.

"Fear is what it's all about," said Dennis. He looked at the others gathered around the table. At Mark. At Diana. At Carl. At Malcolm.

"Fear brings people out of their shell. They feel safe inside that shell. They protect that hiding place with money, power, sex, religion, whatever they hope will keep their sins from being discovered. But nothing and no one can do that forever. The past catches up with all sinners. *We* catch up with them," said Dennis, with a crooked and malevolent smile.

He caught a glimpse of himself in the mirror. He was a good-looking man, handsome and strong. He wore jeans, a blue work shirt, and work boots.

This was a special occasion. The end was near, they all knew it. This was the endgame they had talked about for so long.

"This is my night. This is my chance, my glory," said Dennis firmly. No one said anything.

He knew they all feared him. He knew some of them called him a loose cannon. But, in the end, he knew it would all come down to him. Success or failure. That was exactly the way he wanted it. He was not afraid. And he knew, from experience, that as long as he was not afraid to fail, success would always, in the long run, be his.

He had learned this lesson long ago. As a child. When he'd had no choice. The only thing that had kept him going was his ability to see, to believe, beyond the present. Beyond the hell that he was trapped in at the moment.

"I'd like to propose a toast," said Carl. "To Malcolm. Congratulations on a job well done."

The others raised their glasses in Malcolm's direction, then drank.

"Four down and one to go," said Malcolm.

"At *least*," said Dennis.

Dennis sat staring directly at Malcolm, as though looking through him. Through them all. Dennis was there, and he was *not* there.

Dennis was dangerous. More dangerous than the rest.

When the meeting adjourned, Dennis walked out on the lawn. Toward the lake. Black Water Lake.

For a while he sat alone on the smooth, moist bank. He picked up a stone and skipped it across the water. In the moonlight he could see the ripples undulating out in concentric circles from where the stone had died. Circles within circles. Life was like that. His life was like that. Waves of life emanating out from a single event.

Eventually touching everything. Everyone.

Dennis felt good. He stood and walked closer to the lake, down to the dock. It was . . . ritual.

He got into the small boat and adjusted the oars. Rowed out into the middle of the lake. Looked back toward the shore. Sensed the others looking at him. Even though he couldn't see them.

He knew what he had to do. Knew how to keep a secret.

As he sat there in the middle of the lake, oars idle, in the middle of Black Water, he sensed the presence. It was the presence they all felt. It was the presence that had brought them all together. Made them do what they did.

It was the presence.

It was justice.

It was . . . ritual.

Fourteen

"**M**y sister and I got our tickets in the mail," said Petty as she scooped a nonfat pancake onto Cheney's plate.

"Tickets?"

"To *The Tony Bishop Show*," said Petty, as though Cheney had forgotten Christmas. She started to put a pancake on Elizabeth's plate.

"No thanks," said Elizabeth. Nonfat or not, she was on another diet. Fruits and nuts. After all, who ever saw a fat squirrel?

"I'm a little disappointed, though," said Petty as she put two pancakes on her plate and took the pan back to the sink.

"Why?" said Elizabeth. Cheney quelled the impulse to strangle her.

"Well, we were hoping for the 'Hermaphrodite Beauty Pageant'—very visual—but we got stuck with 'Racist Lesbians' Children.'"

◆ 301

"What?" said Cheney, his mouth full of pancake. The word was out of his mouth before he could think clearly.

"The *TV Guide* said Wednesday was the Hermaphrodite Pageant, but when I called the show, they said Wednesday's topic was children raised by racist lesbians."

Cheney just sat there staring at Petty, unable to speak.

Thankfully, the phone rang. "I'll get it," he said. He went into the living room and picked up the phone. "Hello."

"Cheney?"

"Yes. Cary Ann?"

"Yes. Have you heard from Ray?"

"No, why?"

"Well, he said he was working on something for you. He usually calls me every night when he's out of town."

"Every night?"

"I think he gets lonely."

"Maybe he was working late and didn't want to wake you."

"Maybe," Cary Ann she said weakly. "You think you could find out?"

After a moment's hesitation, Cheney told his ex-wife, "Okay. Where was he yesterday?"

"Pacific Point."

"Any place in particular?"

"No."

"Okay, Cary Ann, I'll look into it."

"Thanks, Cheney."

"Sure," he said, and hung up. He dialed Tony's number. "Tony?"

"Cheney, I was just about to call you. I haven't been able to get hold of Craig, but it's still early."

"Keep me posted."

"Of course. What about Molly?"

"What about her?"

"You want to interview her, or do you want me to?"

"I don't know, Tony."

"It's got to be done."

After a moment, Cheney said, "Yeah, I know. Maybe I'll swing by her place before I head up to Pacific Point."

"Pacific Point?"

"Ray's up there and Cary Ann didn't hear from him last night."

"Craig's from Pacific Point."

"That must be why Ray's there. Probably digging for any bodies Craig's got buried up north."

"He's probably passed out next to some bimbo he picked up in a bar."

"You know anybody up there?"

"No, but I'll call the sheriff and tell him you're coming. When should he expect you?"

"Afternoon sometime, I guess."

"If I miss you at home, I'll call you on your car phone after I talk with the sheriff."

"Thanks," said Cheney, and he hung up.

Molly wasn't happy to see Cheney.

She hadn't opened her veterinary practice for business yet, but her secretary/receptionist was already in and prepping the paperwork for a new day. Molly took Cheney out back where she had a kennel. About a dozen dogs—a couple of dalmatians, three golden retrievers, a shar-pei, a dachshund, and a few breeds which Cheney couldn't quite place—broke into a chorus of yips and yells when the two of them walked out.

Molly led Cheney past the kennels into a field that opened up on a wide expanse of weeds and flowers, above which loomed the San Gabriel mountains. Eventually the dogs stopped barking.

"I really don't want to talk about this anymore," said Molly.

"Neither do I, Molly, but sometimes people have to do things they don't want to do. It's called real life."

"My father is no longer in my life and that's the end of it. It's over."

"Not for me."

"That's unfortunate," she said coolly.

"Molly, you know I would never do anything to hurt you. And I won't. But I *will* find your father's killer."

"That has nothing to do with me."

"Probably not."

"Probably?"

"Okay, it doesn't. And if I didn't absolutely have to ask you these questions, I wouldn't. But I don't have any choice."

"You always have a choice."

Cheney knew that, in certain instances, circumstances and loyalties left a person no options. But he wasn't here to argue the point. "You know anyone by the name of Bridget Colfax?"

"No. Are we done?"

"You're sure?"

"I'm sure."

"Did you ever participate in any group that consisted of yourself and other patients of Dr. Craig?"

"No."

"Were you ever contacted by any of Dr. Craig's patients?"

"No."

"You're positive you've never heard of Bridget Colfax?"

"I already told you no, twice. Who is she?"

"She was your therapist's live-in girlfriend."

"Stanley's?" said Molly, a little surprised.

"Stanley? You call your doctor 'Stanley'?"

"Dr. Craig is very warm. He's more like a friend than a therapist."

"Because?"

"Because he understands."

"Better than the other doctors?"

Molly looked at Cheney soberly. "What does that mean?"

"You saw other doctors, but Stanley was the only one who understood your pain."

"So?"

"Why do you think that was?"

"I'm not sure," said Molly, turning away and looking up toward the mountaintop.

"You're a bright professional woman. Why was it that Stanley was the only therapist who ever really understood your pain?"

After a moment, Molly turned back toward Cheney with a hard look in her eye. "Maybe because he was the only therapist I went to who admitted that he'd been molested himself."

Cheney usually enjoyed the drive up the Pacific Coast Highway. The ocean on his left, the mountains on his right. This time of year the mountains were green and lush, not brown and brittle. Riding in the J30 was like seeing it all from an orchestra seat. But today his heart wasn't in it.

Just as Cheney passed Alice's Restaurant in Malibu,

Tony called and said that Sheriff Oldfield would be expecting him.

"You talk to Craig yet?" asked Cheney.

"Not yet."

"When you do . . . "

"Yeah?"

"Ask him if being molested as a child played any part in his choice of professions."

"I spoke with Ray yesterday," said Oldfield. "Interesting character."

Cheney sat in a green leather chair opposite Sheriff Oldfield. His office was only about three hundred yards from the Pacific. He sat with his feet up on the desk. Two paperweights—one a ceramic bust of Ronald Reagan, the other a large pink conch shell—held down the papers on the desk.

The air smelled like the ocean. The ocean in Pacific Point smelled a lot different than the ocean in Santa Monica Bay, thought Cheney. He inhaled deeply.

"What did you and Ray talk about?" he asked the sheriff.

"He wanted to find out all he could about the Craigs."

"Stanley Craig?"

"The whole family, including Stanley Senior and his father, Oliver."

"What time did he leave your office?"

"I dunno, sometime in the afternoon."

"Did he say where he was going?"

"Nope."

"What did you tell him about Stanley Craig?"

"Little a' this, little a' that. Frankly, your friend seemed disappointed."

"Disappointed?"

"Like I wasn't giving him enough dirt."

"You don't like reporters."

"Do you?"

"I like Ray. He's my friend," said Cheney, with just enough of an edge so that Oldfield would hear a threat, but not enough of one so that he had to openly defend himself.

"If he wasn't your friend, and he was just a reporter, would you like him?"

"I don't know. Look, Sheriff, I'm here to find Ray. You have any idea where he is?"

"Absolutely none."

"What exactly did you tell him?"

"I'm not sure exactly."

"You said you talked about Craig's kinfolk," said Cheney sarcastically.

"Look, there's no reason to get an attitude."

"Oh, really? My friend is missing. You're a cop, and maybe the last person who talked to him yesterday. Now you're sitting here giving me your best Andy of Mayberry impression."

Oldfield thought about acting insulted. But it was hard. Cheney had more weight. And besides, he was right. He told Cheney the details of his conversation with Ray.

"Does Craig have any relatives here in Pacific Point?"

"He's got a sister. Clara. Clara Craig."

"She never married?"

"No."

Cheney looked at Oldfield. The sheriff was useless. Cheney walked out without saying goodbye.

◆   ◆   ◆

"You're the second person from LA in here since yesterday," said Stephen Sample, publisher of the *Pacific Point Lighthouse*.

"Was Ray Malzone the other?"

"Right," said the man with a smile. "How'd you know?"

"I'm a friend of his and I'm looking for him." It was logical that Ray would have gone to the local newspaper office.

"I haven't seen him since yesterday morning."

"You have any idea where he might be?"

"No. When he left here he went to see my uncle—he owns a bar here in town. I talked to my uncle last night and he said he told Mr. Malzone to go see Sheriff Oldfield."

Cheney nodded. "What did Ray ask you about?"

"Stanley Craig. Anything about the family, actually."

"What did you tell him?"

"I didn't know a whole lot. My uncle knows a lot more about Pacific Point—least the old Pacific Point—than I do. But it got me to thinking." Sample walked back to his desk, picked up a yellowed newspaper, then returned and set it down so that the top of the page was right-side-up for Cheney.

"What's this?"

"I did some digging and I came up with this photograph. "

Cheney looked at it for a moment. The photo was of Stanley Craig accepting an award from a local business organization. He looked closer. Then he got the feeling. Goose bumps. Hair standing on end. It was the feeling he always got when the pieces started falling together.

"Who's that with him?"

"That's his sister, Clara," said Sample, pointing to the caption under the picture.

"Where does she live?"

"I don't know. Probably on the estate."

"You got an address?"

Cheney got directions from Sample and walked out of the tiny newspaper office onto the main street of Pacific Point. The sun was hot, but Cheney's blood ran cold. He knew. At least he knew part of it. And he figured that Ray had figured out the rest. Yesterday.

Which might be the reason nobody had heard from him since.

The Round Table was *not* in session.

Dennis sat by himself in a dark room. He could not see the others, and they could not see him. He wanted to be alone.

He was stronger than the others. He knew it and he knew that they knew it, too. He would take it from here. He would be the one to go to war. He would deal with it head on. He was not afraid. The others could kill, if pushed, if motivated in just the right way. Especially if the victim did not know it was coming.

Dennis could look a man in the eye and kill him. He had done so and slept like a baby the same night. That separated him from most people. Soldiers knew what that was like. Knew the exhilaration of looking the enemy in the eye—and killing. At that instant there was what Dennis could only describe as an obscene intimacy. An unspeakable sensation of penetration. It wasn't something Dennis could discuss with other people. Not even the people involved in the Round Table. He knew they didn't feel the way he did about it. How could they?

The police would figure it out. Eventually. They were close. But even when they did . . . it wouldn't make any difference.

Things were changing. Coming to a head. Closing in. The dynamics of the plan were shifting. Which was why Dennis needed to take charge. Now. Fuck the rest of them. They would spook, cave in under real pressure. Dennis would not. He always pulled the others together. Even though they wanted to believe they were strong, they really were weak.

There was only one who was strong. They hated him for it, but that was okay. They feared him more than they hated him. And in the end, that was always enough.

It was late afternoon and already dark by the time Cheney pulled up to the wrought-iron gate on Craig Canyon Road. Stone pillars on both sides of the gate had the number *1* etched in them. The moon was full and it shone over the mountaintop like a brilliant star on top of a Christmas tree.

Cheney had stopped by Bobby Sample's bar and learned that the Craig Canyon estate had been built in the 1930s by Oliver Craig, Stanley Junior's grandfather. Oliver had once owned most of Pacific Point, and most of the people in it. They either worked for him or they were beholden to him or his money in some way.

There was only one property on Craig Canyon Road. Number One didn't take up as much land as it used to. At one time the estate included roughly fifty square miles of the best property in the county. Now most of it had been sold off, some by Stanley Senior and the rest by Stanley Junior. These days the estate was only about a hundred acres, although it included the prime land, the main house, and the stables.

But the stables were empty, the bar owner had told Cheney. The last time he had been up to the estate was nearly thirty years ago, when Senior was still alive. At that time, Bobby Sample was still publishing the local paper. He and his wife had attended the parties, played croquet, admired the high-priced horses, and canoed in the lake, which in those days was ringed by Chinese lanterns.

Since then, according to Sample, no social gathering had been held at Number One.

Cheney got out of his J30, walked up to the gate, opened the call box, and picked up the receiver. It rang.

And rang.

Cheney hung up. He grabbed hold of one of the black wrought-iron bars and gave it a shove. Nothing. The gate was locked and there was no way he could coax it open.

He got back into his car and drove up the road about an eighth of a mile. He parked behind a tree, got out, and walked back to the gate. He scaled it with relative ease and landed gingerly on the other side. Running four times a week has its advantages, he thought as he dusted himself off.

The road inside the gate was long, uphill, and serpentine. From Cheney's vantage point, he still couldn't see the main house through the trees.

He started up the road toward the house, following the winding road through a thick forest, until it finally opened onto a lawn the size of three football fields. Beyond the lawn was a two-story mansion. There were no cars in sight and the house was dark.

Cheney walked to the front door and rang the bell. He heard it echo in the huge empty house. Several times. No one was home. At least, no one was answering the bell.

Cheney went around back and tried the door. It was locked. He tried several windows. All locked. He went back to one of the rear doors and, using a tiny two-piece pick set any cop knew how to use, he opened the door.

Once inside, he gently closed the door and listened. There was only silence, except for a constant ticking that Cheney soon discovered was coming from the grandfather clock in the foyer. The floors were all hardwood, and covered with expensive Oriental rugs.

The living room was bathed in an eerie moonlight that shot up the room with silver and shadow. The staircase was out of another time and place. A time when money was not as important as the place. But in 1995, Cheney felt oddly ill at ease walking up the opulent circular staircase. He had been around money, real money. Cheney even had some fuck-you money of his own. But he had never been around the kind of money that built this place.

At the top of the staircase was a portrait of a man who had many of the same facial features as Stanley Craig. But it was not Stanley Craig and Cheney didn't know if it was Stanley's father or grandfather. He figured it was the grandfather. The eyes were alive in the darkness, in the moonlight, with an arrogance that spanned distance, time, and even death. There was something malignant in the man's eyes. His grandson had not inherited the old man's way with money, nor his empire-building ambition. But that spirit of arrogance had been passed down.

And perhaps, thought Cheney, something much more evil than that.

At the top of the stairs, the hallway went right and left, with several doors on either side. There were no lights on, but in the moonlight Cheney could see easily.

He turned right and headed down the hall. He came to the first door on his right and gently turned the handle. It was unlocked. Cheney reached down under his right pant leg, removed a gun from his ankle holster, and walked into the room.

It was dark. Cheney found the light switch and flipped the overhead light on. The high-ceilinged room was both old and new. Old with a twenty-five-foot vaulted ceiling, window seat, ornate woodwork, and a filigreed music box; new with a flat-screen TV and remote control. It was a woman's room. The bed was all pastels and ruffles. He opened a drawer, which was filled with women's clothing—blouses, brassieres, panties. Other drawers revealed more of the same. Nothing out of the ordinary. Except Cheney had the eerie feeling that no one actually lived here.

He went to the next bedroom and flipped the light switch. No TV, but there was a stereo. All the CD's were classical music. Mahler, Beethoven, Mozart. The room was tidy and it had a—Cheney was going to say that it had a lived-in look. But that wasn't true. It looked as though someone had *been there* recently, but not that they *lived* there.

Cheney walked back into the hall and down to the next room. Walked inside. He hit the light switch and it was more of the same. No TV, but there was a stereo. This time the CD's were all country-and-western. No classical. No sign of anyone feminine.

Cheney walked out into the hallway again and leaned against the wall. Where in the fuck was he? Was this some kind of asylum for Craig's patients? And if so, where were they?

Dennis knew this was the endgame. He checked his watch. The son of a bitch was late. It was then that the headlights sliced the darkness. Dennis slipped behind the tree.

A moment later, Sheriff Oldfield stepped out of his unmarked car—he'd left the city car behind. Dennis had told him to.

"Oldfield," said Dennis in a loud whisper.

Oldfield spun around as though he had been slapped. "That you?" he said into the darkness from where the voice had come.

"Who the fuck do you think," said Dennis, stepping out of the shadows and into the moonlight.

"You 'bout scared the shit outta me."

"He's here."

"I told you he was comin' out here."

"And you did good," said Dennis.

"Keep the money comin', I'm your man."

You're my *something*, thought Dennis. *Man* was not the word that came to mind.

"So what're you gonna do?" said Oldfield.

"Don't worry, I've got it covered."

"I'm not worried. It's just that you wanted me out here. I come all this way, I need to know the plan."

"You don't need to know the plan."

"Why, I mean, if—"

"You're a fuckin' moron."

Oldfield looked at Dennis as though he'd just been told the world was coming to an end in ten minutes. In a way, that was true. It just wasn't going to take that long.

Dennis pulled a nine millimeter automatic with a silencer on its tip from his jacket pocket. He pointed it at Oldfield's face.

"What the fuck! C'mon, man, don't do this!" said Oldfield. He started to back away as Dennis came toward him.

"You know too much."

"I don't know nothin'!" pleaded Oldfield, continuing to back up. He tripped over a log and fell down.

"You're too stupid to be trusted, you fuck!" Dennis kept coming.

"No, please. Please!" screamed Oldfield.

There was a tiny explosion.

Then nothing.

Cheney froze. He thought he heard something in the distance. He listened intently, but heard nothing more. After a moment, he moved down the hall toward a door at the end. He tried the handle and, finding it unlocked as the others had been, walked inside the room. He hit the light switch and saw that he was standing in a medium-sized ballroom. In the center of the ballroom was a large round table, around which were scattered five chairs. It was the largest table Cheney had ever seen, made of mahogany, and cue-ball smooth.

Adorning the walls of the great hall were several portraits, each with a nameplate on the frame. Oliver Craig. His son, Stanley Senior. Stanley Junior. There were several portraits of women whom Cheney did not recognize—all but one.

Cheney sat in a chair at the head of the table. His mind was reeling. He had part of the puzzle. But the rooms . . . Was this the safe house that provided sanctuary for the group he and Tony had hypothesized? Or was there another explanation . . .

It was then that he heard the footsteps on the staircase.

Cheney hurried to the light switch and flipped off the lights. He stood breathlessly, listening.

Waiting.

He heard another sound from down the hall in the direction from which he had just come. Cautiously, Cheney stepped out through the open doorway and padded soundlessly down the carpeted hall. There was a light coming from under the doorway of the first room Cheney had entered. And coming from that same room was the sound of a music box.

Cheney pushed the door open slowly. There on the bed, in dim light, sat a blond-haired figure holding a music box. "Hello," said the shadowed outline, not looking up at him. The voice sounded familiar to Cheney, but he couldn't quite place it.

"Hello."

"Who are you?"

"My name's Cheney. Who are you?"

"My name's Diana."

Cheney moved forward slightly. "Diana, I'd like to—"

"Don't come any closer."

"Why?"

"Because."

"Because why?"

Diana shrugged her shoulders in an adolescent manner.

"Diana?"

"Yes?"

"Are you here alone?"

She did not reply.

"I'd like to help you," said Cheney.

"I don't need any help."

"You and I can go back to Los Angeles—"

"I'm not going anywhere. Not anymore."

"Why?"

"It's over. What we did was important, but now it's over."

"What who did?" asked Cheney.

"All of us—myself, Mark, Carl, Malcolm and Dennis."

"I don't think you understand—"

Suddenly Diana reached over and turned off the lamp next to the bed. The room went dark. Cheney heard muffled noises moving past him, but out of reach. By the time he moved to the light switch and flipped the lights on, the room was empty.

He stepped out into the hall. And waited.

A moment later he heard sounds coming from the room across the hall. Classical music.

Slowly Cheney walked toward the door. He took the handle and twisted slowly. And when he opened the door the world melted into a macabre nightmare.

Mahler's Ninth played in the background. A lantern, the only light, flickered in the corner of the room next to the bed. A man, his back to Cheney, danced a minuet with his lantern-light shadow, which hopped double-size against the wall like an ancient and grotesque ghost. After a few bars of Mahler played out, the man spoke, without turning around. "Hello, Cheney."

"Hello."

"My name's Mark."

Cheney took a step closer.

"I wouldn't do that," warned Mark.

Cheney stopped. The man could see Cheney in a tiny mirror on a desk next to the bed. But the mirror was too small and too far away for Cheney to see the man's face clearly.

"I'm going to take you in, Mark. You know that."

"No, I don't know that. We're doing important work here."

"What kind of work?" said Cheney, trying to keep him talking.

"For the children. The abuse must stop."

"You mean sexual abuse?"

"Yes."

"Mark, you need help."

"The world needs to be educated. That's what this is all about," said the man.

Cheney took a step forward and suddenly Mark blew the lantern flame out. In the dark Cheney moved toward him, but couldn't reach him. He heard scuffling noises. Then silence.

Cheney went back out into the hall. It was dark. He thought he heard a noise on the staircase and he ran toward the sound.

Dennis sensed the trouble. He'd known all along that it would come to this. Him against Cheney. Fuck the others. He heard Cheney above him. Sensed him in the darkness.

He knew Cheney. Had studied him. And he knew that Cheney did not know him.

Dennis was certain he had the upper hand. He knew Cheney was scared and that fear brought a person out of his safety zone. And fear made all men naked.

There was nothing that could protect Cheney now, and Dennis knew it.

Cheney moved cautiously down the staircase, his only comfort the feel of his gun in his right hand. He should have called Tony before he came here, but he'd thought Tony's time would have been better spent interviewing Craig. And who else in the Crestview area could he have called in? And what reasons could he have given? It was all a hunch. A good hunch.

Too good.

At the bottom of the staircase Cheney crept on the balls of his feet, trying not to make a sound. One foot landed on a giant silk Oriental rug. The mansion was filled with a deafening silence. No music box. No Mahler CD. Not even the sound of the wind off the Pacific whispering haunting tunes through the ancient shutters.

Sound. Off to the right. Cheney knelt and aimed his gun into the darkness. Silence.

Cheney moved toward where the sound had been and found himself in a large dining hall. Twenty-four chairs, one long table. This table, too, was smooth, but even in the moonlight Cheney could see a thick layer of dust. In such a rich setting, against the florid-framed giant oils on the walls, such a lack of care seemed almost criminal neglect.

Another sound. A door slammed on the far side of the dining room.

In a crouch Cheney made his way across the room and into a small foyer just off the dining room. It was darker than the other rooms, no windows, just the moonlight filtering in through the slightly open door.

Cheney moved to the door, picked up a broom that lay next to the door, and used it to open the door a little wider.

Nothing but moonlight.

Cheney set the broom down and walked out into the back yard.

In the distance he saw a beautiful lake.

That was when something fell out of the sky, and wet grass jumped up and smacked him in the face like a giant frothing dog.

And then there was just darkness.

When Cheney came to, he was staring up at the full moon. He felt himself rocking and swaying. There was the sound of water slapping against wood. He tried to move his arms and legs, but he couldn't. He was not paralyzed. He had feeling in his limbs, he just couldn't move them.

Cheney shook his head and tried to focus. It all came back to him in pieces.

He was in a small boat. His hands and legs were tied. And there was someone . . . someone he could not quite make out because the person's head was silhouetted against the full moon. Gradually, it all came together.

"Cheney?"

Cheney looked up toward the voice and squinted. "Craig?"

"No. Craig's not here. I'm Dennis."

"But—"

"You're in no position to argue," said the man, as he kicked Cheney's legs.

Cheney winced in pain and looked at his captor. Despite what he had said, the man was, in fact, Stanley Craig, or at least the man Cheney knew as Stanley Craig. Almost. There was a glint of something in this person's eyes. Cheney recognized it, but for a moment he couldn't place it. Then it came to him. He had seen it before, seen people with that look in their eyes howling at the moon.

"Can you feel the presence, Cheney?"

"What?"

"The presence. It's all around us here in Black Water."

"What do you mean, 'the presence'?"

"The oversoul. God," said the man who called himself Dennis.

"What are you talking about?"

The man smiled a crooked, maniacal smile. "God helps those who help themselves," he said in a singsong voice.

"You're crazy, Stanley. You need help."

"You don't get it, do you, Cheney?"

"Get what?"

"It's all about justice."

"It's about murder."

"No, you're wrong. There's strength in the oversoul. In the collective unconscious, I can be who I want to be. I can be who I *need* to be."

"You're Stanley Craig."

"No, I'm Dennis. I *need* to be Dennis."

"Why?"

"So that I can perform the ritual."

"What ritual?"

"The greatest sin a man or woman can commit is to molest a child. It sets in motion a great wheel that rolls over and crushes the souls of innocents for generations to come," said the man, as though reciting from memory.

"It's not your job to purge the world of sin."

"It should be everyone's job. If it was, then I wouldn't have to perform the ritual."

"You mean you wouldn't have to be a murderer."

"I'm *not* a murderer."

"Why did you kill Frank?"

"I didn't kill Frank. Mark did."

"Mark? Is he part of your group?"

"Yes, he's one of us."

"Us?"

"The Round Table."

"Who's in the Round Table?"

"Other parts of my greater self. We're all parts of the collective unconscious. You're part of me and I'm part of you, don't you know that?" The man cocked his head and looked at Cheney, but his eyes were focused on a point well beyond Cheney.

"All I know for sure is that you're a murderer."

Dennis reached over and slapped Cheney hard across the face. "After what Stanley's parents did to him . . . "

Cheney shook off the blow. "What did they do to you, Stanley?"

"My name's not Stanley! I'm Dennis!"

"What did they do to you, Stanley?"

The man took a deep breath and leaned back against the side of the small boat opposite Cheney, who lay helpless. The moonlight rolled across the lake like cartwheeling diamonds.

"They did everything to me, Cheney."

Cheney saw a distinct personality change wash over and transform his captor as he spoke. Suddenly Stanley was back.

"It was both of them. My parents used to like to take the boat out here in the middle of Black Water Lake on the weekends. Just the three of us. And when my father started doing those things to me, he told me it was because I was weak. It was a kind of punishment. And when I cried to my mother, she just slapped me and told me to shut up and stop whining." Craig stopped and smiled sadly. "She told me I was scaring the fish. She'd toss back another beer and just stare out into the water.

"By the next summer, my mother joined my father in . . . punishing me. She took a liking to vodka that summer, and after about ten cocktails out on the lake, she enjoyed having me curl up with her and 'go to sleep.'"

"So you killed your father," said Cheney.

"Wouldn't you?"

Cheney did not respond immediately. He didn't really know the answer. "But you let the farm worker go to jail instead of you."

"It wasn't my fault a jury was stupid enough to send an innocent man to prison."

"He died there."

"I didn't kill him."

"Maybe not directly. What about your mother?"

"She drowned herself shortly after my sister was born."

"Why?"

Stanley looked away, out over the lake, seemingly hypnotized by the lapping water and its rhythmic sound.

"Why?" pressed Cheney.

"She was depressed."

"And guilty?"

"Obviously."

"About Clara?"

"What do you mean?" Stanley looked back at Cheney. Something was changing in his eyes. It was like he was putting on another mask.

"Was Clara really *just* your sister?"

"What do you mean 'just'!" An angry, aggressive Dennis was back in Stanley's body.

"Clara was also your daughter, wasn't she?"

The look in the man's eye flashed insane again and he sat upright in the boat.

"Was Bridget Colfax really your sister Clara?"

The man scrambled across the boat until he straddled Cheney's chest.

"I saw a photograph of you and Clara taken ten years ago. You both look a little different, but Clara and Bridget are the same person."

Madness flared like a backdraft in the man's eyes. "Fuck you!" he screamed.

"You were having sex with your own sister!" shouted Cheney.

"No!" he said, shaking his head side to side. "I never did."

"But Clara was Bridget Colfax. You said she was your girlfriend."

Suddenly Dennis started slipping away again. The anger faded. There was a look of uncertainty in the man's eyes. Stanley was beginning to re-emerge.

"I never had sex with her. I would never have sex with my own sister. I just told you that because . . . "

"Because you're a murderer and you needed an alibi."

"No, no!" The man was becoming confused.

"But you killed Clara! You killed your own sister! Why, Stanley? Why!?"

"No, I never . . . Dennis killed Clara."

"Who?"

"Dennis. He's evil."

"No, Stanley. *You* killed Clara! *You* did!"

Suddenly Dennis came back. And exploded. He picked Cheney up by the collar, dragged him to his feet and threw him into the lake. As he went under, Cheney thought he heard the man laugh. But he wasn't sure.

It could have been a scream.

Cheney felt swallowed up by the water, as though entering the stomach of a giant black beast. Ten seconds later he felt his feet touch the bottom, then he bounced up again slightly. At that point he guessed that his head was about eight feet below the surface. He figured he had about thirty seconds worth of oxygen left in his lungs. He pulled his feet up so that his heels touched his buttocks. Then he slipped his bound hands down and over his bound feet, leaving his hands in front of him. As he did so, his body rocked forward. Cheney felt his face rub up against something . . .

It was Ray Malzone's forehead.

Cheney screamed and, using his hands in a strong paddling motion, he propelled himself toward the surface.

He shot out of the water and yelled at the top of his lungs, his voice echoing in the distance for a full five seconds or more.

There was another voice. "Cheney!"

Suddenly enraged, Cheney slapped the side of the small boat with the palms of his hands, tipping it to one side, causing Craig to lose his balance.

"Cheney!" said the voice again in the darkness.

Then a spotlight shone out on the lake toward Cheney's voice and the commotion in and out of the boat.

Cheney hoisted himself back into the boat and, using his feet, kicked the disoriented Craig overboard. Even though Cheney's hands were still tied, his fingers were laced together so that they could be used to hammer Craig every time his head bobbed out of the water close to the boat.

"Cheney!"

Eventually, Cheney realized that Tony Boston was calling to him over a bullhorn from the boat dock. He thought he heard the sound of a motor boat.

Ten minutes later, Cheney was on shore and Tony and a dozen police officers had Craig in custody. Three officers dragged him across a huge expanse of lawn while he carried on a loud and violent conversation *with himself* regarding which "one of us" was responsible for leading the police to Black Water.

"How did you find me?" asked Cheney, finally free of his bonds and shivering, a blanket wrapped around him.

"When I couldn't find Craig, I ran the information we had on Bridget Colfax. She had a false ID, but the car parked in her space behind her apartment building was registered to Clara Craig of One Craig Canyon Road, Pacific Point. We got a fax of her driver's license from DMV and bingo—Colfax and Craig were the same person. I knew you were here checking on Ray. When I couldn't reach you on your car phone, I got worried."

"I guess I owe you," said Cheney with a smile. And a shiver.

"You and me, we're always even. You know that."

And as the two men walked up toward the main house, Cheney figured that was probably true.

Fifteen

"You're sure you don't mind missing the party?" said Cheney.

"Don't be silly." Elizabeth was curled up on the couch with her husband. She looked up at him. "Funny how much you appreciate something when you almost lose it."

"Not an original piece of philosophy, my dear. Especially coming from a psychiatrist."

"My forte is giving advice, not taking it. I was thinking while we were lying here in each other's arms . . . if I could remember just one piece of advice and practice it every day, I think it would be to appreciate life as it happens, because it'll never come again in exactly the same form."

"You mean you shouldn't take me for granted," said Cheney.

"Or you me."

"Me? Never. I always consider you one helluva piece of . . . well, you know," said Cheney playfully.

"You *are* a romantic son of a bitch," said Elizabeth sarcastically.

"Yeah, but I'm *your* son of a bitch."

Cheney hugged his wife tightly. He sipped a glass of Stag's Leap chardonnay, savoring the oak and vanilla taste. He was less than twenty-four hours back from his watery grave. Air felt good in his lungs, his wife's lips felt exquisite on his own, and this chardonnay tasted better than it ever had.

Cheney set down his glass and asked, "You believe Craig is a genuine multiple personality?"

"I don't know, I've never interviewed him."

"Could he be?"

"It happens. I've never personally had a patient who was a multiple personality, but I've known doctors who've had MP patients."

"I think it's bullshit."

"Maybe. But it just might be brilliant bullshit."

"What do you mean?"

"Frankly, if there is a precedent for such a defense, it grows out of a popular belief that a state of multiple personality can be created as a result of being molested as a child."

"What do you mean?"

"I mean, a child can submerge his real self beneath other personalities more capable of dealing with the pain and sensations the child—the real or native personality—is unable to confront. And current thinking goes that such a dysfunctional process is more likely to occur if the molestation is chronic."

"As Craig contends."

"Yes. That's because the native personality can slip into, if you will, another personality like strapping on a piece of armor in order to protect himself from situations he may be incapable or unwilling to confront.

And the more frequent the episodes, the easier it is to slip in and out of these 'armoring personalities.' And depending upon the frequency and intensity of the incidents, after a while, the native personality may eventually find himself or herself slipping into these other personalities involuntarily, perhaps without even being aware that such a change is taking place. Hence, the multiple personality."

"Do you really believe that the native personality, as you call it, isn't aware of what the other personalities are doing?"

"It's hard to say."

"I'm just asking for your professional opinion."

"Without examining Craig, I couldn't give you a credible opinion on his particular case."

"That's what bothers me."

"What do you mean?"

"These days, I'm convinced that a jury is made up of twelve people too stupid to get out of jury duty. If you, a psychiatrist, are even a little unclear about whether or not such a defense is credible, by the time a high-ticket lawyer gets done singing and dancing and pulling rabbits out of hats, the prosecutors will be lucky if they're not run out of town on a rail for further 'victimizing' Craig."

"That's pretty cynical," said Elizabeth.

"Yeah, well, it's not my problem anymore."

"I'll tell you something, Cheney, if you promise never to mention it again."

"I promise."

"I adore you," she said, looking into her husband's

eyes, grateful for the opportunity to spend another day with the man she loved. The man who loved her more than anyone ever had or ever would.

"And there's something about *you* I've always admired," said Cheney, leaning down and kissing his wife lingeringly on the mouth, their lips peeling away from each other's slowly.

The phone rang. Cheney reached over and answered it. "Cheney here." Pause. "Yes." Pause. "Oh, my God, no."

"Don't get all choked up about this, Derek. I had a good long run and when it's time to go, it's time to go," said Daren Cheney. "Sometimes people get to be like fallen leaves. When a wind comes up, they move around like they're full of life. But just because they move, doesn't mean they're alive."

There were tears in Cheney's eyes as he watched the video. Lanie had called Cheney and told him that Daren had committed suicide. Told him about the tape. Daren had wanted him to watch the tape by himself, so she left him alone.

About fifteen minutes into the tape, Daren Cheney looked into the camera at his son, his eyes tearing for the first time during the unusual monologue. "Finally, there are two things I want you to know. First, I *do* know that you love me. You've told me and shown me in all the ways a good son could show his father. I have no doubt about that. Know that I know." He paused. "I'm sure that'll be important to you, in the next few days especially.

"And second, know that I love you. Period. I love your mom, I love Donald, and I love Erin. But besides your mom, I guess I love you the most. You're my only son and you've made me more proud than any father really has the right to expect from any son." Daren sniffled a little and coughed, righting the emotional ship.

"So, there it is. I love you, Derek.

"Goodbye."

Daren sat silently on his bed and looked into the camera for a short time, then the screen went to static.

Cheney took a deep breath, pointed the remote at the TV, and hit the Off button. After a moment, he took another deep breath and walked out of his father's trailer. Lanie was waiting for him. She looked at Cheney, not knowing how he was going to respond. It could have played out a lot of ways. The two just stood there looking at each other for a moment. Then she hugged Cheney and he hugged her back.

Finally, Cheney said, "Thank you. I think I'm gonna go for a walk." Because that was all he could say without breaking down and bawling like a baby.

Across the Pacific Coast Highway, Cheney walked along the beach, the wind off the ocean whipping his hair. He recalled the last time he had walked the beach with his father. Life, he thought as he walked, tears in his eyes, seemed long, drawn out, full of pain and fear and hardship.

And yet it always seemed to end a couple of days too soon.

The funeral service was the following weekend. Cheney, Elizabeth, Donald, Samantha, Erin, Tony, Lanie and a couple of Daren's cop buddies crowded on board a yacht Cheney had chartered. For several reasons, Cheney tried his best not to make the occasion somber. His father had wrung a lot of life out of his years. And he had gone out under his own steam and on his own terms, even if those terms didn't make everyone else happy. Daren had taught Cheney long ago that no one, under any circumstances, *ever* made everyone happy. *A man's just got to do the right thing as he sees it*. Which is exactly what Daren had done.

Cheney had instructed the owner of the yacht that he wanted to get as close to the Santa Monica pier as possible. The pier was the site of his parents' first date more than fifty years ago. And the waters off the pier were where his mother's ashes had been scattered. Daren had stipulated in his will that his ashes be scattered there as well.

When the ceremony was done, ten-year-old Erin, who was subdued and polite throughout the proceedings, took Cheney's hand and the two of them walked to the back of the boat. As the shoreline began to disappear in the yacht's foamy wake, Cheney held his granddaughter on his knee.

"Will I ever see great grandpa again?"

"Maybe."

"If great grandma's in heaven, and great grandpa's in heaven, then if I go to heaven when I die, I'll see them there, won't I?"

"I suppose."

"Great grandpa was your daddy, wasn't he?"

"Yes, honey, he was."

"Do you miss him?"

"Yes, I do. Very much."

"I know I'd miss my daddy if he had to go to heaven. I just wondered if feelings change when you get to be old like you."

Cheney smiled. "They change, honey, but they never change so much that you don't miss people you love when they're gone."

"Don't leave me, too, grandpa. You promise?"

Cheney picked up Erin and held her in his arms. "I promise." As he watched the sun melting into the

Pacific, holding his granddaughter in his arms, looking back upon the waves that carried his father's ashes out into the great unknown, Cheney thought about love and promises.

And the fact that some promises could never be kept. Such promises were not commitments, but rather well-intentioned hopes and dreams that kept the world from coming apart at the seams.

Sixteen

Stanley Craig's trial didn't start until late October.
By that time, the police had so much physical evidence they would have needed a truck to haul it all into court, or at least that was what Tony told Cheney. The key pieces of physical evidence were Ray's body anchored in Black Water Lake next to a white buoy, and a sealed plastic bag tied to that same buoy that contained items taken from the victims—the unicorn Frank had bought for Lilly; a knife with blood on the blade that matched Andrew Mason's blood type; a country-and-western cassette tape with Calypso McGuire's fingerprints on it; and a photograph of Aubrey Mitchell in happier times with his daughter Cathy. All the items found in the plastic bag also had Craig's fingerprints on them.

But high profile cases in the 1990s were tried at least as much, if not more, in the court of public opinion as they were in a court of law. For months before the gavel fell, Craig's lawyer, Melvin Kleindinst, was on TV so often it seemed as though he had his own series. People got used to seeing him every night. Even his *agent* had been interviewed on *Nightline*.

Craig's defense hinged on three main points. First, Stanley had been molested as a child by both his mother and his father. Second, in order to deal with the horror, young Stanley set up various "personalities" that he employed to shield himself from his parents' heinous behavior. Third, at the time of the various murders, as well as during his "encounter" with *ex*-detective Derek Cheney, Craig was not acting as himself, but rather as one of his other personalities, and therefore was not responsible for his actions.

Cheney laughed out loud when he first heard Kleindinst do his routine. It was during the summer, on one of the local news shows.

But Tony wasn't laughing when he discussed the defense with Cheney the next day. "A no-holds-barred lawyer and twelve impressionable people, anything can happen."

"You can put a tuxedo on a piece of shit, but it's still a piece of shit."

"Yeah," said Tony cynically, "but some people are really impressed by a tux."

Cheney knew it was true. It was a very long and hot summer.

Day after day Kleindinst did his best to obscure the facts. He used reporters and talk show hosts like an artist uses brushes and canvas. By summer's end the image of Craig, the murderer, had been replaced by a portrait of Craig, the victim. He had murdered at least nine people, including his grandparents. He—that is, one of his personalities—admitted traveling to Europe and paying a mechanic to rig their rental car so that it would go over a cliff. Other personalities—the ones he named Mark, Carl, Diana, Malcolm, Dennis—had killed his grandparents, his father, his mother, and his sister, plus at least a half-dozen other victims including Frank and Ray.

Kleindinst argued that, had Craig been raised in a normal environment, or at least in an environment other than the one in which he was raised, such terrifying behavior problems would never have developed. These behavior problems, which ultimately manifested themselves as multiple personalities—"psychological devices which the victim used to cope with his nightmare of a life"—were responsible for the murders. Not the "source personality," as Kleindinst referred to his client.

"The source personality, Stanley, is as befuddled and as outraged as each of you ladies and gentlemen," Kleindinst told the jury. "He devoted his entire life to helping other incest survivors. When he was himself—when he was Stanley—he was the kind of person we would all wish to share a cup of coffee with. The kind of person we would want as a neighbor. He was thoughtful, considerate, and vigilant. Vigilant that our sons and daughters would not be visited by the same unspeakable horrors that devoured any chance at a real and happy life Stanley ever had."

And so it went. Week after week.

Throughout the trial, Cheney and Tony met and talked. The LAPD dug up one revelation after another about Craig, but because of the efforts of a crack team of legal specialists hired by Kleindinst, the DA's office was unable to introduce much of that information into the trial.

One afternoon over lunch, Cheney asked his protégé, "What about the blue ribbons? Ever find out what they meant?"

"Who the fuck knows. It isn't like Craig or 'one of his personalities' is going to step forward and tell us. You want my educated guess?"

Cheney nodded.

"From the beginning, Craig wanted us to tie the murders together. He planned on getting caught and he wanted his arrest to be a big deal. It was like, in his own warped way, he believed he was doing something good."

"At least. He wanted us to *believe* he thought he was doing something important," said Cheney, recalling something Craig had said to him during their encounter in Pacific Point. "He tried to come across as some kind of avenging angel for all molested children."

"Exactly. He didn't want the murders to appear random. He figured that we would give more weight to a serial murder case than to a bunch of random murders."

"He was right."

"He's been right about a lot of things," said Tony. "This fuckin' guy's a player."

He's also a murderer, thought Cheney. A murderer who had taken out two of his best friends. Cheney planned to make sure the man paid for those crimes.

Another thing Tony discovered about Craig was his brilliant manipulation of his sister/daughter. As Clara's guardian and only source of financial support, Craig had cared for her pretty much at his own whim over the years. Due to Clara's real mental problems, or problems manufactured by Craig, and the fact that she was under the influence of several powerful medications, he managed to control her life, much of which was spent in spa/clinics and schools in Europe. She was virtually unknown in Pacific Point or in Los Angeles.

One of Craig's patients, Bridget Colfax, wintered in Europe every year, spending much of her time skiing in Switzerland. Craig knew this. He told Bridget that he was having some work done on his Marina condo and asked if he might have access to her apartment while she was away. Bridget jumped at the chance to please her therapist.

Craig also knew that no matter how smart he was, eventually he would be caught—hence, argued the DA, his defense of multiple personality disorder had been planned from the start.

He had envisioned many possibile scenarios, including the moment when he would be confronted by police and arrested. He needed to buy himself time to fulfill his "endgame" plan. He decided to have Clara masquerade as Bridget. When the police finally confronted him, Craig would first use Clara/Bridget as an alibi, then as a suicide scapegoat.

He knew that the police would investigate the suicide, and eventually discover that the victim wasn't really Bridget Colfax, but Clara. But that would take time, at least twenty-four hours. The endgame scenario, according to Tony, was to be played out on Black Water Lake. There, for Cheney's eyes—and for the record—Craig struck the official madman's pose. No one viewing his actions on the lake that December night could conclude that he was anything other than a raving madman.

Except Tony, Cheney, and the DA, who all concluded that he was not mad, but evil. And quite brilliant. They didn't doubt that he felt that he was some kind of avenger. But they also thought that, being a therapist, Craig had laid the clever groundwork for his own defense from the very beginning.

His strategy, of leading police to incriminating evidence and then setting up a dramatic final scene where he would be dragged away screaming into the night, was nothing short of masterful. Had he been arrested in his Venice office and evidence subsequently discovered, the perception, the defense, would not have been as dramatic, easily demonstrable, nor nearly as strong.

All along, his trump card was Clara. Even if they had him dead-bang, they would have to ask him for an alibi. Clara was his alibi, his escape hatch, allowing him to slip into a change of personality for the last act, his own very visible descent into madness.

The DA's office noted the cold and calculating nature of a man who would so easily sacrifice his own sister, let alone his own daughter, in order to save himself.

But the defense spun that same scenario to their own advantage. How could a man who devoted his entire life to helping people—and they had witnesses to attest to how their lives had been transformed by Craig—actually kill his own sister, whom he loved, cared for both emotionally and financially for nearly thirty years? According to the defense, he did not kill Clara. One of his other personalities did.

The DA's office had heard all kinds of defenses. In LA, if you hung around long enough, you heard it all. Twice. There was obvious self-defense, there was a reasonable fear for one's life, fear of continued spousal battery, on and on. But to coldbloodedly plan to kill a dozen people over a period of years, carry out that plan, and still claim that you weren't responsible . . . that was a new one.

And that's exactly what had the DA's office scared.

That plus the fact that they were up against former prosecutor Kleindinst, the best hired gun in a town full of killers. It seemed ironic to Cheney that it was only because of his inheritance from some of the people he had murdered that Craig could afford such high-priced talent.

Day after day Kleindinst conducted the best defense money could buy. That included "leaked" confessions by "reputable" therapists and friends of some of the murder victims that they had, in fact, molested their children. Cheney noted that no therapist stepped forward to implicate Frank. However, Molly's very public support of Craig made it seem as though Frank was an admitted child molester.

Also, there was the daily radio and TV talk show barrage of child molestation "experts," most of whom were on Kleindinst's payroll, spouting the party line: victims of molestation never lie; what they go through in the media is second only, in terms of violation, to the molestation itself; most people who say that repressed memories are invalid are either misinformed, or perhaps even child molesters themselves, hoping to protect themselves from future prosecution.

Kleindinst was ruthless. He was purposely misleading and confusing. But most of all, he was very, very good.

The day Stanley Craig took the stand, the media ringed the courthouse with vans, satellite dishes, microphones, and miles of cable.

And when he began to weep on the stand, others in the courtroom—described in the media by Kleindinst as "fellow incest survivors"—wept with him.

The next day, when he was confronted with undeniable evidence that he had committed the murders of nearly a dozen people—"under the diabolical control of other personalities"—Craig became hysterical and eventually had to be carried from the courtroom.

The following Monday, when Craig was able to continue, he described, on TV, in front of the world, his encounter with Derek Cheney.

"From your point of view as a trained therapist, was there anything that struck you as odd about Mr. Cheney's behavior?"

"Yes. I recognized the signs."

"The signs?"

"More than most people, I can recognize fellow incest survivors."

Cheney was sitting in the front row behind the prosecutor's table. He felt his muscles tense, felt his teeth start to grind. Tony had told him to expect this. Every witness against Craig had been destroyed or, at least, questions had been raised in the jurors' minds about each witness and his or her motivation.

"Are you saying that Mr. Cheney was molested as a child?" asked Kleindinst of his client.

"Objection," said the prosecutor.

"Sustained," said the judge.

"Why did you become a therapist?" asked the defense attorney.

"Consciously or subconsciously?"

"Either one."

"Because of my background," said Craig.

"Because you were molested."

"Yes."

"And when you met Mr. Cheney, what was your professional opinion of him?"

"Objection."

"Your honor, Mr. Cheney is a key witness against my client. His biases and prejudices go to the core of his ability to be a credible witness."

"Overruled."

"He was obsessed. Good at what he did. Driven."

"Like yourself."

"Yes," said Craig. "I felt a certain . . . bond with him."

Cheney squirmed in his seat. Elizabeth squeezed his hand and tried to hold back her own rage.

"What kind of a bond?"

"It was as though we understood each other."

"Understood each other? In what way?"

"That perhaps we were both driven by the same demons."

"You mean that it is your professional opinion that Mr. Cheney was also a molestation victim, even though he might be in a state of denial." It was very definitely not a question.

The DA rose, but he was too late.

"Yes. And I believe that his father's suicide confirms this suspicion. He killed himself rather than risk being exposed."

The DA was screaming!

The judge banged the gavel at least a dozen times.

The courtroom was on fire and reporters were busy filling their pens with gasoline.

Elizabeth put both her arms around her husband, trying to hold him back. But he was too strong.

The photograph in the *Times* was of Cheney being restrained by two bailiffs. He looked out of control. Craig looked meek.

And Kleindinst, who stood between them, looked like a peacemaker.

When the decision came down a week later, Cheney watched it on TV. He was not surprised to learn that Craig had been acquitted because the jury believed that he was insane at the time of the murders. He was remanded to the custody of the state for a period of observation not to be less than ninety days.

Outside the courtroom, a group of incest survivors wearing T-shirts that read "Free Dr. Craig," carried signs and cheered as he was led away.

Epilogue

C heney and Elizabeth were spending Valentine's Day in Maui. A neighbor had offered them use of a condo, and Elizabeth had insisted they get away. Cheney had been depressed ever since the trial ended in November. And Craig's release from the state hospital February 12th had only made him more so. They no longer talked about the trial. No longer talked about Craig, Frank, or Ray. Cheney's wound had to heal, but for him there seemed to be no closure.

Valentine's Day morning Elizabeth jogged down the beach to the Hilton and returned with the most recent *LA Times*. Cheney had made coffee and toasted a couple of bagels while she was gone.

"How you doing?" said Elizabeth as she sat down in a chair on the patio that looked out over the clear Pacific. It had been nearly four months now since that day in court, but she knew, as a psychiatrist and as a wife, that Cheney was having trouble with his father's death.

And with the Craig verdict.

"I'm okay," said Cheney. He sipped his coffee and looked out at the ocean.

"I brought you the paper."

"Thanks."

"You want the sports page?"

"Sure," he said without looking at her.

Elizabeth separated the sports page from the other sections, slid it across the white wrought-iron table toward Cheney, then took the front page for herself. She scanned it with only casual interest. She was on vacation—from riots, earthquakes, drive-by shootings, and celebrity scandals.

Then something, a name in a headline, caught her eye. And as she read the article her blood ran cold in the hot Maui sun. When she finished, she looked up at her husband, who was still gazing out over the water.

"Cheney," she said tentatively.

"Yes?" he said, not bothering to turn toward her.

"There's an article in the paper . . . "

Cheney was silent.

"It's about Stanley Craig."

Cheney said nothing.

"He was murdered two nights ago."

Silence.

"A few hours before we left LA," she said, almost holding her breath.

After a moment, Cheney turned toward his wife. "He murdered Frank and Ray." Cheney swallowed hard. "And he called my father a child molester in front of the whole world."

For the longest time neither Cheney nor his wife said anything.

After a while, Cheney stood and held out his hand to

Elizabeth. And for the first time since he had met her, he was not sure if she would take it.

After what seemed to Cheney to be an eternity, his wife stood and took his hand. They stepped down off the patio onto the beach and started walking. They walked for more than an hour. And never spoke.

Finally, the beach ran into a mountain of rocks. A dead end. Cheney stopped. Elizabeth stopped and looked at her husband.

And for the second time since they had been married she saw tears in his eyes.

Without a word, Cheney took Elizabeth in his arms, held her as tightly as he could.

Cheney was holding on to the only thing he had left in this world.

Elizabeth was just holding on.

Neither spoke, but all was understood.

And, perhaps, in time . . .

Would be forgiven.